A Week at the Shore

ALSO BY BARBARA DELINSKY

A Week at the Shore

BARBARA DELINSKY

St. Martin's Paperbacks

This is a work of fiction. All of the characters, organizations, and events portrayed in this novel are either products of the author's imagination or are used fictitiously.

Published in the United States by St. Martin's Paperbacks, an imprint of St. Martin's Publishing Group

A WEEK AT THE SHORE

Copyright © 2020 by Barbara Delinsky.

All rights reserved.

For information, address St. Martin's Publishing Group, 120 Broadway, New York, NY 10271.

www.stmartins.com

Library of Congress Catalog Card Number: 2019054413

ISBN: 978-1-250-84694-5

Our books may be purchased in bulk for promotional, educational, or business use. Please contact your local bookseller or the Macmillan Corporate and Premium Sales Department at 1-800-221-7945, ext. 5442, or by email at MacmillanSpecialMarkets@macmillan.com.

Printed in the United States of America

St. Martin's Press hardcover edition / May 2020
St. Martin's Griffin edition / May 2021
St. Martin's Paperbacks edition / June 2022

10 9 8 7 6 5 4 3 2 1

To my readers. I am awed that despite the gazillion other distractions in the world today, you still read my books. For that blessing, you have my eternal thanks—and a promise to give you the best I can possibly write. Deal?

Prologue

I remember the smell of sea salt on my skin and the rolling tumble of the surf. I remember the brilliance of a sun that popped the colors of our towels, boogie boards, and bikinis. I remember my sisters' impatient hands pulling me toward the waves, my mother's appreciative laughter, my father's guarded eyes.

I remember burying body parts until an arm or a leg spewed grand eruptions of sand. I remember moon jellyfish and sea glass and wrack-line seaweed that hid the tiniest perfect spiral whelks. I remember a bonfire on the beach, the smell of singed hot dogs and salty chips, the glow of embers as the sky purpled from east to west over Block Island Sound.

I remember fog, lots and lots of fog—and, cutting through it, the crescendoing growl of a motor when my father's boat left the breakwater. I remember its ghosted image fragmenting bit by bit, like the world we had known, until it was gone. I remember the sound of a gun, at least, I think I did, but it may have been fireworks in Westerly or the slap of a screen door on our porch.

I remember so much. But it is never enough. Nor is it the same as what the others recall.

Chapter 1

Every memory is real, but not all are based on fact. Time, forgetfulness, emotional need—any of these things can chip away at memory. But what if a memory is wrong from the start? What if what you think you saw, isn't what was there at all?

This is why I love my camera. It is *never* wrong. It captures facts and stores them. This frees me to live in the moment and move on to the next with the knowledge that the first is preserved. Since coming to New York, I've documented snowstorms and floods. I've taken pictures of strangers and friends, the streets where I walk, the markets where I shop. I even photographed my way through childbirth—well, until the very end, when my doctor banished my Nikon from the birthing bed. And recording my daughter's life? I have thousands of photos of Joy. On the first day of school each year, we look back at what she wore on the first day of school the year before and the year before that. Inevitably we've forgotten. But there it is in vivid detail.

That isn't to say detail can't be fudged. I do this every day, photographing real estate in a way that shows a home to potential buyers as something bigger, brighter, more alluring. Angles, lenses, creative lighting—these are the stock of my trade. Deceptive, perhaps. But much of marketing is.

Right now, though, after spending my working day photographing a Tribeca condo from every imaginable angle in the shifting city light, I'm playing at home. It's just past nine at night. The skyline isn't fully dark, not this close to the longest day of the year, but the air is heavy and moist, as early June in New York can be, turning what might have been a purple sunset into elongated smudges of gray. Fog is on the move, enfolding my building like a hug from behind, before slipping on past. As I watch, it blankets the Hudson and mists around Fort Lee on the far bank, before drifting north to the George Washington Bridge like just another commuter heading home.

My condo is on the fortieth floor overlooking Riverside Drive. I paid more for it than I should have, but a river view was a must. I've always needed open space, not a lot, just enough. As long as I have that, I can breathe.

Swiveling the head of my tripod lower, I focus on the steady stream of traffic, which grows more vibrant with the deepening dusk. I've taken this same shot hundreds of times—maybe thousands—but it's never the same twice. *Like the tide leaving ripples on sand,* I think as I wait, remote in hand, for the right second.

Photography has taught me how to wait. It has also taught me how to focus on that single subject and ignore everything else. This doesn't come naturally to me. As the middle of three children, I was born with peripheral vision—as in, an acute awareness of my sisters above and below, my parents, our home and friends, and my precarious place in it all. Limiting myself to one scene at a time, as my camera does, has been huge.

The fog thickens on the street below. I wait until diffused headlights and taillights reappear, wait again when I hear a siren, then follow the blue strobe through the shift of vehicles. When I'm content, I turn north, wait for the best mix of fog, steel towers, and double-tiered lights, then shoot again.

"What's the bridge doing?" Joy asks from the far end of the sofa, and I smile. She would know what the Nikon and I see. We're connected that way, my thirteen-year-old daughter and I. And this is a game we often play.

"Floating. I can't see its legs." Leaving the bridge, I find her reflection in the glass. With the rest of the lights off, her tiny book light is little more than a faint glow on the pink baby dolls that were her new favorites from the vintage store in the Village. But that glow isn't as warm as it would have been reflecting off paper.

Suspicious, I slide in beside her, angled to see her book. She starts to close it, makes a small sound, and stops. She knows that I've already seen what she was trying to hide, that her book light is clamped to the edge of *Great Expectations* but that tucked inside the bigger book is her Kindle. Close up now, I see page forty-four of Garth Stein's *The Art of Racing in the Rain*.

"But, but, but," I stutter, tipping my face up to see her, "this was on our *us* reading list. We were supposed to read it *together*." Read it aloud, actually. When Joy was little, I always read aloud with her tucked up close, and somehow I just never stopped. The books have changed, and the older she gets, the more challenged I am to make my voice fit different characters. I'd been looking forward to being a dog.

"Well, I couldn't not read the first page, and then I had to read the second," she reasons. "Isn't that what you always say, that if you want to keep reading, it's the sign of a good book? Olivia Mattson says this one's dumb, like who wants to know what a dog thinks, but I'm not sure how she knows anything about it, because her *totally* self-absorbed mother doesn't read—"

"Joy."

"It's true. Her mother makes lots of money and can afford to buy any book she wants—can afford to buy the *bookstore*—and she doesn't read? And anyway, Olivia has the mind of a squirrel, and squirrels are afraid of dogs. Besides, when Olivia doesn't like something, I do, and here was this book, just sitting in my Kindle library? I was practically crying on page three. You know what happens?"

She isn't really asking. She knows I know, but letting sentences end in the air started along with her period. Even beyond spoilers on Goodreads and the ardor of my friend Chrissie, there was the teary conversation about old dogs that we overheard at the Best Friends Animal Society in Soho.

"It's good, Mom," she confides. "Omigod. It's *sooo* good."

I want to talk about respecting schoolmates. But she happens to be right about Olivia Mattson's mother, who spent the better part of fifteen minutes at a recent back-to-school night lecturing me on how to build my business into something big, how to make my brand *the* brand for real estate photography in Manhattan, which is the last thing I want, since it would mean hiring regular staff, relying on paid ads over word of mouth, and spending less time with Joy.

But that's all beside the point. "What about *Great Expectations*?" I ask. "Your final is next week."

"I'll be ready, you know I will, but if you're playing, why can't I?"

"Because I spent six hours working today to keep you in vegan lip balm, retro clothes, and pomegranate juice, and because I've already graduated from middle school. Besides, I'm the mom and you're not. I get to play. It's a perk of growing up."

I deliberately add the last. My daughter isn't wild about the pressure that comes with being a teenager. Being precocious was cute in a child, not so in middle school, where social conformity is key. She wants to be either totally grown up already and able to speak her mind without being ostracized, or a child forever. We've had the Peter Pan discussion many times.

Rather than take the bait now, she simply says, "Do I have to stop reading this?"

I rub her shoulder with my cheek. Her fresh-from-the-shower curls, still damp and docile, smell of organic mint shampoo. "Nah. We'll pick another to do together. Maybe one where I can be a cat," I joke and, feeling a vibration, pull the phone from my jeans. The call is from the area code where I grew up. Just the sight of it brings a whoosh to the pit of my stomach. And at this hour? Not good. But neither my father's name nor my sister's appears, and I don't recognize the number. Spam? Possibly. Or not. My father isn't well, and given that my sister is ditzy, it could be one of his doctors. Or the hospital. Or neither.

Suspicious of the last, I click into the call expecting a robo-silence, and jerk when my name hits me fast.

"Mallory." Not a question, but a statement in a voice that is deep and tight, familiar but not. The whoosh in my stomach becomes a twist. Rhode Island is a small state, the town of Westerly smaller, its villages even smaller. I tell myself that this voice could belong to any one of the dozens of people I'd known growing up. But my gut says something else.

Standing, I move to the far side of the tripod and say a cautious, "Yes?"

"It's Jack."

I know that, I think, and I barely breathe. Jack Sabathian grew up on the shore, just like us. He was my best friend once, but we haven't talked since I left, and while his voice is older now, I feel the force of memory fighting its way through the tangle of time.

"We have a problem," he barrels on. "Your father was just over here knocking on my door—*banging* on my door, like he'd break it down—and when I opened it, he let me have it." He raises his voice to imitate. *"You no-good bastard, you knew exactly what was going on, didn't you. You probably planned the whole fucking thing with her*—his language, not mine," he puts in before becoming my father again. *"You let me be investigated like I was a murderer, and you didn't say one word, but we both know she didn't die. Tell me where she is. I know you know.* He had a gun, Mallory. He was waving a gun in my face. He swore he didn't own one back then. So either he lied to the DA twenty years ago or he bought it after the fact, but a gun is the last thing a man like that should have. You do know that he's sick—or are you just leavin' the whole thing to Anne—who, by the way, is doing a lousy job, and not just with his care. The house is a mess and the bluff is falling into the sea, but unless she told you that, you wouldn't know, because you haven't been here to check. It isn't your responsibility, is it? Well, hello, Mallory, it *is*. So here's the thing. You need to step up to the plate. If he's talking about that night to me, he's probably talking about it in town. Bay Bluff may be only a tiny corner of Westerly, but the police love the coffee your sister serves in her shop. If he's blabbing, they'll hear—and hey, I'm all for it. He killed my mother? I want it coming out. Do you? 'Course not. So here's a wake-up call," the slightest pause before an accusatory, "Mallory. Either you do something about him, or they will."

I'm spared having to respond by a decisive click, not that I could have spoken, I'm so shaken. That quickly the past is here and now. And the lump in my throat? Huge. Of the many things I've avoided thinking of since leaving Bay Bluff, John MacKay Sabathian is a biggie, but his angry voice brings everything back. I stand unmoving, looking at the foggy city night but seeing the ocean, the bluff, my father's boat leaving the dock and taking with it so so so much more than just Elizabeth.

"Mom," Joy prods with an insistence that says she has called my name several times. My eyes fly to hers. "Who was that?"

I refocus. "No one."

"No one was shouting. He was using your name. He even said *bastard*. I heard it from here."

Leaving the window, I switch on a lamp. I don't want to see the ocean, the bluff, the boat. Jack is right. I'm leaving it all to Anne.

But my daughter is mine. I'm raising her to be different from my past. And she isn't a baby. "It was one of your grandfather's neighbors."

"He only has one. Anne was saying that—remember, when she was here last time with Margo?"

Oh, I remember. We were arguing again about that night—about whether Elizabeth had jumped, fallen, or been tossed off the boat by heavy gales, and whether she could have possibly survived. Joy had already known the basics, but my sisters were full-on into bickering about infidelity, deception, and abandonment. And murder. Murder was the conversation stopper, the horror issue, the visit-breaker.

Since Joy heard all that, I figure she's old enough to hear more. "The guy who called is Jack Sabathian. He's Elizabeth's son."

Her eyes go wide. "What did he say?"

I thumb in Anne's cell, knowing my daughter will listen in. The phone is approaching its fourth ring when my sister picks up.

"Mal?" Her voice was always higher than mine, perky and bright to my down-to-earth sensible, but here she sounds out of breath. I wonder if she was outside chasing after my father.

"What's going on?" I ask as casually as I can.

"Uh . . . now? Not much. You don't usually call at night.

What's up?" She seems innocent enough, but then, my sister is always innocent, thirty-seven going on twelve. I swear, Joy is more savvy.

"Jack Sab just called."

Chapter 2

Anne is silent for a beat before sighing an exaggerated, "*Oh,* God. Jack Sabathian is a pain in the butt. He is *such* an alarmist, you know? He's always telling me what I need to do to the house, and if it isn't about the house, it's about Dad. What's he saying now?"

I relate the conversation, minus the imitation of our father's voice. By the time I'm done, Joy is leaning in, ear to my ear.

"A gun?" Anne echoes. "I have never seen Dad with a gun. Why would he need a gun?" A mumble in the background tells me she isn't alone. I'm quickly annoyed, then as quickly contrite. My sister has a right to be with friends.

"I don't know," I say. "I thought maybe you would. Where is he now?"

"He was reading in the den."

When I left, she doesn't say, but that's what I hear. So she's *out* with friends. A housekeeper comes mornings, I know that much. But this is night, and apparently Dad is alone. If I ask, Anne will insist—as she's done whenever I've asked—that he's fine, that he doesn't need a babysitter, that he likes having time to himself.

To avoid an argument, I ask, "Is he able to read?"

"Of course he is," she scoffs. "Well, maybe not for the long periods he used to, but his nose is always in some law journal."

We all know—at least, Joy and I do—that a nose in a book doesn't necessarily mean reading. But that isn't the issue now. The issue is the phone call I just received. "Would he have gone to Jack's?"

"He could have," she allows, and my mind sees a shrug, like it's no big thing dropping in on a neighbor. "I mean, I don't lock him in when I leave the house. Can you imagine if I did that and there was a fire and he couldn't get out? I'd never forgive myself. The poor guy has gone through so much. He's earned the right to a little dementia, you know?"

Dementia versus Alzheimer's—Anne and I are on opposite sides, but I'm not touching that now either. "Have you heard him talk about what happened that night?" *That night* was a euphemism for what the rest of Rhode Island called the Aldiss-MacKay affair.

"No," she insists. "I told you. He doesn't talk much."

"You said he goes off on rants. What about?"

"Old cases." She brightens. "It's amazing what he remembers, Mal. He can't tell me who came to see him yesterday, but those old cases? He's a gold mine of legal history."

Tom Aldiss had once been a respected judge on the Rhode Island Superior Court. He resigned from the bench six years ago—"resigned" being the word Anne uses, though given his mental decline in the years since, I suspect he was forced out. At seventy-four now, he is often confused. I see him when he and Anne come to New York for the theater, but I don't go to Rhode Island, and he no longer travels well.

"He remembers everything," Anne is saying, "lawyers' names, defendants' names, charges, findings. When he rants, it's in that tone, like he's wearing his robes up there on the bench and is charging the jury on a critical case." Wistful now, she adds, "He was the best judge. These cases haunt him."

The case of the disappearance of Elizabeth MacKay haunts us all.

Hearing that thought, Anne says, "No, Mallory, he doesn't talk about Elizabeth. With all the ranting, he does not. That's why I have trouble believing Jack." Her voice lifts. "Dad comes to the shop a lot now, did I tell you?"

Anne owns a breakfast place in the square that is the heart of Bay Bluff. *Sunny Side Up,* she calls it, apropos of her approach to life, and although I've never been there myself, to hear her tell, it's the place to be.

"I'm glad," I say. "For a while there, he wasn't getting out much."

"He walks down from the house, and, okay, sometimes he winds up at the Clam Shack or the bookstore, but they always point him back to me." She laughs. "Once he came down in his pajamas, it was cute, really. When Joe—you know, from the jeans place, well, actually you don't know because it opened after you left, but trust me, Joe is God's gift to tourism because he carries things tourists don't know they need until they need them—when Joe saw him on the sidewalk in his pajamas, he pulled him inside and dressed him in a shirt and shorts so he was looking *pret*-ty spiffy when he got to my place."

She seems amused. I am appalled. The Tom Aldiss we'd grown up with was a formal man who would never have left the house in his pajamas. He didn't even come down to breakfast *at home* in his pajamas.

"He has a favorite table," Anne cruises on, "and he heads straight there. I mean, it used to be a problem if it was already taken, but by now pretty much everyone knows that it's his, so they leave it open." Half to herself, she says, "That could be dicey with summer people. Maybe I should put a RESERVED sign there. But the shop isn't big, and he doesn't come every day, so I hate to waste the space." She returns to me. "He loves the new girl I hired—did I tell you about her?

She's been in town maybe a month, but it's like she's been here forever. Dad gets all quiet when he sees her. If someone else has taken his table, she calms him down, sets him up at the counter, and brings his coffee and his bacon and eggs and cinnamon toast. He doesn't take his eyes off her."

"What about his hands?"

"What?"

"Sexual harassment."

"Right," Joy whispers. Her school is big on discussing that.

"Christ, Mallory," Anne cries. "She's barely twenty. He doesn't touch her."

"God, I hope not. He was a judge. People know him. They remember that night."

"You remember that night," my sister argues. "It's all you have to measure life here by, but those of us who live here have moved on. No one talks about it. Trust me, there's plenty else to discuss."

For me, as well. "Annie, about tonight. Do you think Jack was telling the truth?"

She grunts. "Who knows. The guy has a major chip on his shoulder when it comes to our family, like we personally ruined his life or something."

"If Dad did have a gun that night—"

"No, Mallory. He didn't. If Dad stands for anything, it's the truth."

"Right." I roll my eyes. "The whole truth and nothing but."

"You and Margo can make fun of those words, but he lived and breathed them. If he said he didn't have a gun that night, he didn't have a gun. Jack has it in for us, is all. Okay, okay, his life changed that night. But so did ours."

"He lost his mother."

"Our parents broke up."

"At least we knew where they were," I reason and am gratified when Anne concedes.

"True. Not knowing what happened to her has to be bad. But at some point, you accept and move on. Jack spends hours on the beach near his boat. It's like he wants to be ready in case he sees his mother in the waves—can you imagine, after twenty years? I feel sorry for the guy. He's delusional. And he says Dad's demented? *Sheesh*."

"Jack can't be all that demented if he's a successful veterinarian."

"Who told you he is?"

"You. How else would I know about Jack?"

"Margo," Anne says. "She always liked him."

I sigh. "Annie, Margo is living very happily with her husband and sons in Chicago. I doubt she's keeping up with Jack. By the way, the *Sun Times* loves her. Her blog is huge. Do you ever read it?"

"No."

It is a period meant to end the discussion, and even though I want to pursue it—to pursue anything that might bridge the gap between my sisters—this isn't the time. "Jack said Dad was referring to Elizabeth. Does he ever do that when he's with you?"

"No."

"What about the house? Jack said it needed work."

"I'm telling you, Mallory, Jack is as clueless as Dad. The house is fine. I have someone who does upkeep. He was in last week working on the plumbing, which, of course, good ole Jack Sab can't see because no way would I let him in the house. My guy can do anything." There is another murmur in the background, then Anne's muffled, "You *can*," before she tells me, "He's a jack-of-all-trades, Dad would say."

The murmur had been male, and unless my inference is all wrong, the male Anne is with is her jack-of-all-trades in the flesh. That thought, paired with her breathlessness at the start of my call, brings a more worrisome one. When it comes to men, my sister Anne has notoriously poor taste.

Trying to tease, I say, "Okay, Annie, who's there?"

"No one."

"Bill," comes the low voice, apparently with an ear to Anne's phone as Joy's ear is to mine.

"Bill who?" I ask.

"Houseman," Anne says a little too innocently and adds, "Do you remember him?"

"*Billy* Houseman?" How can I not? Billy Houseman had been bad news around town from the time we were kids. "Anne," I warn.

"He's Bill now, new name, new leaf, new image. He's a good guy, Mallory. But, hey, I gotta run."

"Home to check on Dad?"

"Hint, hint," Joy breathes.

Anne says, "In a bit. Don't be a worrywart. I'm on top of this. Plus, you're not here, your choice. So don't criticize me, okay?"

She has a point there. But so do I. "I worry about you, Annie."

"I'm fine, okay? Try trusting me for a change?" Billy— *Bill*—says something, but I can't make it out, and then Anne says, "Talk soon. Bye," and ends the call.

I stare at my phone, then at Joy. "Why is everyone hanging up on me tonight?"

"Maybe because you're not going along, so now you know what it's like for me," she charges. "People want you to say what they want to hear, and when you don't, they forget being nice." Her brashness withers, face grows worried. "What if he does something? You know. Papa. With a gun." Her green eyes have gone forest-dark.

"We don't know that he has one."

"Your guy said he did. Is he more reliable than Anne?"

"Most anyone is," I remark and immediately feel guilt. "Anne means well. She just sees the world in a way that isn't always realistic."

"And the guy?"

"Jack was always honest." Brutally so. Which is why he and I haven't talked in twenty years. Our parting was brutally bad.

"So if Papa has a gun," my daughter says, "there could be trouble. We need to go there, Mom."

I go there all the time. Thundering waves are a soundtrack for every dream I have. The thought of *physically* going there, though, gives me heartburn.

Setting off for the kitchen, I call, "When? This is not a good time to travel."

Joy is close behind. "Why not?"

"You have finals, for one thing, and for another, I have work." I run the sink faucet hot. Dinner had been takeout of a veggie quiche, whose melt-over had burned onto the rim of the pie plate in which I'd heated it. I'd left it soaking, knowing it would be a hassle to clean, but I'm suddenly in the mood to scrub.

Joy leans into the counter, which means very close to me in our tiny kitchen. She is barely an inch shorter than my five-six, though her curls more than make up the difference. Those curls were damp when we settled in at the window, but air-drying, they've grown bigger by the minute. Seeming fragile beneath them, she says, "School finishes next week—"

"—and your internship starts right after that."

"Scooping kitty litter in a cat café," she drones.

I glance her way in surprise. "I thought you wanted that job."

"I do, but it's only a couple of hours a day, no pay—"

"Of course, no pay, you're only thirteen, and what about Willard?" Her piano teacher.

"He'll be away, too, remember? This is perfect, Mom. No school, no piano, no need for me to be at the cat café exactly next week. You cut back on bookings to spend time with me.

Why don't we spend it together with your family in Rhode Island?"

I pump hard at the soap dispenser. "I've explained to you why we don't."

"Conflicting loyalties, I know, you want to stay neutral. But how can we not do anything? He's your father, and what if he does have a gun? I mean, Anne doesn't see every little thing he does; she was out of the house just now, right? Besides, he could have bought one online and been home alone when it was delivered, so she wouldn't know. Guns kill, Mom. He could kill himself or kill Anne or kill the *housekeeper*?"

I shoot her a punishing look. She's almost as bad as Anne sometimes—imagining things like *what if I locked him in and there was a fire in the house?*

I work at a burnt-on piece of crust with the tough side of the sponge, needing suds but getting few. "Do you *see* how ineffective this dish detergent is?"

That quickly, Joy is the appeaser. "But we're doing a good thing here, Mom. See how compact the bottle is, no wasted plastic—and not tested on animals? If everyone on the planet signed on, the world would be a better place."

I send a dry thanks to the head of her school, who, since taking the job two years ago, had made The Environment as much a part of the curriculum as Singapore math and Robotics—and hey, I'm all for going green. I recycle. I refill my reusable water bottle. I pay bills online. There are times, though when being PC sucks.

"Right," I say and drop the sponge. After refilling the pie plate with hot water, I wipe my hands on the linen towel. Not paper. Linen.

"What about Papa and his gun?" Joy asks, following me into the hall.

At our closet laundry room, I open the dryer. "We don't

know that he has one." I begin sorting still-warm clothes into a double basket, Joy's on the left, mine on the right.

"But what if he does? What if he takes it into town and starts shooting the place up? Or decides to kill your neighbor? What if he did kill Elizabeth—"

"He did not." I may have issues with my father. I may question his compliance with the truth, the whole truth, and nothing but. But I refuse to believe he is capable of murder.

"But what if he has a gun *now*? What if he *uses* it?"

"Don't ask that. Don't even think it."

Joy takes over the sorting, but she doesn't back down—she rarely does, which is both her greatest strength and her worst curse, in part because she is logical enough to be annoying as hell. I should leave her to the job and walk away. But the truth is, I want her opinion.

Actually, I need it. She's all I have.

"He's your father," she says now. "And Anne's your sister. And that house is where you grew up. Not all the memories are bad, some are good—like hide-and-seek in your mother's potting shed—so why can't you focus on the good stuff?" She's sounding younger as she drops the last of the items in the basket and turns wounded eyes on me. "I've never been there, Mom. It's less than three hours away, and I've never been there? That's embarrassing. And even if all of the above wasn't true, it's the *beach*? We *love* the beach."

Basket on hip, I head for her room. "We were in Jamaica in February and spent last Thanksgiving in Anguilla." Our travel expenses were paid by the owners of the houses I photographed. "Those beaches are soft and warm. Beaches on the New England coast are neither."

"Those beaches were for work," Joy argues as I dump her things on her pillow, where she'll have to address them before she sleeps. "This would be a vacation."

"Going home will not be a vacation, Joy. Trust me on that."

"Okay, so let's go for a weekend, just a weekend?"

We could, I concede on the way to my room. I've considered that before, but always veto it when I start to hyperventilate. Okay. That's an exaggeration. I'm not hyperventilating now. But the knots in my stomach are real. It's an ingrained thing, a legacy of my childhood when I was always afraid I'd do something wrong, provoke Dad, piss someone off.

And then there's my mother. She's been dead a while, but I imagine her up there looking down, watching, waiting, wondering what I'll do, whether I'll flip sides now that she's gone. Maybe my father is doing the same thing in his judgmental way. Or not. I've often thought it would be nice if, in his diminished state of whatever, he mellowed. When I was growing up, it was his way or the highway.

Margo chose the highway, me the median strip in an attempt to be neutral, because I want my family to love me. I want to have a relationship with my sisters once my father is gone, and that means finding common ground. Common ground is right here in New York. When they visit, I knock myself out planning fun things to do. That's the thing about fun. Each round is a deposit in a memory bank that earns interest over time.

At least, that's the theory.

But Joy isn't into it. Having followed me into my bedroom, she is the dog with a bone. "He's the only grandfather I have, and I've met him, like, three times? Is that fair? He could be dead this time next year. He could be dead this time next *month*."

I begin folding my clothes straight from the basket.

"He could be dead this time next *week*, Mom."

She isn't telling me anything I haven't told myself a dozen times since I saw my father last. But if I go home now, Margo will never speak to me again. If I go home now, Anne will expect that I'll always go home. If I go home now, I'll be subjecting myself to the godawful insecurity that I've worked so hard to overcome. I'm a capable woman—a good photographer, a good mom. I've built a life in New York. I belong here. Just thinking of Bay Bluff has me walking a tightrope again.

It isn't your responsibility, is it? Jack Sabathian asked. *Well, it is, Mallory.* And for a minute, my conscience flickers. Where does conflict avoidance end and responsibility kick in?

But that was Jack speaking. He couldn't begin to understand my dilemma back then, and he certainly can't today.

Joy can. Giving her time to think about it, I go into the bathroom to wash my face. But suddenly hers is in the mirror with mine. Her skin is a little darker, her eyes green to my amber, her body leaner, though that could be her thirteen to my thirty-nine, or her love of kiwi versus my love of anything fried—like fried clams, of which the best, *the* best, were sizzled up fresh at the Clam Shack back home.

"Mom," she calls with impatience, because she can see my mind wandering again and wants it on her. All maturity is gone now. She is my little girl, the daughter I chose to have when it was arguably a selfish thing to do, the one I love more than life and whose mental well-being is key.

"I want to go," she insists, falling back on the one argument she knows will prick me. "My father is just a number, meaning no grandparents or aunts and uncles or cousins from him, so your family is all I have. I'm them—this hair, these eyes. And I love the beach. I want to go, Mom. Is scooping kitty poop *really* more important than that?"

Chapter 3

Rain can be a nightmare for me. It isn't so bad when I'm photographing a high-rise condo, but when it comes to a free-standing home, curb appeal counts. Downpours can depress even the most elegant property, often in ways Photoshop can't fix.

I'm not working now, though, so rain is just fine. It's good actually—keeps traffic from moving too fast. Cruising along to light classical, which Joy loves as much as I do, I have no problem when we hit a third major tie-up. Delaying our arrival is okay by me.

The wipers aren't as frantic now that we've slowed. They're actually syncing with Handel's "Water Music," to which my daughter's fingers were playing along until two minutes ago, when she stopped to check Waze. We've just crossed into Connecticut. The wail of an approaching ambulance confirms an accident ahead, and the app is pushing an alternate route.

"Here, Mom—here it is—turn here," Joy instructs with enough insistence to make me nostalgic for the days when she sat in the backseat preoccupied with a snack pack of Goldfish. "Follow that car."

When I don't, she shoots me a baffled look that only deepens when I smile. But how not to? My daughter is a splash of color—totally, outrageously Joy, impatient face and all. Her hair is piled in an off-center topknot held by a turquoise scrunchie. Her tank top is red-and-white striped and cropped at the midriff, and her jean shorts have the kind of high waist the eighties loved. Ever the optimist, she's wearing a bathing suit beneath.

"Weather.com says it'll be nice in Westerly," she had announced shortly after dawn, wanting to leave then. When I vetoed that, we agreed on nine. Then I got a call from my favorite Sotheby's broker, and by the time I was done with her edits, it was closer to noon.

Trying to catch the spirit of vacation despite my own private storm, I'm wearing a tee shirt and shorts minus the swimsuit. My hair, a paler brown and less curly than Joy's, is in a ponytail minus the scrunchie. My flip-flops are plain gray to her orange glitter.

Joy has sunk back in her seat, staring at me hard.

"What," I say.

"You don't want to get there."

"Would I be going if I did not?" I ask, but I'm playing with words. Going home is one thing, wanting to go home another. This trip is largely a concession to my daughter, who is in a rush to reach Bay Bluff. I am not.

I stay on I-95N. Not only does bad traffic put off what I don't want to do, but it tells Joy that the drive isn't quite the *easy-peasy 137 miles* she's said a gazillion times of late.

Besides, I do love driving, which is why I pay a huge monthly fee for my space. A car comes in handy when I'm photographing houses in Dutchess County or Long Island, and on weekends, Joy and I take road trips to explore the art center in Cornwall, hike trails in Stony Brook, or kayak in Smithtown.

Now we're driving to Rhode Island. Not my choice. Well, yes, my choice, because I am the ultimate chooser in our family of two. But between my conscience and my daughter, there wasn't much choice at all. It's been ten days since Jack Sabathian's call, and while there hasn't been a second, the first one haunts me.

"Whoa," says Joy when we reach the accident. Morbid curiosity keeps her turning to look back as we move ahead. Finally, flopping forward, she says, "I'm not driving. Ever." In my periphery, I see her glance at her phone, and not for the first time. She must have texted a friend before we left and is awaiting a reply.

If history serves, she's in for a wait. Joy is on the fringe of the texting group, for which I'm thrilled, though she is not. She once told me about being in the lunchroom and sitting alone with her sunflower-butter sandwich because she couldn't stand the *smell* of the *crap* the others were eating. I figure she told them that. Both the school counselor, who loves Joy's spunk, and Chrissie, who is a psychologist, claim that Joy is mature for her age and that the others will catch up. I worry about the harm done until that happens. It's about self-esteem.

Deliberately, I relax my hands on the wheel, but still my heart bleeds. Every child needs a best friend at her back. I had my sisters, Margo the fearless and Anne the ray of sun. Joy is a lonely only, sitting by herself in a lunchroom full of kids. And now a silent phone? This is why I agreed to a week, rather than a weekend, at the beach. Rhode Island will be a diversion.

We're listening to Ed Sheeran now. She had thumbed him in before dropping her phone, and I know there's defiance in her choice. *I can't wait to go home,* he sings in "Castle on the Hill," which has been her anthem since we decided on this trip. Little does she know that while I'm okay with that line, the ones that follow grip me more. *I was younger then, take me back to when I found my heart and broke it here.* But she hasn't a clue.

Greenwich falls behind us, then Stamford. As Vivaldi

rises through the speakers, Joy's fingers play the notes. "Do you remember this highway from growing up?" she asks.

We're approaching Darien. "I do."

"Going to New York."

"And Philadelphia. And Washington."

"All five of you?"

"Uh-huh. My father believed that our education needed theater and museums and history, so we'd take 'culture trips,' he called them." The memory opens. "We were packed in a Jeep Wagoneer. It had wood on the sides, a really pretty car. The three of us were in back, me in the middle so those two didn't fight. We didn't have movies to distract us."

"What about music?"

"Nope. Dad said that was for a concert hall. So we'd play games, like I Spy, or looking for license plates from different states. Margo was always testing him, laughing or singing, and we'd be giggling, so he'd end up yelling at us anyway. Mom would tell him we weren't doing any harm, so he'd yell at her. It went downhill from there."

Joy considers that as we pass a horse trailer with two tails hanging out the back. She turns to follow, looking for horse eyes through the narrow slats. "So those trips weren't fun?"

"Actually, they *were*," I recall. "It was backseat against front, three of us against Dad."

She thinks about that to a quieter Brahms as we pass Norwalk. Then, sounding unsure, like she's only now considering what we might find when we arrive in Bay Bluff, she says, "But being old and all, he's mellowed, right?"

"Anne says he has," I grant, though, that wasn't my take-away from Jack's call. If Dad is worse—if he's irrational, or, God forbid, does have a gun—

But those are ifs, and Anne has said no to them all. If I seriously thought Joy was in danger, we wouldn't be headed to see the man now.

"I'm starved," she announces. The avocado wrap we'd

shared before leaving, which would have spoiled if left behind in the fridge—has clearly worn off. "How much longer?"

"Ninety minutes, give or take. I can stop—"

"No. I want to wait. You said Bay Bluff has great places to eat."

"It does." I've Googled it. Of course I have. My favorite eatery is still there. "Great fried clams."

"Fried is bad."

"This fried is good. Trust me, babe."

She doesn't argue, mainly because she is checking her phone again, which she hides behind a show of changing the station. Her hand is quickly tapping the beat of Maroon 5 on her thigh.

The rain has let up, but the sky remains thick. "So," she invites, "what did Margo say?" When I'm silent, I feel her stare. "You didn't call her?"

"I decided not to. I didn't want to argue with her. You want to go, and that's that. Besides, it's not like we'll be there long." One week. I'm booked for a job in the city the Saturday after this one.

"She'll be angry if she finds out. Won't Anne tell her?"

I hesitate several seconds too long.

"Oh, no, Mom. You didn't tell her either? We agreed that you'd call."

"I made an executive decision not to," I say in my most executive tone. "If she knows we're coming, she'll rush to fix the house or search for a gun. If we really want to know what's happening there, we have to surprise her." Besides, once I called her, I would be committed. But right up until the minute we left, I wanted the option of changing my mind— which I've done a dozen times in the last few days. It's about those memories.

And here comes another, triggered by nothing more than a sign to Westport. Mom wanted to stop there. When Dad refused, they argued. After Elizabeth's disappearance, when their marriage crumbled, we realized that he'd had a lover there.

Disconcerted by how quickly the angst returns, I focus on the music—Sheeran again, "Perfect" this time. I tell Joy about a friend who lived in Fairfield, an innocent enough memory. But by the time we pass Bridgeport, I'm back on the Aldiss family road trip. This time it's my needing a bathroom and Daddy refusing to stop. Then, as we approach New Haven, I remember being rejected from Yale and Daddy blaming it on my portfolio, since, he claimed, photography wasn't "real art." Coming up on New London, where I did go to college, I remember the stomach cramps I used to have heading home for vacation. I'm not feeling full-out cramps now, just small knots of apprehension.

Another hunger complaint comes from Joy as we pass Mystic. It's after two, and I would have been hungry myself had it not been for those knots, but when I offer to stop, she says, "It's only twenty minutes more, Mom," like I was the one who had complained, like I'd been complaining for the last *hour*. Hunger is her version of *Are we there yet?*

We are closing in. Leaving I-95, we're on Route 234, a.k.a. Pequot Trail, which is a name I used to love, though now it brings us closer to the last place I want to be. Pawcatuck slows us down, same old for a Friday afternoon in June, but too soon we cross into Rhode Island, pass under the railroad bridge, and find ourselves in downtown Westerly.

Turn back! cries my scared little self. But it's too late. Way too late.

Muscle memory takes over then, well, of a sort. I know these roads like the back of my hand; know which ones to take to skirt the worst of the downtown traffic and, after that, which ones lead to the sea. Little has changed in the years I've been gone, a fact that eases me in an odd kind of way. I see the same modest houses, the same gas station and hair salon. What used to be a strip mall has become a shopping center with a supermarket, a CVS, and Urgent Care, but the languor of seaside New England remains.

Joy turns off the radio and watches it all with the same awe she might show the Grand Canyon, which amuses me. This is no Grand Canyon. We are in understated Yankee territory here, a stiff backbone in the most unassuming of homes. Wood siding is uniformly on a gray scale, green lawns are neatly mowed, and while the occasional shrub patch has been left wild by a mutinous owner, the rest are neatly trimmed. Even the ancient maples and oaks, whose Puritanical primness hides motel cottages from prying eyes, are limbed with lavish green leaves in a way that suggests Old World wealth.

We pass a small independent pharmacy, a florist with purple petunias cascading from hooks on the porch, a cemetery stretching so far that my sisters and I always believed strangers came here from miles away just to be buried near the sea. I'm thinking that it's really very sweet—when we hit the BAY BLUFF ANIMAL HOSPITAL, and my qualms return. There are no names on the signpost, no John Sabathian DVM or some such. But it has to be his, doesn't it? How many vets are there in a small shore town?

This is the first visible reminder of what I'm walking into, and it shatters my poise. I dread being here, but feel guilt at not having come sooner. I'm afraid of what I'll find when I get to the house, but feel an overriding responsibility for whatever it is. I'm having second thoughts about surprising Anne and not calling Margo. And seeing my father? That's the worst. My relationship with him has always been iffy. And now? He may be angry to see me, or pleased that I've come. He may not recognize me at all.

Deep down, though, driving along these streets, I feel a touch of excitement. For all the emotional baggage this place brings, I loved it once. The Rhode Island shore and I have a past, and it isn't all bad.

Take Gendy Scoops, I realize, smiling when I see the rambling white house with sea green awnings. "Gendy was an old lady," I tell Joy, "but this looks rehabbed. Her kids must run it now. Or their kids. Summers, we hung out here."

"Not in Bay Bluff?"

"Bay Bluff didn't have an ice cream shop. Besides, everyone knew everyone in Bay Bluff, so if we didn't want spies reporting to our parents, we came here."

The bikes out front now have thick tires that make the ride over back roads easier. There are cars, too, and people eating ice cream under huge umbrellas that match the sea green of the awnings. The sky is a blanket of clouds with the occasional spot of blue, but the pavement is dry. Joy was right about that.

The final approach is lush with the rich green of oaks, the blue of hydrangeas that thrive in sea air, the fountains of ornamental grass that had become a landscaping mainstay. We pass the same three-way intersection that I remember, the same signs for Misquamicut and Watch Hill. Another several minutes in, and the houses start swelling in size.

"Crazy," Joy murmurs when we pass a particularly grand one.

"That was there before, but the next one's new." I point ahead. "And that one." These are expensive homes, with expensive cars parked in expensive circular drives. No overgrown shrubs here. All is as pruned as the salty air allows.

Bay Bluff is its own little peninsula halfway between Misquamicut and Watch Hill. A small, weatherworn sign with an arrow marks the turnoff, so that if you don't know to look for it, you miss it. We used to joke that the arrow was flipping the bird to anyone who hadn't been invited to town, but now I wonder if I'm welcome here myself. Is home always home? Why, then, does my mind see ENTER AT YOUR OWN RISK in that arrow?

Tucking the warning away, I drive on past banks of

mailboxes at dirt driveways that burrow off into the trees. Once the road has angled along the peninsula, we pass homes I remember—the Mahoneys, the Santangelos, the Wrights, all still here in some generational form, to judge from the names on mailboxes. These houses have been updated with gables, turrets, and glass, and, to a one, their cedar shakes are weathered a deliberately stylish gray.

"Beach," Joy cries when houses give way to diagonal parking, not quite filled but almost, and beyond that sand and surf. "Put down your window," she orders, straining against her seat belt to see out my side.

Slowing, I do it as much for her as for me, and the warm salt air billows in, as if it was just waiting for the invite. No matter how much beach air I've breathed in the last twenty years, this is different. It smells of time and fish and a gazillion grains of sand that have washed through kelp, cradled crustaceans, or human toes. And still, it fills me with an odd . . . *purity.* How to explain?

Rather than try, I leave my window down. The tide is out, reducing the thunder of surf to a tuneful roll as the waves spill like dominoes down the shore. We pass a grove of stunted trees and shrubs, and while the green is dulled here, wild beach roses more than compensate.

Then those are gone, too, and we reach the square, which is as close to a center of town as Bay Bluff can claim. Slowing down, I'm impressed in spite of myself. When I left, only a handful of shops skirted a central patch of scruffy grass, but there are more than a dozen shops now, and the patch of grass has become a deck of pebbles hosting a large bench, whiskey barrels filled with blood-orange lantana, and a pair of gaslights. When I left, the shops had a freestanding feel, but the square's corners are now pergolas to the sea, and the gaps between shops have been filled. Awnings and signage are of a style. Sidewalks have been widened for picnic tables outside eateries—and those? I can't see details from the car, and with another car behind me I have to keep rolling, but there are three separate clusters of tables, all comfortably filled this mid-afternoon.

For a place that supposedly doesn't give a fig whether people come or not, it's an inviting little secret. Actually, not so much a secret, to judge from the flock of visitors milling in a splash of T-shirts and shorts, flip-flops and hats.

Feeling an inkling of pride, I ask Joy, "What do you think?"

"I need food," she declares, which translates into *Stop here, stop now,* and even though the voice of wisdom says we should go to the house first, I've been promising Joy we'd have lunch.

So I park in the lot just beyond the square—once dirt, now neat gravel—pull my ponytail through a ball cap and slip on large sunglasses. By the time I've grabbed my camera, Joy is at my door, brows raised. "Seriously, Mom? Sunglasses?"

"For the glare," I say and climb out.

Glare? she might have echoed and added another *seriously*? Instead, humoring me, she reaches back into the car to snatch her own sunglasses from the console. They are identical to mine. We bought them last February in Jamaica, and while large and round is more her look than mine, they happen to offer the right amount of shade.

That quickly, she is gone off to explore. I close the door and, for an instant, leaving New York in the car, I can't move. I'm hit by an unexpected moment, the balmy scent of my childhood is that strong around me. No, it isn't the same at other beaches, and purity is a dodge. What's different here is memory, which hugs me with myriad arms before I can think to raise my guard. Held in its grip, I remember the ripeness of sea-soaked bathing suits, the smell of fresh fish at the docks, the sweetness of full bellies in a delicate crust—and above it, the screech of gulls, the slap of a screen door, and always, muted or clear, the roll of the waves.

From the parking lot, I can't see those waves over a string of dunes. But I do see things to save. Flipping the glasses to my head and the camera to my eye, I photograph the blur-of-color Joy makes as she strides past the Clam Shack's weathered-gray siding. Distracted by that siding, I close in on its texture, then back away again to shoot shadows that sharpen as a cloud gives way to blue. Lowering the camera, I replace the shades, but as soon as I round the corner, there's more photo bait. Glasses up, camera to eye, I take pictures of a family of four in blue BAY BLUFF T-shirts, newly bought, folds still fresh. I zoom in for close-ups of the town name, momentarily an ironic *Bay Buff* when the teenage boy wearing it reaches to scratch his back. Shifting focus, I spot three dogs sitting like a trio of old men on the bench in the center of the square.

Dogs are safer than seeing people I recognize, although there haven't been any of the latter yet. There will be. That was the danger of stopping here first and the wisdom of ball cap, glasses, and camera. I haven't changed much in twenty years. I still wear my hair long, it's still light brown, and the ends still frizz in ocean air. I'm still five-six, still 125 pounds—okay, before breakfast and naked, but my point stands. Twenty years isn't that long a time.

Uh-oh, and yup, there's the first. Deana Smith is a descendant of the granite quarrying Smiths whose historic importance is Westerly lore. Classmates like me added envy to the lore; Deanna had such a handle on guys, grades, and looks that it wasn't fair. My camera follows her down the sidewalk until she disappears under the SMITH REAL ESTATE sign, which explains her skirt and blouse, formal for Bay Bluff, but make sense if she's a realtor. Likewise, Deana herself. She was the kind of outgoing that would make for a successful broker—knew everyone and everything, and would definitely recognize me. If she does, she'll tell whomever she meets, which won't be good.

But she hasn't seen me. I'm under a ball cap and behind camera and glasses, am I not?

Not chancing that she might look out her front window and find a camera aimed her way, I quickly shift focus all the way to the corner, where—whoa—a camera is focused on me. I don't move. Turning and running would be a sure sign of guilt. Besides, do I actually know whether this guy, who is tall and narrow in loose shorts and a baggy tee, is looking at me, rather than at the parking lot behind me? Does he actually know that I'm focused on him rather than on the periwinkle-covered pergola or the ocean beyond?

I squeeze the shutter release. When he continues to keep his camera aimed at me, it becomes a contest. I'm not quite sure where my defiance is from, but I feel something proprietary for Bay Bluff. This is *my* town. *He* is the outsider.

Zooming in, I take another shot. Then, lowering my camera, I simply stare at him. I'm afraid he took a picture of that, too.

I'm used to people taking pictures of people. What better place for street photography than New York, where faces are nameless and diverse? The same can't be said for Bay Bluff. I'm starting to wonder about that when he lowers his camera and studies the screen on the back. He looks to be barely thirty, which makes him younger than me, but no way is he thinking MILF thoughts. I don't radiate sexuality. Never have.

Sure enough, he raises the camera again, focusing this time on the dogs on the bench. After taking several shots, he checks the LED screen again. Then he looks around, apparently feels he's taken enough, adjusts the camera strap on his shoulder and heads back through the pergola toward the beach.

Dismissing him as a random tourist, I raise my own camera again and turn to the other side of the square. There my lens finds SUNNY SIDE UP with its eponymous sign and, since it's after two, a CLOSED card on the door. The shop is much as I imagined it would be, meaning yellow and fresh. It is flanked by a bookstore with as many bright toys in the window as books, and a sand-colored shell shop, both holdovers from my time here. Farther along, I see a deli, its patrons eating thick sandwiches on the patio. At the foot of the square, a beach shop hawks boogie boards, a stack of folding chairs, and blow-up toys ranging from simple rings to Wonder Woman. Next comes Smith Real Estate. And after that, oh Lord, the penny candy store, another holdover from my childhood, and wouldn't you know, Joy is glued to its window, which is nearly as colorful as she is. How not to immortalize that? I bracket several shots, then, when I see that she sees me, lower my camera. She sprints over.

"Mom." Her eyes are wide with excitement, her voice breathless as she grabs my hand. "You have to see this." She pulls me down the south side of the square to a shop between the Clam Shack and Small Plates. The latter is apparently a seaside version of tapas, serving small portions of lobster salad, slaw, sliders, and skins, if the low prices on the chalkboard outside are a clue. I don't have time to study the menu further, though, because she draws me into a store between the eateries. *Jeans and Joe.*

It occurs to me that Joe is the guy Anne mentioned, the one who dressed Dad when he wandered down from the bluff in his PJs. Jeans are displayed in the window, but they are way outnumbered by BAY BLUFF gear. This is where the family in blue got their shirts, but I'm stunned that my daughter wants this, rather than organic yogurt raisins or coconut smiles. She has never liked tourist gear, always considers it tacky. Before I can remind her of that, though, she slides her sunglasses to the top of her head and leads me past stacks of beach towels and blankets, shelves of branded mugs and picture frames, racks of T-shirts and tank tops and bathing suits. With uncanny precision, she extracts two hoodie sweatshirts, one women's S, one M. Both are bright red with the town's name splashed on the front in large white letters.

"Can we?" she asks, and, yes, it's a question, though I see dire hope in her eyes, and it's a killer.

She's getting the sweatshirt, of course. I'm a sucker for dire hope, and this is a unique circumstance. Still, I ask, "When will you ever wear this?"

"Now. Feel the wind? And tomorrow, and the day after that? We didn't bring anything for the cool, and besides, I'll wear it back home."

"You will not," I remark. I don't feel much wind now and, sure, wind can funnel down avenues in New York and fall comes in three months and winter after that. But once we're back, she'll think this tacky again.

"I *will* wear it. I *love* this place. It's my roots."

"Whose roots?" I tease, thinking hers are in New York. But that isn't really true. In the deepest sense, her roots are here. Because my roots are here. So I'm wrong.

Oh, yes, I'm wrong. No parent is perfect. When Joy was a baby, I spoiled her, the result being a nightmarish terrible twos. Getting through it was a slog that lasted until she was five, but we both emerged on the other side a little smarter. She learned that when I say certain things a certain way, that's how it is. I learned to hold firm when it really matters and to be flexible when it does not. A stubborn parent creates a stubborn child. A parent who refuses to admit a mistake creates a child who can't.

Gracious in victory, Joy simply smiles. And again, I feel a twinge of pride, this time that she does like the place of my birth. Distracted by the pleasure of that, I take both sweatshirts and make for the cash register.

Too late, I realize my error. Behind it stands a man I've definitely seen before, and from the way he is looking at me, the recognition is mutual. I need my shades. But they're hooked on the neck of my tee, and putting them on here, now, inside, would be a tip-off.

Since this isn't a kid working a summer job, I'm guessing that this is Joe-the-owner. He is roughly my age and height, with an auburn man-bun and a sunburned nose. I'm struggling to place him, when he turns the same puzzled gaze on Joy, and it strikes me that he may see the family resemblance even more so in her. Joy has the same dark hair as Margo and Anne, the same forest green eyes, while mine are lighter on both counts. That said, we all have Mom's heart-shaped face.

A name comes to me then. Joey DiMinico. He was Margo's year in school, a fact that Anne failed to mention when she told me of the Joe who dressed Dad. Of course, he would find us familiar. He sees the twenty-years-older Anne every day.

This could be a problem, I realize. The last thing I want is for him to pick up the phone and call her before we get to the house ourselves.

"Just arrived?" he asks.

"We have," I say with an exaggerated flourish that I hope suggests tourist glee. "How much do I owe you?" Since he hasn't connected the final dots, I search my wallet for cash, rather than handing over my credit card with a neon ALDISS emblazoned on the front.

While Joy dives into her sweatshirt, I hand over a fifty and, leaving my hand waiting for change, half turn to watch her dance to the front of the store.

"First time?" he asks as I pocket the change.

Risking rudeness, I simply lose myself in my own sweatshirt. Good to look like every other tourist, right? By the time I join Joy on the sidewalk, my sunglasses are in place. What I see through them, though, brings me to a dead halt.

It's a ghost not ten feet away and closing in.

But no. The image in my mind is of a woman who, had

she lived, would have been in her late sixties. This girl may have the same blond hair and gray eyes, the same tall, athletic build, but she can't be twenty yet.

So no, this person isn't Elizabeth MacKay. It's just the power of suggestion in my nostalgic mind, active now that I'm back here for the first time in so long.

The girl smiles—a different smile, I see—and passes us by.

Then my phone rings, and Anne's name lights up the screen.

Chapter 4

In the space of a heartbeat, I wonder why my sister is calling at this very minute—whether someone did recognize me, even the man with the camera—and *why* didn't I play it safe and go to the house first? But Joy wanted to stop.

Nope. Can't blame Joy. I wanted to stop, too.

And besides, it's done.

"Hey, Annie," I say casually and brace for her dismay.

Her voice is muted but urgent, and not the words I expected. "Dad fell. He was climbing the ladder to get something from the attic and lost his footing. I've told him those steps aren't safe. I've told him *so* many times that I can *get* things from the attic for him, all he needs to do is to ask. But he doesn't listen. When did he *ever* listen? He is the most stubborn man—"

"Was he hurt?" I interrupt to ask, and Joy moves closer.

"Broken wrist. It's a simple break, and at least it's his left arm, so he can still write and brush his teeth and feed himself. Can you imagine if it'd been his right? I suppose it wouldn't have been that big a deal, just someone coming in to help him do those things while I'm gone. But his balance isn't good, Mal. I hear this from tons of people whose parents are starting to age."

I defer the aging issue. "Have they set it?"

"They're about to," she says, clearly at the hospital, hence her muted voice. "They're giving him a waterproof cast. That'll be one less worry."

"Where are you?"

"Urgent Care." She is instantly defensive. "It's ten minutes from the house—and I knew it wasn't major, so if you're thinking I should have gone to Westerly Hospital and waited forever, don't say it. Twenty minutes was bad enough. Dad kept getting up from his chair and going to the desk to ask when Dr. Cronin would arrive. Remember Cronin? His old PCP? Who died ten years ago?" I didn't know he had died, just one more thing I had missed, but Anne says, "Dad has the patience of a three-year-old."

"Is it the Urgent Care at the crossroads?"

There is a short pause, then a cautious, "Yes . . ." Clearly, she wonders how I know, since it was not there when I left town.

"I'll be right there."

"What do you mean?"

"Joy and I are in Bay Bluff."

Her voice jumps. "You are? Where? Since when?"

"We just got here."

"At the *house*?"

"No. The square. We couldn't resist stopping."

"Why didn't you say you were coming? I mean, how fair is that, Mallory? You haven't been home in years and you just show up? The house is a mess. If I'd known, I'd have cleaned, I'd have aired out your room, I'd have been prepared." Here's the chastisement, though it sounds more like hurt.

Feeling guilty for that, I say a soft, "I wanted to surprise you, Annie. We can be at Urgent Care in fifteen minutes."

"It'll take you eight."

"Yes, but my daughter hasn't eaten since breakfast. We'll get something to go. Should I get something for you and Dad?"

Since the answer to that is a *no,* Joy and I wolf down our own lunches as we drive—a veggie burger for her, fried clams (could not resist) for me. The wolfing down is starvation on Joy's part, nervousness on mine. I haven't seen my father in three years, and, forget Alzheimer's disease or dementia or even just ordinary old age, the man terrifies me. He always has, which is probably the major reason I haven't been back to see him sooner.

Parking in the lot outside Urgent Care, we run up the steps and down the porch to the wavy glass door. We're barely into the reception area when my father and sister emerge from an inner office.

Given that he has a fresh white cast on his left hand, Dad stands remarkably tall. He wears ironed khakis and a button-down shirt whose left sleeve is rolled to clear the cast. His silver hair is vaguely disheveled, but his posture picks up the slack. It is commanding, a warning to anyone who may be in his way, and certainly enough to intimidate me. I've been waiting for his illness to soften that, but it hasn't done it yet. His eyes are blue, faded from what they were a few years back, but authoritative nonetheless. His stride keeps him the half-step ahead of Anne that always seemed his due.

My sister is wearing a yellow tank top, short denim coveralls, and fuchsia high tops. With a burgundy streak in tousled dark hair, she looks as funky as my daughter.

She is reaching forward to keep a guiding hand on his elbow, though his purposeful manner implies he knows exactly where he is and why. This is encouraging. Not so the fact that he glances at us and doesn't react.

My stomach dips under the weight of this particular memory, the one where he looks past me at Margo or Anne. That worked evenings when a jury's prolonged deliberations nastied his mood. I was happy to be out of his sight then. Other times, I would have killed for a loving word.

Anne quickly pulls him to a stop. "Look who's here,

Daddy! It's Mallory and Joy, come to surprise us. Isn't that super?"

"Hi, Daddy," I say, stretching up to brush a kiss on his cheek.

He seems puzzled, unable to place me. I'm wondering if maybe it's just disbelief, when Anne breaks the moment by giving me a hug.

"You look fabulous, Mallory. And Joy?" The deliberateness with which she repeats our names says she's helping Dad out. In the three years since he saw my daughter last, she has certainly changed.

Joy is shy, standing close to me when her grandfather's gaze finally leaves my face and finds hers, and what takes place then is the best I'd hoped for. His features soften, brows rise in pleased surprise, eyes light with something akin to hope.

Encouraged, Joy kisses him as I had done. "Hi, Papa," she says.

He smiles and touches her cheek with his good hand. "Margo. You're here. All the way from San Antonio?"

"New York," Joy says lightly, ignoring the *Margo*. "We just drove up. I'm sorry about your wrist."

But he's frowning. "Not San Antonio? Did you move?"

Anne says, "Daddy, Margo lives in Chicago. This is Mallory's daughter, Joy."

"Mallory's?" He does look at me, clearly making the connection with my name, but he's confused.

I put an arm around Joy's shoulder and smile. "My daughter."

"You're married? When? Why did I not know? Does no one tell me these things?"

Anne rescues me with a quick, "Okay, Daddy, we can talk about this when we get home. There are other people here, and we're in the way." The reception area is barely full, but the excuse is enough to get us moving again.

We are barely out the door and on the porch, though, when my father snags Joy's hand. "Margo, with me," he says. "I don't see her enough."

"Our back seat is available," Anne offers with an inquiring look at Joy, who quickly looks at me. I'm not sure if her expression is a *May I?* or a *HELP!* So I waggle a finger between us and hold up my hands, as in, either way is fine.

It's a moot point, since my father is already leading her down the porch. Trailing them, I watch her slide into the back seat of Anne's Volvo. It is actually Dad's car and likely on its last frugal legs, but at least Anne is driving. Last time Dad drove, he phoned Anne in a panic when he couldn't start the car. She laughed telling me the story—*he got confused, forgot how, kept trying to start it like it was his old wagon*—and while that might in fact be a common aging problem, seventy-two isn't terribly old. Forgetting how to start the car is one thing, forgetting how to brake in traffic something else. Though the latter hasn't yet happened, Anne promised me that she wouldn't let him drive.

She hides the keys, makes it a game. She tells me this often, like she's handling a child. The fact that my father doesn't call his buddy at the local garage, whom he once helped with a DUI and who then did every last bit of service on our cars for free, puzzles me. Maybe Dad doesn't think of hot-wiring the car. Maybe the buddy is retired or dead. Maybe Dad doesn't want to drive because he has nowhere to go.

Whatever, he takes the passenger's seat without a fuss. As soon as the door is shut, he swivels to look back at Joy. I see this through the window, see that he stays that way as the Volvo backs around and heads out.

Alone in my car, I follow them back to Bay Bluff. Gravel has been strewn over pavement, a summer ritual that hasn't changed. Under the hot sun, it will embed itself in the tar, adding traction for winter's ice. In the here and now, it adds crunch to a soundtrack whose background is, always and forever, the sea.

My car climbs. The shrubbery now is more dense than I remember, a wealth of sea grass, myrtle, and juniper, with scrub pines interspersed, all a safe bet against the ocean wind. After a minute, two houses rise against the hazy sky like a pair of standing stones.

Though separated by several hundred feet of gravel and grass, the houses are clearly a pair. They were commissioned by Tom Aldiss and Elizabeth MacKay within months of each other and designed by the same architect. That was more than forty years ago, which is how long our families have been entwined.

Since the bluff stands high above the sea, cresting it offers a breathtaking view. I might have stopped to take it in, if the Volvo wasn't already at the house. My father waits for Joy to climb out, then takes her hand and leads her to the front steps.

I'm not sure what they talked about in the car, or whether they talked at all. But the look Joy shoots me over her shoulder is definitely amused. I'm guessing she loves being coddled. I may have coddled her when she was little, but it's been a long time since I led her around. Hell, she stopped letting me do it. Papa, apparently, is something else.

Wanting her back by my side—my family, my safety, my *need*—I climb out to follow, but pause with a hand on the roof of the car. The house stands above a fieldstone skirt, and is wide rather than tall, with turrets front and rear. Its sides are clad in cedar shakes—and yes, the shakes buckle in spots. Yes, several shutters could be straighter. Still, my heart trumpets, because this house is a handsome thing.

That said, I'm not quite ready to go inside and greet the memories waiting there like a party of long lost relatives.

Needing a boost before I confront them, I follow the timeworn path between heather the color of slate, to the staircase that leads to the beach. The wood here is just plain weathered, ragged both underfoot and on the handrails, but other than the splinter risk, it feels solid enough.

Walk, don't run! my mother calls. So I descend one step at a time, inhaling more deeply the lower I get. At the bottom step, I do the little dance of kicking off my flip-flops, and sink into the sand. It is cooler than it will be in another month, and damp enough after last night's rain so that I don't sink in far, but it feels wonderfully familiar. Likewise the smell. There is nothing to dilute it here—no food, no people, no cars. It is pure ocean, pure . . . pure.

A man-made barrier of rocks forms a breakfront protecting the dock, whose planks range in color, old to new. The whole of it is held in place by thick pilings, and stretches well out over the water. Two boats are tied here, my father's on the right, Jack's on the left. Both are powerboats of average length and beam; both are new to me, clearly purchased in the years since I've been gone. Still, the sight of them takes me back in time, way back past that one awful night to boat picnics and sunset cruises and trips to Newport or Montauk or the Vineyard.

Inevitably, though, that one awful night looms. Where had my father and Elizabeth been headed? *Just out,* he said in annoyance when we asked, and when the authorities asked, he said Jamestown. *Just for a ride,* he replied when they asked him why, and the story never changed.

I wonder if we'll get anything more now, then wonder if it matters. The more immediate question is whether he currently owns a gun.

But I don't want to think about that, either. Taking a deep, salty breath, I hold it in my lungs until it eases my upset.

Walking to the spot where the sand is shiny and hard, I wiggle my toes as the water bubbles in, trickles out, advances again and retreats. A tiny voice in my head tells me to go back up to the house. But if there is a problem, Joy will come looking for me. And didn't she want to get to know her grandfather? Besides, Anne is with them.

Leaving the water's edge, I walk several yards onto the dock and sit with my legs hanging over the side. My feet don't quite touch the water, which means it's low tide. When we were kids, this was a measure of our growth, much like a mark on the kitchen wall. Another measure? How quickly we could scramble up the bluff without using the stairs. There were always footholds. But no more, I realize, looking back. The rocks we used then now lie in a straggly line at its base.

The bluff is eroding. The stairway seems to be holding the soil in place, but on either side of it, gravelly sediment flows over what used to be pure sand. The Sabathian side of the bluff, where plantings anchor the gravel, fares better.

Beach maintenance. Another thing to consider.

But not now. Now I simply listen. Though the breakwater gentles the surf, the greater ocean still resonates as it gathers, spills, and ebbs. I hear the soft ding of ships' bells, a slightly different tone from each boat, in sync one minute, not so the next, and the percussive thump of the bumpers that hang between the boats and the dock. Combined this way, these sounds are unique. They are the lullaby of my childhood, the one that scores my Manhattan dreams, as pure here as the smell of the sea.

A gust of wind whips at the loose ends of my hair. Grateful for my Bay Bluff sweatshirt, I start to pull up the hood. But that will hide too much of the shore experience, and in this instant, that is what I need. Instead, I pull its sleeves over my hands, press them against the dock, and focus on the horizon.

Focus. Camera. Back in the car.

But I veto that thought, too. For these few moments at least, I want nothing between myself and the sea. On a clear day, we could always see Block Island and, on an extra clear day, the tip of Long Island. Today a broken haze hovers over the ocean, allowing only cracks of sunlight to splinter through and gild the waves.

Just shy of the horizon, I see two boats, one with sails, one not. Their paths approach, cross, and separate. I can't hear them, not even the distant rumble of a motor, the breeze is that stiff. I do hear another sound, though—a faint jangle, land-based, and growing louder fast.

Looking toward the Sabathian side, I see a dog coming at me on the run. It is medium-sized and powerfully built, though the power is strictly in its body. In comparison, its legs are spindly. It is shorthaired, so much the color of wet sand that it might have blended in, if the sand offered up anything as mean-looking as this.

Time to go to the house, I sing to myself. But it's too late. The dog is racing past the firepit, heading for me. It closes in even as I evaluate my odds of escape.

It isn't that I don't like dogs. But this one doesn't look friendly, and the last thing I want is to have to return to Urgent Care for stitches and a shot.

Trapped, I hold very still. The dog stops at the end of the dock where it, too, holds still.

Distracted by movement down the beach, I dare a glance there. The man approaching us is tall and as solid of body, if far, far more long-legged than the dog. He doesn't run, clearly isn't alarmed, or is simply testing me to see if I'll blink. All I do, very carefully, is ignore the wild thudding of my heart and, very slowly, turn on my bottom so that I'm facing the threat.

Stopping at the dog, he scrubs its head with his fingers. "Good guy," he says.

"Is that a pit bull?" I call in disbelief.

"Could be," he calls back in the deep voice that I know. I want to hear amusement. But no. It's challenge.

"Do you own it?"

"Yes."

"Why?"

"Why a pit bull? Because no one else wants him and he needs a home. Pit bulls are the most misunderstood dogs."

"Tell that to the mother whose three-year-old was mauled by one," I say. A story to that effect had recently appeared on my Twitter feed. It wasn't the first I had read.

"If a dog is trained to fight, it fights," he states. "If a child rushes it, it gets scared. When an animal, any animal, is threatened, it defends itself. I repeat. Misunderstood." He has the gall to approach me on the dock, and I continue to hold still. Not that I think he'll attack. John Sabathian is a pacifist. Physical abuse was never our problem. Our problem—*my* problem—is that my legs won't work, because I don't know what to do. Stay, leave, walk, run, listen, love, argue, reason, accuse? The past contained all that and more. But this isn't the past.

He comes close enough so that I have to tip my head up. His face is older, its lower third sporting a stylishly thin, half-scruff beard. Though his hair is shorter, hitting his nape rather than his shoulders, it is the same every-shade-of-chestnut-give-or-take that it was. The grooves between his brows have deepened, no surprise there. He was always a frowner. That said, he looks good.

"I didn't think you'd come," he says in a lower voice now that he is close.

I try to think up something witty about command performances or wild accusations or for-old-time's-sake corn, but nothing seems right. I simply say, "I didn't either."

"Why did you?"

"A gun can be lethal." *Like a pit bull,* I think, with a pointed look at the dog. But the creature, which has followed Jack onto the dock, is looking up at him with adoration. Clearly, it doesn't judge me to be a threat. It doesn't even look my way when I maneuver my legs around and stand.

Pulling a treat from his pocket, Jack rewards it for its

docility. The dog sits and chews in a surprisingly well-mannered way, then closes its mouth, and turns placid eyes on me. I suppose it can't help being jowly. Or having bloodshot eyes or ears that hang like limp lettuce.

"Is this your only dog?" I ask, thinking that if he's a vet, he may have a houseful.

"Right now. They come and go."

"Get adopted?"

"Or die. Some of my clients can't deal when their pets get sick. I can."

"Are you a shelter?"

"Just a vet. But the line between the two isn't set in stone. I care about animals. I do what I can to make their lives better."

He sounds genuine enough, but I struggle to reconcile the past with this. He hadn't been the most social sort. What was on his mind was on his tongue, no filter in sight. Joy is like that too often for comfort. That said, there is a case to be made that Jack was my model of how not to raise an only child. Consideration of others was never his strong suit.

That he is now considerate of animals raises a curious point. "You didn't have pets when we were kids."

"Your memory sucks. I had rabbits. You don't remember my hutch? But no. You wouldn't. You were afraid of me. You wouldn't come close."

I half expect to see a mocking twitch at the corner of his mouth. But he is stating a fact. I do remember being afraid of him at first.

Unafraid now, I say, "I meant cat or dog."

His mouth does twitch now, but with self-disdain. "My parents were overwhelmed with just me. They couldn't have handled a house pet."

"You weren't that bad."

"I was that bad."

"Mom!"

My eyes fly to the bluff. Joy is running down the steps.

"Walk, don't run!" I shout and, given cause, jog down the dock and across the wet sand. I'm slightly breathless when we meet. "Everything okay?"

Her curls have grown ten-fold, but her dark green eyes are bright. "Well, Papa forgot I was there and got obsessed with a crossword puzzle, and Anne is racing around trying to clean up. I mean, Mom, like the place is a pigsty?" Her gaze shifts past me, voice guarded. "Who's that?" When she sees the dog, she sidles closer to me, which says something about the look of this dog.

Jack approaches us, nothing shy about the man. I'm thinking that I need to formally introduce them—am thinking, actually, that this is the last situation I want to be in and that I need to return to the house *now*—when Joy asks in a none-too-friendly tone, "Are you the guy who called on the phone?"

He stares at her, then at me. I'm not sure if he's wondering why she called me *Mom,* or, having moved beyond that, is asking, *Do I need to answer this twerp?*

"This is my daughter, Joy," I tell him. "Joy, Jack. Yes, he's the one who called."

"Is that a pit bull?" she asks, even more accusatory than I had been minutes before.

"Yes."

"They're vicious."

"They're misunderstood," he repeats. His voice doesn't gentle because she's a child. I remember this about Jack. He was always quick to argue, and once riled, he didn't back down from a fight. *Rather like a pit bull,* I think. But, really, what do I know about pit bulls, or Jack Sabathian after twenty long years?

"Will he bite me?" Joy asks.

"If you pick up a stick and come at him, he might."

"What if I try to pet him?"

"Go ahead. Just put your hand out so he can see you mean no harm."

She does that, inching it closer to the dog. I want to pull her back, but don't want to teach her fear, and if Jack is watching, she'll be safe. A vet wouldn't stand by and let a mad dog bite a child, not even a vet with an ax to grind.

The dog barely looks at her hand but continues to stare into her eyes.

"Poor thing," she says. "He's so ugly."

"Joy," I protest. She's right. But I've taught her not to be mean.

That said, she is the type of child whose big heart bleeds as much for ugliness as for the rape of natural resources. Still holding out her hand, she moves closer. The dog sniffs it and waits. Very lightly, she strokes its head. When she looks back at me with wide eyes and a smile, I feel a spray of pride.

Eyes returning to the dog, she continues to pet it. "Don't pit bulls have stand-up ears?"

"Some do," Jack says, gentling now. Animals are clearly his thing. "Some are gray. Some are black. Some are brown with white markings. They're all different, like people."

"Why does he look so sad?"

This dog's eyes are indeed soulful. I'm touched by that myself.

"Maybe because he's used to being pre-judged. Maybe because he's used to being abused."

She gasps. "*Was* he?"

"Oh yeah. He was beaten and abandoned, then turned in to a shelter that would have euthanized him if the humane society hadn't rescued him."

"What kind of shelter would euthanize a poor, abused dog?" Joy asks with disdain.

"The kind that sees an abused pet as damaged goods. Or that has too many other abused dogs, too many intractable dogs, too many dogs, period. Rescue operations go on all the time. They bring animals to parts of the country like this. We're bigger with spay and neuter here than in some parts of the country, so we have fewer unwanted litters and therefore more room in shelters for adoptable pets."

Her hand has moved to the dog's chin. "What's his name?"

"Guy."

As in, *Good Guy,* I realize, and am thinking that's an awful name for a dog, when Joy says, "That's an awful name for a dog." I don't look at her. I know the kind of face she's making, have seen it often enough when she finds something distasteful. "It's what everybody calls everybody. If he's a survivor, he needs something special like . . . like Phoenix."

"Phoenix," Jack repeats. He is making a face, too. I can hear it, though I don't look at him. My eyes are glued on the dog. Abused pets can turn in an instant.

But Jack doesn't yield. "Phoenix is no good. He wouldn't answer to that."

Joy has seen as many muzzled dogs on the streets of New York as I have, but she clearly doesn't feel threatened, either by this one or by Jack. "Then Griffin. Or Jagger."

"He knows Guy."

"Or Knox. You know, like the fort? I can't believe he would have been killed," she says as she cups the dog's chin. "He's so sweet."

"Shows the power of ignorance," Jack resumes, and I hear renewed purpose, even relief to be on safer ground again. "People make assumptions that are just plain wrong."

I look up at that, because it's clearly addressed to me, but before I can fully take in what he's said, he has refocused on Joy.

"Maybe they just don't know the truth," she says.

"Or don't want to know."

"How could someone not want to know that cruelty is bad?"

"They don't define it that way," I put in, playing devil's advocate. "They don't call it cruelty. They call it discipline. Or punishment."

"Which is a lie," Jack says, and his voice is tight again. "Some people just can't be honest. They can't see that they're being driven by anger. Or revenge." He holds my gaze now, and I know we're not talking about dogs. Last time he and I talked face-to-face, there had been anger on both sides. His mother was gone. We didn't know if she was dead, involuntarily missing, or willfully absent. All we knew was that my father was driving the boat from which she disappeared. The police investigation was done; the district attorney deemed the incident an accident. My father was cleared, but Elizabeth MacKay remained gone.

Jack was angry at me for being an Aldiss. I was angry at him for blaming me for that.

So I understand anger. But the idea of revenge appalls me. "Revenge for *what*?"

His eyes are dark and do not blink. "Things that go wrong with their own lives."

"Revenge on a *dog*?" asks Joy.

He darts her a quick glance before returning to me, like he's right back where we were twenty years ago, just the two of us. "Sometimes people dream things up. They come up with bizarre theories to excuse their own failure."

"Failure in *what*?" I ask more sharply than I should have with Joy right there, but I didn't see failure in my father. He had been frantic when he returned to shore that night. He had sped to the dock and barely tied the boat before he was out and running along the shore, searching for Elizabeth. He was shouting for the rest of us to come, desperate to get as many people looking as possible. He had been so upset that, of course, my mother and sister had assumed the wrong thing.

"Failure in life," he accuses. "Failure in love."

Joy is looking back and forth, confused. "What is he talking about, Mom?"

I suck in a deep breath, needing a moment and trying to make it look casual. I can't believe how quickly this has surfaced. But then, I'm not the one living in Elizabeth Mac-Kay's house with the detritus of the life she left behind. She was troubled. We all knew that. It was one of the few memories on which we agreed.

Chapter 5

Jack Sabathian has his mind set. I can see it in the lines between his eyes, which could as well be carved in stone. I won't win this argument. The best I can do is to extricate my daughter and me from what will only grow more contentious the longer we stay.

That said, I might have glanced at my watch in feigned surprise and made a polite excuse about needing to see to my father or help Anne or unpack. But I refuse to feign anything in front of this man—refuse to be the apologist, especially since it was *my* peaceful reunion with the water that *he* disturbed.

Instead, I sing a definitive, "Oooo-kay, this is going nowhere." Grabbing a handful of Joy's sweatshirt, I pull her toward the stairs.

We've barely taken two steps, though, when she pulls free and turns back. "You're a vet, right?" she asks Jack, just to let him know she knows, because she doesn't wait for an answer. "Can I work for you?"

"Joy!" I cry, beside her again. "Let's *go*." I hook an arm in hers, but she won't budge, simply turns wounded green eyes on me.

"I'm serious, Mom? If I was in New York, I'd be working at the shelter. What's the difference?"

"The difference—*es*," I say in a low, close voice that I hope stresses my own seriousness, since I am very much so. Seeing this man on the beach—fighting a tangle of memories—is exactly why I haven't been here for twenty years. Well, one of the reasons. The rest are up at the house. I came down here first, actually stopped at the square first to superimpose good thoughts on bad. And look what happened. I agreed to this trip because my daughter wanted it, but she needs to be a little sensitive to *my* needs. "The differences," I say, "are that we came here to spend time together on the beach and to spend time with your grandfather and your aunt, *and* we're only here for a week, and *he* isn't a *shelter*."

"What kind of work?" comes Jack's low voice.

"Thanks, but she's not interested," I say without looking his way. My eyes are on Joy, trying to drill in all that I can't say.

But the ocean must be drowning it out—either that, or stubbornness has turned her momentarily deaf, because my daughter doesn't hear a word I'm not saying. "I *am* interested," she insists and, breaking eye contact with me, tells Jack, "I'll do anything you need done? I can play with animals or feed them or change their water or scoop their poop—and I don't want pay, this is *totally* volunteer."

"Joy—"

"Volunteer, Mom," she assures me, "so it can be two hours a day for the next five days. I mean, you'll be busy cleaning Papa's house, trust me, there are piles of things *everywhere* and someone has to go through them, and just now? When I tried to move one book, *one* book off the sofa so he could sit, he told me not to touch anything and went to the only uncluttered chair in the place. So there's lots of sorting out to do, which takes someone who knows what's good and what isn't *and* who can deal with Papa—and can I really do *that*?"

"*No,*" I hiss. I can't believe that she's raised all of this in front of Jack, toward whom I hitch my head. "But *he* doesn't need an intern."

"I do," Jack asserts.

"No," I tell him and tighten my fingers on Joy's arm like I had when she was four and kicking and screaming at the pond in Central Park because she didn't want to leave. I remember being mortified because other children were well-behaved, remember being horrified having to drag her because she was too big for me to bodily lift, remember being terrified that the police would cite me for child abuse, remember realizing that I'd brought this on myself by being too permissive. It was a pivotal moment in my life as a parent.

Use your words, I would beg her, and oh yeah, doesn't *that* come back to bite me now.

"I really want to, Mom, and why does it have to be only a week? There is nothing in New York that I have to do. I mean, they won't miss me at the cat shelter, and I can do my summer reading here as well as there, and don't even *think* piano, because let's face it, I'm no Mozart. And anyway, really, don't we both deserve more than just a week off?"

"Life isn't about what we deserve," I say. "It's about what survival demands. I can't take time off. I have a job."

"You said you were cutting back."

"Not cutting *out.*"

"Oooo-kay," Joy says as I had earlier, "so you can go back and I'll stay. Annie is here, and Papa. The times I wanted to go to summer camp, you wouldn't let me, but I'm older now, and this is different, Mom. This is Bay Bluff. This is *family.*"

Softly, I say, "We'll discuss this later," and tack on a more urgent, "Please?"

Grinning a grin that smacks of victory, she bobs on the tips of her toes and gives me a quick hug—though I have no idea why, since I am not giving in. And still there's something akin to triumph in the look she shoots Jack. "I'll get back to you," she tells him like a CEO, and she's the one to lead now, taking my arm, calling back, "BTW, I like your dog!"

We're at the top of the stairs before I say, "That was not fair, Joy. There's a whole lot you don't know."

"Why are you angry?"

"Because there's *a whole lot you don't know*," I repeat and pause to let her precede me on the narrow path through the heather.

"So tell me."

"Jack used to be my best friend. Now he is not."

This message she gets. "*Tell* me," she invites, eyes widening with the salacious interest of a BFF. Only she isn't my BFF. Well, she is. But she's also my daughter. And she's only thirteen. So I really can't talk about all that.

"Later," I say, though I hate it when people use that word. Later can mean later. Or it can mean when I feel like it, or I don't want to, or never. For me, right now, it is all of the above in an I-can't-deal-with-this way.

"Well, I do like his dog," Joy remarks.

"That's fine. That's allowed." Hoping we're over a hump, I come alongside her, link our fingers, and look up at the house. "What do you think of it?"

Following my gaze, she tips her head and considers. "It's cool. Grand, actually."

"Not grand," I say. Grand is twice the size, with twice the windows and chimneys. Grand has stone on the front and a circular drive passing beneath a *porte cochere*. Grand is what we'd seen on the drive into town. The Aldiss house isn't that. But it does have location.

"Very beachy," she says. "I love the turrets."

"One's in the living room, one's in the master bedroom, and one's in the stairwell leading to the second floor. Did you go up there?"

"Not yet." She glances at the Sabathian house. "His doesn't have turrets."

"It does, only square," I say, but absently. I'm caught up now by the wide steps leading to the front porch. "We used to take family pictures here each year."

"Seriously? I want to *see*."

"You will." I don't say later, because I do mean it this time.

"We don't have any pictures of little you in New York," she complains as we start up the steps.

"No. We should." Leaving here twenty years before, I hadn't wanted reminders. Actually, I hadn't realized twenty years would pass before I returned. "Omigod, the rockers. Still rocking. Know how many sunsets we saw from here?" These were good memories. Letting them open, a morning glory unfurling, I drop Joy's hand, rush to the nearest rocker, and plop down.

"Mom."

She wants to go inside, but I'm not ready. Closing my eyes, I rock. Wood creaks on wood, a long familiar, eternally soothing sound.

Then comes another creak, this one the screen door. "Here you are," Anne says. I open my eyes to find her rubbing her hands together. "Okay. Dinner. I'm grilling steak, but are you still not eating meat, Joy?"

Mercifully, Joy is gracious. "It's okay. I'll eat whatever else you have."

"Your grandfather likes brown rice with his steak. Does that work for you?"

"Awesome," she says and reaches for my hand.

I want to resist. I could stay out here forever, where there's freedom and fresh air. But I can only put off the inevitable so long. Letting myself be pulled from the rocker, I take the screen door from Anne and follow them inside.

I don't want to be here . . . don't want to be here . . . don't want to . . .

The thought reverberates outward from my brain to my nerve endings, because nothing here has changed, not the misty seascape on the wall, the time-stained Berber underfoot, the slant of late-day light spilling through mullioned glass—and not my sense of being an outlier in this house.

But I am here. And wallowing in the why of it accomplishes nothing.

Tamping down my unease, I breathe deeply of the sea smell that may be more faint here than outside, but that walls can't completely block. Salt air works for me. I cling to it for strength as I look around.

The large front hall spills into the living room, both as dark with wood and fabric as ever, both as handsome—or potentially so, because my daughter is right. The place is a mess. Once there was plenty of sitting space. Now, newspapers, magazines, and books sit where we used to. Dirty glasses and mugs litter a side table seconds before Anne sweeps them up.

All of that is secondary, though, to the man in his chair. Seeing him here, I'm apprehensive as I wasn't at Urgent Care. Here is home, which makes it different. I want him to recognize me. I want him to smile and be glad that I've come and say that he's missed me. I want him to love me.

Well, *that* thought just slipped out. I push it away, but the point remains. I haven't realized how high the stakes are— haven't allowed myself to dwell on them, but now that I'm here, they hit me in the face. I want so much.

Dad's chair is a large leather wingback thing whose claw feet must have put down roots through the carpet and into the floorboards by now. He always loved that chair. There was something throne-like about its placement, in that it gave him a view of the entire room. The rest of us knew not to sit in it, unless he and Mom were both gone, at which point we would fight over who would sit there. Well, Margo and Anne fought. I waited until they lost interest before sneaking in and curling up on the indented cushions with the smell of leather, Tom Aldiss, and a book.

"I need to talk with Papa," I whisper to Joy and cross to him. When he lifts his eyes, I squat down with a hand on the nail heads outlining the chair's leather arm. This steadies me as his sharp look does not. He is the only one of us with blue eyes; like Mom, we girls all have versions of green. Mom had wanted a boy, if only to maximize the chance of having one of her children looking like Tom. One of Margo's sons has blue eyes. But so does her husband.

"Hi, Daddy."

His sharp look—startled, perhaps—softens with a smile. "How are you?"

It's a polite smile, but it's something. "I'm good. And you?"

"I'm good, too." He pauses, remembers. "Except for this." He twitches the cast.

"Those attic stairs are treacherous."

"Attic stairs?" he mocks, like I'm daft. "It wasn't the attic stairs. I was running out to the car and tripped on a rock. Your mother always warns me not to run, but do I listen?"

He's gotten the tense wrong with regard to my mother, and certainly the details of the accident. But the story he tells is credible enough. "Does it hurt?"

"No." He dismisses the matter with a loud, "How's San Antonio?"

"We're in New York, Joy and I." I hitch my head toward the door, but she has gone out to get our bags from the car. "My daughter."

He scowls. "Well, I know that. Why do you people think I can't remember things? I didn't get where I am today with a bad mind." He returns to his paper.

"Whatcha reading?"

"I'm not read-ing." He enunciates the word the way he always used to when he disagreed with something I said.

"I'm doing the cross-word puz-zle. People without memories can't do those, in case you're wondering."

"I'm sure your memory is fine," I say in an effort to appease.

He glares at me. "And if it isn't? And if it *isn't*? I have a right to forget things once in a while. I'm seventy-two, for chrissake." His brows are still menacing when they come together. They're more gray than his silver hair, and messier. "Don't you have something else to do?"

I certainly do, like ask him if he has a gun. But his own question is so Tom Aldiss—ornery at a time when Tom Aldiss is fading, that I leave the moment alone. Besides, Joy is coming through the front door with the bags. So I rise and go to help.

The stairs to the second floor hug the round turret walls, and while worn carpet runners mute sound, the creaks beneath it have multiplied since last I was here. I know. I used to be intimate with those creaks. When we were growing up, staying out late involved risk. Mom wasn't bad; she would often appear at her door to see which one of us it was and put a finger to her lips in warning before slipping back inside.

"Omigod, Mom, these are *amazing*," Joy breathes before I can dredge up the consequences of Dad being the one to find us.

Having stopped several steps behind me, she is studying the photos on the wall—because here they are as they always were, lining the turret, our front porch shots from the beginning of time. Funny, how I would have walked past them. I've seen them so many times in my life that they're like wallpaper, and my mind is elsewhere. Now I see what my daughter sees, no wallpaper these.

The earliest are black-and-white close-ups of Mom, Dad, and Margo, labeled 1978 and 1979 in white marker, very small and slanted in the lower right-hand corner. Come 1980,

I'm the one in Mom's arms, and while the year remains marked in white, the photos are in color.

Well, were in color. In those first days of color photography, the materials were primitive. These prints aren't even in direct sunlight, but their colors have faded. Looking ahead, the color deepens as the materials improve. But the transition is an interesting one from mono- to polychromatic.

"Poor you," Joy wails. Having deposited her bag on the stair, she is pointing at 1982. "Anne's the baby in Papa's arms, and there you are, stuck on the ground, holding onto your mother's leg. You don't look happy."

I study the shot. Margo, tall at age four, stands between my parents. Her back was as ramrod straight then as now. Anne is cuddling into Dad, the wisps of dark hair on her one-year-old head buried against his throat. And yes, there I am at age two beside Mom. No, not happy. Her hand around my shoulder isn't enough. I want to be held.

"And this one," Joy effuses, pointing at the picture taken two years later. I was four, still with Mom's hand on my shoulder, but facing front, chin raised, more confident. Or is that chin-tilt defiance? Or resignation? Whatever, Anne was on her feet but leaning into Dad's side much as she had snuggled in infancy. Margo still stood straight between them.

"If you're the middle child, why aren't you in the middle?" Joy asks.

"It just started this way and stayed this way." I wave at the photos up the line. "We always took the same spots."

"Just took them?"

"We were placed at first, then it became habit."

"Who placed you?"

"Mom—Dad—I don't remember." I'm trying to, when Joy follows up with a question that opens a whole other door.

"Who took the photos?"

"Elizabeth."

"*That* Elizabeth? Was she a photographer?"

"No, but since she lived next door, it was easy. We had a cookout together every Fourth of July. Her taking our family shot became a tradition."

"Was she related to Papa?"

"No."

"But they built houses here at the same time."

"Coincidence," I say, though I've never been sure. Margo insists that Dad and Elizabeth were lovers who decided to marry other people and came to regret it. But that's Margo. Me, I'll grant that they knew each other, liked each other, even loved each other once, but after they married others, that was done. I never wanted to think that Dad would cheat on Mom. Or that Mom would put up with it.

I mean, seriously, what husband would keep a lover living right next door? What wife wouldn't suspect and object? What daughter wouldn't be able to figure it out?

Me. For all the times I felt there was an answer just out of my reach, I could never wrap my fingers around it and pull it clear.

I'm feeling the frustration of this when, having lifted her bag, Joy begins climbing stairs to study more pictures. They go three-quarters of the way to the second floor before yielding to bare wall.

She gets that one fast. "The pictures stopped when Elizabeth died."

"Uh-huh." I try to make light of it. But Joy gets this, too.

"There were no pictures to take. The family scattered."

It hadn't been instant, like a single day and then—whooosh—gone. Elizabeth fell overboard in early July. There were headlines—some salacious—and a search, followed by a police investigation. Even after the case was judged an accidental drowning and closed, the search for Elizabeth went on. Dad hired investigators. He was obsessed. So was Jack, who was convinced that the investigation had been tainted—whitewashed was the word he used—by Dad's prominence, and that Dad's obsession was akin to Shakespeare's lady protesting too much.

Mom was in so much pain that I could never talk about it with her. I didn't want to make things worse by asking questions. And, really, it wasn't a mystery. She was humiliated. Who wouldn't be, given the headlines?

I returned to college in late August. Margo stayed a little longer to support Mom, leaving only after her own classes had begun. Mom lasted another month before filing for divorce and moving back to her hometown in Illinois.

None of us three ever returned. Margo met Dan during her last year at U Chicago, and since Mom was nearby, she stayed out there. I graduated, moved to Manhattan, and took a job with a commercial photographer. One of our clients, the editor of a food magazine, was putting her condo on the market and wanted photos as appealing as the ones we'd made of a chocolate ganache cake with raspberry drizzle. Her broker became my first recurring client.

There was no point in coming home. I had Anne down to visit me, often to meet up with Mom, though she would never breathe a word of that in Bay Bluff. Dad being Dad, divided loyalties weren't allowed. His truth was the whole truth. If we couldn't live with it, well, that was that. No, I didn't take sides—I assiduously did not. But Mom needed me more than he ever had. She loved me more than he ever had. Did I really have a choice?

Mom blossomed once she was free of Dad. Though we didn't see each other often—she was busy, I was busy—we grew closer. Her death was a blow.

"Yup. The family scattered," I tell Joy as we continue up the stairs.

My parents' bedroom is—was—down the hall to the left. Margo's bedroom was near theirs. They had initially planned it as a nursery with the intention of moving out one child when another came along. I remember hearing Mom say that, but when I repeated it once to Margo, her vehemence taught me to never say it again. It was what it was. Margo's room stayed Margo's room, evolving in style from infancy to childhood to adolescence. Anne and I, arriving within a year of each other, had rooms down the hall to the right.

I lead Joy toward mine. The door is slightly ajar and seeming to breathe. When I push it wide, I see that Anne has opened both windows to air out the place. There is still a mustiness, but the ocean breeze is doing its thing.

"Your. Room," Joy declares with a mega-smile. Having dropped her bag on the double bed, she wraps an elbow around one of its tall pine posts and slowly swivels.

Little has changed here either. The same plaid quilt covers the bed, the same corduroy covers the armchair. The desk where I did homework has the same brass lamp arching over a collection of papers and books. For a split second, I think the latter are a spillover from downstairs—but no, this room hasn't been touched since I left, other than by the breeze that is currently etching striations in the dust.

Nope. The mess here is all mine. These books are from my freshman year in college, deposited when I came home that horrid summer and never removed. Now they seem like fragments of a different era, relics not to be disturbed—and still, feeling a kind of morbid curiosity, I touch a cover, a spine.

Joy distracts me with a reverential whisper. "This place is a *gallery*."

Looking around, I have to agree. Photographs are my wallpaper, covering most every inch of space. I had come to take them for granted, like the family photos in the turret—just more of those things in life that we see so often we don't see at all.

But Joy's eye is fresh. Definitely, a gallery. Unlike the formal family shots climbing the stairs, these are candids of Margo and Anne, Mom and Margo, Dad and Mom. There is a shot of two high school friends taken from behind, hung here not because of my closeness to them but the beauty of the composition as they sit in the dunes.

"Well, *he* is cool," Joy remarks. It is Jack in profile as he looks out to sea. His hair is longer, his features less marked. He might have been sixteen at the time, but his gaze seems prophetic.

"I told you," I remind her, lest she start imagining, "we were good friends."

"When you get past the hair, he kind of looks the same."

But I move on. "Tennis," I say, pointing at a grouping of shots in which I'm running, arching into a serve, leaping sideways for a volley, executing a doublehanded backhand with a ferocious look on my face. "I was pretty good."

"You never play now."

"No time, no place."

"Who took these?"

She is probably wondering if it was Elizabeth again, but it definitely was not. "My mother."

"You never said she was into photography?"

"She was into lots of things—y'know, trying out bridge, then photography, even conversational *Italian* until she found what she liked."

"Accounting," Joy says, having heard this part of the story before.

"She was actually an old hand at it. Bills, taxes, you name it, she did it in the shadow of the toughest critic of all."

"Papa?" Joy asks with interest.

"Definitely Papa."

"Why didn't he just do it himself?"

"Go ask."

"I will."

"Don't!" I quickly cry. My *go ask* had been a throwaway expression, but I should have known better. As much of a role model as Jack Sab was about how not to raise an only child, my daughter is still a work in progress. "Those are the kind of memories we don't need to dredge up. Besides, it worked to Mom's advantage. Once she was back in Chicago after the divorce, she went to school, which she would never have done here. She became a CPA, and she was good at it. She knew how to handle difficult men," I add, because this is on the short list of the things my sisters and I do agree on.

"Yay for the girl," Joy declares.

"Absolutely," I second, because while she's sincere, I have a point to make, here in this house, where my mother was held back in so many regards. "She built a career when she was in her forties and competing against men in their twenties. We should all be so strong."

"Did she teach you photography?"

"No, but I took over her equipment and found what worked for me."

"Was Papa okay with that?"

She surprises me. "What do you mean?"

"It was your Mom's thing, and they got divorced."

"Uh . . . uh . . . that's an interesting question." I've always clumped his dislike of my art with his general disapproval of what I did. He desperately wanted a son. I was the second disappointment for him in that sense. Though he and I had shared intermittent moments of connection, I always felt it was a lost cause. I was never quite good enough.

So maybe his annoyance with Mom was to blame for this part of it, at least. Crossing to the bookshelf, I take her camera—my very first—from the next-to-top shelf. "Could never give this away," I murmur with a swell of affection. I brush the dust from the top with my thumb, savoring the old familiar feel of the shutter speed dial, the film winder, the on-off lever.

"This is *ancient*," Joy says.

"Not really. At least, not in years. The technology of picture-taking has grown so fast that it just *seems* ancient."

Returning the camera to its shelf with a gentle stroke and a promise to hold it again later, I return to the other photos it helped me make. People pictures aside, the rest are black-and-white shots of the beach, many taken from the very same spot at the base of the bluff, but so different, one to the next, that I impress myself.

"This is what our condo is missing," Joy states.

"My pictures are on the wall there."

"But they aren't old ones, like ones with history?"

"Don't confuse black-and-white with old, sweetie. Besides, I have black-and-white shots hanging at home."

"I know, Mom, but, I mean, look at these? These pictures tell a story." She is focused on a grouping of seascapes above the bed.

Her comment is innocent enough. But when I look at her, something squeezes my heart. Here she is, my daughter, in the bedroom where my own childhood was spent—and how *not* to think of my mother in this, too? Joy was a toddler when she died, too young for them to know one another, and still Mom helped me raise her. *What would my mother do?* I often asked myself when I didn't know how to handle my child's quirks. Eleanor Aldiss had been a single mom too, in her way.

Standing in this place now, I'm caught in dusty little cobwebs of happiness, grief, confusion and purpose. But there's something else. For not the first time today, I feel pride, because Joy is right. These pictures do tell a story. The fact that she gets this brings tears to my eyes.

Wrapping my arms around her from behind, I rest my chin on her shoulder and inhale her sweet scent.

"The ocean," Joy breathes in a way that says she's imagining the stories. "Time. Fog. Sand." She angles to meet my eyes. "I want to see more people pictures."

"You will. They're in the attic."

She lights up. But my mind is a step ahead. I'm wondering why my father went up there this morning, only to stumble on the way down and break his wrist.

The word *gun* comes to mind.

Access to the attic is through the closet in the spare bedroom. Since that room is directly across the hall from mine, I'm quickly there. I see the same large, eyelet-covered bed, the same bench at its foot, the same dresser. And the closet. Its door is open to a tangle of hangers collected over the years, lit now by the attic light falling through the open hatch. Bisecting its beam, the stairs slant to a point just inches above the wood floor. These stairs, too, are wood, and while they're secured by a metal frame and therefore sturdy, they are narrow. I understand why Dad lost his footing. Lord knew we all had done it once or twice.

Several books lie scattered at the foot of the stairs. They are blue leather and vaguely warped, but as familiar to me as the old camera in my room.

"Lawyer's Diaries," I tell Joy. Crouching, I finger the once bright, now dull lettering on the front. "Dad wrote in them every night."

Joy squats beside me and lifts one. "1996. Crazy." She flips it open.

I flip it shut. "Confidential."

Her eyes meet mine, her face an adorably bemused *where-did-that-come-from* mask. "Seriously? After so long? Like I'll recognize names—or even understand what's in there? What is in there?"

"I don't know. I never saw. Touch Thomas Aldiss's diaries, and he swatted you away. And not just me. Any of us."

"State secrets," Joy intones with the drama of a girl who has read a thriller or two. "Classified information."

"Nothing as glamorous as that," says Anne from the door of the room. She has pulled her hair into a ponytail but looks only marginally more conventional. The burgundy streak snakes back from her left temple. "There are dates, appointment reminders, notes about clients when he was in private practice and about cases when he was on the bench."

"So you've looked inside them?" Joy asks.

"Oh yeah." My sister has one hand on the door frame and appears to feel no guilt. "He allowed us to look. He just chose which pages we could see, and he had to do that. I mean, legally. He couldn't show us everything. What kind of lawyer would do that? What kind of *judge*?" To me, she says, "You remember him as a disciplinarian, but he wasn't always so strict."

I'm thinking that Margo would have something pithy to say about that, when Anne tells Joy, "Papa loves music. Will you go down and play the piano for him?"

Joy laughs. "On what?"

There was a silent beat. "Duh."

"I didn't see a piano."

"You didn't look past the front rooms. Try the conservatory."

I'm the one who laughs now. "The conservatory? That's rich. Joy, she means the sunroom, out the door at the back of the living room. And she's right. He'll love it."

"Did Margo play the piano?" Joy asks me.

"Nope."

Breaking into a bright smile, she jauntily pushes to her feet. I catch her hand as she starts to breeze past me, but when she eyes me in question, I pause. How to explain that I don't want her to leave me alone in this house, that she is my confidence here, physical proof that I've done plenty right?

But I'm not going into that now, not with Anne at the door. So I just mime a kiss and release her hand.

Anne watches after her until we hear her skip down the stairs. Then, pushing her hands deep into her coverall pockets, she enters the room. "I didn't want to talk in front of her. I'm really glad you're here, Mal."

She stops short of saying something, simply presses her

lips together and looks at the fallen books. As I wait for whatever it is that she doesn't want Joy to hear, I gather them up and, climbing the stairs just enough, slide them onto the attic floor. The attic is something to search. There are photos there that Joy wants to see, and other personal mementos of mine. There may be a gun.

Behind me, Anne remains quiet, but she wouldn't have come up here for nothing. After backing down the steps with care, I turn to face her.

Chapter 6

"I wasn't sure you'd ever come back," she says. The hands in her pockets bring her shoulders together, giving the illusion of a shrug. Clearly, she's unsure of the me who is here.

"I wasn't either." I glance at the attic. "Remember how we used to play there?"

When she breaks into a smile, I relax a little. This is the Anne I want to see. Sunny side up starts with her face. "The attic was our clubhouse. Margo was the president, you kept the records, I did the food. Even then."

"By the way, your shop looks adorable," I say. I'm not trying to butter her up. Well, yes. I am. I know there's a "but" behind that smile and want to put her at ease. "I love the logo."

"I love the whole place."

"A lot of work?"

"Nah. It's just breakfast and lunch."

Giving her time to elaborate, I pull up the bottom section of stairs. It creaks as it folds, but soon enough the base covers the hatch with only a short piece of rope hanging to lower it again.

Anne is too quiet. Normally, she would go on about Sunny Side Up, which is why I raised the issue. The shop is something she does well. But she is definitely uneasy.

Gently, I say, "I'm not here to cause trouble, Annie. That's the last thing I want."

Her eyes hold mine. They're the same dark green as Joy's when she's scared. "What's the first?"

I consider. How to prioritize? "Seeing Dad, I guess." *So how did that work for ya?* a voice inside me asks, and I wince. "He didn't look pleased."

"He was unsettled, is all. He didn't expect you to come. If I'd known ahead of time, I could have prepared him."

"How bad is he?"

She wrinkles her nose. "Not bad at all. You'll see. He eats, he sleeps, he walks, he talks. He does everything he normally did, except work."

"And remember who Joy is."

"But he does," she enthuses with a new light in her eyes. "He kept looking back at her in the car and saying, 'Mallory's daughter, Mallory's daughter,' like he didn't believe she was here—and he said it in a really excited way. He loves that you brought her."

I hoped that. The alternative was that his repetition of who she is was an attempt to drum it in so that he didn't forget again.

"His memory isn't what it used to be," Anne goes on. "He wants to see the three of us here, and Joy looks like Margo. It was wishful thinking, is all."

He isn't the only one suffering from that. I cross to the window. The beauty of being on the bluff is that every window has a striking view. This one is part ocean, part land. I want to focus on the ocean half, which is more open, certainly more soothing to me, but that's the coward's way. Land is where the people are. Sure, open ocean can be lethal, but so can people. Is my father a murderer, or is he not? The answer isn't out there in the deep blue. It's here on land.

Returning, I sit on the bench at the foot of the bed and pat the spot beside me, like I would do at home with Joy.

Seeming grateful for the invitation, Anne comes right over and sits close enough beside me that our arms touch. And there's a memory here, too.

For an instant, we're conspirators again. I whisper, "Remember ganging up on Margo?"

She whispers back, "Oh yeah." We're both eyeing the closed hatch. "She'd be up there ordering us around, and we'd sit here so quiet, *so* quiet that she'd finally come to the door and look down and see us and hit the roof that we hadn't already come back with her peanut butter Triscuits."

"We'd just stare up at her."

"It took two of us to defy her."

"She wasn't always bad."

"She was imperious."

"And where did she get that?" I ask, the words slipping out before I can think better of it.

Anne angles away to face me. "Don't blame Dad. If he was imperious, it was because Mom needed direction. Mom was a ditz."

"Only when she was with Dad. He didn't take kindly to competent women."

"But he has a heart, Mal. He suffered when the family broke apart. He's been lonely."

There are a number of things I might say to that, the first involving my mother, who did not *need* direction. She proved that ten times over after the divorce. She was a strong woman held down by an authoritarian thumb. Why she allowed it was another of the questions I wanted to ask, but that would take us off topic.

Levelly, I say, "I'm just trying to explain why Margo grew to be forceful. She wasn't the boy Dad wanted, but he pushed her to accomplish. When she refused to go into law, there was a huge scene. Remember?"

"It wasn't a huge scene. It was a discussion. He was perfectly reasonable. He said she had choices, and he ended it by saying she should do what she wants."

Those might have been the words, but the tone was something else. I remember anger and shouting. I remember a level of hostility that drove me from the living room and had me hiding in my bedroom for hours. But that was me. I hated fights. Margo welcomed them, and Anne? Anne was always able to simply tune out the bad.

"I'm just saying," I try to explain, since Margo isn't here to defend herself, "that in some regards, she had it worse than we did. His expectations for her were high."

Anne gives a twisted smile. "Oh yeah. Expectations. He had none for me. That made it easy."

She tosses off the statement like it's a good thing, but I wonder. The lightness is a cover for what sounds like hurt. Either that's new, or I was simply too wound up in my own thoughts to see it before.

Wanting the space between us gone, I loop my arm through hers and lean just that little bit her way. "How is he about that now?"

"Expectations? Good, actually. He has mellowed, Mal. Blame it on memory if you want, but he doesn't hold grudges the way he used to. And as for Sunny Side Up? He doesn't know what to do with someone who owns an eatery, so he's open-minded."

"Does he ask you questions about it?"

"Sometimes, like how do I know to fry his eggs over easy or where do I get these terrific mugs. He doesn't ask about the money part of it. I'm not sure he can relate to that."

"To running a business?" I ask in surprise. "Business law was his specialty in private practice."

"I think it's just the fact that I'm doing it. He still relates to business, at least, to hear his remarks when he's going through the *Wall Street Journal*."

"So he does read it?"

"Well, he must if he's able to repeat what he does. He still gets it, Mal. Just not," she hesitates, "all the time." Her back stiffens, eyes sharpen. "But I know what you're thinking, and you're wrong. This is *not* cause for dragging him to an Alzheimer's specialist. He's seventy-two. Everyone who's seventy-two forgets things. By the time you reach that age there's so much junk crammed in the brain that stuff just overflows and is lost. Dad does not have Alzheimer's disease. I don't want him labeled that way. So if that's why you're here—"

"It's not, Annie, not."

"But you're worried that I'm not taking care of him."

"No. I'm worried that he's doing things behind your back."

"Like buying a gun? I told you Jack was dreaming that up, but okay," she nods, "I searched the house anyway. I checked his bedroom and the kitchen. I looked inside planters in the conservatory and under cushions in the living room and behind hats and gloves in the hall closet. I looked behind books—I'm telling you, I looked everywhere I could think of where he might have hidden a gun, but there was nothing. Nothing."

I glance at the hatch. "Not up there?"

"Especially not there." She seems wounded that I suggested it. "That's the first place I checked, because he likes going up. I think there's something about the oldness of what's there, or maybe the smell of time, and his *diaries,* he loves reading those. This isn't the first time he's brought a few down." Her voice has risen. "So, yeah, it was the *first* place I checked. That would be an obvious place to hide a gun, right? But there isn't one up there. And here's another thing, Mallory. He's so forgetful that I honestly think if he stashed a gun somewhere, he'd forget where it is."

Which returns us to his mental health. "There's medication for that."

Her eyes flare. "Not. Alzheimer's."

"It's *okay,* Annie," I try to soothe her. "It doesn't have to be Alzheimer's, doesn't have to be dementia at all, it can simply be memory loss, but unless you go to the right doctor, you won't get the right help."

"Will you tell him that?" She is indignant now. "Will you convince him that his mind is failing and he needs help? Will you take him there?"

"Yes."

Anne barks out a laugh. "And you seriously think he'll agree to it?" Pulling free, she stands. As she looks down at me, her drawn-back dark hair with its burgundy streak seems too stark, her jaw too tight. I barely have time to brace myself, when she says, "See, that's what I hate, Mallory. You don't see him every day, like haven't spent any significant time with him in *twenty years,* but suddenly you're an expert?"

Put that way, I feel totally wrong—both for having abandoned Anne and for disagreeing with what she's chosen to do on her own. But there's a flip side. Gently, sensibly, pleadingly, I say, "No, I'm not an expert, and you're right, I haven't spent enough time with him to know much. But because I *don't* see him every day, I can see the change since I saw him last."

"Since you saw him last." She rolls her eyes and sighs, though she is anything but relaxed. "So he's three years older. So he forgets things. So he doesn't want to go places. So he's sometimes depressed, because he actually loved Mom and she's gone, and he actually loved Margo, and he actually loved you, and all he's got now is me. So I try to make things easier for him, and if that means overlooking small stuff, I do. I don't care if he sits reading in his chair for hours. I don't care if he's turning pages just for the heck of it. That doesn't mean he's sick."

Put that way, it doesn't. Unless he isn't reading at all, because the words make no sense. Unless he's depressed because he knows his mind is rotting. Unless he doesn't want to go places because he fears he'll meet friends whose names he can't remember.

"And *besides,*" Anne says, "do you think I haven't thought of these things? Do you think I haven't searched the web to compare him with other people his age? Do you think I haven't read and reread the symptoms of Alzheimer's disease? I'm not stupid, Mallory. I know the possibilities. I just refuse to assume the worst because other people think they know better—"

"I don't—"

"You *do,* but how *can* you? How can *anyone*? It's impossible to diagnose Alzheimer's for sure until a person is dead, and—here's a flash—Dad isn't dead. He's still living, and he may live for a long time. Am I supposed to treat him like he has one foot in the grave? I refuse to do that. I'm living here with him, trying to keep up his spirits, trying to make his life easy and pleasant, even fun. So if you suddenly think you have all the answers, let's hear them."

She juts out her chin, rounds her eyes in demand, and stands there, waiting.

I hold up my hands, half-afraid to speak. I always think of Anne as young, because she acts it and dresses it and is just that little bit younger than me. But there's something weary in her now. Something *wary.* The Anne staring at me is someone new.

"Why did you come?" she finally asks. "If it's because you want to see whether I'm taking care of things, you can head back to New York in the morning. Everything's fine here." She turns to leave, then swivels back. "And anyway, how long *are* you staying?"

"Joy wants to stay the week. Actually," I try to make a joke of it, "she wants to stay the whole summer."

Anne looks horrified. "The *whole* summer? You can't do that."

"No. I can't." But her tone annoys me. It is everything I've always dreaded about this place, the sense of not belonging. Annoys me? *Infuriates* me. This is as much my house as Anne's. Technically, I can stay as long as I want. "Part of the reason I'm here," I tell her, doing my best to sound conciliatory while I make my point, "is because you made me feel guilty when we talked on the phone. I can't stay here long—I have to be back at work a week from tomorrow—but I thought you'd want my help, even for a little while."

"Not if it comes with strings."

"Like my forcing you to do what you don't want to do? Have I ever done that?"

"Not in words." Accusatory eyes finish the sentence.

I should have hedged and apologized and reassured her. But *not in words* rubs me the wrong way, too. *Not in words* is what I most detest about this place. *Not in words* is all that I didn't understand about why I am who I am. My parents didn't discuss things. As a parent now, I do. As an *adult* now, I do. And Anne's accusation is wrong.

Perhaps unwisely, but unable to hold it in, I say, "That's your insecurity speaking."

She jerks back. "Insecurity? I am not insecure. I know who I am and what I'm doing and who I'm doing it with, which also means I can date who I want." The last is a clear reference to Billy Houseman. "I'm not a child, so if you think you can treat me like Joy, you can turn right around and drive back to New York tonight. Don't even bother to unpack. You can get dinner on the road."

I barely have time to stand before she storms out.

What to do? I don't belong here. Anne's outburst validates my having stayed away for so long.

That said, alone in this barren bedroom, I feel a great emptiness. Anne is my little sister. In all those years we lived here together, we never went at each other this way. Granted, what happened twenty years ago fractured us. Granted, my life is light years removed from Anne's. I'm a different person now. Apparently, she is, too. She resents me. Deeply.

What to do? She is angry. She doesn't mean what she said—well, maybe she does mean the words, but certainly not the hatred I felt receiving them. And if I take her advice and leave tonight? My father won't know the difference. He'll forget I was here. I've seen the house, and it's not falling down, as Jack implied, and he has seen me, too. I came, I saw, I checked off that box.

But is Dad a murderer? Is he a danger to Anne or Jack or some other innocent in town?

What to do? I'm still standing in the guest bedroom, not knowing where my steps should lead, when I hear faint strains of the piano drifting up the stairs, around the turret, and along the hall. Crossing to the door, I lean against the jamb and listen to Joy, who is tentative at first, then more confident. She is playing by heart—no, no prodigy, but she does have an ear for music. I recognize Beethoven's "Moonlight Sonata," though there is a slight deviation in the usual rhythm. Joy is being Joy, either simply feeling the music or knowing that I need soothing. I listen, breathe deeply and feel calmer.

We'll stay here, of course. She would be crushed if I dragged her away from something she has just discovered and so badly wants. She has just as much a right to this place as I do, and if Anne doesn't like it, that's *her* problem.

Actually, it's my problem. By the time dinner is done, I realize that. I try to make conversation with Dad—ask how his wrist feels, whether he's read anything good, whether he'll take me to Sunny Side Up for breakfast tomorrow—but he answers each with a yes or a no. When nothing follows, I try to make conversation with Anne—ask whether she hires more help for the summer, mention that I saw Deanna Smith and Joey DiMinico and a blonde-haired woman, girl actually, who looked so much like Elizabeth MacKay that I got the chills. Dad doesn't react to the Elizabeth mention, and my sister simply says that her name is Lily and that she works at the shop.

"Lily?" I ask, startled. I realize that this must be the woman Dad stares at. "Short for Elizabeth?" The coincidence would be too much.

"Short for Amelia," Anne states. "Amelia Ackerman from Boise, Idaho." Her stare tells me that she knows what I'm thinking and am wrong.

On the plus side, Anne has served the steak presliced for all of us, so that Dad can easily handle it without using his left hand. I have to give her points for foresight.

And they both do talk to Joy, even my father, who asks surprisingly good questions. *How long have you studied the piano? Where do you go to school? What's your favorite subject?* They're sensible questions, the kind any grandparent might ask, to which Anne looks smug. Me? I'm relieved to hear him this way. I don't want him to have Alzheimer's disease. I don't want him to have dementia, period.

Then, abruptly and wordlessly, he stands and leaves the table. We've barely finished our steak. Fresh-from-the-oven brownies are cooling on the stove for dessert.

Joy watches him go with a look of alarm, before glancing at me, then at Anne. "Was it something I said?"

"No, hon, he's just tired," Anne explains. "He gets like that sometimes."

"The way he just picked up and left, that was weird," Joy says.

My sister snickers. "Not with my father. He engages and disengages at will. He was always that way," she says, shooting me a look that dares me to disagree.

I can't. Yes, Dad always did what he wanted when he wanted, to hell with social norms. We assumed it was just an authoritative personality doing its own thing. In this instance, though, it could be that the effort to be "normal" has exhausted him, which happens to those with Alzheimer's, I've read.

But right now, that's neither here nor there. As I load the dishwasher, while beside me, not three feet away, a silent Anne cuts into the brownie pan, I'm thinking that this week could be tough. Between my father and her, I'm invisible.

Okay. So this week isn't about me. It isn't even about whether Dad shot Elizabeth. This week is about Joy.

Still, how not to take it personally, given my history here? I don't need, don't *want* to be the center of attention, but I can only ask so many questions about Anne, about Dad, about Bay Bluff, before silence sets in. Back in New York, Joy has plenty to say at my slightest suggestion, has plenty to initiate herself, and when silence settles there, it's a comfortable one. This one is not. Aren't they curious about my life? Do they care at all that I'm here?

The brownies are yummy, as I knew they would be. Anne always knew her way around a kitchen, even when we were kids. And the vanilla ice cream she scoops on top, quickly melting on the brownie's warmth? I have two helpings, I am that desperate to show Anne that I appreciate her efforts. But it isn't until I tell her Joy and I will finish cleaning up, that she brightens. Tossing the dish towel aside with a flourish, she announces that she's going out, tells us—me—not to wait up, and breezes out the back door.

Joy stares after her, before turning baffled eyes on me. "Did she even tell Papa she was leaving?"

Of course not. Doing that would have ruined the drama of her exit. *Take care of everything here,* her flourish said. *Everything.*

Feeling newly responsible, I go looking for my father. He is asleep in his chair, head back, mouth open. I watch him for a minute, seeing so much older a man than the one in my memories that I feel a great sadness.

But he needs to be in bed. "Daddy," I whisper, gently shaking his arm.

He comes awake with a jolt, looks around, then straight at me with piercing, if faded blue eyes. He knows just where he is. I'm the only thing out of place. "Mallory?" he asks, curious.

He knows my face. And curious is better than disappointed. My heart leaps. "It *is* me."

He considers that with a frown, studying me for so long I have to fight not to squirm like a frightened child. Then his eyes clear and sadden.

In a voice that is filled with regret, he says, "It was guilt."

I wait for more. Terrified that he'll leave it there, I gently coax, "What was?"

"Why she left. We had an agreement. Neither of us would tell."

My heart beats faster. "Tell what?"

"What she did. Why she did it. We made a pact. I wouldn't tell about her, if she didn't tell about me. Many couples do that. They have to, to survive. When there are children involved, and reputations . . ." His gaze clouds and, like his voice, drifts away.

Agreement. Pact. Children. The words reverberate, fading in and out. He's talking about Elizabeth, of course. Or is he? My rational mind has a second rational interpretation, but it's so abhorrent that I chalk it up to fear. I need more. I *feel* more. There's a memory here, but I can't touch it.

"Dad," I whisper. His eyes fly to mine. "Do you know where she went?"

He looks back at me. "Who?" he asks, as though just now joining the discussion.

And for several beats, I can't answer. There's something about that memory. Try as I might, though, I get nowhere. All that's left is common sense in the here and now.

"Elizabeth," I say.

"Elizabeth," he repeats and is suddenly back. "How would I know that? I've told you time and again. She was on the boat one minute and off it the next. Why are you bringing up Elizabeth?"

I swallow. "Well, you mentioned her, so I thought . . ."

"Thought what?" he barks.

The man with answers is gone. Whether willfully or beyond his control, the moment of confession is lost. Releasing a breath, I say as gently as I can, "Why don't you go to bed?"

He scowls at his watch. "I never go to bed this early."

"You were just sleeping—"

"I was not. I'm not old, and I'm not sick." He flicks me away. "Go. Now. I have reading to do before morning."

Backing off, I rejoin Joy at the archway and take her hand. "We'll be outside," I call his way. "Let me know if you need anything."

"What would I need?" my father shouts. "I have everything I need, and if I need something, I can get it myself. I'm perfectly capable of doing that, you know. A broken wrist doesn't make me infirm."

Absurdly, his outburst works for me. My father was always moody, quick to anger, a stickler for what he sees as fact. But I have my daughter with me now. She is *my* fact. Leaving the man and my little bits of memory behind, I continue onto the deeply-shadowed porch.

"Is he always like that?" Joy asks when the screen door slaps shut.

"No. He's angry."

"Because we're here?"

"Because we haven't been here before. And because he probably does not have reading to do. And because he can't remember things he wants to, and he knows that his life is narrowing in. Getting older can be beautiful or not." I tug her down beside me on the steps and drawl, "Aren't you glad we're here?"

A pair of geese pass overhead, honking in laughter.

Joy isn't laughing. "I *am*. We don't get this in New York." She is staring out across the darkening heather toward the ocean. "I can't imagine seeing this every day. It must have been awesome." The dying sun is edging the horizon's clouds an orangey pink. Closer to shore, the surf has settled into a gentle gather-and-break. Sage is in the air, carried in from the bluff on the breeze.

I need my camera.

No. Some experiences are better experienced in the flesh. Some memories are better formed firsthand, and sitting here arm to arm, hip to hip with my daughter as the sun sets is one.

"So much can change," I whisper, since speaking louder seems sacrilegious, "but this stays the same."

Joy's mind has wandered. "Papa likes the piano. He came in while I was playing, just stood there listening—I mean, right at the end of the keyboard, and he was staring at my hands, like he'd never seen hands before and wanted to see what they could do? So naturally, I got nervous. My fingers started to stutter."

I smile. "I thought you did that on purpose. It sounded like improv."

"Nuh-uh. Just mess up. Why does he have a piano? I mean, like, who plays?"

"No one. But hope dies hard. He thought learning to play was a must for girls, so he bought a piano. None of us took the bait."

"He didn't make you?"

"Oh, he tried. But after a few weeks of our practicing while he was home, he caved. Now you've come along to play his piano the way it should be played. I'd say his wait was worth it."

She leans into me and says with a pout, "You say that because you love me."

"I say it because it's true." And because I do know she loves hearing it.

"So who said things like that to you when you were growing up here?"

"Uh . . . my mother?" When Joy slides me a *you-don't-sound-sure* look, I say with greater conviction, "My mother."

Seeming satisfied with that, she rests her head on my shoulder. The purpling sky soothes. "This is so nice," she says, and it is. My daughter keeps me in the present, which is where I want to be.

Then, upstairs in my bedroom, she falls asleep, and my grip on the present wavers. While she breathes deeply, her warmth pressed to my arm, I lie awake thinking of this room, this house, the people my family had been back then. I hear flutters in the attic—bats we kids knew, just *knew*—and my eyes fix on the ceiling, waiting for something to break through and whip around in the dark. When nothing does, just as nothing did then, I close my eyes again and listen to the ocean in real time, rather than dreams. It is as beautiful, as soothing as I remember.

After a while, I hear my father's footsteps on the stairs. Slipping from bed, I creep to the door and put my ear to the wood. It occurs to me to go out there and see if he needs help with his cast. But I can't begin to imagine helping this man undress. He was never a touchy-feely guy. If he held my hand when I was a child, it was to lead me somewhere, not to impart warmth. He never dressed me, never tied a ribbon in my hair. I don't recall whether he ever actually hugged me.

His door closes. Quietly I return to the bed and am about to climb in, when I pause. Changing my mind, I go to the window. The heather is a dark blur, the Sabathian house even darker. Memories of this knock at the door of my mind, good ones right up until the end. So many nights I stood watch at this spot, eyes glued to the second floor window, wondering if Jack was awake and would signal. Standing here now, I have a clear vision of his Maglite's burst—three-one-one, repeated twice in quick succession.

It is a minute before I realize that I'm not imagining it.

Chapter 7

I hold my breath. The signal comes again.

Quickly, silently, I pull my Bay Bluff sweatshirt over the loose tee I sleep in and hop into sweatpants, one leg, then the other. Flip-flops in hand, I tiptoe to the door, open it carefully and, after checking to be sure Joy is still asleep, inch it closed.

Avoiding creaks, my bare feet whisper down the stairs and run lightly through the kitchen and mudroom to the side door, the one we always took to the beach. It isn't until the cool air hits me that I stop dead still.

This has all been pure habit, true muscle memory. From the time I was fifteen and found Jack, until I was nineteen and left home, I responded to that light. Now, at thirty-nine, I wonder what in the hell I'm doing. The signal? *Our* signal? After all this time, all this acrimony? If I go down to the beach, what do I hope to find?

I don't know. That's the thing.

But I had seen his light. And there is no way I can *not* respond.

Slipping on my flip-flops, I walk along the side path at a more adult pace, giving myself plenty of time to rethink what I'm doing. But I can't find a reason to turn back. If I've misinterpreted the signal, I'll be alone on the beach. If not, well, I'll find out why he sent it in the first place.

The moon is a slim cradle that comes and goes through fingers of clouds. Though there's enough light to see, I hold the railing as I take the stairs, because my eyes aren't on my feet. They're searching the beach. It isn't until I'm at the bottom and starting toward the Sabathian side that a dark figure takes shape at the end. Fortunately, he's well before the outcropping of rocks that used to hide us from the world. I'm not sure I could have dealt with those particular memories.

He doesn't meet me halfway. No. He's making me commit. But then, he always did. Jack understood that I wanted to please. His mission was to make me take a stand—which, of course, I did when Elizabeth couldn't be found. Unfortunately, my stand wasn't compatible with his.

His hands are under the tails of a tee, tucked in the pockets of his shorts. Arms, legs, and feet are all bare, all long and well-formed. This is not memory. This is fact.

I pass the firepit, which is a murky saucer in a field of dim sand. When I'm just close enough, I stop. *You called?* I might have quipped had our recent history not been so taut, but my insides are in a knot. I have no idea what to expect.

Another throwback? He is chewing on the corner of his mouth. Good. So I'm not the only one feeling weird. That was one of the things we used to talk about all the time—feeling weird in one's own home—because if I had family issues, Jack's were worse. I'd seen firsthand his attempts to get his parents' attention. But his father was forever distracted by one intellectual cause or another. And his mother? Self-absorbed. Her disappearance would have poured salt on the wound of being her son, for sure. For *sure,* her disappearance would have exaggerated his long-running sense of abandonment.

Realizing that, I feel the urge to fill the awkward silence

with consoling words, even to touch his arm. But I'm afraid to reach out lest I be bitten. Like dog, like man.

Speaking of which, I ask, "Where's your dog?"

"Sleeping. Where's your daughter?"

"Same."

A tiny wave breaks, rolling our way in a whisper meant as backdrop alone, because we're the main attraction, Jack Sab and me. I've broken the silence by speaking first, and I can easily make other conversation. Middle children are practiced at lessening awkward moments, and here in my hometown I'm the middle child. But I've been away for a long time, been a different person for that long time. And I didn't call this meeting.

So I wrap my arms around my middle, clutching the folds of the sweatshirt, and wait.

Finally he says, "I overstepped with her. Did I screw up?"

The words are right, even if the tone isn't exactly apologetic. But then, I don't know how to be with him, either.

"No," I say, grateful for the statement regardless. "I'll just tell her it won't work."

"It will on my end. I can always use help."

"We're only here a week. Is it worth training her for that little?"

"Training?" he mocks. "To give love to frightened pets who are caged up, waiting for treatment, feeling abandoned? She was a fast learner when it came to my dog. Where'd she come from, by the way?"

Startled, I'm silent for a breath. Then I echo, "Come from?" I hope he doesn't mean what I think. "New York. With me."

"But who's her father?"

Bingo. That's my Jack, filtered not. There are any number of answers I might give to succinctly end the conversation. Lord knew, I've used many of them over the years. But strangers with inappropriate questions are one thing, Jack Sabathian another. I never lied to him. He might have thought it. But what I said about my father was what I believed.

Honestly now, I say, "I have no idea."

"Really? *You?*"

I don't bother to answer. He's thinking I was drunk, which goes to show how faulty memory can be. I didn't drink. Never had. There was nothing spontaneous or irresponsible or un-planned about conceiving Joy, and it had been worth every terrifying minute.

"One-night stand?" he asks.

"Sperm donor," I reply.

That draws a curious half smile splitting dark stubble, which the moon appears just in time to reveal. "Seriously?"

"Why not?"

"Because," he says without missing a beat, "you can have any man you want. Why use a donor?"

"Maybe," I say without missing my own beat, "because I don't like the men who want me, but I wanted a child."

"Does she know?"

"Absolutely. Joy and I know how to communicate. I told her as soon as she was old enough to understand." *Not making the same mistakes my parents did,* my mind adds, and he hears that part, too.

His voice is faintly subdued. "Was it hard?"

"The telling? No harder than explaining adoption. 'Mommy had a gazillion choices, but she wanted *you.*'"

"It's different from adoption."

"You know what I mean. There's a similar issue of *Doesn't he want to know who I am?*"

I feel a niggling of guilt, thinking of all the times my daughter has asked this. But no. She accepts. She understands, and only in part from the books we read of the why-don't-I-have-a-daddy type. In time she came to see how many of her friends were being raised by single parents, making me no different at all. But my niggling remains. It's the guilt that

I feel, me, personally. It's in subjecting my daughter to the same insecurity I felt myself about my own roots.

But this is the memory that's just beyond my grasp, and curt Jack isn't done with his questions.

"Doesn't he? Want to know her?"

"He doesn't know she exists," I snap, annoyed that he has so quickly dredged up my guilt. "That's how it works. You see characteristics and a number, never a name. Why are you making a big deal about this, Jack?"

He doesn't have an answer for that. But the fact that he's been so blunt gets me going. He wants me to stand up for myself? Fine. Fair is fair. "So *do* you know where Elizabeth is?"

He stares at me, then looks away and scratches the back of his head. By the time he returns, he is quiet. "Not one word since she disappeared from your father's boat. How 'bout you? Did you find the gun?"

"We just got here. I haven't had time to look. Do you think she's dead then?"

"What else can I think? She was never a family person, but what kind of mother would leave her husband and son without a word?" His voice is deeper than when we were kids but vulnerable still, even after all these years. "I mean, no note, no call, no email, no text. Ever."

Again, I think to touch him. Again, I hold back. But I do feel his pain. My sensitivity to him hasn't changed. "Your dad heard nothing?"

He makes a throaty sound that doesn't quite mesh with the tranquility of the sleepy waves trickling close by our feet. "He'd be the last one to hear. They barely talked. He could have been a renter in the house, for all she cared."

"Did he look for her?"

"He? No. He just waited to see if she'd show up. He was like that. Mr. Passive. Me? Yeah, I looked. All that fall, I looked. I drove from one little coast town to the next. I read their newspapers and talked with their cops. I figured that if she'd washed up somewhere with no memory, someone would report it. Same if a boat picked her up, and she didn't know who she was."

"How could anyone for miles not know who she was?" I ask, astounded. "Okay, twenty years ago Google wasn't what it is now. But her disappearance made headlines."

"Yeah, well, I kept asking myself that, too," he says, hanging a hand on the back of his neck while his dark eyes hold mine, "only not everyone reads the paper or watches the news. Some people live with their heads in the sand."

Like ignoring dementia? Ignoring the risk of a gun?

He may not be thinking those things at all. I'm probably being oversensitive. But he was headed in this direction earlier, when Joy was here, and it was a dead-end street. "Please don't go there again," I beg and, in a more coolheaded voice, return to the larger discussion. "Wouldn't her body have washed up somewhere?"

"Not if it was weighted."

"Weighted?"

"We all watched *The Sopranos.*"

I'm appalled. It isn't that he didn't talk about murder back then, or that I haven't considered it lately myself. But a gun is one thing. *Weighted* is something else. *Weighted* means tying something heavy to a body and pushing it overboard. *Weighted* means premeditated.

I wish I could see his eyes to know if he's serious, but the sliver of moon isn't cooperating just then. "You're saying my father shot her, then made sure the body would never surface? That is *sick,* Jack." Turning, I start back toward the dock.

"Still running away?" he calls in a taunt that stops my flight.

He's right. I whip back, needing this discussion. "He wouldn't kill her. He loved her."

"Lovers kill. They kill all the time."

"I didn't say they were lovers. I said he loved her. There's a difference."

"You don't think they had sex?"

"Maybe before they were married, but not after. I remember us all together—cookouts, boat rides, even just sitting here on the beach. There were no secret looks, no sneaking off."

"No? I remember my father barely talking to yours and your mother barely talking to mine. I remember your father touching my mother's hand. I remember her touching his arm. Did they touch their own spouses? Ever?"

They did. Of course, they did.

At least, I think they did. Suddenly, though, as I struggle to see it, I'm not sure. "No?" I ask, wondering if I had missed something there.

But my indecision is short-lived. Of the other, I am entirely sure. "My father didn't kill her. He was as frantic as any of us looking for her that night on the beach."

"Sure he was," Jack says. His head is lowered, eyes on his foot as his heel drills a hole in the sand. "He was afraid she'd wash up with a bullet in her head."

The image makes me flinch, it's that vivid. "And where was the blood? The boat was clean."

His head comes up, eyes on mine. "Boats can be washed. Or maybe he pushed her into the water and shot her there. That'd *really* be clean."

"You are sick." I'm about to turn and walk—not run—walk away, when he holds up a conciliatory hand.

"Okay. Maybe it wasn't that. But put yourself in my shoes. I've spent twenty years trying to figure out where she went and why. So forget family. Think business. She founded a company. She loved it more than anything on earth. There's no way she would deliberately walk away from that, even if it was going downhill—*especially* if it was going downhill."

"Was it?" I ask. That would be a new twist, though not surprising. Elizabeth had been on the ground floor of electronics, creating a computer in the mid-seventies that was small and powerful. Unfortunately, her company was similarly small. It couldn't begin to compete with the Apples of the world.

Jack looks like he hadn't meant to blurt it out. But he isn't a liar any more than I am. "Yes," he admits.

"Couldn't that be a motive?"

"For her to jump ship and leave the mess for someone else to clean up? She wasn't a quitter."

"She quit on her family."

"You can only quit if you've signed on, but she never did with us. Know how many business trips she took? How many days at a time she was gone? How many important life events she missed, like birthdays and anniversaries and football playoffs and—" He stopped the list with a sputter. "Besides, where would she go?"

"Margo remembers seeing a second boat—"

"Which the Coast Guard couldn't find. If Margo saw something, it was a mirage. So where would my mother go?"

"Did you talk with her family?"

Hands on his hips, he faces me straight on. "Of course, I did. I'm not stupid, Mallory."

I forgive him the tone. "I'm as frustrated as you are."

"No way."

"Yes way. What happened to your mother directly impacts my father. You don't think I've wondered for twenty years? You don't think the not-knowing is part of what kept me away?"

He is quiet.

I sigh. "So. Her family. Any clue?"

"Nah. They were estranged."

"But she kept their name when she got married."

"She didn't want to take my father's name. Says something right there, y'know? Not that a name ties you to family either way. I used to see cousins when I was a kid, so things were fine at first, but then something happened. I never knew the cause."

"Did you ask?"

He snorts. Of course, he asked. Jack Sabathian wouldn't not ask.

"What did they say?"

"Nothing. My mother said nothing. My cousins said nothing. My uncle, Mom's only sibling, refused to talk with me on the phone, so I tracked him down, went all the way to friggin' Tallahassee. He refused to talk about it even in person, just him and me, and I badgered. Didn't get anywhere."

But he'd made the effort. From the sound of it, he had gone well beyond what the local police or my father and his private investigators had done. I have to give Jack credit for that. "I'm sorry. It'd be nice to know."

"Yeah, well, life doesn't always work that way."

I do know that. Ten years after my parents divorced, Margo called in a tearful rant about an auto accident that she claimed Mom wouldn't have been anywhere near if Dad hadn't made her feel so unwanted that she dated anyone who asked, including a guy with a history of DUIs. An auto accident. She was dead before I could ask her about all the things I didn't know.

Which is about me. But we are talking about Jack. "Where's your dad now?"

"Berkeley. He gave it a couple of years here, but the memories were hard to take."

"I'd have thought you'd leave, too."

Bending, he picks up a rock and wings it into the sea. "And let your father off the hook?" he asks almost distractedly. "Are you kidding? I want him to see me here in this house, year after year after year, and remember the family he destroyed."

I can't imagine nurturing that kind of bitterness. "How do you do that—live with constant anger?"

A piece of driftwood is bobbing in the shallows. Sloshing over, he catches it and lobs it toward the firepit. Then he straightens and puts his hands on his hips, thumbs bearing the weight while his fingers lie long and loose against the cotton tee. He takes a visible breath. "My work helps. Animals appreciate what you do for them. Pets give the unconditional love parents can't."

I want to tell him that what I feel for Joy is unconditional to the extreme. But Elizabeth never felt that. Nor, really, did my mother, or she'd have answered the questions I lacked the courage to ask.

With mention of Jack's work, we've come full circle, but I don't want to leave him just yet. I always felt a connection to the boy he used to be. Time and adversity haven't changed that. I hated the anger between us twenty years ago and would give anything to replace those memories with kinder ones. It has nothing to do with my being the peacemaker and everything to do with my feelings for Jack. The past may be over. But I want us to be friends.

Returning to the splotch of a firepit, I sit on one of the logs at its edge and hug my knees.

He continues to stand for a while, ankle-deep in the surf as he studies the midnight sky on the far horizon. Looking for Elizabeth, as Anne claims? No. He's looking there because it's beautiful, because it puts provincial Bay Bluff in context and reminds us that we're part of a larger world. Way back when, we used to look at that horizon and imagine the places we'd go and the things we'd share. I know he has gone places since. I googled him after he called, of course I did. He got his degree in veterinary medicine at UC Davis, one of the best, and I'm sure he didn't limit his travels to California. I'm sure he traveled. But I refuse to believe it was the same as we imagined, because I went places, too. It wasn't worse without him. Just different.

But this is history, and here we are in Bay Bluff eyeing that same horizon. We often talked about the comfort of the sea. Surprising, given the circumstances, I feel it now.

Apparently Jack does, too, because, after several minutes, he joins me at the firepit. Once upon a time, we shared a log. Margo would glare each time, and while I cared, Jack did not. Now, though, he sits one log over with his legs sprawled.

We don't talk. I might have remembered nights when this fire blazed and we were all here, or nights when it was just Jack and me. But I don't want to remember. Right now, I'm the me who lives in the moment, and this moment is nostalgic in an undemanding way.

"Why did you call me?" I ask. I haven't planned to speak, but there is my voice.

And then his. "Because I felt bad. I shouldn't interfere with your daughter—"

"I mean in New York. After my father showed up at your house. Why did you call me and not Margo or Anne?"

"Because you're the only one in the family with brains."

"That's not true." Margo is the intellect of the family, and Anne is running a successful restaurant.

"The only one with common sense."

"They have it."

"Not when it comes to your parents."

"And I do?" I make a guttural sound. "*That's* rich." When it comes to my parents, I'm raw emotion in an airtight jar.

"Well, you're the only one I trust," he states in the deep voice that I'd loved once.

And okay. Yes. Maybe that's what I need to hear. Maybe I need to know that a little of the past remains for him, too.

If I say it, of course, he may deny it, or start in on my father again. So I just nod and lower my arms around my legs, folding my body in two.

"Cold?" he asks.

I shake my head, and focus on the waves. Their rhythm is a lullaby—sweet, soothing, elementary—that takes me back in the best of ways. And I'm definitely back there when I feel Jack's foot brush mine, warmth in the night chill as he shifts his legs. Was it accident or intention? I don't know. But I don't move, barely breathe. That one glancing touch brings so many memories that I'm momentarily engulfed.

"Your father knows."

Pop. The bubble bursts. Convinced that I imagined his touch, I turn my head so that my cheek rests on my thigh. His face is in profile—the nose that is too sharp for beauty but so reflects his manner as to be laughable—his bearded jaw, chin, and upper lip—the protrusion of his brow that tells of a frown.

He turns to me, fully rational and in control. "He knows what happened that night. If we assume my mother's dead, he's the only witness left. That's another reason I called you. He's losing it. Someone needs to get the truth out of him before it's gone."

So. His major concern when he called me in New York wasn't the gun. The gun was an excuse. His worry is that the way things are going, my father's mind will shrivel up and crush everything inside, just take it right away. He's thinking Alzheimer's, too, I know he is. And I want to discuss this with him. But we're already in agreement here. He wants answers about his mother; I want answers about mine.

I try to think how to approach my father. "It's a sensitive topic."

"It needs to be done."

"Anne is protective."

"Anne is overprotective."

Which means I need to work directly with Dad. "He puts up a wall when I'm around. I'm walking on eggshells."

"It's just asking questions."

"He doesn't like questions, especially intrusive ones."

"Would you rather he take it all to the grave?"

"Of course not." I want to know whether my father loved my mother, whether he loved *me,* and if not, why not, and he's the only one who can say. "I just have to figure out the best way to do it."

"Time's running out," Jack warns.

"I know."

"So do it. Isn't that why you're here?"

It isn't why I've come. I've come for Joy. At least, that was the premise. But seeing Dad again, seeing this place, even being here on the beach where so many watershed moments occurred, I feel a deeper calling. Yes, it's about retrieving the past.

"Mallory," he says in the forceful way he always had.

"I will."

I want to say I am resolved to act, but all I can think of as I walk back to the house is that confronting my father won't be fun. I remind myself that I'm an adult now, a mother, and a professional. When it comes to this man, though, I'm still a child. And suddenly into that childhood moment comes a memory. It's a recurring dream that I put behind me when I left Bay Bluff and haven't allowed in for years. In it, my mother goes off somewhere, leaving us three alone with Dad, who keeps doubling his normal size. Margo and Anne don't seem to see it, despite my yelling and pointing and jumping up and down. They're not afraid. But I am. I don't want my father to see me and attack. So I make myself invisible by becoming a butterfly—no, an ant—no, an *owl,* emerging only at night when everyone else is asleep.

Coming so soon after thinking myself an owl, I'm wide-awake when I reach the house. Anne's car is back, but since she isn't downstairs, I assume she's in bed. I'm sorry for that. I would have liked to ease the awkwardness between us. We used to talk after dates. Not that I've been on a date. But she had. A date? A party? A sleeping-with sans sleep? Whatever, I want to know more about Billy Houseman.

Resigned for now to failure in that, I take my laptop from the kitchen and turn on a small lamp in the living room. After moving just enough books aside so that I can curl into a corner of the sofa, I pull up Margo's latest column. She typically writes about family issues in response to correspondence from readers. Too often to be coincidental, I see our family in her words.

This one is a case in point. It is a poignant piece about the prospect of Father's Day when one has no father to toast, and while the focus is on fathers who have died, I can easily guess she's thinking of us. She talks about sadness, about the emptiness of the chair at the head of the table and the clothes gathering dust in the closet. She talks about celebrating the man a father once was and doing something to make him proud. *Accept what you can't change by changing what you can't accept,* she advises—and at first read, it sounds preposterous. A dead person is dead, right? When she launches into honoring memories by living the best of who that person was, though, I see where she's headed. She isn't thinking of Dad. She's thinking of Mom. Having been to Margo's house multiple times, I've seen how she keeps fresh peonies, year round, in a clear vase on her kitchen island. Mom did that, though where either of them found peonies in the middle of winter was anyone's guess.

I'm not there yet with regard to Mom. With regard to Dad, though? *Accept what you can't change by changing what you can't accept.*

I cannot accept that I'll never know the truths I seek. And

while my solution is less honorable than Margo's, she isn't here, is she? That means I can avoid confrontation by becoming a snoop.

When I wake up Saturday morning, Joy is gone. A note lies on the pillow. *Taking Papa down the hill for breakfast. Come when you wake up.*

I will. First, though, I'm hunting for a gun.

Chapter 8

Feeling like a thief, I work quickly and with an ear out for anyone who might return. Since Dad spends most of his time in the living room, that's where I start. But there's no gun under a cushion, behind a book, or in a drawer. I blouse out the floor-to-ceiling drapes, hung so long ago by Mom, and find traces of dust that the vacuum missed but no gun, not even cleverly tucked into a wide hem. At the front hall closet, I grope through hats, scarves, and gloves above, in coat pockets and sleeves mid-level, and rubbers and boots below. The dining room, too, is a bust; neither the silver drawer nor any of the linen drawers hold a gun. I'm checking the last of my mother's decorative vases when my phone vibrates.

Seeing Chrissie's name, I feel an immediate lift. Chrissie Perez is one of those friends who doesn't go ultra-far back in my life but whose friendship goes deep. We met seven years ago, sweating on adjacent stair climbers at the gym, and just . . . clicked. In the years since, Joy and I have been to her place for more Sunday brunches than I can count. Chrissie, her husband, and her three-year-old son are as close to family as we get in New York.

"Chrissie," I breathe in relief.

"Just wondering how you're doing."

"Funny you should ask," I sing, tucking the phone between my shoulder and ear. "As we speak, I'm looking for a gun."

"*The* gun?"

"Yup. Our dining room always had a slew of vases. None are transparent, which makes them plausible hiding places. My mother used to fill every one with flowers from the garden." I peer into a trio of squat ones, all empty. "When there were no flowers, it would be greens, and when there were no greens, it would be sticks. Even the sticks were stunning. They were in the tallest vases." Plunging my arm into one of those tall ones, I sweep my fingers around its hollow base. "She was an artist."

"You never told me that."

"She said she wasn't, which is why I got her camera equipment. And after that there was the whole accounting thing, which was practical and methodical and worked so well for her that I forgot about the flowers." Retrieving my hand from the last vase, I look around. "There's no gun in this room. Lots of memories"—for which I have no time, so I head for the kitchen—"but no gun."

"What about the kitchen?" Chrissie asks. We do think alike. "Lots of places to hide something there."

"Too many," I decide, casting a discouraged look around. "I don't have long, and there are too many cabinets and drawers to check quickly. Besides, between Anne and the housekeeper, would he risk hiding anything here?"

"What about his bedroom? That would be the obvious place."

"Yes," I say, holding the phone to my ear as I zip up the stairs. Halfway down the hall, though, I stop. "I can't go there."

"Why not?"

"It's his room."

"That's the point."

"No. It's *his* room. The *judge's* room. Searching there would be a violation."

"Mal. He's your dad. And you're looking for a murder weapon."

"Potential," I correct and, resolved, start forward, only to stop after a step. "If I find the gun elsewhere, I won't have to search his room at all. And besides, isn't the attic a more likely place to hide a gun? He was up there yesterday. He probably goes there a lot. Reading Lawyer's Diaries could be his cover."

Still with the phone to my ear, I enter the guest room and pull down the hatch. The stuffiness hits me when I'm barely halfway up the ladder, and this is familiar. Memorial Day to Labor Day, the attic absorbed enough daytime sun to retain heat through the night.

"You okay?" Chrissie asks softly.

I sigh. "Just remembering."

"Is it hard?"

"No," I say, then, "Yes." I could tell her about my father mistaking Joy for Margo, about Anne's annoyance with me, about seeing Jack Sabathian. Chrissie would be able to place it all, I've told her that much. She's a good listener. So am I, which is why I know about the growing pains in her marriage, her struggle to have a baby, and her mother's resistance to her biracial husband and child. We give mutual therapy, Chrissie and I.

But the attic is mine. I need both hands and speakerphone won't do. "Can we talk another time?" I ask.

"Of course. I'm here."

"Dante and Kian good?"

"We're good. Call whenever."

"Thanks, Chrissie."

After pocketing the phone, I gather the books from yesterday and return them to the shelving that holds the others.

They fit neatly into their slots—1996, 1997, 1998. And yes, I wonder why he was looking at those. Of course, I wonder. But there's so much else here, too. Standing back, I study the collection as a whole. It's an impressive one, spanning forty years. Some lawyers would burn outdated diaries after a time. Not Dad. He kept every one.

Where to start? Well, here is 2000, looking no different from the others—same faded blue leather, same worn spine. This was the year Elizabeth disappeared. I wonder if he mentions it inside, if he gives a clue to something he hasn't shared with the world. Slipping the book from its slot, I weigh the spine in my palm. I'm breaking a rule. But the cause justifies the means, right?

Quick, before I lose my nerve, I open to the center pages, where summer would be. The entries are sparse, but I remind myself that this makes sense. He was a judge by this time, so there would be none of the notes about client meetings or the billing records he kept in private practice. The notes of a judge relate to cases being heard, motions to read and rule on, meetings with lawyers in chambers. But this was summer. Big cases weren't tried in the summer. Everyone— jurors, judges, clerks—resented being confined. A skeletal staff remained, and Dad was often on call.

But he was also home a lot. And *that* was a slippery slope. It would begin with us out of school and Dad planted on the porch reading a law journal, a newly-submitted brief, or the biography of one historical figure or another. Occasionally he joined us on the beach and actually seemed to enjoy it. He taught me how to swim. I do remember that, rather a tough-love kind of throw-her-into-the-water experience, but he did the same with my sisters, and he did reward us with smiles when we got it right. He had us picking up surf clams. He led us to hidden rocks where blue mussels clung, and set us to harvesting enough for dinner. He taught us to recognize the color of a rip tide and how to swim at an angle to escape it—taught us the difference between a rip current and the less dangerous undertow. And he was animated, totally into what he said.

These memories are good ones. I can complain all I want about his authoritarianism, but we did have fun. Because he liked doing these things. This explained why we lived at the shore. Tom Aldiss had grown up vacationing on Cape Cod and had dreamed of becoming successful enough to buy a shore place himself, which he had. He took pride in our house. And the boat? His escape. Rarely did a day pass when he wasn't out on the ocean. Fog, wind, rough surf—he handled it all with the skill of a man who had learned as a boy.

Those summer days, he took us on boat trips, and on road trips like the ones I described to Joy. I remember Mom cooking chili, which he loved, using tomatoes from the garden—actually from the greenhouse nook of the potting shed, which was as much hers as the boat was his. He loved grilled steak, so she grilled steak. And made clam chowder from the clams we gathered. And boiled lobster.

These memories, too, are good. Sure, we chafed in the backseat of the car, and quickly learned that if we didn't have a destination, spending hours on the boat while Dad stood tall at the helm with his ball cap clipped to his collar so that it wouldn't blow into the sea was boring as hell. Still, when he was happy, we were happy. Even Mom. She didn't have to make clam chowder from scratch, when she could as easily have bought homemade in town. But she did it for him. That was proof of love. Wasn't it?

Then Dad grew antsy. At its onset, he would walk around with his hands in his pockets, never quite able to settle down. When it worsened, he would find fault with Monopoly, shout snide answers to Trivial Pursuit from across the room, pontificate on the superiority of William Faulkner to whatever we were reading, and if we were on the beach doing nothing at all, he would complain about that.

Margo likened him to a caged bear. I remember that image clear as day. I didn't entirely agree with it—even at his worst, Dad was more disciplined than a bear. I did agree, though, that he seemed to dislike his life.

Not that he would write about that in a Lawyer's Diary. The page of Aldiss-MacKay is blank, as is the entire week that followed. On the pages for the week after that, his sprawling script refers to a national meeting of judges—Dallas, it says, though I don't see any sign that he actually went.

The investigation was in full swing by that time, and with his being on top of the detectives and the detectives being on top of him and the local press watching it all, he hadn't gone far. But I see no reference to any of that. It's like he saw this diary as his legacy, and didn't want it tainted by even the slightest untoward scrawl.

Did that make him guilty of a crime? Of course not. Closing the diary, I return it to its slot and glance at the ones he'd been holding when he fell. Those may tell more. But more of what? I don't know what I'm looking for, which makes the search absurd.

Whatever, there is no gun in these books. Determined, I quickly search behind other bookshelves and between stacks of files. I run a palm over brown folders with the label of Dad's law firm on the front, but all is smooth and flat. I feel through Dad's old suits, hanging on a metal rack, but find nothing resembling a gun in any pocket.

There are other boxes. Mom was organized. She used to label cartons for us to fill—ANNE'S SCHOOL PAPERS, MALLORY'S PHOTOGRAPHS—and though Margo took her own things when she left, ours remain.

The stuffiness is starting to get to me. I'm also thinking I ought to head into town. But how to resist MALLORY'S PHOTOGRAPHS? Just for a second?

Pulling the top flap free of the opposite corner under which it's wedged, I pull it open. The faintly vinegar-y smell takes me right back. It's from the fixer I used to print pictures, lodged as deeply in my memory as in these prints. When I used a darkroom, in those days before digital, my hands chronically carried this smell.

The carton is packed with photos. The top one is of the ocean, yet another view at another time, this one with the golden light of the sun gilding the scalloped waves, or so my mind's eye sees in this black-and-white shot. There are others of the beach—a spiral whelk, a knot of seaweed, a piece of sea glass. Shots of Jack are tucked in at the side, and while I sift through the others, I leave him be for now.

A camera is the keeper of memories, Mom used to say. And there she is, smiling at me as she flips burgers on the back porch. She loves me there. I know she does. For that alone, my eyes cling to her face. Joy resembles her so much that it's frightening. No. It's wondrous. But the issue of resemblance passes quickly, because this is my mother's face. Sure, I have shots of her taken in the years after we left. I'm a photographer, for goodness sake. But a shot of Mom at Margo's place in Chicago or mine in New York isn't the same as one from my growing up years in Bay Bluff. That face is the one I remember. I haven't seen it in twenty years. Back here now in Bay Bluff for the first time, I miss her more than ever.

I don't recall the moment when I took that picture, don't recall whether Dad was around or not. He used to wave my camera away, like it was a beach fly, so I'm guessing he was off somewhere else when this picture was shot.

Mom's face reflects that. She is relaxed, her green eyes smiling right along with her mouth. Those eyes in that heart-shaped face radiate love. I feel it now in ways I've maybe forgotten. She loved me openly. But only when Dad wasn't around. I've imagined every reason why, but only one makes sense. It's obvious, isn't it? Only it does *not* make sense, not based on what I remember.

"*Tom,*" *my mother hisses with hushed urgency.* "*Don't do that.*"

"*Do what?*"

"*Treat her that way.*"

"*I'm fine to her.*"

"*You're critical of her. You hold her to a different standard.*"

"*She's a middle child. She lets the others go first. She needs to harden up.*"

"*She needs to be loved.*"

"*Don't go there, Ellie. We've talked about this. I have three daughters. I love them all.*"

I was ten, standing in the shadows when this conversation took place, and I've replayed it hundreds of times since. *I have three daughters. I love them all.* There were words after that, but I was already slipping away. These were the ones I wanted. For years, I clung to them as proof that I wasn't a mistake. Even when I tried to retrieve the others, these were the ones I heard.

Then I left home and became a different person, and the memory shimmered with doubt. Was that challenge on the part of my mother, who rarely challenged my father? Was that deference on the part of my father, who rarely deferred to anyone? Was there an element of rote in their exchange, like the words were part of a script that had to be repeated to be believed? *We've talked about this.* What had that meant? Was it a general statement of parenting, or a specific reference to something unique to these parents?

Each time I've seen my father in recent years, I feel apart, and oh, I know. I'm likely transferring childhood feelings to the present. But then there are those other words, spoken right before I slipped away. At times I think I remember a phrase or two. But it may as well be imagination as fear.

My mother knew the whole truth. With her gone, it's impossible to confirm.

With that thought, I realize that I've had enough for now. Now I need Joy. She is my unconditional love, no questions asked.

Closing the carton, one flap under the other, I turn to leave only to glance past, then return to, the end of the attic that holds *things*. Most are stacked on and around the high chair in which each of us once sat, in which our children would have sat had our lives not been pulled apart. Crossing there, I can't resist touching the crocheted crib blanket that is tucked under an oversized bear on the seat of a bouncer. My breath hitches when I spot, half-hidden behind these things, the tiny table and chairs that we used for coloring, and on top of those, a pile of games—Candy Land, Monopoly, Sorry! and—*omigod,* Where In the World is Carmen Sandiego! I *loved* that game.

But those memories are for another time. Joy is in town with the grandfather she barely knows, the aunt who'll be running from kitchen to table and back, and a slew of utter strangers eating bacon and eggs. I've dallied long enough. She needs me.

She needs *me*? my thoughts mock as I return to my room. Hah! Joy Aldiss is irreverent enough to know how to handle herself. She doesn't need me.

I need her.

Quickly pulling on a tank top, shorts, and flip-flops, I grab my camera and trot down the stairs. It's not yet nine, hopefully early enough to still find Dad at Sunny Side Up staring at the new server. When I'm nearing the front door, though, I hear sounds from the kitchen.

Backtracking, I peer around the corner from the hall to find a woman at work. The silver hair piled on the top of her head barely moves as she bends to the dishwasher, gathers clean dishes, and straightens, bends, gathers, and straightens. She wears slim jeans and a loose blouse. Her back is to me.

What had Anne told me about the housekeeper? Not much other than that she is a local and needs the work.

Not wanting to startle her, I knock on the jamb, then do it louder when my first raps are lost in the clatter of forks and spoons being returned to a drawer. When she whips around, I realize that the white hair is stunning but misleading. Her skin is smooth. She can't be more than sixty.

Her eyes go wide when she sees me. She isn't frightened, exactly, but clearly surprised.

To put her at ease, I say a cheery, "Hello. I'm Mallory." When there is no response, I raise my brows. "Anne's sister?"

"I know," she says. Her voice is quiet but, while not exactly hostile, far from warm.

Rolling my eyes in a *duh* kind of way, I smile. "Pictures going up the stairs."

"You haven't changed," she says, but I realize she's not talking about the pictures. She remembers me from the past.

And isn't this awkward? She is vaguely familiar to me, like Joey DiMinico was yesterday, but I can't place her. He's my contemporary. This woman is closer to my parents' age.

I grimace, embarrassed. "I'm sorry. You are . . . ?"

"Lina Aiello," she says and, for the first time, I hear the trace of an accent, so faint that it would appear only when saying something learned in childhood from a parent with a stronger accent. Fully a third of Westerly is of Italian descent, immigrants brought here generations ago to help quarry granite. When the quarries closed, they became a vital part of nearly every aspect of the local economy, fully assimilated even as they stayed close to their church, the saint from the Italian town where their forebears were born, and their *soppressata*. Thanks to Italian friends, I knew what the Feast of the Seven Fishes was about. I remember sneaking *pizzelle* home, hiding it in my bedroom, eating little bits each day. Thanks to those joyous Christmas Eves, I knew the potential of family warmth.

"Aiello?" I repeat, scouring my memory until I feel a warm suspicion. "Danny?" I ask with a smile, because if the memory is correct, it is pleasing. Danny wasn't a close friend, certainly not close enough for me to be invited to his home. But we shared a love of American literature and coffee chip ice cream at Gendy's, so we got along well.

Lina's eyes move over my face. It's like she's looking for something, though, for the life of me, I don't know what.

"How is Danny?" I ask.

"He's fine."

"What's he doing?"

"Teaching English."

I clap in delight. "Perfect. He was made for that. Will you give him my best?" I might have liked a nod, but she is still searching my face. I wait for her to speak. When she doesn't, I raise my brows again. This time, my smile is forced. "Is . . . something wrong?"

Very quietly, she says, "You look like your mother, is all."

"My daughter even more so. You'll see her, I'm sure. It's like seeing a ghost." Truth be told, now that I say the words, Lina Aiello is the pale one, clearly unsettled by me.

Time to leave. I start to turn, then stop. It strikes me that if this woman is here every day, she could be a help. "I haven't seen my father in a while. How's he been?"

"Fine," she replies.

"Does he talk to you?"

"Sometimes."

"Anything of substance?"

"No."

I take a different tack. "Do you clean his room?" When she nods, I tip my head and, like I've just thought of it, ask, "Have you ever seen a gun there?"

Gentle as I've kept my tone, her eyes are alarmed. "A gun? No."

"Not on a bookshelf or in a drawer?"

"I'd never open a drawer. That's not my business. I dust, is all."

Her alarm could be guilt, if she's protecting Dad, but my gut says that's not it. Her response to this feels more spontaneous than the guarded one she's shown up to now.

"Okay," I say easily. "I just wondered. He's confused sometimes, so a gun is the last thing he should have. If you see one, will you tell Anne?" She nods but says nothing, and that's my cue. "Nice to meet you," I say and add a genuine, "Thank you for helping around here, Lina. It's much appreciated."

Heading out the front door, I pause at my car. On one hand, I could drive. That would be fastest, and I'm so late already that I'm surprised Joy hasn't texted to make sure I'm alive. On the other hand, it's barely a ten-minute walk down the hill. Since the road is the only way to the square, if Dad and Joy are heading home, they won't get past me. If I walk, I get exercise. If I walk, I get the Bay Bluff experience.

So I pull on my ball cap and sunglasses, thread the Nikon over my shoulder, and set off at an easy jog. The air is warm, the breeze grazing my skin. This isn't the kind of day that gnarled the scrub pine with its twisted form at the very top of the road; that would be one where an angry wind spewed seawater in the name of rain. This day is hazy but kind, and how not to stop to memorialize that pine? As many times as I've photographed homes with man-made topiaries in glorious display at the front, this shaping is Mother Nature's doing.

Glasses to my head, camera to my eye, I bracket my shots, then move around the tree and take several more. The exposure is tricky. With the sun rising from the ocean behind me, it is a matter of shadow and light in extremes. Inspired, I tilt the screen, raise the camera over my head, and shoot the pine against the lighter green of the ground foliage, perhaps not as dramatic as the silhouetted shots, but a more realistic rendition. Unable to resist, I return the camera to my eye and move in for several close-ups of the twist of a branch.

I could spend hours with this pine alone. Realizing that, I shoulder the camera with a vow to return and resume my jog. It's an easy downhill stretch. Near the bottom are two driveways that lead to homes on the side of the bluff. There used to be a single mailbox at each, but the lower one now has three. I'll have to ask Anne about that.

I'll also have to ask her about Lina Aiello—well, not about Lina, per se, but about whom else I might run into. I've been gone a long time. If Anne can refresh my memory, I might be able to recognize some of the people I see and avoid the awkwardness I felt with Lina. I've forgotten how small Bay Bluff is.

As soon as I round the curve in the road, the square appears, and I slow to a walk. The parking lot holds a smattering of compacts, SUVs, and pickups. The Volvo is likely parked behind the eatery; Anne would have driven to work, not only to get there quickly but to avoid tempting Dad with wheels. As I approach, another pickup appears, this one with the logo of a construction company. Two men climb out and head for the yellow beacon of Sunny Side Up. They're barely at the door when it opens and a family of four explodes from inside, two children breaking into a run, like they'd been caged and are suddenly free.

Shouting their names—*Liam! Ava!*—their parents run after them. I watch for only a second before spotting Jack Sabathian and his dog.

Chapter 9

They are at a picnic table on the edge of the square. The man sits on its top with his elbows on splayed knees, while the dog sits on the bench seat with its short, sandy-haired body pressed to his leg. As I watch, Jack tightens the leash while the children pass.

I consider what to do myself.

Still running? he asked me last night. If I were, I would study my phone like I was checking a crucial message and make for my sister's shop as if I hadn't seen him there at all. But that would be ridiculous, with Jack now the only human in the square. Giving the picnic table a comfortably wide berth, I circle to the front. Both heads follow me around.

Jack is wearing mirrored sunglasses, so I can't see his eyes. I do know they're gray, but what shade? While his nose is blade-straight, his body solid, and his opinions either for or against with no room for doubt, his eyes can go darker or lighter, harder or softer, iron to pewter to dove. They are a paradox, the only part of him that lacks absolutism.

Well, there is his hair, I concede. Despite the occasional strands of gray in his beard, I see no gray on his head. In a nod to memory, its chestnut is perpetually streaked, more so under the June sun, and while it is inches shorter than it was, it still has enough length to form waves. That hair is the devil's lure.

I focus on the dog. "Smart move, the leash," I remark.

Jack is stroking the dog's ear, drawing it between forefinger and thumb with soothing repetition. "It's for his own protection. Kids can be lethal."

"But there are always kids here. It's the way of the square. So why bring him?"

"Training. He's learning that not everyone is a danger." He takes off the shades, drops them on the table, and adds with what I see now is amusement, "Want to give him a pat?"

My hands are busy, one holding the camera strap on my shoulder, the other wiping sweat from my neck. Sweat is trickling between my breasts as well, but I'm not going there with Jack so close. "Thanks, but I'm good. Maybe another time."

His eyes chide me. "Let him get to know you. Your daughter wasn't afraid."

"I'm not afraid."

"You are."

I'm about to deny it. But why? "Okay. I am. I'm used to goldendoodles, cockapoos, and cheagles. They're all smaller." But we both know the problem isn't size. Jack's dog is smaller than many of the designer breeds my friends have in New York. "There's something about the way he's tugging on that leash."

"He wants to sniff your hand. Don't worry. He just had breakfast. He won't eat you until that's worn off."

"Good to know," I say, but those bloodshot eyes are begging for something, and I do feel for the poor thing.

Jack's voice comes low and coaxing. "Make his day, Mallory. Let him know you won't hurt him."

Trusting Jack because, well, because I do, I extend a hand. Guy sniffs it, looks at me with those woeful eyes, and then, apparently having sent his message, loses interest. Putting his jowly muzzle on Jack's thigh, he closes his eyes.

"Looks like I made a big impression," I remark.

"That's the best kind," Jack replies and lifts a tall coffee to his mouth. His palm covers most of the lid, while his long fingers splay over the front. I raise my sunglasses to my cap, but the logo stays the same.

"Starbucks?" I ask in mild disbelief. Bay Bluff prides itself on homegrown coffee. It prides itself on fresh burgers and in-house chips. At least, it used to.

He takes a drink, then says, "There's one near work."

Which raises another issue. The Jack Sabathian of old would have slept late unless the house was burning down. Granted, in this chapter of his life, he is a professional with a practice to run. Still. "You work weekends?" I ask, but redundantly. His scrub top is dark green and still pressed despite spatters of something fresh in the area of his abs. Studying them, I wince. "Those look ugly."

"It was," he says. "A family cat was hit by a car. I got the call at five this morning and did what I could, but I'm not sure she'll survive. My partner is with her now. I'll check back later." He sounds like he's trying to be matter-of-fact, but that groove on his forehead says he's discouraged, which puts me to shame. Sure, he could have changed his shirt before being seen in public by people who have just eaten breakfast, though it is in the nature of Jack to make statements. Still, criticizing bloodstains earned by a lifesaver? *Shallow, Mal. Shallow.*

"I'm sorry."

He squeezes my elbow so unexpectedly that by the time I realize what he's done, his hand is back on Guy's head. He frowns and says a quiet, "I understand that some pets have to be outdoors. By definition, a barn cat is an outdoor cat. But this isn't a barn cat. She's a longtime pet that goes in and out of the house at will. That's asking for trouble.

Dogs, fine," he says, running a hand along the pit bull's sleek flank. When the dog opens its eyes and smiles—I swear, it does—he smiles back. "They have to be walked. But cats are safer staying indoors. The alternative is inviting trouble." His smile fades. "Lately it's been coyotes. The small animals they grab are often found dead or close to, in which case the best I can do is put them out of their misery. Or they're not found at all." He presses his lips together and inhales through his nose. Exhaling, he says, "Then it's just wondering what happened." Ashy eyes meet mine. "Guess I'm the expert at that, right?"

His rancor isn't what it was yesterday, but I know he's thinking about Elizabeth. My presence has to be bringing it back.

"You were right, what you said," I grant him by way of apology. "I can't imagine what that's like."

He isn't surprised that I've followed his thoughts. We were always on the same wavelength, Jack Sab and me. Still, I'm startled when he says, "I'm sorry about your mother. She shouldn't have died that way. It must have been hard for you, being in New York."

Funny. My first thought when I learned that my mother had died was to call Jack. Joy was too young to understand, and my friends didn't know my mom. Jack did. He knew that I loved her with the kind of love that never, ever died. Most anyone could guess that. At the same time, I blamed her for things I didn't understand. Only Jack knew that. But we were enemies by the time she died and couldn't talk. I'm not sure we can now, either. So I simply wrap my arms around my middle and nod.

"Did you ever ask—" he started.

"No."

"She never explained—"

"No. We should have had all the time in the world, but she was here one minute and gone the next. Who knew that would happen?" I look around, seeking comfort in the sun-soaked glory of the square. Tables are clean and waiting—glass-top rounds outside Small Plates, square-top woods at The Deli, long picnic tables, like Jack's, fronting the Clam Shack. The door to the bookstore has just opened. Another car pulls into the lot with the crackle of tires on gravel. I smell the sea and bacon, and it is rich to me in the way of childhood memories. But my mother's childhood memories were elsewhere.

"She wouldn't have wanted to come back here," I say as much for my own sake as for Jack's. Lord knew we had debated long and hard, but bringing her back just didn't make sense. "Margo and I were both gone, and Annie wasn't about to visit her grave. My father always overshadowed her, and after—well, *after*—people didn't know what to say to her, so she was a victim of that night, too." I feel the same sense of resignation now as I felt then. "We buried her with her parents in Illinois."

Jack sets down the coffee and flexes his hand. It wants to touch me—pure habit again, I know, because I feel it, too. Our relationship was a physical one, and it went beyond sex. We touched easily and often, satisfying a need that no one else in our lives filled.

Times have changed. But his eyes don't seem to remember that. Their warmth makes me want to cry.

"Was she finally happy?" he asks.

Swallowing, I manage to say, "Yes. Finally fulfilled."

"That's good."

I take a minute to recompose myself, thinking of my mother and Jack. My stomach clenches around the memory, causing an involuntary grunt. "You're being very generous. She wasn't particularly nice to you."

"She thought her husband was having an affair with my mother. How was she supposed to act?"

I could more easily understand if Jack hadn't looked just like Elizabeth's husband. "Like it wasn't your fault?"

Tearing his eyes from mine, he looks down and gives a sad laugh. "Like human nature forgives and forgets?" His thumb glides back and forth over the drinking hole on the lid of his coffee. He takes a drink and lowers the cup, then, seeming to realize, offers it to me. I take a sip and hand it back, by which time he is staring into the distance. "But I'm a fine one to talk."

About forgiving and forgetting? And here he is outside Sunny Side Up, which is pretty much the headquarters of his nemesis. "So you're just . . . hanging out here on your way back from work?"

He shrugs.

"Do you know my father is inside?" I ask.

"Sure do. I have spies."

"Spies?"

He snorts. "Friends, Mal. Employees. Clients. Small towns are small towns. People love dredging it up. Hell, I could care less, but if you're waiting for him, don't. He sits in there for hours. He won't be out any time soon."

"Do you ever go inside?"

"Nope."

"Just sit out here."

"When I have time." The words are barely out, though, when his manner shifts. It is so subtle that the tilt of his spine, the lift of his chin, or the focus of his eyes might have been missed by someone who didn't know him. When it comes to body language, though, I'm still attuned to Jack's.

Looking over my shoulder, I see Amelia Ackerman from Boise, Idaho, a.k.a. Lily, who looks exactly like Jack's mother, emerging from the pergola between the still-closed deli and the beach shop. She is with a man I've seen before, and this time, I remember where. He's the same one I saw here yesterday, the one wearing baggy shorts and a loose tee, the one who may or may not have been taking pictures of me but who is definitely walking beside Lily. Just to be sure I'm not mistaken, I pull my camera around and, sliding up beside Jack, scroll back to yesterday's shots.

Zooming in on the one I want, I offer him the camera. "Who is he?"

Shading the screen with a hand, he leans close. My instinct is to lean away, not because I don't like his nearness, but because I do. He smells of soap, which he has obviously used after operating on the cat. Sure, there's the bloody shirt. But that's Jack. His hair is short enough to be messed and still look good. His face is tanned and scruff-chic, skin moist in the heat.

"More to the point," he murmurs, "who is she." It isn't a question. He knows.

I do pull back now. "Who is she?"

Chewing on the corner of his mouth, he considers that. Then he nods, seeming to accept that he has to say it aloud. "My mother's brother's granddaughter. Amazing thing, genetics."

"Wow," I breathe, studying the girl in this new light. The blonde hair is in a ponytail, the long legs in athletic shorts, the height putting her eye-to-eye with the man. They've started down the sidewalk toward Sunny Side Up, so I figure she's on her way to work. "Why is she here? I mean, I know what she's doing while she's here, but why *here*?"

He returns his elbows to his knees. "She says she's tracing her family tree. She thought it would be fun to explore this branch."

"You don't believe her."

"Not for a minute. Fun? There's been too much hard feeling. Something bad happened back then. Why else would there be zero communication? Fast forward to this spring. Anne advertises for summer help in the local paper, and

Amelia answers. It sounds innocent enough, but one look at her wearing my mother's face, and you know it was not."

"Maybe it is. Maybe she doesn't feel her grandfather's animosity."

"And her mother doesn't share it?" he asks. "Fat chance of that. I always liked Kim, but after my mother disappeared, she wouldn't talk with me either."

"Lily looks eighteen."

"Try twenty-two. She just graduated from Boise State with a degree in journalism. So what's she doing working as a waitress?"

He has a point. But there is a plausible counterpoint. "Breathing?" I offer. "Taking time to decide what she wants to do? It's not uncommon. I have friends whose kids take gap years after high school or college just to lie low until they decide what comes next."

"Maybe she knows what comes next, which is write a book about what happened to her family." He says it like I should know what he's talking about. Only I don't.

"What happened to her family?"

"Financial ruin," he says but without satisfaction. Whatever resentment he holds toward Elizabeth's mother's family for not cooperating with him in his search, is apparently separate from this. "Her grandfather—my mother's brother—invested everything he had in a deer farm in upstate New York. He imported a breed of deer that supposedly produced better meat. Venison was in demand in Europe, and he didn't see why it shouldn't be in demand here."

"It wasn't?"

Jack shrugs. "Don't know if the problem was on the marketing end or the breeding end, but it never took off. When he finally folded, he was up to his ears in debt. Home, farm, equipment—everything sold at auction for a fraction of what it was worth."

"How awful."

"You'd think."

"You don't?" I ask in surprise.

"Oh, I do. I just have trouble dredging up sympathy for a family who still has the man in the flesh. They couldn't've cared less that my mother was gone."

I could understand his resentment. "But why would Lily come here to write a book about what happened there?"

"Yeah, well, that's a good question. I'm guessing they asked my mother for financial help and she refused."

"Did you ever ask Elizabeth about it?"

"Hell, I didn't *know* about it until after she disappeared. So," he drawls and returns to his list of possible explanations for why Lily is in Bay Bluff, "maybe she suspects there was a connection and is here to do research. Maybe she doesn't even need to do research because she already knows what really happened. Maybe she knows damn well how much she looks like my mother and wants everyone in town to know it, too. Maybe she's here to haunt me. Maybe she's here to haunt your father."

I'm looking at him through the last of this, but only at the end does he realize it. Then he turns to me in quick dismay. "No?"

"No to which part? There are lots of them here."

Eyes the color of slate search my face. "You pick."

"Okay." I consider the options. "She's been here . . . how long?"

"Five weeks."

"And she's questioned how many people?"

"None."

"So she's not researching a book. That'd be way too much wasted time. Has she talked with you?"

"Oh yeah. I confronted her the first time I saw her."

"What did she say?"

"She told me right off who she was, but she claims to know nothing about my mother."

"What do your spies say?"

His mouth quirks. "That she went to Boise State because it was cheap, that she was engaged to be married before breaking it off, and that her mother doesn't know she's here."

"She volunteers this?" I ask in surprise.

"So my spies say. She likes to talk." He murmurs the last as a heads-up. Lily has seen us and is trotting over. His posture doesn't change, though I sense that is deliberate. He is the image of nonchalance, which must run in the family, because when Guy raises his head, Lily doesn't show an iota of a qualm. She may have experience with pit bulls. More likely, she's met this one before.

"Hey, you all," she says, and after giving the dog a head scratch with her left, offers her right hand to me. "I'm Lily. You must be Anne's sister. I heard you were here."

"So quickly?"

"Well, yeah, when I called Anne to say I'd be late, she said your daughter could help out 'til I got here. So here I am."

We shake hands, though I'm not sure I manage an actual smile. Totally aside from the fact of wondering whether Lily Ackerman is in town to hurt my father, the girl is even more like Elizabeth up close. I can't help but stare.

"Sorry," I say when I realize what I'm doing.

Her smile is kind. "You're not the first. Strong genes," she remarks with a quick look at Jack. I'm thinking that she may be afraid of him, when she reaches back for the man in the baggy tee. "Nick White, Mallory Aldiss." In lieu of introducing Jack, she tells me, "Jack and Nick met last week." Softening, she says to Nick, "I'd better go in." And off she goes.

Awkward in her wake, Nick nods to us and heads back toward the beach.

Once he's out of earshot, I make a face. "That was weird."

"What?"

"Is he a boyfriend?"

"He's a private investigator."

"She hired an investigator?" I ask in alarm.

"She didn't. I did."

I lean away. "You? To pin something on my father?"

"Nah. I've hired snoops before to do that, and they've come up with zip. I hired this one to follow her."

"And how's *that* workin' for ya?" I mutter. When Jack snickers, I add, "Looks like they're a pair. Is that the way he works?"

"No. That just happened. I'm not supposed to know the extent of it, but Christ, they were all over each other at the beach the other day."

"Which you know how? Ah. Spies. Right. Is he still on your payroll?"

Eyes smiling, Jack bobs his head side to side. "For now."

"What does that mean?"

He sighs. "It means, Mallory, that I'm not a total shit. If they're together, he's not going to give me anything of value. If they're together, they're together." He sits forward again, putting his forearms on his thighs and linking his hands.

"And you don't want to ruin it?"

"Why would I? I'm not a monster. I just want to make sure she's not here to make trouble for me. If she wants to make trouble for your father, great."

I ignore that. "She seems guileless. If she likes to talk and may not have much more of a filter than her uncle—"

"Cousin."

"—cousin, wouldn't she have already spilled something to someone if she was here to nose around? She knows that she looks like your mother, so yes, she may be sticking it to my dad, but maybe that's not a bad thing. Maybe it's just another way of jarring his memory so that something spills out."

There is no change in Jack's body. I would know. Our arms and thighs are touching. But I do sense a shift in mood. Sure enough, when I look at him, the grooves on his forehead are deep. His eyes meet mine, but only long enough for me to see the shadows there, before he looks away. He seems to be considering what I've said—something about my father's memory or about Lily's motives—no, not either of those but something else—actually considering whether to broach it, because he's chewing on the corner of his mouth again. I'm watching that when he murmurs, "Maybe my mother sent her."

My eyes fly to his. The words don't fit a man who is an educated professional, who has established a successful business and screams *survivor* from every pore. That man should have accepted what logic insists. And still, I sense that he needs me to say it.

I jiggle my leg against his, just the tiniest bit. He is wearing shorts, and his skin is warm, not gorilla hairy but enough to add abrasion. I always liked being able to feel that difference between us. "Oh, Jack," I say softly, "you know that's not true."

"You think she's definitely dead," he whispers, eyes haunted.

Hope dies hard, I know. But I've never seen this vulnerability before in Jack Sabathian. Add the sun glinting off unruly hair, and he could be ten years old. My heart breaks as I nod.

He nods back. After a minute, he returns to rubbing the dog's ear with his thumb. I think of the soothing that comes from touching a rabbit's foot, a lucky penny, even rosary beads. He clearly gets something from Guy's silky ear. When he finally speaks, his voice holds surrender. "She drowned. It's the only thing that makes sense. The question is how she got in the water."

And there we are, back at Square One. I don't look at him, don't want to see accusation. It's been nice sitting here talking with him.

"I've missed this," he says quietly. "Never had it with anyone else. The easy talk. The honesty. The silence."

"Not even your wife?" I ask.

He seems startled by the question, perhaps uncomfortable, like he's cheated on me and is caught, which is both sad and adorable at the same time. "Anne told you?" he asks.

I nod. "With pleasure."

"It didn't last. Did she tell you that, too?"

I nod again. "What happened?"

"You."

"Me."

"She didn't measure up." Before I can make an evasive maneuver, he is pressing his face to the back of my neck.

"Jack."

He inhales as he pulls away, and eyes me with expectance.

"What was that for?" I can't be angry, not after what he just said. But I'm curious.

"Remembering," he says with a sad smile. "It was good, Mal."

"Uh-huh, until it wasn't. Do you remember why we broke up?"

"I remember why you ran away."

"I didn't run—"

"You did. You didn't stay to talk it through. A few bad words—"

"A *few*?" I cry. It was more than a few. It had been a torrent, coming from the person I most trusted in the world, and it had sent me into a downward spiral of loneliness and doubt. I spent months trying to recover from that argument. The memory of it, even now, is painful. "You called my father a murderer and my mother a coward. You called Margo a ballbuster and Anne stupid. You called me a basket case who couldn't make up her mind what she wanted. You called me spineless. You said I was crippled by my father. You said I was damaged—*permanently* damaged, you said, if memory stands—and you said it when you knew I was falling apart, knew my family was falling apart, knew I was *crushed*. Do you know the meaning of love, Jack? Love means you put another's pain even above your own. I was in pain, and you were too obsessed with yourself to see it. *You're abandoning me,* you said. Well, no, Jack. *You* abandoned *me.* For you, it was only about the Sabathians, but I had family, too. I had issues and fears, and you were blind to everything but—" I stop. "What is that *smile* about?" It is triumphant.

"I love it when you're passionate."

I gape at him. "You do not. That's what set us off twenty years ago."

"No," he says, still smiling, "what set us off was shock. We'd never argued before. We threw words at each other, and at the worst possible time. But now? Now is deliberate and rational. You never did it like this back before that night, but I wanted you to. Has living in New York given you balls?"

Rational? Hah! If I were another type of person, I'd have hit him. It might be the resurgence of those memories and my need to lash back for those ugly words. It might be his smugness. Or the fact that this man has the ability to so quickly strip me raw.

But I'm no hitter. Physical violence gives me a panic attack. Words—now, words are another thing entirely. I don't even bother to move away, because what I have to say can be said inches from his gorgeous face.

"Listen, bud," fury keeps my voice low, "living in New York gave me nothing that I didn't work my tail off for. And I sure as hell didn't do it for you. I've been with men who are kinder than you. I've been with men who are smarter and more successful. I've been with a *ton* of men."

"But you didn't want any of them."

"And I don't want you. You are not why I came back, Jack. My family is. So call me crippled or damaged or spineless, if calling me names gives you a rush, but I'd wager I'm a lot happier than you are right now."

My phone dings. His phone dings. We both reach, raise, read.

Where r u? Joy texts.

Almost there, I text back and slide off the table at the same time as Jack. "My daughter calls," I say. "Gotta run."

"Me, too. My cat calls."

I might mock the fact of daughter versus cat, or say, *See, it's always about you,* if it weren't for the concern in his voice, which I do hear precisely because I loved him once. But no more.

Without another word, we walk off in opposite directions, which is a metaphor if ever there was one.

Chapter 10

The interior of Sunny Side Up is as yellow as its name implies—yellow walls, yellow tables, yellow art. Still annoyed at Jack, I would have preferred a calmer blue or green, even my New York black. I'm not feeling terribly sunny.

Then I see Joy, and my mood lifts. She is a rainbow of color, with a short bar apron tied around her waist, and moves from table to table with carafes of coffee in each hand, one regular, one decaf, all the while chatting and smiling and topping off cups with aplomb. She is underage. She is inexperienced. But she is adorably happy.

My father sits alone in the front right corner of the shop. A newspaper lies open before him, and he does look to be reading, to judge from his glasses and the movement of the eyes behind them. I know that once I sit with him, all hope of anonymity is gone. But if I'd wanted to be anonymous, I wouldn't be here now, would I?

Besides, connecting with my father is preferable to dwelling on Jack.

Setting my sunglasses and camera on an empty patch of the table, I slide into what must have been Joy's chair, given the remains of a green smoothie and the uneaten half of a piece of avocado toast. "Hey, Dad."

He looks up in surprise and just stares at first, hitting me with the awful possibility that he won't recognize me here. I'm about to take off the ball cap to help him out, when he removes his reading glasses, breaks into a smile, and says, "Hello, middle one."

I'm stunned. "Middle one," which he had always thought a clever takeoff on "little one," was his nickname for me in those fond moments that were so few and far between.

I had forgotten.

But this was a *nice* memory.

More confident with him on my side, I push Jack from mind and relax. "Sorry I'm late. I meant to get here sooner, but, well, vacation and all." No lie there, though far safer than mentioning the search for a gun or time with Jack. "How's your wrist?"

"Fine," he says. But he is studying me like I'm the clue in a crossword puzzle that has him stumped.

"My hair's a mess," I try, explaining the ball cap. When we were kids, hats at the table were forbidden. In a place like this, though, I'm far from the only one wearing a cap. Ocean air? Humidity? Vacation? Skimming past the other hats, I spot my daughter. "Looks like Joy is keeping busy." The words are barely out when she heads over.

His blue eyes actually soften. "She's a good child," he says, and again I hear fondness. Of all the things he doesn't know in his current state, he should know this. Joy isn't just a good child. She's the *best*.

Leaning in to kiss my cheek, my *best* child scolds in a whisper, "I was worried, Mom. Like, I was starting to think something popped, you know, burst in your head and you didn't wake up?" She straightens with her server smile in place and asks in a server voice, "Coffee?" Before I can reply, she has righted a clean mug from an unused place setting and is filling it to the top. She knows I take it black—just as I know, with quick remorse, that she worries when I'm not where she expects me to be. I'm all she has.

At least, I always have been. She has barely finished topping off my father's coffee, when Anne waves her over, and she's off—but not before bending to me and murmuring, "You need to tell your sister plastic straws are bad. I mean, where has she been? Didn't she get the memo? She uses them like they're air."

Smiling, I watch her go. Anne may be part of the family she's always wanted, but that doesn't mean she gets a free pass, which actually raises another issue. "Is it legal for Joy to be working?" I ask my father.

He is frowning at the spoon in his hand. Grabbing the cream, I add some and gesture for him to stir. In the process of doing that, he seems to have forgotten the question. So I repeat it.

"Is it legal for her to be working?"

"Is that what she's doing?" he asks back.

"Well, pouring coffee." But I have to amend that when I see her turn from the window with a plated breakfast in each hand. "And serving food. Are there liability issues for the shop since she's underage?"

The question hangs there, but I'm distracted watching her. She sets the plates down before a Vineyard Vines pair, and wipes her palms on her apron while they talk. From there, she turns to clear a nearby table whose occupants have left. She certainly seems to know what she's doing.

My father hasn't answered.

Again, I repeat the question. "Is liability a problem?"

"What does Anne say?" he asks—and it strikes me that he doesn't remember the law. Too quickly, he adds, "She's only helping until the other one comes."

Well, that does make sense. It also raises an issue I want to discuss. "I met her—Lily—outside. She must be in the kitchen by now. Amazing how much she looks like Elizabeth." When he doesn't react, I ask, "Do you know why she's here?" I've heard Jack's thoughts. I want to know his.

"Why do any of them come?" He grapples with the question. "She needed a job. For summer. I think she has something else for the fall." It's another plausible statement, but in the next instant, he looks stricken. He presses his lips together and looks at me in desperation. He is clearly trying to remember what that something else is.

"Is her family struggling?" I ask.

"Struggling?"

"With money?"

"I think. Yes."

"Do you know why?" When his blues sharpen, I soften the question. "What do her parents do for a living?"

He draws back. "How would I know?"

His voice is too loud. I drop mine even more in the hope he will take the hint. "Do you know that she is Elizabeth's great-niece?"

"Objection!" he bellows. "That is irrelevant to the point. The prosecution has no business raising it."

I grasp his cast and say a hushed, "I know. You're right. Question withdrawn." To my relief he lets it rest. Truth be told, I don't care what Lily plans for the fall. I care about making this man comfortable. Opting for distraction, I gesture at the plate before me. "Is this Joy's breakfast?"

He regards the half-eaten avocado toast. "I believe."

Taking the fork, I set to finishing what my daughter has left. Between bites, aiming for light conversation, I say, "I also met Lina. She seems nice. How did you come to hire her?"

He lifts the newspaper and, using his full right hand and the fingers of the left that are free above the cast, shakes it into its proper folds. When he has it right, he sets it aside. "Hire who?"

"Lina. Your housekeeper?"

"I know who Lina is," he snaps but he doesn't answer the

question, seems to have forgotten that, too. Having settled the newspaper, his focus is on the kitchen.

As I eat, I try to guess at his thoughts. The good thing is that his outburst didn't draw attention. No one in the shop is paying him much heed. But that may be the bad thing, too. He is used to being noticed. He used to thrive on it. When Elizabeth disappeared, people weren't sure what to say and gave him space, but Anne told me things are back to normal. If so, he should be the retired judge holding court right here, with a reverent audience greeting him on their way in or out.

That isn't happening. Only locals would recognize him, of course. Looking around to decide how many of those are here now, I spot Deanna Smith. She is sitting with a family of four, but quickly rises and weaves between tables to Dad's.

"Mallory." I barely have time to set down my fork when she gives me a hug. "I heard you were here." Addressing my father, she aims a sideways finger at me and says, "Does she look amazing, or what?" Then she's back to me. "New York, huh? Photography, huh? *Real estate,* huh?" She grins at the last, seeming pleased that we finally have something in common.

I'm not sure where she got her information, whether it is newly obtained or older. It would make sense to think she may have occasionally asked Anne about me, and there's no reason Anne wouldn't tell. Nor is there reason for me to be nervous that I've been discovered, since I knew what I was doing when I sat down with Dad. Still the past returns.

I remember Deanna in grade school, always the head of the pack. Come middle school, she was a woman while we were still girls. By high school, she was head cheerleader *and* president of the class. Around Deanna, I felt out of my element. But when I try now to conjure something she might have done to make me feel that way, I can't—which suggests the problem was me. She loved the limelight, I avoided it.

She partied, I studied. She was the one everyone wanted to be with, I was not. Sure, my father was a judge, but that could have gone either way—been a source of status or a cause for distance. Margo certainly had plenty of friends. Me, not so much. And I hadn't minded. I didn't want to be noticed. To be noticed was to risk criticism, and Lord knew, I had enough of that at home.

But I don't want to be that Mallory now. I want to be the one with a good career and a super daughter and a Facebook page followed by real friends. Sitting straighter, I say an upbeat, "Yup, real estate photography. And look at you, gorgeous, as always. Sophisticated. Successful." I glance at her table. "Clients?"

"Yes." She drops her voice. "I'm sorry. I'd love to talk. Actually, I want to milk your brain for ideas that can help me sell. The middle market is fine, but the high end? I'll bet you do a lot of that. Around here, lately, it's a tough sell," she hitches her head to indicate her current clients and adds in a whisper, "even with unlimited money in startups. Can we talk another time?"

"Sure," I say, which restores her grin. I hate that I love being in her sights, but I do.

Holding up a be-right-back finger, she returns to her table and is right back with a business card. "Do you have one?"

Not here. Nope. Naturally, not. She is chic, and I'm sweaty. What else is new?

But hey, I'm on vacation. I've earned the right to travel light. "Back at the house," I say and, taking my father's pen from the breast pocket of his shirt, write my phone number on a paper napkin. "Not fancy, but it'll get you to my phone."

Grinning, she scrunches herself up, like she's controlling excitement, then gives a little wave and rejoins her clients.

I start to return Dad's pen but pause. Taking it from his pocket had been reflex, but there was an intimacy to the gesture. And why not? He was my father. He always kept a pen there, and he never minded when we borrowed it. If we dared to walk off with it, well, that was something else.

Gingerly, I slip it back into his pocket. "That was nice," I say, meaning Deanna stopping by.

But he is still focused on the kitchen, and his expression is dark. I never knew what to say when he was this way before, and I'm even more unsure now. So I sip my coffee and try not to make things worse.

Then the darkness lifts. I know even before I turn that Lily is on her way.

"Hey there, Judge," she says with a big Elizabeth smile. "How're you doing today?"

He raises his silver brows. "Not bad. Not bad. Where you been?"

"I overslept. Your granddaughter is adorable."

"Granddaughter."

She tosses back a glance. "Joy?"

"Huh. Joy."

"She was good to fill in for me, but I'd better see who needs food."

"Amazing," I say once she is gone, because the resemblance truly is. "Did you know she was coming to town?"

"Should I?"

"Did she call you ahead of time?"

"Why would she do that?"

"Maybe just to let you know."

"Why would she do that?" he repeats, but he is growing agitated. Not wanting him to raise his voice again, I let it go.

That is when Anne stops by. She is nearly as colorful as Joy, though her eyes are nowhere near as warm. "Everything all right here?" she asks. Always an open book, my sister, I see concern for Dad and annoyance for me.

Ignoring it, I say a bright, "It is. I love your place."

She relaxes some. "So do I. So does Joy. Is it okay if she hangs around?"

"Uh, sure. If you're good with it."

"She knows how to pour coffee," she says but apparently hears something in the kitchen and turns to leave. "You okay, Dad?"

He waves her off with a hand.

She is no sooner gone when two men approach. They're Dad's age, but while he is more formal in a pressed shirt and khakis, they wear tee shirts and shorts. I should know them, but the names won't come, and when I glance at Dad, he's rustling through his folded newspaper, clearly as clueless as me.

So I grin at the men and pray. "Hello."

"Hi theya," says the taller of the two with a distinctly coastal accent. Fisherman? Not at this time of day. House painters? Ditto. "Just want to welcome you back. It's been a while."

"Twenty years," I admit and wince in both apology and invitation.

"Howard Hartley." He hooks a thumb sideways. "My brother Don. We used to do the landscaping around your place."

"Ahhhhh," I say with a relieved laugh as memory returns. "The Hartley Brothers. Used to?"

"Our sons do the daily now."

"Mikey and John," I come up with, pleased with myself.

"They still go to your place." He turns to my father and tips two fingers off his brow. "Morning, Judge."

My father sets down the paper. "Howard. Don."

"How're you doing today?"

"Couldn't be better." He turns to me. "Aren't we supposed to be back at the house?"

We aren't. But I give him props for coming up with a plausible cause for escape. Not about to deny him, I reach for my camera. Then I have a thought. "The bluff is in rough shape. Have your sons mentioned it?"

Don answers. "Sure have. The state mentions it, too. You got those letters, didn't you, Judge?"

If something came in the mail, my father doesn't remember. Nor does he care to discuss it, says the irked look on his face. While we watch, he pushes out of the chair and strides off.

"Sorry," I mouth to the men, but I'm thinking I need to follow him. He shouldn't be out there alone. Seeming to understand, the pair melt away.

I gather my things, then pause. Do we pay? Do we not? Do we tip or not? The table looks bare without something.

"Go," Anne murmurs. Her hands come around to remove our plates. "He's my father. I don't charge him. Take his glasses. He leaves them here every time."

"Can he walk home, or should I take your car?"

"Walk. He needs the exercise. And if you want to put in plantings on the bluff, there are people who'll do it cheaper than Mikey and John. I'm on top of this, Mallory."

"You've talked with someone?"

"It's on my to-do list."

"Okay." I can't argue with that. "What about Joy?" She is on the far side of the room, again with a carafe in each hand.

"If she gets bored, I'll send her home."

Nodding, I slip the glasses into my pocket and hurry after my father. At first I don't see him and feel a mild panic as I look from the square to the road. And then there's the ocean, which could be dangerous for a man who may or may not remember its dangers, which doesn't speak well for said man living a single staircase away from the ocean and possibly being able to wander there in the middle of the night. I'm wondering if Anne has taken precautions against that—if she has the doors alarmed in a way that would alert her to one opening in the wee hours—when he appears on the far end of the parking lot, apparently having taken the pergola route around.

"Dad!" I call, running to catch up. "Wait."

He actually slows down and lets me catch up. "Thought you'd never get here," he says in a crusty voice that makes me smile. It's a memory-waker, that voice. And while not all the memories are good, the straight shot back to my childhood is impossible to avoid in this place.

"They're nice guys," I say as I fall into step beside him.

He clicks his tongue. "They charge too much. They charge me more because of who I am."

"Really? But they keep the grounds around the house looking good," I say in an attempt to appease. "And we do need to do something about the erosion problem."

"It's called bluff retreat," he lectures. "The waves come in higher each storm. When they retreat, they take more of the bluff with them. Bluff retreat," he repeats in a shout, then waves a dismissive hand. "The state sends letters about beach restitution, but *I'm* not hauling sand to *my* beach. All we need is a little vegetation to dry out the bluff soil and hold it in place."

I am astounded by the coherence of his speech. It's the most he's said at one time since I arrived, and other than *restitution* where *restoration* should be, it makes sense.

"Then we should put some in. I'll bet—" I was about to say that I'd bet Jack could advise us on it, since the Sabathian side of the bluff, with its plantings, was faring far better than ours. But mentioning the Sabathian name might set him off.

"Bet what?" he asks, sending me a sharp look. He knows what I was going to say. The man is astute that way, and that's the good and bad of it. He knows what you want. But then he does what *he* wants.

I revise my thought, deleting the Sabathian name. "I'll bet it wouldn't cost much to have the Hartleys do it."

"We can do it. Nothing to it. You buy a plant, dig a hole, drop it in. Unless you're afraid of physical labor."

I think of the miles I clock walking from our condo to the market to Joy's school, the hours I spend in the gym, and the vacuum I push, the sheets I change, the dozens of shelves I wipe down to remove every last crumb each and every time Joy sees a single cockroach. Afraid of physical labor?

"I am not. I'd be happy to plant whatever needs to be planted while I'm here, and Joy would be glad to help. What you need to do is to make sure Anne is on board."

He looks at me in surprise. I'm not usually as assertive with him. In this case, though, assertive is also practical, so I don't take it back. And then, just as his eyes return to the road, my phone chimes. Joy would text, so I know it's not her. Same with close friends. The realtors I work with know I'm away, unless it's a new contact, which I wouldn't want to miss. Lifting my phone, I shade the screen with a hand.

Margo? I re-angle the screen to make sure I'm seeing it right, but her name remains, which is worrisome. I'm usually the one who calls her, not the other way around, and the timing couldn't be worse. If she's calling, though, something may be wrong, so I answer.

"Hey. Everything okay?"

"Fine, great, actually, because I'm in the city. I thought I'd stop by."

"In New York?" I ask in alarm and switch the phone to the far ear.

"Last minute girlfriend weekend. Joanie scored tickets to *Hamilton,* which I missed when it was in Chicago, so the three of us just took off. Are you free?"

Free? Omigod. If she could see me now, she wouldn't be pleased. Nor would Dad, if he knew I was talking to my sister. Granted, he's focused on the road, trudging along in his boat shoes, one foot striking pavement, then the next. There's a deliberateness to it, like he wants to be sure he does it right. Trying not to watch, I wander toward the trio of mailboxes to give myself, my sister, and my phone more room.

"I'm not in the city," I tell Margo softly. "I'm sorry. How long will you be there?"

"Just the weekend. Where are you?" she asks, indignant, like we'd had plans and I stood her up. Had it been anyone else, I'd be offended. But this is quintessential Margo, imperious to the core.

I get a mirror attitude in the other ear. Dad has followed me over. "Who is that?"

Rolling my eyes, as if the caller is no one special, I say into the phone, "You're leaving Sunday?"

"Will you be back?"

"Before then? Noooo." I drag out the word in honest regret. "I'm *so* sorry. I'd have loved to have you over."

"Where are you?" she asks again.

"Who *is* that?" Dad repeats, this time in a voice that is too loud, too close, and too gruff.

Margo is silent for a beat. Finally, with dawning horror, she says, "I know that voice, and it isn't one I want to hear. Where are you?"

I hesitate a minute too long.

"Mallory." Her words come hard and fast. "Are you seriously at the Bluff? What are you *doing* there?"

"Can't talk now," I say, pressing the phone tight to my ear. "Can I call you later?"

"What's going on?"

"Nothing. Really. Joy loves the beach."

"*That* beach? You do know Mom would be turning over in her grave."

"Actually, no," I shoot back, furious to be put on the defensive when I am so trying to do the right thing, "I don't know that, because we never had that particular discussion. It was always you saying it. I have my daughter to think of now. Please don't pass judgment on me." I've said too much already, but another thought comes and for the life of me I can't hold it in. "'Accept what you can't change by changing what you can't accept.'"

"What in the hell does that mean?"

"You tell me. You wrote it. This. Week."

"See? That's why you shouldn't be there. You don't sound like yourself. Go to that place, and you change. He's a *lawyer*. He knows how to make his case."

"It isn't that."

"Then what is it?"

His age, his mind, the house, the bluff, Anne, Jack, my memory, the truth—it is so many things that I don't know where to begin, and that's even apart from the issue of a gun. So I sigh, lower my eyes to the gravel road, and say a quiet, "It's complicated."

"You do know this will ruin my weekend."

If it does, I think, *that's your doing.* But saying it will only make things worse. The spoken word is like bleach. Use it with purple socks—as I mistakenly did once with Joy's—and though the socks may be wearable, they are never the same.

I keep my mouth shut.

"Okay," Margo concedes, because I hear voices on her end. "Talk later."

I want to tell her to have fun, but I'd have to apologize if I say more, and I refuse to apologize. I've spent a *lifetime* apologizing. And I'm in the right here.

So I nod, which she can't see, return the phone to my pocket, and try to put the discussion out of my head. It's about compartmentalizing. I'm good at that in the city, where anonymity makes for easy diversion. Here, everywhere I look— now at the boulders off the road on the right, where my sisters and I used to sit finishing off our penny candy so that our parents didn't know how much we'd bought—I see memories.

Dad stumbles. I reach out to steady him, but he catches

himself. Has he actually pulled his arm away so that I don't help?

"Your sister," he growls.

I consider lying. He can't have heard that clearly, and the truth will cause him distress. But a lie will cause me distress. "Yes. My sister."

I prepare for him to attack her as he had so long ago. The words were angry and ugly in those awful days. I thought I'd buried them, but three break through. *Traitor. Ingrate. Self-centered imbecile.*

Words. Always words. Like knives coming from Jack and arrows from my dad.

But he doesn't speak, just plods along, breathing heavily now. The road has started to climb, and he is leaning into it, shoulders rounded as they never used to do. The shape of him cries defeat. He seems very much alone.

Taking pity on him, I walk close enough so that he can't miss me, far enough so that our arms don't touch. He stops once, frowns at the path ahead, and, half to himself, says a breathy, "Is this right?"

It's a minute before I realize that he is serious, several beats again before I accept that he is confused. More than anything else I've seen of him since we arrived, this is the most upsetting. Having lived on the bluff so long, he has taken this road thousands of times. It is the only way to the top of the bluff, hence the only one he could possibly take home. *Confused* is a serious problem.

Making light of it, I say, "The house is just ahead. Boy, is this road ever steep."

He resumes his plodding, but I see that he is bracing the cast against his belt.

"Does your wrist hurt?"

He doesn't respond. His mind is elsewhere. After several steps, he says under his breath, "Sometimes I think she sent her."

My first thought is Margo, since my sister was our last touchpoint. But there is a gentleness to his voice that redirects me. "Elizabeth sent Lily?"

He shoots me an uncertain look, and I think of Jack asking the same, still wondering and wishing. As angry as I can be with either one of them for past attacks, my heart goes out to them both.

"Elizabeth is dead, Dad," I say gently. "We agreed on that. Unless you know something we don't?"

"Oh yeah," he snorts, though his breathing is heavy, "I know lots that you don't. But not about her."

I wait for him to elaborate, perhaps to go off on something having to do, if not with Elizabeth, then with the law or my mother or even Margo.

We are nearing the top of the road. The house has appeared and grows taller with each step. But he has slowed even more. When he stops entirely, he straightens, puts his hands on his lower back and stretches. He is panting.

"Are you okay?" I ask.

"No. I am not."

Now that I look, he is pale, and there's that breathing. I reach for my phone. "I'll call for help—"

"No." Straightening, he starts walking again. His steps are slow, his eyes on the house like it's the goal of his life. "I need to tell you." He shoots me a glance to make sure I'm listening.

And I hear a confession coming.

Chapter 11

My pulse trips over the possibilities—Elizabeth, my mother, me—but I've left one out.

"I know what's happening," he says in short breaths. "To my mind. What I have."

Quickly, I recalibrate. I'm not stricken; he is only confirming my suspicions. But his tone is the shocker. There is resignation even in his breathlessness, and resignation is *so* not my father. Belligerence, yes. Resentment, yes. Defiance, yes. But not resignation.

"I can't remember," he goes on in his soft huffing. "Words. Names. Where to be. What to do."

He shoots me another glance, but my childhood training is ingrained. I know not to speak, just to listen. That said, I could swear his glance held shame and as his daughter, as a human being, I'm heartsick.

I want to tell him that what he has isn't his fault. But he is slogging on now, just that foot or two ahead of me, up the last of the hill to the crest. Once there, he points at the front steps. Veering in front of me so sharply that I have to stop short, he crosses the last distance and lowers himself to the wood.

Now that he's stopped, the sound of his breathing is even

louder. I'm not sure if it's the hill, the heat, or the hell in his mind, but he is clearly in distress.

Dropping down on the step, I face him and urge softly, "Go on."

He puts his forearms on his thighs, lean fingers tightly linked, and waits for his breathing to slow. That breathing scares me. But my first priority is his mind. Distract him with another problem, like shortness of breath, and I risk losing him.

"It won't get better," he finally says.

"There's medication—"

"No drugs."

"There are ways to slow it down."

"I don't want that."

"Not to live longer?"

He shakes his head. "Not happening."

"Living longer? It can. If drugs slow it down and then a cure is found—"

"It's too late for me."

"How do you know that? Listen to you now. You are totally coherent."

His breathing is starting to level. He knows enough to give it a minute more, pulling air in and blowing it out. With the last, longer exhalation comes sadness. A tragic smile shapes his mouth, but it does nothing to cushion the words. "It comes and goes. Sometimes I'm good, other times I put a shoe on the wrong, uh, uh, side. I know it feels wrong, but I don't know why." He darts a look around, as if someone is listening, and speaks in a more confidential tone. "I can be at Anne's and not know anyone there. It's a foreign place. I can't remember names." He gives a humorless laugh. "Always that. Names are hard."

"You knew Howard and Don."

"You did. I repeated you."

"You know about bluff retreat."

"I do not. I know about law, and the law in this case is clear. The law dictates," he declares, "that planting can only be done within twenty feet of a public building. For anything else, you petition the state for a variance. Do you have one of those?"

"Uh . . . uh . . ."

His voice lowers again. "Now you're angry."

"I'm not. I'm just trying to follow. It's a lot to take in." Afraid that he's leaving me, I scramble for more. "Does Anne know about this?"

"About what?"

I tap my head.

His hand cuts a no.

"What about your doctor?"

He repeats the motion, but is suddenly up from the stairs and walking toward the ocean end of the house. I feel a moment's panic, imagining him going down and walking into the sea, farther and farther, until it swallows him up.

Rather than head for the stairway, though, he rounds the house and enters the backyard. Friends were always amazed that we had one, since, technically, the ocean was our backyard. But not every day was a beach day, and we were kids. We used to have a swing set here, though it fared worse than the gnarled scrub pine on the road. The Hartleys would have to sand it each year when they groomed the paths.

Shrubs still bordered the house in beds that my mother carved out. They were salt-tolerant ones, like blue juniper, dark green holly, and silver thorn, and aside from the occasional large-scale replacement, when she stood over the Hartleys telling them exactly what to put where, the shrub beds were all hers. She also planted daisies, black-eyed Susans, and varieties of lilies and irises that could live near the sea.

Early mornings, late afternoons, mid-days when Dad was home and we were in each other's hair, she escaped to the potting shed. It was her refuge. In the years since we left, especially since she died, I've often pictured her here.

I remember her humming as she unpotted new accent plants and repotted old ones. I remember how she would smile as she watched the sky lighten the windows in the greenhouse nook, and how she would gather us all in the backyard to oooh and ahhh over the fruits of her labor. I remember the pride Dad took in the landscaping when we had friends, colleagues, even clients here for cookouts.

Actually, no. I don't. Remember, that is. These are wish-it-were memories, meaning, likely not true. My mother couldn't hold a tune, she had us digging and lifting more than oooohing and ahhhing, and as for Dad showing pride? I do not recall that.

Yet here he is now, striding over the grass to the potting shed. It is small, little more than eight by ten feet, its wood frame a sea-worn gray and roughened by age, its windows streaked with sand. The greenhouse nook is a wall of glass that curves into the roof facing south for the most sun. The other walls have normal windows, albeit small ones to allow for storage inside. Even then, Dad complained that all the glass made the shed more vulnerable in high winds, but other than one hurricane when several broke, Mom's guardian angel kept them safe.

This was her happy place. No wish-it-were memory this one. She may not have smiled at the sun or sung to her plants, but the potting shed was her domain. Dad did not step foot in it.

He doesn't now, simply opens the full Dutch door, which moves with surprising ease given the neglect of the rest, and, holding himself straight, looks inside. What little I can see past him doesn't appear to have been touched in years. But there is nothing warped about that door.

He's been here before, I realize and feel a pang of sentiment. Missing my mother? I picture him standing here talking with her, asking about the iris she just planted or the loam she uses to bolster the soil. But of course, he didn't do either.

Annoyed by that, I ask, "Why have you told me this, Dad?"

He shoots me a startled look. "What?"

"About your mind. You could have told Anne. Why me?"

He says nothing for a minute, just gazes into the shed. Finally, seeming wistful, he sighs. "She loved gardening."

I'm not sure if I've lost him on the Alzheimer's vein, but I do like this one. "Yes."

"I come here sometimes," he says. "It's quiet."

It was. The memory of that motivates me, and, slipping past him, I enter. I always marveled that wood and glass could mute the shore sounds this well without insulation. But it was like this place was of earth, and within these walls, earth overrode water, birds, even the guttural rumble of double outboards too close to shore.

Quiet. Yes. Here is the table on which my mother worked, the shelves of stacked pots and watering cans, the trowels and clippers and other hand tools on hooks. The wheelbarrow still holds remnants of dirt from her very last planting here, but on top of that are neatly folded knee pads and a hat. A stained aluminum ladder slants against the wall along with a lineup of shovels, rakes, and hoes. Cobwebs are everywhere, but they only add to the ethereality. There is something sacred about this place, as rightly there should be. My mother is here.

Tearing up, I hold my arms close to my sides.

"I come here sometimes," my father repeats from the door.

I swallow. "I understand why," I say, then realize that no, I do not understand why. He cheated on my mother for years, if not in body then in mind. He kept her tied to this life as his subordinate. He was the cause of her worst humiliation. For all these reasons, I need to understand more.

I turn to him to ask, but his blue eyes are moist. Tears? From Judge Thomas Aldiss, my very formal, detached, world-unto-himself father? I'm horrified. I don't know how to deal with vulnerability in this man.

"I don't want to forget her," he says.

"Who?"

"Your mom." He pauses. "My mom. You girls. Elizabeth."

I could have done without the last, but even so, I hear an invitation. A dozen questions pop into my mind, and though I'm desperate to ask, I fear that peppering him will only drive him to silence again.

In that instant, though, I have a thought. It's a brilliant one, actually. Returning to the door, I dare grasp his arms. "You don't have to forget, Dad. I could write it all down."

He pulls in his chin. "Write what down?"

"Your memories. Your story. People do this all the time now. I've read about it. Some even hire videographers, but I could video us myself." He is staring at me, impossible to read. "Or not," I relent to make it less threatening. "It could be just you and me talking, no video, maybe even here in this shed. You talk, I write. That way when you think you're forgetting, you have a refresher. You can just pick up my notes and read."

"I can't read," he mutters. "The words . . . mix up."

Reminded, I take his glasses from my pocket and slip them into his alongside the pen. "We can have your prescription checked."

"It isn't my eyes," he barks. "It's my brain."

"Then someone can read it to you," I say without reacting to his remark. Of *course,* it's his brain, and it won't get better. That's why my writing his life is a brilliant idea. "You don't need to share it with anyone. You can just put it in the attic, but you'll know it's there in case you want to check on something."

He is silent for a beat. "Check on something."

"That's right."

"Check on what?"

"Whatever you want to tell me. You've lived a full life, Dad. You have stories in you. There are stories from your time in private practice, and stories from your time on the bench. Remember when you defended that man who concocted an elaborate scheme to steal his own mother's inheritance—his own *mother's*?"

"Elvin Anderson," he says without missing a beat.

"Yes." I'm thrilled that he remembers, at least when it comes to work. Anne is right about that. "People think law is boring, but it wasn't for you. You handled interesting cases."

He nods, clicks his tongue, says nothing.

"And then there's the personal stuff. You could tell us about what this shed means to you. You could talk about Mom, like what you were feeling when you first met her. You could talk about the house or the bluff or the town. You could talk about Elizabeth. You wouldn't want these things to be lost."

"No," he murmurs, and, almost amused, arches a silver brow. "I could tell you about John Doe."

"John Doe?" Everyman? An anonymous client? A corpse?

"John Doe."

Okay. I bite. "What about John Doe?"

But he is suddenly frowning, staring past me at the peg-board where Mom's garden gloves hang from hooks. There are three pairs. Each is a different color, though what with dirt and time, the colors have begun to blend. "She forgot them."

"I think she figured she wouldn't have time to garden. You know she went back to school." Dad's paying her tuition was a contentious part of their divorce. He didn't see why he needed to pay for her to learn a skill if he was giving her alimony so that she didn't have to work. She wanted both. She got both. He wasn't pleased.

Memory of that shows on his face. "Such a ridiculous

thing. And then she jumped off the boat. She's hiding some-where to punish me."

I give him a minute to rethink. When he simply scowls at the peg-board in silence, I say a gentle, "Mom isn't hiding, Dad. She died. You know she was living in Chicago when she left here. There was a car crash."

Frightened eyes meet mine. "Margo?"

"Eleanor."

"Chicago?"

I nod

"Not Albany?" he asks.

"No."

"Not John Doe?"

"No. Mom. She was identified at the scene. Her identity was never in question."

"Ah," he says, opening his mouth in an exaggerated fash-ion to let the word out. Then, seeming to have had enough, he turns and strides off.

How had we ever played hide-and-seek in this potting shed? Alone here now, I take in the whole of it. It's smaller than I remember—but isn't that always the case? Life through a child's eye has to be supersized to hold the huge wealth of possibility she sees. I would squeeze under the wheelbarrow or flatten myself behind the ladder when it was draped by one of Mom's shirts. I would make myself long and narrow behind the coils of hose on the lowest shelf, praying those coils weren't snakes.

Hah. Snakes. Not part of my memory, but something I can hear now coming from my daughter's mouth.

Without conscious intent, I raise my camera and start shooting. Odd, but I've never photographed the potting shed before. The exterior, yes. But not here inside. I work quickly, snapping the whole of it, then individual parts, and all the while I feel a pressing need to preserve something that might soon be gone. It was a ridiculous thought. This shed will likely outlive us all. And still, I hurry to memorialize and keep it forever.

Like my father's thoughts.

There's no sign of him, not at the ocean edge, in the yard, or through the kitchen window. And for a minute I feel guilty, thinking that I should have followed him the instant he left. But I can't crowd him in. If I do that, he'll never talk. And that is what I want. It doesn't matter whether I record what he says or write it down. I won't be publishing a book on the life and times of Thomas Aldiss. All I want is more information than I've gotten so far.

There is a difference though, between crowding him and making sure he's all right. Needing to do the latter, I enter the kitchen through the beach door. Lina isn't here, although I see a loaf of bread, a head of lettuce, and a bowl of what looks like chicken salad on the counter, if the denuded rotisserie chicken is any indication. Chicken salad was always Dad's favorite.

I'm heading for the hall, when I hear voices. One is Dad's, meaning he's safe with Lina. That's all I need by way of permission to play.

The late-morning sun is high above, and while clouds drift, its heat is strong enough that I welcome the breeze on my skin. Heading for the beach stairs, I start down, then sit, brace my elbows on my knees, and lift the camera to my eye. The surf is up, making for more dramatic shots. I take several at a fast shutter speed to freeze the high tumble of the waves, and think to go for blur with a slower speed, but there is simply too much light. A tripod at twilight would work for that. For now, I continue down the steps.

As the surf recedes, my eye catches tiny jigglings in the sand. Stepping out of my flip-flops at the foot of the stairs, I cross the beach and squat as another wave breaks. Left behind in the ebbing is a squadron of sand crabs scrabbling to dig in. When we were kids, we used to catch them in flat-topped nets and give them to Dad as bait. Wanting to capture something of that memory, I photograph through several more breaking waves, bunches more crabs, farther out ruffles of surf, still farther ocean. I could photograph here forever. Sinking onto my bottom, elbows on knees again, I take a panoramic sweep of the ocean. That's when, scanning far left, I see Jack.

Chapter 12

Sitting all the way down the beach near the Sabathian stairs, Jack is bare-footed, bare-legged, bare-chested. He is staring at the horizon, which, compared to the clear overhead, is a ripple of murk. The dog's head rises between his bent knees, muzzle aimed seaward as well, and their profiles are in such perfect alignment that I can't resist. Zooming in, I take a handful of shots, then move closer to the bluff to capture them outlined against the sea.

I've barely lowered the camera when Jack turns his head. I don't know if he's seen me taking pictures, but now that I've been spotted, disappearing is pointless.

His eyes hold mine. They're too far away for me to know what shade of gray they are. But the set of his brow suggests deep grooves between his eyes. And I remember the words we spoke in the square.

I should be riled up, should be offended all over again, should be ready to shout right back at him if he dares shout something even remotely offensive. I want to be bold, if only to prove how different I am now from the person who left here years ago.

But I can't muster anger. I said my piece back at the square. The best way to prove its truth is to be self-confident and move on. Besides, the words that weigh on me more are the ones my father said. Not that he said anything I didn't know. Just that his saying them makes them real, and their reality hollows me out.

Time has taught me that the best antidote to hollowness is activity. In the early years after I'd left Bay Bluff, when I missed my mother, missed my family, missed Jack, I immersed myself in whatever mind-absorbing project I could find. Sometimes it had to do with work, sometimes the condo, sometimes friends. I was running away for sure. But what good would come of obsessing over things that had to be?

Needing something consuming to combat the hollowness now, I consider going to the house and fighting to get Dad to talk about something relevant. That would be worthwhile. So would searching deeper in his diaries for clues. Or sorting through old pictures. Or looking for that damn gun in the potting shed, though I cannot imagine that he would ever hide it in Mom's sacred place.

There's something about the way Jack is staring at me, though, that holds me in place. Forget shouting insults. If I want to prove self-possession, approaching him now would be a good way.

Being casual about it, I walk down the beach, or try. The tide is out, and with the sun high and the breeze up, the sand closest to the bluff has dried, meaning that I sink deeper, and the walking is hard. With as much dignity as wading through soft sand allows, I pass the firepit in a diagonal cut toward the water. He watches me the entire way, but what I initially took for challenge isn't that on closer look. There's something about his bare shoulders, and his features, even the placement of his hand on the dog's back that has a slump to it.

Then I remember his parting words and realize that what I see is Jack subdued.

"The cat?" I ask when I'm close enough to be heard over the breeze and the waves.

He stares at me for a minute longer, then looks out over the water and does something with his mouth, like he's trying to clean off a bad taste. "Couldn't save her."

All too clearly, I remember the blood on his shirt. "You tried. That's something."

After a negligent shrug, he stretches his neck side to side. It's the dog who is watching me, bloodshot eyes pleading, begging me to say something to make his person feel better. I'm trying to decide what that should be, when the surf gives a thunderous crash.

I wait for the sound to die. "I'm sorry."

Jack nods. "It happens."

"That doesn't make it easy. The frustration must be awful."

He darts me a look. "Try anger."

"Anger?"

"At the car that hit her. At the family that couldn't keep her secure. And at myself. Maybe if I'd focused on her lungs. Maybe if I'd stabilized her before trying surgery. Maybe if I'd spared her the pain and euthanized her at the start. I knew her chances were slim."

You tried, I want to repeat, but the words clearly hadn't done much. "Were you trying to swim it off?" His hair and shorts are damp, and the sand spattering his lower legs says they'd been wet as well. When all he does is snort, I say, "Didn't help? Not even a little?"

"For the time I was out there, yeah, the waves are that strong. Come ashore, though, and it's waiting right fucking here." He finally turns his head, eyes finding my breasts. "Sex would help."

He is serious.

I am suddenly, acutely aware that he isn't dressed, and that I desperately wish he were. Jack Sabathian wearing nothing but shorts is a sight to behold. My sisters thought him too rough, though Margo said this only after it became clear that he wasn't interested in her. Rough, to them, meant too much of everything—height, breadth, physicality. It meant too brawny. It meant un-refined, though that had nothing to do with upbringing, or physique, and everything to do with attitude. Same with outspoken and abrasive. None of that had ever put me off.

All these years later, I feel the physical pull. It doesn't help that his eyes have gone lower. It is all I can do not to press my legs together. But sex with no relationship behind it? Oh, I did that a time or two in New York—well protected, thank you—when I found a man hyper-attractive, but the details elude my memory. What I do remember is the emptiness of it. To feel that emptiness with Jack would break my heart. Better to preserve the memories we had than to dilute them with something less.

"Uh, no." My voice lifts, gentle but firm.

His eyes rise. "Why not?"

"Because that was then."

"But it was good."

"It was." I have to give him that. "Well, after the first time."

He seems surprised that I've dared mention it. Then he breaks into a sheepish grin. "What the hell did I know about being with a virgin? I wanted to make it good for you—for you, of all people—but I had no idea how. I barely knew how to use my own equipment, let alone understand yours."

"Are you kidding?" I shoot back, because compared to what I'd known, he was the Oracle. "You were nineteen. You'd been sexually active for five years." He lost his virginity to an upper-class girl in a supply closet at school, which was clichéd as hell, but quintessential Jack. Had he been caught, there would have been all hell to pay, and he would have had his parents' attention. That was always his goal. Except when it came to him and me. We were a secret. Since I didn't dare ask my mother about birth control lest she tell my father, who would say I was too young and place me under house arrest, Jack used condoms. And his parents? His dad wouldn't have said much, but his mom would have been on her high horse about *not* doing *that* with *Tom's* daughter, for God's sake.

"Those girls were experienced," Jack insists. "I just followed their lead. It was a physical experience that never reached the brain. Zero emotion, zero finesse. Did I ever tell you otherwise?"

"No."

So there, says the arch of his brow. And while I don't like his smugness, at least he looks better than he did moments before. I'm not about to have sex with him, but arguing about it is fine.

"So." His stubbled chin is on his shoulder, which has bits of sand as well. "No sex?"

"No sex."

Straightening, he shoves his hair back with a handful of fingers. "Then help me feel better about losing a beautiful tangerine cat whose owners are devastated. What's that old Bobby Frost quote?"

Despite the irreverent nickname, I know who he means. I used to share Robert Frost with him, as I've done now with Joy. She isn't into poetry yet. But she will be. She takes pop lyrics seriously, and aren't they a form of poetry?

"In three words I can sum up everything I've learned about life: it goes on," I quote.

"It goes on," he repeats and, putting his dark head to Guy's, scrubs the dog's neck with both hands.

Quitting while I'm ahead, I cross back over the sand, wading where it is dry, toward the stairs. Short of it, though, I stop, drawn again to the stark difference between Jack's side of the bluff and ours. While ours is crumbling down to the beach, his is intact. Because of the plantings he put in? Even my untutored eye can see that they are strategically placed and varied.

"The key is using plants with root systems that grow deep and wide, and that do it fast." His voice comes from behind and is even. It isn't smug, just a statement of fact.

"Did you do the planting?" I ask, not quite looking back. I'm well aware of him without the visual.

"Me and Mike Hartley. He owed me for helping his dog through an immune deficiency issue, so we did an in-kind swap." Coming close to my shoulder, he points at various spots where thick clumps of tall green blades rise from the slope. "That's switchgrass. It's the first thing you try, because its root system is made to order." He gestures at other plants. "Goldenrod. Beach plum. Bayberry."

I repeat them silently. Despite my mother's aptitude, plants have never been my thing. Photography, yes. But the few times I've tried to grow herbs or houseplants or even get an avocado to sprout for Joy's sake, I've bombed. "Anne says she'll take care of this, but I'm thinking I can give her a nudge. Mike, huh?"

"I'll help you plant."

I laugh at that. "My dad nearly had a fit when I mentioned hiring the Hartleys. Think he'd feel better if I hired you?"

"Would he know?"

And isn't that the question of the day? I drop a hand and, startled, snatch it back when it hits the dog's head. Guy. Now that I know he is there, I let my fingertips graze his sandy fur and look up at Jack. I have to squint; the visor of my ball cap runs out when I tip my head back, which I do, he's that close. Jack was always much taller than me. In spite of the different roads we've taken and the memories that keep us apart, I am still drawn to that. And yes, to his body. He has aged well. Call him too coarse, too tanned, too ripped. But there is something about his solidity that offers comfort.

"Mallory."

My eyes fly up from his chest.

"No sex?"

"No sex." I swallow. I should take a step away. But I do crave comfort. "I want to talk about my father. We walked back from town together. I'm not sure if he was deliberately looking for the opportunity or if it was a spontaneous moment, but he said he knows his mind is going."

"No surprise there," he says. "Tom is a smart guy. The only surprise is that he spoke the word aloud."

"He didn't. Not the word. But a spot-on description. He is perfectly lucid about what he wants, which is no doctors, no medicine, no prolonging the inevitable."

"Would he rush it?" When I look at him blankly, he asks, "Is he suicidal?"

"I don't think so."

"Any mention of the gun?"

"No."

"Or anything else?"

"Like pills or a noose? Hell, he could just jump off the bluff."

"Wouldn't work on your side," Jack remarks, reaching for a stick that is caught in his vegetation. "It would crumble under his feet, so he'd just slide down the hill." Turning away, he hurls the stick, sending it end over end in a high arc toward his end of the beach. Guy shoots after it.

Suicide? Would he? What would I do, if it was me in his place? "What is it like, knowing you have something that'll eat at your mind, piece by piece? Knowing that it's only a matter of time before you don't know the people around you? Knowing that your mind may be gone but your body lives on? That he won't even be able to do the most intimate things for himself. Maybe he's obsessing about that. Maybe he doesn't have Alzheimer's at all, but is worried he does, since his mind has always been his claim to fame. Maybe he's just clinically depressed?"

I look to Jack's face for the answer, but he is watching his dog leap for the stick, juggle it in his jaws to secure it, and race back.

"Jack? Do you think he is?"

"Clinically depressed? No. He has Alzheimer's. It's the memory thing."

"Have you talked with him, I mean, other than the night he banged on your door?"

"I didn't talk with him then. He did the talking. And no, I haven't talked with him. Other people tell me. He's at the breakfast shop every morning. When he walks into the place and looks around like he has no clue what he's doing there . . . No, hon, it isn't only depression." Bending to take the stick from Guy, he straightens, hauls back, and hurls it again. The movement is nearly as beautiful as the surprising flow of his barrel-bodied dog.

After several beats, he glances my way. His expression is one I haven't seen him wear. "I don't envy Tom. Don't envy anyone who has that disease. At some point, though, it won't be as hard on him as it is on you. Or Anne. Or Lina."

I hear what he's saying in an intellectual way, even vaguely register the concession he's making to say something kind about Tom Aldiss, but my emotions keep returning to "hon." I'm sure it just slipped out, like the words of a childhood song. The fact that it doesn't mean anything strikes me as infinitely sad.

But it is what it is. As Bobby Frost advises, life goes on. So I start walking toward the waves as Guy lopes to Jack with the stick. Seconds later, he's off following the arc of another throw.

I cross hard sand, then wet sand spotted with odd pieces of kelp and a broken shell or two. When my toes touch water, I watch the play of bubbles over them as another wave ebbs. Jack's legs materialize in my periphery, close enough for me to say, "What do you know about Lina Aiello?"

His feet are at a ninety-degree angle to mine. He's clearly

watching the dog as he speaks. "That she's your father's housekeeper. That she needs the work because she needs money. That I was tempted to pay her to snoop, but didn't trust that she wouldn't go right back to your father with it."

"I mean, what do you know about *her*? She seems a little odd."

"Odd how?"

"She kept staring at me."

"She was probably thinking of her daughter. Both kids live away. The dad's been dead for years."

"Who was the dad?" I search what I remember of Danny, but our relationship never really left school.

"Roberto," Jack says.

I catch a breath and smile. "Omigod. Roberto Aiello." The key turns, memory opens, and there he is. "He was a gardener. He did our lawn before the Hartleys."

"He helped build the potting shed. He and your mom worked side by side in the dirt. Your mom adored him."

I smile fondly, then pause. Something in his tone sucks the fond from my smile. I squint up. "Excuse me?"

"Your mom adored him."

"What are you saying, Jack?"

If it is what I think, his eyes will be the bald gray of a seal. The sun is over his head, though, highlighting the tangle of his hair but shadowing his eyes. All I know is that he holds my gaze. "Small towns, small minds. There are always people who speculate."

"About me?" I ask, grabbing at wisps of hair blowing into my mouth.

"About your mother. After the marriage fell apart and you all left, the talk went wild. Tom had an affair with my mother or with his law clerk or with the wife of the guy who fixes his car. Your mother had an affair with Roberto or with the roofer who replaced your slate or with the pharmacist who was getting his own divorce."

It was one thing for Anne and me to wonder about Mom, knowing that Margo would rebut whatever we said. It was another thing to imagine it on the lips of strangers.

I am alternately offended and alarmed. "You're saying she was with our *gardener*?"

Guy has returned. This time, Jack sends the stick skimming lower over the shallows. The dog bounds in and out of the foam. "I'm not saying it," he argues. "I'm saying his name was mentioned."

"They really talked about my mother that way?"

"Didn't you?"

"That was different." I feel an immense loyalty on my mother's behalf. "I can wonder all I want—it's my life, my identity—but *they* have no right to do it. She was a beautiful person who was stuck in a lousy marriage."

He grunts. "Yeah, well, seems like everyone is lately."

"That's not true. My best friend in New York has a great marriage, in part because her parents had a bad one. She consciously decided that history would not repeat itself." The thought of Chrissie usually makes me stronger, but I can't get past a certain vulnerability. In a small voice, I ask, "Roberto Aiello?"

"He was a good-looking guy. Tall, dark hair, tanned."

"I don't tan well." But I do remember his hands. Large and knobby, they were showing my mother how to deadhead the rhododendron. I wince, look at Jack, and whisper, "Do you think it was him?"

A wave thunders in as I say the words, and as soon as they're out, the breeze whips them off. Which is good. I don't want them here.

But I do want an opinion, and Jack always has that.

So once the waves quiet, I prompt. "Jack?"

"I don't know. But it would explain Lina staring at you— you know, if she was looking for something of him in your face."

Needing to move, I splash my way down the water line.

"But hey," he calls after me, "she could just be wondering. She could have heard the talk, too."

Having a different father has always been my greatest fear. It's the only thing that explains Tom Aldiss's manner toward me. I'm not the first child of a troubled marriage who has wondered this. But seeing an actual face? Doing the math and realizing the timing works?

Jack splashes alongside. "It wouldn't be a terrible thing."

"It *would*. All those times he was at our house? Did he know? Did he look at me funny? Did he teach *me* how to deadhead the rhodies?" I look up at Jack. "Am I related to Danny? Did I even know his sister?"

"She was younger."

"I don't remember a thing. Did I deliberately not? Like, a defense mechanism?" I had an awful thought. "And what about the roofer? Did my mother adore him, too?"

"Mal—"

"Or the pharmacist? Mr. *Hennessey*? Omigod!"

Jack takes my arms in a soothing way. "Don't believe gossip. Idle tongues wag."

"But you know I've always wondered. You know I had doubts. Did you bring this up out of spite?"

His hands tighten. "No. Trust me. No."

"So is the pharmacist still around? Or the roofer? Do I look like either of them?"

"You look like your mother, and Hennessey is around, but the roofer's long gone."

"And Lina Aiello is a widow, meaning Robert is dead. What do I do now?"

"You could ask your father."

Shrugging off his hold, I raise both arms and cross them over my ball cap. It's sheer self-protection, followed immediately by the idea that I should return to New York and forget I'd ever come. But there's no comfort in that option. I won't be able to forget. There's no going back. The cat's out of the bag.

"Ask your father," Jack says.

I look at him then. And oh, yes, his eyes are seal gray, which means kingly, which means imperative. I take one breath, then another, and fold my arms, putting my hands where his had been moments before. When I feel sufficiently calmed, I say, "I suggested that to him. Not about whether he's my father. But whether I could write things down for him so he doesn't forget. I figured I could slip in personal questions and he wouldn't notice the difference. He looked like he was considering it, then he just walked away. I didn't want to push."

"Maybe you should."

"And if that makes him shut down completely? Then I'll be nowhere." I see the look on his face and know exactly what he's thinking. "Okay. Yup. You're right. We're nowhere now. But there's a way to do this, and there's a *way* to do this— and do not," I warn softly, "tell me I need to take a stand. This isn't indecision, Jack. It's diplomacy. It's a strategic plan. If I push too hard, my father will know exactly why I'm pushing. Believe me, I'll keep at him, especially now that I know he knows and he knows I know, or he did for a few minutes there—and especially since I now have three names permanently embedded in my mind, thank you, John Sabathian." In my distress, I stumble on a different thought. "He said he hasn't told Anne what he has. Should I?"

"Why wouldn't you?"

"Because we've argued about it before. I say Alzheimer's, she says old age. We've gone back and forth ad infinitum. If I say Dad confirms it, she'll say I'm lying."

"Anne?" he asks in disbelief. "Sunny Side Up Anne? She thinks *me* the liar, not you."

"She's changed. When we were kids, she was cheery about everything. Then came that night—not even that night, but the years since. She still has sunny moods. But other times not so much, at least when it comes to Margo and Mom and me. She's still naïve. But she's also defensive. I thought she'd be happy that I was coming back to help. Only she doesn't see it as help. She sees it as interference. So if Dad won't see a doctor or consider medication, maybe there's no point in telling her." My mind races on. "But then when he gets worse, which we know he will, she may blame me for not saying something. And what about his breathing? The guy's in lousy shape. He was totally winded walking up the hill." I grimace at Jack. "Think something's wrong?"

"I wouldn't know."

"You're a doctor."

"I'm a vet. Animals are different from people. Maybe he's out of shape because he doesn't get enough exercise?"

"Mom!"

I look back at the stairs to see Joy waving excitedly, then leaping from the second stair to the sand and running toward us with increasing speed as the sand hardens.

At the same time, Guy has broken from Jack and, with a growl that is separate and distinct from the rumble of the surf, races to meet her.

Will he bite me? Joy asked yesterday.

If you pick up a stick and come at him, he might.

There was no stick, but in the dog's eye, she is coming at him.

"No!" I cry, racing after the dog. "Joy! Stop!"

Jack is that much farther ahead, shouting orders to the dog, and when that does nothing, shouting them to Joy. As the distance between them shortens, I envision the dog leaping at my daughter's throat with open jaws.

Either she heard us. Or she, too, remembers what Jack said yesterday. She stops short, her eyes on the dog, and holds her arms out at the sides. I'm guessing she is terrified. Or maybe it's just me who is terrified.

Whatever, there is enough of a break in the action for Jack to reach Guy. One hand wraps around the dog's collar, the other arm around his chest. I'm passing them to reach Joy if only to put myself between her and the dog, when Jack snags my waist.

"I have this," he murmurs and pulls me behind him.

I'm not stupid. He is the pit bull expert, not me. That doesn't keep me from shaking.

Jack's voice is calm but firm. "Good Guy. Atta boy. *Good* Guy. She won't hurt you. She's excited, is all." He lifts his voice to Joy. It is gentle, but holds the same quiet command. "Come closer."

"I can't."

"Yes, you can. I'm holding him. He won't hurt you."

"I'm sorry, I'm so sorry, I just had such a good time working at Anne's and got to the house and Mom wasn't there and then here you all are at the beach, and I just forgot—" She stopped short. Her large eyes are on Guy.

"Come closer, Joy," Jack repeats quietly. "It's important for Guy."

The dog should be panting from the run, but instead stands still as stone. He is deadeye focused on Joy, who, despite the baby steps she takes, is nearly as still.

Not me, though. My pulse is racing, hands fisted against my throat. As I watch, all I can think, absurdly, is that we need a dog treat, why doesn't Jack have a dog treat, where are the dog treats—and when none appear from the pockets of Jack's shorts, I think of the gun that he claims my father has. If I had a gun in my hand, I wouldn't feel so helpless.

"That's right," Jack coaxes as Joy nears. "Good Guy," he murmurs at the dog's ear. "See, she's more frightened than you are."

"He's frightened?" Joy asks.

"Absolutely. Where he came from, someone rushing at him was not a good thing. He was trained to attack if he wanted to live. So now we have to retrain him. It's about trust. He's learning, but he has setbacks."

"I'm sooo sorry," Joy whispers, this time to the dog.

"Hold out your hand," Jack says. "He'll recognize you."

Her hand is remarkably steady. I hold my breath until the dog has sniffed, identified, and pushed his head under her hand. With the wag of his tail, the moment is over, the tension gone.

I'm slower to relax than Joy. Vaguely, I'm aware of a discussion between Jack and her, but I'm having a mother moment in which the world is filled with danger that can at any time take away my child. I want to shout *No!* when Joy kneels on the sand. I want to restrain the dog myself when Jack lets go and steps back. And when Guy sidles close to Joy, his blonde body wagging, I wait.

"They're fine." Jack is standing beside me now. "No need to panic."

"Of course, there's need," I argue, but I'm still weak in the knees. "Dogs kill children."

"That wouldn't have happened. I'm right here."

"Like you'd have been able to stop it?"

"I would have. Can't you trust me on this?"

I feel his eyes on me, but my own don't leave Joy. "I could see the headlines, Jack. Girl mauled to death on Rhode Island beach."

"That would not have happened. My dog is not a danger if common sense is applied. Look at him, Mallory. *Look* at him."

I take my eyes from Joy to find the dog's woeful ones on me. I could swear he is apologizing.

"Joy knows she shouldn't have charged him."

"She didn't charge him. She was running toward us."

"Same difference in his eyes. Now he's learned that she won't hurt him. So he's come another step in his training."

"This is about your dog being trained?" I ask in disbelief,

and give a dry laugh. "Sorry, but that doesn't work for me. The world is full of things I can't control. This is one I can. You have no right to use my child that way."

"I sure as hell do. This is my beach. She was running toward my dog on my beach against my orders."

"She's my daughter!" I cry. How else to explain my feelings?

But suddenly Jack is facing me, blocking my view of Joy and Guy. His voice is deep and low, as menacing as Guy's growl minutes before. "Yeah, well, she should have been mine. Do you really think I'd have let anything hurt her?"

Chapter 13

Jack is right. Joy should have been his. When I was picking a father for her, the qualities I'd looked for in a donor were the ones I had loved in him. Had it not been for our parents, she *would* have been his.

But your parents weren't the only ones at fault, Chrissie said in the gentle way of a therapist pointing out the obvious to a friend. We were at lunch last week. I was still debating whether to come home, and was trying to explain to her how intense it might be.

She was right, of course. We can blame the Aldiss-MacKay thing all we want. But Jack and I were the ones who had argued. We were the ones who had let our emotions build a wall. *We* were the ones who had turned our backs on each other at the worst possible time in our lives.

It is mid-afternoon now. Joy and I are back on the beach, slathered in sunscreen and lying on our stomachs reading, when Jack and his dog appear at his end and head for the dock. My daughter turns over, sits up, and adjusts her wide-brim hat to watch them, but neither the shadow of the brim nor her sunglasses can keep her thoughts from me.

"No," I say preemptively, barely looking up.

"Why not? I'd love to go for a boat ride, and that boat is so cool. I'll bet Jack's a really good boater."

He is. Absolutely. But Joy is not going on his boat without me, and right now I need a little distance. Jack Sabathian doesn't prevaricate. Discussions with him touch on core truths, and that last remark he made before stalking off this morning is only one. I'm still grappling with thoughts of the gardener, the roofer, and the pharmacist. I need a break.

Even though I don't look at the boat, I easily imagine Jack watching us as he readies to leave. "We'll get Anne to take us on Papa's boat," I tell Joy. "It's cool, too."

"But she's not here, and he's going out now, and just think of how neat it would be to have bonding time with Guy?"

"We weren't invited, sweetie. I think Jack wants to be alone."

"Really? You think that? How do you know?"

"Because the clinic lost an animal this morning. He needs time to process."

She is quiet for only a minute. "Well, I could help. I could untie ropes or raise a sail—"

"No sail, honey. It's gas all the way."

"Okay, so I could hold the wheel while he fixes the engine. I could wipe splashes off the deck. I could make sure Guy doesn't fall overboard."

I glance back. "Look at the horizon. See those clouds?"

"They're not here."

"They could be soon. Check out the weather on the Vineyard."

Of course, her phone is with her. It always is, just like Lip Smackers were when I was her age—and isn't *that* a memory, come to me here, where Nilla Mint Frost was my go-to. Oh boy, did Dad hate the sight of those tubes. He called them hotbeds of germs, though, compared to an iPhone, they were totally benign. If she isn't checking Snapchat, she's scrolling through Instagram or checking Houseparty, waiting for an invite. Since we arrived, she hasn't texted anyone but me, meaning none of her friends have texted back. Good to give her something practical to do with the phone.

Raising it, she searches Dark Sky for Martha's Vineyard, which lies due east, in the direction of those clouds. "Rain? *How?*"

"The ocean is like that. Storms rise out of nowhere."

"He would turn around before it rains. Please, Mom?"

"No." Next to my book, in the shadow of my own wide-brim hat, my phone lights. *She should have been.*

No doubt what Jack means.

But she isn't, I type and send.

Joy is fixated on the boat. "I thought we came here to do different things."

It's not too late, he texts.

"We came here to spend time with your grandfather."

"Who is taking a nap," she replies with disdain.

"Which is why we're at the beach. If you're bored, we can head back to the city tomorrow."

Dream on, I type and send.

"Oh-ho, no," Joy laughs. "We're staying here. Things are just getting interesting."

Her tone is too cocksure for comfort. She knows something I don't.

I look up at her, but she's still facing the boat. The engine starts, then idles while Jack releases the last of his lines. I don't have to look to know this. I lived it too many times to forget. "What things?" I ask.

"Anne's boyfriend is coming to dinner."

Jack's boat leaves the dock with a huge, crescendoing growl.

My goal for dinner is to mend fences with Anne. I usually know the right thing to say to people, but I'm not doing so well with her. She liked that I like her shop, but when I mentioned our bluff and the Hartleys, the good will vanished. She's my sister. I accept that our memories of childhood differ. I accept that she resents Margo and me for abandoning Dad. I accept that his health creates a dilemma. But there has to be common ground.

Determined to find it, I join her in the kitchen early to see what I can do to help. Billy—*Bill,* Mallory, *Bill*—Houseman is there with her. From the moment Joy said he'd be coming, I repressed the thought. With so many other battles to fight, I can't afford one about Bill. But here he is.

How to deal with him in a way that doesn't worsen my relationship with Anne?

I remember him having greasy hair and a stringy beard, wearing jeans that sagged and biker boots. I remember him holding a can of beer in his hand, always a can of beer. He had attitude written all over him, and he reinforced it with petty crimes, from shoplifting to "borrowing" people's cars to painting graffiti on the schoolyard wall. I remember him being a smoker.

He isn't smoking now. Nor do I smell it on him. His hair is short, his five o'clock shadow respectable enough. He wears nice-fitting jeans, an untucked shirt rolled at the cuffs, and flip-flops, and he holds a bottle of what looks like craft beer. The only thing I see that is even remotely rebellious is his ink. It covers both arms and climbs one side of his neck.

Even with that, he looks reputable. I might guess that he'd done it just for tonight, except that he seems at ease with himself. In fact, that's the one thing that hasn't changed about him—the insolent look. He knows that I remember the old Billy and is daring me to comment.

I smile and extend my hand. "Bill. Wow. It's been a while."

He hesitates, wary, before saying a measured, "It has. How're you doing, Mallory?"

"Great. It's really something being back here."

"Is that good or bad?" Anne asks over her shoulder. She is at the sink husking corn.

Crossing the floor, I nudge her aside. "I can do this. As long as it doesn't involve cooking, you're safe." When she raises her hands and steps back, I continue with the ear she was working on and say to Bill, "Thanks for helping out with the house. It looks good. Is that what you do? Home repair? Property management?"

"Nah. Fixing things is fun. I'm a correctional officer."

I did not expect that. "Really?" I ask, looking back, but that lazy grin gives nothing away.

"You mean, being on the outside rather than the inside?" he says, summing up my surprise. "It's true."

Anne has been clanging metal in a low cabinet. Emerging with the largest pot, she plunks it on the counter. "How's that for a shock?"

"Hey, Annie, I'm glad." I pull several pieces of silk from the corn and drop them in the sink with the husks. "I'm impressed. He cleans up good."

She does laugh at that, kicking sideways to jab Bill's leg with her foot.

"Fine," he grumbles. "You win."

I look from one to the other. "Win?"

"She said you'd be sweet, I said bitchy."

"Why would you think that?" I ask him.

"Because you always were."

"Really?"

He nods.

"Bitchy?" I ask in dismay.

He nods again.

"If I was bitchy to you, I'm sorry. Maybe what you took for bitchiness was terror? You did that, y'know, terrified people."

"I still do. That's why I'm good at what I do."

"I'm sure," I say with a convinced look, then ask Anne,

who is opening a large cardboard box, "What're we having with the corn?"

"Lobster. And cornbread. And grain salad. Is Joy okay with that?"

"Everything but the lobster. Don't let her see you put them in the pot. She'll have nightmares when they scrabble to get out."

"Are you talking about me?" Joy says, swinging into the kitchen. To judge from the red on her cheeks and nose, she got too much sun, but she is freshly showered, has her wet hair in a top knot, and is wearing a tee shirt with a huge fried egg on the front. When she sees my eyes on the egg, she proudly twirls to show me her back, where SUNNY SIDE UP is written in large letters.

"I like it," I say, but she is twitching her nose and, before I can stop her, she is peering into Anne's box.

"Omigod," she breathes. "They're *moving*." The smile leaves her voice, and she looks at Anne. "You're going to boil them alive, aren't you? That's awful. I can't be in this room." She is starting to turn when she sees Bill. Her eyes go straight to his arms, one of which is bringing beer to his mouth, the other propped on the counter on full display. "Omigod," she repeats. Her eyes go to his face. I want to say that, yes, there's an element of terror. But no, she isn't frightened. The f-word she is, is fascinated.

"Those are amazing," she says with awe. "I'm Joy, by the way. When did you get them?"

"A long time ago."

"How long did it take? I mean, all that had to take a crazy load of time. What is this one? Wait, wait—are these your own designs? My Spanish teacher has a biggie," she forms a circle with both hands, "but it's on her shoulder, and she usually covers it up, and hers is nowhere near as gorgeous as yours. So, *did* you design these yourself?" She reaches out, almost touching him but not quite. Her eyes rise to his. "Did it *hurt*?"

Bill looks overwhelmed. Anne is suppressing a grin.

I come forward. "Know what we need, Joy? Flowers." Grateful that the clippers are still in the same old tool drawer, I hand them over. "Cut lots for the lots of vases in the dining room."

"We're eating in the dining room?" Joy asks, eyes as wide at that thought as at the tattoos, and I feel a pang. We eat in Chrissie's dining room, but rarely our own. Joy equates dining room with family, which is different in her mind from just us two.

"Uh," I look quickly at Anne, who gestures, *Sure.*

"O-*kay,*" Joy agrees and heads out, but not before telling Bill, "We aren't done with this conversation."

He waits until the screen door slaps before squinting at me. "Where did she come from?"

I simply raise a hand to say, *Don't ask,* and return to the corn.

Having slept through much of the afternoon, my father is in better shape than I've yet seen him. Maybe it's having dinner in the dining room on a large mahogany table done up with linen napkins and the family silver. Maybe it's having lobster. Maybe it's seeing all those vases filled with flowers— and I do mean filled. Joy went overboard, and while her experience is limited to the tiny garden behind Chrissie's brownstone or bunches of flowers from Whole Foods, she has a knack. One vase holds red phlox, another orange and yellow gerbera daisies. The two largest vases sprout fans of purple-blue Russian sage, the three smallest offer nosegays of violets and buttercups.

My mother's arrangements were more refined. But Dad appreciates Joy's. He moves from one to the next in patent admiration. Nothing on his face suggests worry, as it would if he had left a gun in the one vase I might have skimmed too quickly, or, for that matter, anywhere else in this room. His good mood may be that he feels safe here.

It may also be having people around this table, and, for a split second, I wish Margo were here to feel the nostalgia I do. If she could open her mind to the memories in this room, she might soften. She might agree with me that family is worth saving. She might commit to finding a path forward with Anne.

She might even get an understanding of what Dad's life is like—might even feel a drop of compassion for the man. His world has shrunk, his family is dispersed. I'm not sure whether Anne actually eats dinner with him each night, or whether she just sees that he's fed before she leaves. Whatever, I'm guessing that five for dinner is more than usual.

Of course, that could have the opposite effect, which is why it's probably better that Margo is at her pre-theater dinner in Manhattan. Typically, Alzheimer's patients are stressed by new or challenging things. Seeing Margo might freak him out.

That said, he greets Bill with a handshake and calls him by name, suggesting he's been here before. And I'm glad. Bill is a surprise. He seems to calm Anne. For that alone, I like him. Moreover, the guy here today is a huge improvement over the one I remember when we were growing up. I won't say he's charming, since I can't call a discussion of inmates at a medium security prison in Cranston charming. He supervises the carpentry shop there, and while I ask a question or two, they go nowhere fun. And there's still the matter of the tattoos, at which Joy continues to slide surreptitious glances. He does, though, tell my father about the legal battle an inmate is waging against a conviction that was based on the testimony of a single eyewitness.

"Tricky thing, eyewitness testimony," Dad says. He is studying his lobster, not sure where to begin, then jiggling one of the feelers in uncertainty. But he does remember the law. "If the initial identity is made from a police sketch, a witness is more apt to confirm the accused in person, whether he believes it or not. He may not want to be wrong. He may be swayed by a prosecutor who promises lenience or even immunity on a charge of, say, aiding-and-abetting. Let's face it, eyewitnesses aren't always good people, especially if they're hanging around places where crimes take place."

"What if they are good people?" Joy asks. I try to catch her eye to keep her from breaking Dad's momentum, but she's on a riff. "What if there's just one person who survives an awful crime, like a school shooting, and she has to iden- tify the suspect?"

"Oh sweetie," Anne says as I would have if she hadn't beat me to it.

Seeming unaware how tragic it is that a thirteen-year-old knows to ask this, my father lifts his lobster fork and, dis- passionately, says, "That scenario introduces other ques- tions, like the effect of trauma. Terror can color eyewitness testimony. And if the witness is injured during the event and loses consciousness, his recollection may be spotty."

"Emotion," I say without meaning to, but if Joy thinks of school shootings, I think of that night, right here, twenty years ago. In the aftermath, we were all highly emotional.

My father either doesn't hear or can't compute. "Then you have the matter of time between the crime and the trial. And memory. It isn't stored in the brain intact. It has to be recon- structed. The mind retrieves pieces and puts them together. There's room for error."

What he says makes so much sense that I wonder if he and I are wrong and Anne right. He may not have Alzheimer's at all. Right now, he is perfectly lucid.

But then, setting the fork aside, he frowns and looks around the table. Anne is sucking sweet scraps of meat from the feelers, while Bill has forcefully bent the tail backward and is tugging chunks of meat out with a regular fork. Joy is holding her corn in both hands and eating it row by careful row. I twist off a claw.

Watching me, Dad twists off a claw.

"I never thought of memory that way," I say, working at the meat. When no one speaks, I realize that either I take the bait, or the opportunity is lost. "Is that what you do, Dad—fit pieces together?"

He removes a piece of meat, dunks it in butter, and eats it. Almost absently, he says, "It is."

"Do you do it when you think back on that night out on the boat?" I dare ask. I'm aware that Anne has paused to listen.

"Of course, I do," he says. "I'm the only eyewitness to what happened to Eleanor."

"Elizabeth," I whisper.

"Elizabeth," he whispers back—and how pathetic it is that despite his mistake, I'm pleased that he and I connect.

"It was a long time ago, Dad," Anne says.

He frowns. "There are so many pieces. I forget some and remember others. Like the weather. Like the sky this afternoon."

Joy sits up. "Sunny here but stormy in the Vineyard?"

Again, his eyes seek out mine. "It was foggy when we left. I remember that. I hadn't wanted to go out at all, but she wanted to talk. I didn't think we'd go far. And we didn't. But the wind got strong all of a sudden, and the snow . . . the rain came."

He pauses, seeming stymied. I hold my breath, willing his mind to clear.

"Buckets," he finally says. "I've never seen anything like it. Buckets. We were going up and down, all over the place. I was struggling to hold the boat steady. It was so bad that I tossed her a flak jacket."

Life jacket, he means, but no one corrects him.

"I told her to put it on, but I don't know if she did. I couldn't watch her and manage the boat. I remember—" He uses both arms, one with cast, one not, to wrench an imaginary steering wheel to the right. "I had to head us into a wave that was coming in sideways or we'd capsize, and when I finally got us righted and I looked back, she was gone."

"The Coast Guard confirmed micro-bursts," I say, wanting him to know that this was corroborated.

But my remark ticks him off. His blue eyes cut me. "The Coast Guard wasn't there. The Coast Guard didn't know what it was like. The Coast Guard had no idea how strong those waves were." He is reliving it in angry bursts. In the next instant, he quiets and averts his eyes, seeming bewildered. "Then it was done. Gone. Calm again. But I couldn't find her."

"We know, Daddy," Anne says. "You looked. We all looked."

I work on my salad—quinoa, farro, spinach, and feta— and recoup from what I feel is a dressing down. Which is absurd. But this is what I remember growing up here. After a minute of telling myself that it's all right, that I can take a scolding if that's what it takes to jog his memory, I have the courage to ask, "Why didn't you want to go out in the first place?"

"The weather."

"But she insisted. What did she want to talk about?"

"The estate."

"You mean her house?"

"The family estate."

"Her family estate?" I specify to make sure we understand.

He sighs. "Yes, Margo. For God's sake, ask John Doe. He knows all about it."

Anne and I exchange a glance. Calling me Margo isn't the worst part here. It's John Doe. He was a frequent presence when Dad was on the bench. And this is his second reference.

"John Doe?" I ask.

He gives a single nod, like that ends it, and casted wrist and all, deftly removes the tail meat from the lobster, at this moment knowing what to do without having to think.

"Who is John Doe?" Anne asks.

Eyes on his meal, he continues to eat.

I glance again at Anne, who shoots me a baffled look.

"Is John Doe a real person?" Joy asks with such innocence that I bless her little heart. If anyone can get away with a follow-up in this, she can.

"Oh he's real," Dad says and reaches for his corn.

"How can a parent name a child John Doe? John Doe is in books and movies and on TV. It's what you call an unidentified person lying in a morgue, or an unidentified suspect in a crime. I mean, what does that say about someone who actually has the name? That he's a nobody? If I had that name, I'd do whatever I had to do to be a somebody." She turns to Bill. "Your guys must know all about John Doe."

"Some do," Bill says.

"Are any of them named John Doe?"

"Nope."

"But lots of guys in prison have tattoos, right? Is that where you got yours? Are there people who do them right there, like, tattooists?"

"Tattoo artists," he says, "and there are some. It's all undercover, so they have to improvise tools."

"Like how?"

"They use a stapler. Melted Styrofoam. Soot. It's disgusting. Inmates pay them by trading food or smokes or maybe money if they have a phone and can transfer it. There's no sterilization or anything, so there's a lot of infection. I didn't get my tats in prison. I wouldn't be so dumb."

"Where did you get them?"

"Joy," I caution.

She turns innocent green eyes on me. "What, Mom. This is *interesting*."

"You're not getting a tattoo."

"I'm just asking him about his."

"Don't get one," says Bill.

Her head swings to his, loosened curls flying to follow. "Why not? You've done okay with them."

"In a prison?" he asks. "That where you want to work?" She has no answer.

Grateful for that, at least, I take a closer look at Bill. He is earnest in a way I wouldn't have thought Billy Houseman could be. But no, he's not Billy. He's Bill.

And my father eats. No reaction to mention of tattoos, which he verbally denounced many times, or to prisons, which once would have sparked a lecture about the evils of going near one. Rather, he puts one forkful of salad carefully in his mouth, chews, then goes for another.

Bill tells Joy, "I got these when I was nineteen and doing nothin' good with my life. Then I decided to change that. So I started at CCRI. Community college. Only courses cost, and I had to eat. Teachers hire research assistants. I wanted one of those jobs. But they didn't want me. They looked at my tats and figured I wouldn't be a good worker."

"Seriously?" Joy asks. "I see people with tattoos all the time."

"Sure, you do, and some of 'em would say the same thing as me. Times have changed, but not that much. Get a tattoo before you know what you want to do with your life, and it can hurt your chances. Want to be a teacher? Or a nurse? Or, Christ, a politician, and sleeves like mine'd be the kiss of death."

"I don't want a whole armful," Joy drawls in concession. "Maybe just one?"

"You already have one," Anne says. Her voice is fond, and I'm sure it's sincere. The issues Anne has with me have never spilled over onto my daughter. But I cringe, knowing what's coming.

Joy goes very still. Only her eyes move, shooting me a horrified look.

"Anne," I caution. "Not a tattoo. A birthmark. And not something to discuss here."

But Anne doesn't have a thirteen-year-old daughter. She doesn't know how sensitive they are about their bodies, even girls as bold and unfettered as Joy. And in front of two men, neither of whom she knows well, one the prim grandfather she wants to impress, the other a man she clearly thinks is super cool?

"It's beautiful," Anne argues, speaking to me, which is another sign that she doesn't know my daughter. Joy is old enough to be addressed directly. But Anne is seeing the baby whose diaper she changed and the toddler who played naked on a deserted Maine beach. She has seen the J-shaped mark low on Joy's groin. We never made a big thing of it. But she forgets that Joy is now pubescent. Apparently, too, Anne forgets when she was that age with a body whose inborn quirks seemed different in the light of womanhood.

"It's her initial," she says with enthusiasm. "It's unique. It sets her apart. Isn't that what a tattoo does—except that she inherited hers from Mom, which makes it *really* special." Finally acknowledging Joy, she adds, "I wish I had one like that. I could have used the connection."

Bill has a hand on her arm, though I'm not sure whether he is trying to comfort her or get her to stop.

"Mom?" Joy begs.

"Enough, Anne," I say.

"Doe is in Albany," my father puts in.

His interruption has to be one of the kindest things he's ever done for me. I doubt it was intentional, but the timing couldn't be better. All eyes go to him.

"John Doe?" I say.

"Yes."

"A real person?"

"Of course he's real. Would I mention him if he wasn't? What is wrong with you? Can you not hear me?"

I wither.

But Anne is smiling at him, indulgent. "Do you remember the case, Daddy?"

His silver brows come together. "Of course I remember the case. I told you. It was the estate."

"Elizabeth's?" I whisper, because withering under the press of the past is a luxury I can't afford. My gut says we're getting somewhere here.

He doesn't answer.

"Daddy?" Anne invites.

With a long-suffering sigh, he puts down his fork and looks at her. "It's about robbing Peter to pay Paul." Brows up, he turns to Joy and is off on a wave of lucidity. "Know that one? It goes back to the Reformation. They were building two churches, St. Peter's in Rome and St. Paul's in London. To pay for the building, there was the Peter tax and the Paul tax. People in London would've had to pay two taxes, one for each church. But they couldn't afford that. So they just paid for the one near them. They didn't pay Peter in order to pay Paul. Robbed Peter to pay Paul. Took from Peter to pay Paul."

"That's a great story," Anne says because he's told it so well. I wait for her to ask Dad what it means in the current context. When she doesn't, I do.

"And?" I coax gently.

Eyeing me in annoyance, he turns his good hand one way, then the other. "Peter. Paul." He repeats, hand and voice. "Peter. Paul."

"But how does it relate to what we're talking about?"

He glares. "What're we talking about?"

"Elizabeth's estate."

He stills. "Are you trying to trap me?"

"No, of course not, I'm just confused."

He sputters a laugh. "*You're* confused. That's a good one."

The parable has to apply. My father was never one to quote scripture to us, was never religious at all. He knew history. Maybe that's where the Peter-Paul story came from. But it has to relate to Elizabeth. Same with John Doe.

I want to run this by Jack.

But we're barely done with the lobster when Anne is corralling us to go to Gendy's for ice cream, and once she mentions it, Joy forgets to be miffed about the birthmark. We pile into Bill's pickup, Dad up front with him and we three women shoulder to shoulder in the extended cab.

Joy is beside herself with excitement, whispering to the side, "Omigod, Mom, I've always wanted to ride in a pickup." She touches the roof, the carpeting, the leather seat. "Who knew it was so gorgeous?"

"Guzzles gas," I whisper back.

"Well, I *get* that, but it's still cool."

She also gives this new rendition of the rambling white house that is Gendy Scoops a pass on not being a nut-free facility, and, citing the need for historical reference, orders the traditional banana split after seeing another come through the takeout window. To look at her eating it, you'd think she'd never had ice cream before. But then, it isn't only ice cream. It's banana. And one scoop each of Heath bar crunch, cookies and cream, and mint chocolate chip, her three slightly nontraditional choices. And caramel sauce and crushed peanuts. And whipped cream. And a cherry. She eats the whole thing herself, refusing to give me more than a taste.

Dad is preoccupied eating a single scoop of strawberry ice cream with his plastic spoon, one engrossed bite at a time.

Anne and Bill share a hot fudge sundae.

And me? I'm on a wild ride down memory lane, first studying the menu, which hasn't changed, then admiring the sweet, round white table where we sit under a sea green umbrella in the lingering light of day. I have a chocolate frappe, my usual back then, and snap pictures with my phone until Joy grabs it and slides it under her thigh, which is what I often do with her phone when it outstays its welcome at dinner.

Unfortunately, it is still beneath her leg when it vibrates, which means that she is the one to pull it out and read the text on the screen. Aloud.

Talked with PI. Where are you?

Chapter 14

Talked with PI. Where are you?

Joy looks at me. She has seen who sent the text and is curious. "PI? Like, private investigator? What's Jack talking about?"

What to say? *What to say?* I draw a blank, then scramble for an excuse. Joy isn't the only one awaiting an answer. There's Anne and Bill, and likely even Dad, who is looking at me along with the others.

I want to tell the truth, but don't know what that is. Jack's talk with Nick White could have been initiated by either one of them. It could be about the PI's growing affection for Lily. It could be that Nick has learned something from her, which could be about Lily or Elizabeth or Elizabeth's family or Tom. It could be about something else entirely.

Declaring ignorance is the only thing that may get me off the hook. Of course, it only postpones the inevitable. Everyone here will expect me to ask him and report back to them. I mean, forget texting him back now. I'm sure as hell not doing it with everyone watching. What was he *thinking*, sending a text like that?

Actually, he was thinking that my phone was in my possession.

Retrieving it from Joy, I tell her, "I have no idea what he's talking about," which, of course, isn't enough for Anne, who looks horrified.

"Did Jack hire a private investigator?"

"Yes," I admit. "He wanted to know why Lily Ackerman is here."

"She's working for me," Anne retorts. "That's why she's here."

"Do you know that she's Elizabeth's grand-niece?" I ask, trying to sound curious, rather than confrontational. Daring a glance at my father, I find him staring at me. Listening? Absorbing? Understanding? Any of these things would be good. If he joins in the discussion, he may add to it.

"Of course I know," Anne replies. "I'm not blind, and despite what you think, Mal, I'm not irresponsible."

"I never—"

"She and I Skyped before I hired her—Skyped *twice,* because I saw what she looked like the first time and wanted to know more. I care about the shop—and the town—*and* my family. If I felt she was coming here to cause trouble, I would never have hired her. Can't you trust me in this, at least?"

I reach across the table and grasp her forearm. "I do, Anne. But you need to trust me, too. I didn't ask Jack to hire a private investigator. That's totally his business."

"But you're texting with him. How long's *that* been going on? I thought you and he were done."

"We *are* done. He got my number to call me in New York, so now that he has it, he texts. We all text."

"Not with an enemy of the family," she declares in too loud a voice.

Leaning in, I lower my own. The other tables are filled with people Anne has to know, and though we're outside, where the sound of a passing car mixes with cricket chirps, caws of crows in overhanging trees waiting for crumbs, and the distant surf, Gendy's patio isn't large.

"Jack is not an enemy of the family," I say.

Anne makes a throaty sound. "He's a pain in the butt. Didn't I tell you that? He's still living in the past. He wants someone to pay for his mother committing suicide." The words barely settle on the table when she asks, "He's going after Dad. It's what he's always wanted. Why else would he hire a private investigator? And don't say it's about Lily. Lily is as innocent as Joy."

Dad, no longer looking at me, has finished his ice cream. After pushing the empty cup aside, he uses his napkin to wipe the small space where it was.

"Yes, it's about his mother," I tell Anne in an urgent whisper. "He never got closure. Her family won't talk with him, and suddenly a relative shows up claiming she knows nothing. He wants to be sure."

Anne sits back, pulling her arm free. Accusation is in her eyes and her voice. "You've discussed all this with him."

I sigh. "He talked."

"Is he why you came back?"

"Annie," I chide.

"He is," she accuses.

"No," I insist, but her metal chair is already scraping back on bluestone, and in seconds she is striding toward the truck.

Bill has turned to watch her, a raised hand frozen midair. He clearly doesn't know what to do.

I do. Catching Joy's eye as I get up, I gesture at the empties on the table. "Put these in the trash, babe, and take Papa to the salt pond?" I point to a break in the trees. "It's just down that path. Sunset there will be gorgeous. Let me talk with Anne." She barely nods, when I take off.

"Wait up, Anne," I call. My flip-flops slap the heels of my feet as I trot across the gravel lot toward the truck.

She whirls to face me, arms folded, face tight. In her emotion, I see the intensity of Margo, the anguish of Mom. But

Anne is so laid-back. At least, that's how I always saw her.
Was it true? Or did I simply want it to be?

"You came back for him," she repeats the charge, green
eyes granite-hard.

"I came back for you."

"You came back because he's feeding you lies, and you
believe him."

"That's not *true*. I came back for *you*."

"But he was the one who got you back. Nothing I said all
those years could do it, and I tried, Mallory, I tried until I
finally gave up." Her eyes well, and therein lies my younger
sister, the sweet one, the naïve one, the one who wore vulnerability just under the rose-colored glasses. "Why did
you come back? What is he telling you? Is he turning you
against us?"

"No. *No*. Annie, listen to me," I cry, clutching the hem
of her tank in an attempt to connect us one way, at least.
"You're my sister. You're why I'm here." I want to touch her
but am afraid she'll pull away. That would hurt me more
than the sight of her tears. My own eyes may be dry, but my
heart cries. "I came back because Jack was blunt about Dad.
He said I was dumping it all on your shoulders, and he was
right."

She doesn't blink. "I told you about Dad. I told you his
memory wasn't good. I told you his moods were up and
down."

"But you kept saying you had it under control."

Her eyes widen. "So it's *my* fault you stayed away?"

"No, Anne," I sigh. "No." Taking the risk, needing to at-
tach us somehow, I cup her shoulders and look into her eyes.
"It's my fault. It was easier to stay in New York. Easier
to believe what you were saying. Easier to look the other
way."

"Yeah, looking the other way, straight at Margo. I'm all
alone here, and you two are ultra-close."

My stomach dips. The years peel away, and suddenly we're in a little girl moment, competing to hold Margo's hand, pair with her on a rubber raft, partner with her playing Trivial Pursuit—or, for that matter, competing for the red Life Saver, the yellow horse on the carousel, or Mom's lap. Anne was always more vocal and me more submissive, but she's wrong now.

"I'm no closer to her than I am to you," I inform her.

"You both left. You both sided with Mom—and, okay, I understand she's your mother and she was starting all over again, but he's your father!"

"Is he?" I ask without thinking, my own vulnerability that close to the surface.

Anne recoils. "What does *that* mean?"

"Nothing." Pushing my hands into my hair, I gather it at the crown, then let it fall in a way meant to convey nonchalance. "I mean, he always made me feel different, like I was doing everything wrong, like I didn't belong here. It's just me being upset."

But she doesn't blink. "So, you said that figuratively?"

Yes, of course, I did, I want to cry. But the words don't come.

"Literally?" she whispers, seeming terrified. Not even the shards of late-day sun that spill gold across the parking lot can hide the fact that her face has lost color.

I'm guessing mine has, too. Bouncing this off Jack is one thing, sharing it with my sister is another. With her, it's more real. In the silence, though, I realize it's time. I also wonder if she hasn't ever wondered about this herself.

She's certainly wondering now. Dry now, her eyes are a window to somewhere else entirely. When she refocuses, her voice is tenuous. "Do you remember the hammock on the porch?"

I'm startled by the change of topic. "Our porch? Of course."

"Remember how you and I would lie there together and listen to the gulls and the waves?"

"Of course."

"Remember—" she starts, but something on the side catches her eye. She waves a hand to shoo it away. Bill. That's all he gets, a wave, and I have to say that I'm glad. This is between Anne and me. "Remember the game we played," she continues sotto voce, "like we were hiding there and no one knew?"

"I *do*." We heard things we weren't supposed to hear, like what early Christmas gifts Mom had bought or what Margo's stomach cramps were about or . . . a memory returns, why Roberto Aiello was no longer around.

Distrust. The word pops into my mind. But who said it? When? *Why?*

I'm searching, when Anne says, "Remember when Mom was talking with Shelly Markham?"

"Shelly Markham," I echo, testing the name after so many years. I conjure a reedy woman in jeans and a barn jacket. "She was here a lot. She was Mom's best friend. Is she still around?"

"Gone to Florida, but do you remember when she and Mom were working in the garden? And they were talking about marriage?"

I don't, but Anne clearly does. I'm starting to feel as frightened as she looks. "What were they saying?"

"That it was hard. That you married someone and then learned the bad things, but you were stuck? Maybe those weren't their exact words, but that's the gist of it."

"You remember this? How old were we?"

"Nine or ten, maybe eleven. I haven't thought about it in years, but I remember being upset about something else Shelly said." Her eyes sharpen, like she is readying for my reaction. "She said that at least Mom had you. You were her special gift."

"She *said* that?" I ask. I don't remember it at all.

"I was angry. I mean, we were always competing—"

"You were. Not me."

"Okay, I was competing, and to hear someone say you were Mom's special gift? I ran off and didn't talk to you for a week."

"I do not remember that," I say.

"Maybe it was only for the rest of the day," she concedes, "and I seriously haven't thought about this in years, not until you said what you just did."

About Tom Aldiss not being my father. But I'm hung up on what Anne claims to have overheard. "Special gift?" I repeat. "What did she mean?"

"I don't know. But *I* was supposed to have been her special gift, the one who came last and was another girl, which Dad did not want. He should have treated *me* different, but he didn't."

I glance around the parking lot. There's no sign of my father or Joy. Or Bill. The sky is a deeper blue than it was earlier. And Anne has mentioned different treatment.

"Then, I wasn't imagining it?" I ask in a tentative voice. "The way he treated me?"

Very slowly, she shakes her head. "He wanted Margo to achieve like he had, and he just babied me, like he'd given up on the boy thing and thought I was cute. You, you were in between." She stares at me, puzzled, then looks away.

I wait. A family crosses the parking lot. We watch them enter an SUV, four doors opening and closing in rapid succession. After the engine starts, I step closer. "What, Anne?"

She looks back at me fast. "I knew there was a reason. I knew Mom wasn't all into the marriage. She cheated on him."

"We don't know—"

"Look at the *facts*," she cries. "If you have a different father, she cheated."

"Margo says *he* cheated—and, by the way, I've never, ever said anything to Margo about this."

"If he cheated, it's because she did."

"Anne—" I start, then stop, remembering what he said to me yesterday. *We had an agreement. Neither of us would tell.*

There's so much we don't know. I wish Mom was alive to give answers. I wish Dad was of sound mind and approachable. I wish I *remembered* more.

I'm guessing my sister's thoughts are similar, because her anger fizzles. She is whispering again, and I understand that, too. It's not that anyone is close by, just that whispering is less threatening. "How long have you wondered about this?"

"Oh, God," I roll my eyes, "since I was a teenager and had no idea why he was always so down on me. I mean, there were good times. But the bad times are the ones I remember."

"I didn't know."

"And I didn't say back then, because it sounded so absurd. But I'm not a bad person, Anne. I've learned that. People like me. Joy loves me. There is no one else in this world who treats me like he did."

She looks like she wants to argue. Loyalty to Dad has been her credo. I hear a touch of challenge when she asks, "If he isn't your biological, who is?"

I shrug, not ready to share the possibilities, much less their source.

"You look like us."

"I look like Mom. We all do. Her genes must be the dominant ones."

"Is that why you stayed away all those years, y'know, because we aren't sisters?"

I pull her close. Once her initial stiffness fades, I say a soft, "We *are* sisters. We have the same blood. Look at Joy. She's probably more like you than she is like me. Nothing will ever change that."

She nods against my shoulder.

"And no," I go on, "it's not why I stayed away." Drawing back, I look her in the eye. "Well, maybe Dad is. He never said he wanted me here—and don't defend him, you know it's true. But it was me, Anne. Really. When I left, I didn't know who I was. I had to find out."

"You made a life in New York."

"With Joy, but no family."

"You have Chrissie."

"She's not like you and me. I want what we had before, Annie. I want us to be close."

She sinks against the truck, seeming younger and more vulnerable. I join her there, my arm flush to hers as we look back at Gendy's, where the last splinters of sun have faded and lights now outline the sprawling house.

"What about Jack?" she asks.

"Definitely not family, and definitely not why I came back. I mean it."

"You loved him. I assumed he was it for you."

"Me, too," I admit, allowing myself to remember that night and the horror that followed. "But we said awful things to each other. We *believed* awful things of each other. People who are meant to be together don't fall apart like that. And he didn't chase me to New York, did he." It wasn't a question. "Didn't contact me once all these years."

"What was it like seeing him again?"

How to sum that up in a word or two or even three? I settle on, "Confusing."

"Confusing, how?"

"Past to present. He's the same, but different."

"Do you like him?"

"I don't know him."

"Is he a danger to us?"

"Nah," I say without having to wonder. "At least, not directly. He isn't malicious, Anne. He wants answers about his mother. If those answers incriminate Dad, then yes, he's a danger."

Anne smiled sadly. "You still call him Dad."

"I don't know for sure that he isn't. He's the only father I've ever had."

Anne initiates the hug this time. "I'm sorry, Mallory. You're so calm about this, but I'm reeling."

"I'm not calm," I say, clinging to her. "I'm terrified. It's just that I've had time to get used to the idea."

"DNA test?"

"Dad would never go for that."

"We could take a hair from his brush."

"Not as reliable."

She draws back, eyes compassionate in a way that makes me feel there's hope for us yet. "You've read up on this."

"Oh, yes," I say, but with a lightness that wasn't there before. I feel *so* much better having told her this. Jack knows. Chrissie knows. But my sister is different from them. The fact that she's moved past the *mom-cheated* place gives me courage. "He knows, Annie. The answers are somewhere in that mind of his. We need to ask."

"*I'm* not doing that," she drawls. "He thinks I'm flakey. You'd be better at it. What about asking Margo if she knows? She was the closest to Mom all those years. Maybe Mom said something to her."

"If Margo knew, wouldn't she have said something to me, especially after Mom died?"

"Not if she thought it would wreck you."

She's right, insightful in this. How many times have I told myself that it isn't worth the heartache of going public with my fears? "I could ask her. I will. But I need to talk with Jack first."

With a half turn, Anne clutches my arm. Her eyes are large and intense. "Don't flip, Mal. Please don't."

"Flip?"

"To Jack. Or Margo. I want you on my side."

"This isn't about taking sides."

"It is. With families as broken as ours, it always is."

The salt pond behind Gendy's is connected to the sea only at times of heavy runoff from streams or tidal storm surge. Half a mile long and far shorter across, it is bordered on the land side by trees and modest homes, on the ocean side by a salt marsh. Power boating is regulated to protect the habitat, but a pair of kayaks glide by as we emerge from the path.

The beach is shallow and starting to darken under a purpling sky. Bill is sprawled in a weathered Adirondack chair a bit down the beach, but Joy and Dad are farther still, walking hand in hand—which, coming after mention of broken families, is a pleasure to see.

"Whoa," says Anne. "Who initiated that?"

I squeeze her arm. Sisters do think alike. "I was wondering the same thing."

"Dad."

"Joy."

"He really likes her."

"She really likes him."

Anne snorts and says a dry, "*She* didn't grow up with him."

"Nope. But she's desperate for family."

"So am I," Anne says and sets off to join them.

So am I, I think but don't follow her. Rather, sinking down near the water line, I ruffle my hand over strands of eelgrass to expose the tiny stones and shells beneath. My thumb and forefinger single out an oyster drill. Cupping it in my palm, I brush off bits of dark sand, and trace it from its pointed spire, over its small ribbed shell, to its flared outer lip. When the snail is alive, its tongue reaches out past that lip to drill into oysters and suck out the meat. I cringe thinking about it—would never tell Joy that these sweet little snails are vicious predators, though, even here in the eelgrass, I see shells with tell-tale round holes. That said, this one's swirls of amber and white are definitely something to photograph.

I'm wishing I had my camera with me now, when my phone vibrates. Pulling it from my pocket, I look at the screen. The good news is, no one else sees it this time. The bad news is, well, bad news.

Chapter 15

Cops know. Where are you?

I stare at the words for a frightened minute, then type, *Know what?*

Lily, you, Tom's mind. Can we talk?

We're at Gendy's. Twenty minutes?

On the beach.

Though Anne doesn't see my screen, she knows the texts are from Jack. Trusting from his earlier one that my meeting him is necessity rather than choice, she challenges Joy to a game of Scrabble. I remain in the living room long enough to see my delighted daughter open the ancient board with reverence, and to warn Anne that Joy is good at the game, before heading to the beach.

Jack is sitting at the far end of the dock, his back to me, legs hanging over the edge. Leaving my flip-flops at the stairs, I cross the sand and am about to step onto the wood planks when time pauses. Jack, the dock, the breeze in his hair, the low near-night light, the sea—nostalgia hits me hard. When he and I were a thing, I never felt alone. If life was about taking sides, he was always on mine. I may be stronger now, may be my own woman, but I feel a wanting that I haven't felt in years. Yes, it's physical. Of *course*, it's physical. When they talk about chemical attraction, Jack Sabathian is it for me. Beyond that, though, the wanting I feel now is emotional.

But not to be explored here. This meeting is about business.

To drive that point home, I leave a fair space between us when I sit. "What happened?"

He flicks me a glance. Enough of twilight remains to shadow the grooves between his eyes. "Nick White quit. He called to say he couldn't work for me—conflict of interest, and all. He also said he's being watched by our men in blue."

"Watched?"

"Questioned. They think it's suspicious that all of a sudden Lily is here, he's here, you're here. They know Tom's mind is failing. They think something's going on, and they want to be in on it."

"Like, reopening the investigation?" I ask in alarm.

"If warranted," Jack says.

"Whatever would warrant it? Whatever is new?"

"You tell me."

"Absolutely nothing. I haven't found any sign of a gun—and, okay, I'm sure he has one if you saw it," I add, because Jack wouldn't imagine something like that, "but if he used a gun on your mother, would he have kept it all this time? Really? He was bullheaded, not stupid. He knew the penalty for murder, so even if he shot your mother, he would have ditched the gun. If he has one now, it's new. Maybe he bought it to protect himself. Maybe he imagines that a defendant he once sentenced to jail is out now and hell-bent on revenge. He rambles. He talks about old cases. He carries on about John Doe, like he's reliving his time on the bench." I search Jack's face. He isn't disagreeing with anything I've said. "Has Nick learned something?"

"That he's willing to share?" he asks dryly. "Only that it's about family money."

"It?"

"The reason my mother and her brother were estranged."
His hands grip the edge of the dock as he stares out into the
darkness. "Lily isn't as innocent as she looks. Seems her
specialty in school wasn't just journalism, it was investigative journalism. She tracked her grandfather's problems to the
collapse of the family estate. It was supposed to have money
in it but did not."

The estate. I feel a niggling. "Nick told you this?"

"Yeah. He said it was on my dime, so he owed it to me."
He exhales a vexed breath. "Not that it tells me much."

"It may." I zero in on the niggling. "My father mentioned
her family estate. That's when he went off about John Doe.
John Doe? Albany?"

His head turns fast. After staring at me for a minute, he
swears softly, yanks his legs from the water, and, grabbing
my hand, pulls me up. I have to scramble as he walks full
stride down the dock and across the beach, but I'm willing
to do that if something I've said helps.

The closer we get to his house, though, the greater my
qualms. This isn't where I want to be—not with my memories, not with Jack in the flesh. But I can't quite pull my hand
free. I know what he wants and right now, it isn't me. It's his
computer. And I want to see what he finds.

The Sabathian stairs are at the far end of the bluff. Not
straight like ours, they tack midway around a scrub pine.
Same pine as twenty years ago? Looks it. Same stone path
leading to the same back stairs, same open deck, same kitchen
door. But that's where same ends. The kitchen, once as traditional as ours, is now white and steel. Also redone, the hall
is pale gray and mirrored, and the living room's cushiony up-
holstered furniture has been replaced with pieces that are
modern and sleek. Shelves piled with books offer the only
warmth, but they're tiny islands in a sea of gloss.

The wife, I think, looking around in dismay.

Jack says a chagrined, "Yeah," and scrubs the back of his head. "Not exactly me, is it."

I'm spared answering by what sounds like a herd overhead but turns out to be Guy, who gallops down the stairs and leaps at Jack, who scrubs at his flanks before setting him down. I'm thinking the dog should be taught not to greet a person that way, when Jack moves on to the chrome plank of a desk. As furniture goes, it's no warmer than the rest, but at least the strew of books, papers, electronics, and chargers make it look used.

Parking himself on a black swivel chair, he types on a laptop, checks the large desktop, then returns to the keyboard. By now, I'm at his elbow watching the big screen. Guy is on his other side, mercifully unimpressed by my presence.

"Not John Doe," he sees. "Ronald Doe, Esquire, with law offices in Albany, New York, better known as Ron Doe, which is the name I do know." He turns to me. "He specialized in wills and estates. My mother worked with him after her father died. Since she was the business brain in the family, she was the executor of the family estate." He types more, waits, reads. Then he sags back in the chair and rests his outside hand on Guy's head.

Having seen what he has, I sag against the edge of the desk. "Dead. But there have to be records somewhere. Did he have law partners?"

Jack's mind is there as I ask it, his body forward, fingers typing again. I watch the screen as he waits, but the answer disappoints. Ronald Doe was a single practitioner. His office closed fifteen years ago, soon after he died.

"Were there any papers from him among your mother's things?" I ask.

"Y'd think. If she was the executor. When my uncle's family wouldn't talk with me, I searched our house long and hard. There should have been something, *anything* about the estate."

"Unless she destroyed them." I regret the words as soon as they're out. They vilify his mom. He may be furious.

More resigned than angry, though, he echoes, "Unless she destroyed them."

Not wanting to dwell there, I rush on. "You recognized the name Ron Doe. What do you remember?"

Facing the screen, he chews on the corner of his mouth. When he returns to me, his gray eyes are foggy. "Just a vague . . . distaste. She went to Albany. She had meetings with the lawyer. She came home upset."

"Did he do the work for her own company?"

"No. She used your father's law partner for that."

"But she told my father about Ron Doe—at least we assume that's who he meant by John Doe. Or maybe not? Dad also went off on a riff about Peter and Paul—you know, the old saying about robbing Peter to pay Paul, but I have no idea where that fits in to any of this."

Jack has gone still. When he finally speaks, his voice is low. "Peter is her brother. Paul is your father's partner."

"Paul Schuster?" I know that name well. Paul was often at our house when I was growing up. I recall a pleasant man, the yin to Dad's yang, or yang to Dad's yin. Whichever, he was the more amenable of the two. There were several other lawyers on the letterhead, but Aldiss and Schuster were the name partners. Paul was married briefly, had no children, and was therefore often at our house for holidays. He made a mean apple pie—actually made it himself.

Lost in thought, Jack runs a finger back and forth on the stubble over his lip.

"Is he still around?" I ask.

He nods.

"I'll call him."

"Robbing Peter to pay Paul," he says. "It has to mean something."

"I don't know if he'll talk, client confidentiality and all, but it's worth a try." I pause, cautious. "What, exactly, do we want him to say?"

"Why my mother went missing. Whether she was upset enough to commit suicide. What your father meant by robbing Peter to pay Paul." He is frowning, the grooves between his eyes pronounced.

"What," I whisper.

His eyes meet mine, then dart away. "There's an obvious meaning. If you take it literally."

Yes. The question is whether he trusts me enough to risk airing it aloud.

"Between you and me?" I offer, because I am desperate for that trust.

When he finally speaks, his voice is raspy, as if a broken tone is less condemning than a full one. "What if my mother bolstered her business with money from the family estate that might have helped her brother? Wouldn't that be robbing Peter to pay Paul?"

"There's nothing illegal in it."

"Maybe. Maybe not." Tilting back in the chair, angled just a tad toward me, he pushes both hands through his hair, leaves them on the back of his head, and raises reluctant eyes. "If she committed suicide—" He stops and clears his throat. "If she deliberately jumped from that boat in the middle of a micro-burst, it would have been because she was in mental pain. People don't do things like that unless they are. But she didn't have a history of mental illness. She wasn't in therapy. She wasn't taking antidepressants. But if she did take money that could have saved her brother, she'd feel guilty. If her brother lost everything because he didn't have that money, she'd be devastated. If her business failed in spite of what she took, she'd be destroyed."

"That's a lot of ifs," I say, though what he outlines sounds frighteningly plausible. "But could she just take the money?

Most estates spell out who gets what and how it has to be distributed. Can an executor just help himself?"

"No. A co-executor, likely Ron Doe, would have a say. In theory."

I get the "in theory" part. That would occur if Elizabeth committed fraud, but neither of us is going there yet. "Where does my father fit in? Did he know about her family money?"

"He had to. They were too close for him not to."

"You still think they were lovers."

He startles me by reaching for my hand. He had held it from the dock to the house, but he isn't leading me now. He wants the comfort that a link between us brings. I can't fight that.

"Nah," he confesses, watching the weave of our fingers. His skin is warm, fingers dwarfing mine in the old protective way. "You're right. Likely before they were married. Not after."

It's definitely a concession. Way back when, he wouldn't admit to even the slightest chance that my father was anything but the devil incarnate.

We let it sit. After a minute, I squeeze his hand and pull mine free. Passing Guy, who is asleep under the desk, I approach the sleek sofa on the far side of the room, fold my arms, and study the wall. A modern oil hangs there, but I can't figure out what it is. "A seascape?"

"They say."

"Remember what used to be here?"

He is beside me now, staring at the wall as I am. "Yup. A real seascape. Painted by Dante Bowen."

"Local artist."

"Lots of color and emotion."

I look up at him. "What did you do with it?"

"It's in the attic. I couldn't give it away. Couldn't give any of them away. They're part of my childhood." I expect sarcasm, but hear only sadness. He's thinking it's the best part, and how pathetic it is that a piece of art should be that.

Feeling the aloneness that always haunted him, I slip an arm through his. "Joy loved seeing the family pictures climbing our stairs. Remember? Your mom took them."

He smiles crookedly. "Oh yeah."

"They tell a story, the psychology of photography and all." I was always on that farthest end from my father. Always. "So what was my father's role in what happened that night?" I ask, knowing that Jack will follow my thoughts. "If Elizabeth was guilty of something, did he know? If she deliberately jumped off the boat, did he know she planned to do it?"

"An accessory?" Jack asks with a sad-eyed look.

I move my head enough to confirm. "You could say."

"I can't. He can. Will he?"

"Talk? I don't know."

"Guess."

I want to punt. In spite of everything, I do feel a loyalty to Tom Aldiss. Sure, Jack has granted him a reprieve from being the bad guy. But if he is trusting me with his worst fears about his mother, I have to do the same. "He mentioned guilt. He said that was why she left. He said they had a pact not to tell."

"Pact."

"But was it with your mother or mine? He goes in and out, Jack—is lucid one minute and not the next. The upside of his being lucid is he'll remember what happened on the boat. The downside is he'll remember a pact and won't talk. If he's half-confused, he might."

"How can you make him half-confused?" Jack asks with only the smallest quirk of his lips.

"By badgering him. When he gets flustered, he gets confused. I hate to do it." I put my heart in my eyes. "He's an old man, Jack. He knows what's happening to him, and he isn't happy." When Jack opens his mouth, I say, "I know, I know. What he's keeping secret is making everyone else *un*-happy. But it's hard for me."

"Could the police do it?" he asks, and while I hear compassion, the worst of memory drowns it out. It isn't just the police. Where the police go, the media follow, and while there were no lies in the articles they printed, they were painful to read. Those pieces were speculative, asking questions we were asking ourselves. Unfortunately, what the media speculated about went public.

I don't want that again.

Slipping my arm free, I turn and look around the room. The books help, with their colorful mix of hard and soft covers. Spines of the latter are cracked multiple times—and there's another one in the shadow of the angular sofa arm, open and face down, an active one, for sure. Neither of Jack's parents were readers, and I can't imagine the wife doing this much reading in the short time she was here, which means the books are his, which is interesting. He never used to read. Teenage rebellion prohibited reading as an art form. If he does it now, I'm guessing loneliness drives him to it. Either that, or maturity, neither of which have to do with the décor here, I decide and refocus on that.

Even aside from the Dante Bowen original, I miss the way this house used to be—miss the big furniture, the colorful pillows, the sense of time and place and purpose. Sure, my condo in New York has the same modern feel as this. But that's New York, where the chaos of life outside demands simplicity inside. Here on the bluff, it isn't a matter of chaos and simplicity, but survival. The ocean is beyond our control. The counterpoint is softness, comfort, and warmth.

Feeling a chill, I wander into the hall. The dining room, straight ahead, is more of the cool modern that Jack's wife apparently liked.

Coming up from behind, Jack is quiet. "She never understood this place. She wanted to make it into somewhere else."

"Didn't she know what she was marrying into?"

"She thought she could change it."

How can you stand it? I want to ask, but stark negativity isn't my style. Instead, I look back at him in sympathy.

"You think I'm not changeable," he says.

"It's not that. You can change. But this is *so* . . ." I look around in despair.

". . . not me. Is it you?"

He's asking about my life in New York, and New York is home to me now. But home can be where you spend your time, which is different from where you come from and who you are. Here in Bay Bluff, no. This isn't me.

I place my hand on the newel post, which is square to our round. Similarly, the banister has a blocky feel, but then, everything about this house is more angular than ours, from those square turrets on down. Still, the memories I have of being in this house aren't edgy. Despite everything that happened at the end, my memories here are soft and warm, even hot. There were times, when Jack's parents were away, that he and I spent hours in his room. Making love in a bed was a luxury. Having a mattress beneath us was a far cry from doing it on the beach at night or, worse, in a hidden cave. We couldn't go to a motel. We didn't dare. We tried to cushion ourselves with towels, but dry sand was everywhere, wet sand was clammy, and caves? Caves are stone, and stone is unforgiving.

Not Jack's bed, though. His bed was wonderful.

"I've missed you," he whispers, so close that I feel the heat of his body. Without conscious intent, I lean back into it. Jack always had a wild smell to him—part attitude, part life at the edge of the sea, part innate essence. It circles me now, right along with his arms at my waist. When he kisses my neck,

I think to move away but can't. The breath that follows the kiss is against my cheek, the voice deep and hoarse. "My old room is the same. I wouldn't let her touch it. Come up with me."

"I can't," I whisper.

"Not even a quickie?"

"Please no, Jack."

"We could forget about all this, just go with it, just get lost in each other like we used to."

Slowly, I shake my head.

"When we make love," he persists, "I forget everything else. Don't you ever want that again?"

"Yes, but we're adults now. Sex for the sake of sex doesn't work for me anymore. It has to mean more. It has to lead somewhere."

"It could," he says.

I tell myself to move away. All I do, though, is shake my head again.

"Why not?"

"Because I can't have that and then leave, and my life isn't here."

"You'd leave me again?"

It's such a needy male comment that I want to laugh. Except, nothing here is funny, and answering this remark would take hours. It would ruin the moment, and I'm not ready for that. His hands are stroking my waist now, thumbs teasing. And I'm aching as I haven't with any other man.

Reaching behind, I circle his neck, then, when I feel his hands full-on me, I whisper his name. And do I ever know where this will lead if I don't stop soon? Turning in his arms, I grab that gorgeous, mussed, chestnut-colored hair and pull him in for a kiss. Just one. A full kiss, like he used to give.

And full it is. It positively consumes my mouth, covering, opening, tasting. I need hard and fast, even punishing, but this kiss takes its time. Surrounded by scruff, it is still butter-smooth and, in its thoroughness, ten times better than I remember.

Only when it ends, when I draw back with my fingers still in his hair and look into eyes that are electric gray, cheeks that are flushed above the stubble, lips that are moist, do I realize how close our bodies are. My breasts are crushed to his chest, while his hands on the small of my back press my lower body to his. Jack Sabathian is well-endowed, and I feel every inch. *This* is punishment for my leaving. He is showing me everything I lost.

"Don't say it," I beg, breathing too fast.

But he can't help himself. It's the honesty that I love about him, the honesty that I hate. "Stay, sweetheart. Stay in Bay Bluff."

Shaking my head, I say, "Too late." My voice is too loud, but I need it to drown out the stubborn hum in my body. Knowing I'm losing my grip on what little of me remains when I'm in this place, I break away. Running through the kitchen—yes, running, which is what you do when you're scared—I go out the back door to the small deck at the top of the stairs. There I stop. I breathe in. Deeply. Of the night ocean, of sand, of marine life that I can't begin to see.

Far out, a boat moves through the waves, single lights front and back. Though the sound of its motor is swallowed by the shush-and-break of the surf, not so the hooks that jangle on the dock closer in or the breeze that stirs the tall grasses on this side of the bluff.

I hear all of this, then the quiet opening and closing of the door, and feel Jack beside me, even before he speaks.

"I was wrong, the things I said back then, Mal. I was taking it out on you that your father was there and knew what happened."

Had *he* recovered from that little kiss? If so, he was stronger than me. The sweet salt air has stabilized me, but arousal is still just a thought away. Consciously pushing it farther, I ask, "But does he? He's been consistent from the start. He was fighting to control the boat in a squall, and when he looked back, she was gone. You want to blame him—"

"—but I can't. I accept that. Something was going on with my mother. I just wish your father could explain it."

"I'll keep asking."

"But you're only here a week. What if that isn't enough? What if he doesn't say anything? Will you still run away to New York?"

I shoot him a warning look. "Careful, Jack. If I run to New York, it's to my home. My life is there. My daughter's life is there. I cleared things to come here for a week, but next Saturday is booked. I have people lined up. If I'm not back, the realtors I work with will go elsewhere."

"No loyalty?" he asks, part inquiry, part scorn.

But I understand my clients. Many have become friends. "It's about the bottom line. I work with high-end realtors who have high-end clients. They want results and they want them now. Besides, I love what I do."

"It shows. Your pictures are top-notch. I love what you do."

Closing my eyes, I drop my chin to my chest. "You're not helping."

"Only because you don't want to hear what I'm saying," he insists. "You've stayed in New York all these years because no one was arguing against it. You choose to raise Joy there because being alone means you're the one in control. You grew up trying to please everyone else, but when you're there, there's no one to please but you and Joy. The decisions are yours."

Of all the things I've considered, even discussed with Chrissie, the idea that I chose New York for that reason isn't one. I never thought of myself as controlling. Never thought of myself as wanting to be.

"Didn't consider that?" he asks. "Not in twenty years?"

I don't take offense. He's overlooking one major factor. "I

wasn't exactly sitting around doing nothing. I made a home for myself. I built a career. I made friends. I raised a child."

"An amazing child."

"She is," I agree, and because he's said that, I admit, "You may be right about why I stay in New York." Turning, I lean back against the railing. "But that doesn't change things. Why I did what I did is beside the point. It's done. My life is there, yours is here. My father is here, your mother is gone. Two people went out on the boat that night, only one returned. I can badger Dad, but we may never learn anything more. What then?"

He stands right-angled to me. "Then we move on."

"Can we? Here?" I gesture at the darkness behind. "I look at the dock and remember that night. I look at the firepit and remember two families around it. When I think of summer, it's all of us on the beach. When I think of the Fourth of July, it's both families in town. The memories won't go away. And then there's the way we fought. We said horrible things—"

"—that were angry and vengeful and wrong. So we botched it once—"

"—not once. Multiple times. We had three weeks of fights before I left."

"One. We had one. It just went on for three weeks."

I have to smile. Standing on principle is classic Jack Sabathian. "Fine, one that went on for three weeks, but I couldn't get through to you and you couldn't get through to me. It was our first big fight, and we failed."

"It was about catastrophic events."

"Life *is*. And we failed."

"Okay, but haven't we grown?"

"Have we?" I ask. On one hand, we've both grown tremendously. I'm a professional photographer with a high-functioning daughter, and Jack is a doctor of veterinary medicine with a successful practice. On the other hand, we're hung up on the same unanswered questions.

"I have," he insists.

And I think of Robert Frost. *Freedom lies in being bold,* he wrote. Maybe the only path to freedom from the past is being bold. "Prove it. What are you going to do about the police?"

"Talk with them."

"And say what?" I ask.

"That Lily Ackerman is new to the whole situation, that she doesn't know anything more than any of us and is asking the same questions we all asked twenty years ago. That you're in town to introduce your daughter to Bay Bluff. That your father was a fine judge, but his memory isn't what it was. That talking with him is pointless and smearing him now would be a disgrace. I'll say that I'm the one who's most affected by my mother's disappearance, and that I've accepted the fact that she fell off that boat and drowned. I'll remind them that I looked for years, that I worked with two different investigators, but that there's nothing more. I'll tell them that they'd be wasting their time and taxpayers' money to reopen the case."

He's covered it all. But then, I never doubted Jack's quickness. "Will they listen?"

"Of course they will." He slants me a smile. "I take care of their pets. We're talking"—he squints, tallies—"five dogs, three cats, two horses, six guinea pigs, and a tortoise, all that in a small department." His grin is smug. "They adore me."

"And you'd use that relationship to get what you want?" I ask, trying not to succumb to that grin, though it makes my insides curl. Jack is a contradiction of arrogance and vulnerability that I always found appealing. This hasn't changed.

"Of course I will," he insists. "It's the way the world works."

"So," I test, "you don't want me to call Paul Schuster tomorrow?"

"Oh, I do," he says, like there's no contradiction here.

"I do my part, you do yours. It's about covering all the bases. It's about us being in control. The more we learn, the more we have. I'm tired of questions, Mallory."

"Maybe the police asking would get it out."

"And hurt you all over again? I made that mistake twenty years ago. Not making it now."

Of all the things he has said about us, this touches me most deeply. I'm fighting the reasons why as I walk back across the sand, so I'm too distracted to notice Anne, who sits at the top of the stairs, blending into the night with her purple tee and shorts and her tousled dark hair with its burgundy streak. Since she doesn't call out, I don't see her until I'm straightening with my flip-flops in hand.

Factoring in time for an expression of surprise, I have about twenty seconds to decide what to say.

Chapter 16

What to say?

If I tell Anne that Lily is digging into the past, she may fire the girl, which I don't want. Lily needs the job. And we need whatever information she unearths. So no to that.

If I tell her about Ronald Doe, I'll have to get into the whole thing about Elizabeth's estate, in which case Anne may jump to the worst conclusion and go to the police herself. So no to that, too.

I can tell her some of what Jack and I discussed, and what I say will be true. But it won't be the whole truth. Then again, does that matter? We were raised on the truth, the whole truth, and nothing but. Looking at our lives now, though, with everyone either hiding something, looking the other way, or simply forgetting, that mantra is a joke.

Anne begged me not to side with Jack, and I'm not doing that. He and I will check things out, then share with the others. The danger, of course, is that Anne learns what I've hidden first, in which case the fragile détente she and I found earlier this evening may break.

What to do?

"So?" she asks when I'm far enough up the stairs that she doesn't have to shout over the sound of the surf. "What did Jack say?"

"The PI is quitting." I climb the last few steps and sit beside her on the dry planks. "He says he likes Lily too much."

"But he's sticking around?"

"I guess."

"Will he be trouble?"

"As in, going after Dad? I doubt it. What can he find?" I change the subject before she can answer. "Where's Joy?"

"At the piano with Dad. He asked her to play. He remembered she could. It's really good for him that she's here, Mal. And it's good for me, too. Can she come to the shop with me tomorrow morning?"

"Sure. She had an awesome time there."

"It's awesome having her there." She sounds wistful. "My niece."

I wiggle closer to her. "You'd be a good mom, Annie."

"You think so?" she asks.

"Of course." But I sense her uncertainty. "Don't you?"

As dark as the night is, I know that her eyes are a clear, honest green. Her voice is clear as well. "I'm not the most realistic person. Would I know what's going on with my child, or just see what I want to see?"

I'm relieved that she knows this. She's never expressed it before, certainly not to me. It's definitely an admission.

Taking her hand, I face her. "You, sister, have bought into the image you created. Sunny Side Up? That's optimism, and there's nothing wrong with it. But just the fact that you asked this question is an answer. You'd know what was going on with your child, because you'd know to look deeper. You'd know to be realistic when realistic counts. Besides," I add, grinning, "you'd have me to point things out."

"Promise?" she begs. "I'm going to need you."

My thoughts falter. There's an urgency in her voice, an immediacy that suggests something beyond the hypothetical. She neither denies it nor looks away.

Cautiously, I ask, "Need? Present tense? As in . . . now?"

"In seven months."

My heart thuds. I put a hand there. "Omigod. Annie. Seriously?"

She nods.

"Pregnant?"

Eyes wider, she nods again.

I slip an arm around her waist. "That's terrific!"

"Is it?" she worries. "I haven't told Bill yet. I keep thinking I'm not really pregnant or I'll lose it, and then I won't have to put him to the test. I'm not sure he wants to be tied down."

I remember the way he reached for her at Gendy's when she abruptly left the table. The spontaneity of the gesture said something. "He adores you."

"But he didn't ask for this. Birth control was my responsibility. If I force something on him, it could drive him away."

She is right about that. Lord knew, in the course of my own decision-making, I'd met potential dads who didn't want to be dads. Before meeting Bill, I'd have guessed he was one of them. Even expecting the worst, though, I've been impressed. Granted, I haven't seen much. And his past isn't stellar. And what he may like about Anne is the legitimacy of the Aldiss name. And his ink is way too much. But he did say the right thing about that to Joy. And he treats my sister with respect.

"You won't drive him away," I tell her, "and if you do, that says something about him."

"But then I'll be alone, just me and Dad. He thinks pregnant and unmarried is the height of immorality. Remember the awful things he said to you when you told him you were having Joy?"

Do I ever. "But it helped me prioritize what I wanted. Do you want this baby?"

"I stopped using birth control."

Deliberate, then. Like me. I feel a connection to her in that. "So, it's done."

She continues to eye me plaintively. Still, I'm taken off-guard when she whispers, "What would Mom say?" Having distanced herself from our mother all those years ago, the fact that she cares touches me.

Smiling, I say, "Mom was a different person once she left here. She decided what she wanted and went for it. Isn't that what you've done?"

"Is it?"

"Absolutely. You have a successful business. No one told you to do that. And now a child?"

"But it's scary. Were you scared?"

"Terrified. But you can do it, Anne, I know you can. And you *won't* be alone."

Her eyes fill with a different doubt. "Would you really help? I mean, especially if we're only half-sisters? I'm sorry, but I'm really struggling with that. What if you have a whole other family? What if there's some man out there who knows you're his daughter and who's been watching you all these years?"

"Without saying a word?"

"Maybe, for some reason, he can't."

"Maybe he's dead," I suggest as I often have when my mind jumps on this train.

"But if it's Roberto, there's Danny and Tina—"

"—neither of whom have ever approached me about being related."

"What if they don't know? What if it's someone else entirely, someone rich and wonderful and just waiting for the right time?" Her voice suggests a fairy tale shade, but I'm more realistic than that.

"What if it's a one-night stand whose name Mom wouldn't even remember, especially if she was tipsy," I counter, "and since Mom didn't usually drink, one martini could have done it, and we both know she and Dad were unhappy. I've considered the angles, Annie. I've wondered for years. Part of me always wanted it, because it would explain why Dad treated me differently. It would be the reason I was always wrong in his eyes—the reason why I was always standing at the very edge of the family photos, hiding from him in the shadow of Mom."

She looks surprised, like she hadn't remembered it that way. "Were you? Always?"

"Just look at those photos."

"That's so *sad*."

"But I have a good life. I've made it a good one."

"Still."

"*No*. There's a theoretical life. And there's a real one. You're my real one."

Anne looks like she might cry. "But you're happy in New York. How can you help me if you're there?"

"I can be back and forth," I say, because I would want to help her raise a baby. Half-sister or not, yes, I would—though as soon as the words are out, I feel a qualm. I avoided Bay Bluff for twenty years. Do I seriously want to commit to regular trips back? One thing I do know. "Joy will be beside herself."

Anne gasps. "Omigod. Don't tell her yet. And don't tell Margo. And *whatever* you do, do not tell Dad." As soon as I raise a hand in pledge, she asks, "About Dad? Will you watch him tomorrow morning? Lina isn't in on Sundays, so I always worry when I have to leave, but Sundays are big at the shop. If I leave early with Joy, will you walk him down for breakfast?"

That's the plan. I'm not sure whether Joy is woken by excitement or the alarm on her phone, but she is already dressed when I crack open an eye. After she kisses me goodbye and leaves the room, I try to go back to sleep. But my mind has jump-started and is racing on a track crammed with thoughts. Jack, my parentage, new info on Elizabeth, Anne pregnant—had I expected any of this when I left New York? No. But here it is.

Craving a little immersion in what has always steadied me, I pull on my Bay Bluff sweatshirt, grab my Nikon, and, with no sign Dad is up yet, I go to the beach. I do leave a note on the kitchen table, though whether he'll notice it or even be able to read it is up for grabs. I would be safer waiting for him inside. But my memories are vivid. The beach at dawn is too special to miss.

Sunrise is different from sunset, a crescendo in the day's symphony, rather than its denouement, and our eastern exposure is prime. I'm not discouraged by narrow strips of clouds between me and the sun. Their purples and pinks are dramatic.

While the ocean gently gathers, rolls, and retreats, I photograph the scene in thirds—beach, water, and sky—then in simple halves of sky and waves. Avoiding the two boats, which introduce elements I don't want, I stretch out on my stomach on the dewy dock and, putting the camera on the wood, photograph its narrowing arm reaching into the brightening horizon.

Sunrise comes fast. I'm always amazed at that, but then, when I'm engrossed, I lose track of time.

Elbows on the wood, I turn my head the smallest bit. East-facing windows on the Sabathian house reflect the rising sun. Ours must be, too. But Jack isn't in our house. He's in his, likely in bed.

Unable to resist, I take a picture, just one, though whether it will bring pleasure or pain once I'm back in New York is up for grabs.

Back on the beach, I shoot the wrack line with its new offerings, singling out several shells and a length of kelp. The light has blossomed into a fragile yellow when I see my father making his cautious way down the stairs. He looks typically Tom Aldiss, meaning too formal in his button-down and khakis. His silver hair, though thinner than it used to be, barely blows. For each normal step he takes, on the next he places one shoe first, then the other beside it, like a very young child.

Straightening from the surf, I smile and wave. He doesn't smile, but he does lift his cast in greeting. We meet at the bottom of the stairs, where he promptly heads for one of the beach chairs. Sinking into it, he is winded.

"Are you okay?" I ask. With so much else to think about, I've forgotten about this.

But he dismisses any problem with the wave of his hand. "Fine. Fine. I saw your note," he murmurs. Then he eyes my camera. "You still doing that?"

I don't take offense, don't even brace for an attack. I'm more confident now than I was back then, when I read attacks into most everything he said. Maybe, having discussed my connection to him now with Anne and Jack, I'm that little bit shielded from hurt. Whatever, he did raise me as his—gave me his name, a home, food, clothes, orthodontia, college. The least I can do by way of thanks is to indulge him his moods.

"Still doing it," I confirm. "Professionally." Perching on the edge of the second chaise, I turn on my camera and pull up the last shot I made. "I took this just now." Shading the screen with my hand, I show him the shot.

He dips his head to see better. "It's just a slipper shell."

"But look at its coloring. The sweep of the design is stunning. Nature is a miracle. Isn't that what you used to say?"

"Your mother was the one who said that."

No. He said it. I remember clearly. He said it during beach lessons—or so we thought of them, since he piled in so much information—and he said it more than once. But I wasn't about to argue with him. Here was one memory that worked either way.

I hold the image before him for another few seconds. When he rights his head, visibly unconvinced, I set the Nikon on the webbing behind me. "I do real estate photography. Brokers hire me when they put homes on the market. So much of the shopping experience is online now. The pictures have to be good."

"You can't make much money."

"Enough to support us." Mom left me money, though there's no point in telling him that. I would give most anything to have her, not her money. But at least the bequest allows me to spend more time with Joy.

"Where do you live?" he asks in a *please-remind-me* way.

"New York," I say, then, because he seems relatively fresh and because I have an agenda, I add, "How's Paul?"

"Paul?"

"Schuster."

"He's good."

"Do you ever see him?"

"Sure do. At the office." The flick of a frown here. "Well, I used to."

"Is he still practicing?"

He nods. "We're a team, Paul and me."

"Then he's still around," I say, just to be sure.

"Yes. Well," he pauses, frowns, "maybe no. I don't know."

I want to ask whether Paul ever visits him, and if not, why not. "I'd love to say hi while I'm here. Is the office phone the same?"

He starts to speak, then stops and slips me an apologetic look that breaks my heart.

Gently, I say, "There's medication, Dad. It can help your memory."

But he's waving a hand *no* before I'm done. "No doctors. No pills."

Frustrated, I try, "Research is—"

"No," he insists and, dismissing the subject, lifts his head to a trio of gulls that are flying toward pickings on larger stretches of beach.

Anne is pregnant, I want to say. *You'd have a grandchild growing up here. Don't you want to be part of that?* But this isn't my news to share.

Following his gaze, I, too, watch the gulls. The beauty of their flight soothes our moods. And it's pleasant, sitting here with him, cushioned in the smell of the sea. I tell myself to be silent. Only there's so much I want to know. And having him alone is an opportunity.

Casually, like it's just popped into my head, I ask, "Paul represented Elizabeth, didn't he?"

His eyes fly to mine, faded blues alert. "Why do you ask?"

"No special reason. I was just thinking about her business, like what happened to it after she went missing."

"Like? *Like?* I hate that." I begin to fear I've lost him, when he mutters, "The thing shut down. It wasn't worth much."

"Ever?"

"Once. But a few bad moves killed it. Bad moves," he repeats before seeming to catch up with the thought again. "She fell behind."

"Did that upset her?"

He considers, then nods.

"Enough so that she would deliberately jump from the boat?"

"Boat?"

"That night. Was it suicide?"

He lowers his legs from the chaise and pushes himself up. Standing, he braces his good hand on his lower back and leans sideways to ease a crick. When he straightens, he is facing the bluff. Quietly, he says, "I don't remember," and turns tormented eyes my way. "Wouldn't I remember something like that? She told me everything else. I've never been so close to someone."

"You loved her," I say, giving him permission to admit it.

"I loved her," he repeats.

"Why didn't you marry her instead of Mom?"

He considers that and shrugs. "She doesn't want me. Besides, I want family. She wants work."

That makes sense, given the way she treated her husband and son, but before I can ask more, he is on his way to the stairs. With a foot on the first, he stops, considering the right side of the bluff, then ours on the left.

He gestures at ours. "Why is this side so bad?"

I remember his articulate discussion of beach erosion yesterday, but clearly he doesn't. "That side has plantings to keep the bluff from eroding."

"Why not this side?"

"Because . . . because it just doesn't yet. I'm happy to do it. Would you mind?"

"Why in the hell would I mind?" he barks, that simply agreeing to the fix. I think of the analogy, plants-to-bluff like medicine-to-brain, but I have no time to raise it. His mood has shifted. He is already starting up the stairs, grumbling, "Why hasn't your mother done it? Where the hell is she anyway?"

Ignoring his questions, I take the stairs at a trot. "Are you hungry?"

"Yes."

"We can have breakfast here or at the square."

He doesn't respond, simply aims for the road. And yes, we can walk. Walking down is easy. But I remember how breathless he was yesterday on the walk back up.

So I run inside for my keys and, sliding quickly behind the wheel, start the car. Stopping several paces ahead of him, I lower the window just as he draws even with me. "Climb in, Dad."

He seems startled to see me. Bending just that little bit, he squints. "Margo?"

"Mallory. Climb in." He climbs in. "Seat belt?" I prompt.

But he either doesn't want it or can't process the request. "I tried to help her."

I coast slowly down the hill with my foot on the brake. "Elizabeth?"

"She was upset. Upset," he repeats as he searches for the next thought. "Afraid. She was afraid to lose everything. I had to help."

"What did you do?"

He considers that, but either he can't recall or doesn't want to say. Hooking his elbow on the open window, he turns away from me and looks out.

"Dad?" So close. I know the answer is there. I want it. But he remains silent, and the square is in view. Frustrated, I try the Aiellos. "Seeing Lina yesterday got my mind working. I remember her husband, Roberto. Did you know him at all?"

He is silent so long I'm about to give up, when, without looking my way, he says, "Gardener."

"Yes. Roberto Aiello."

He does turn now, seeming puzzled. "Do I know him?"

He would, if the man had an affair with my mother—unless he didn't know or doesn't remember. But here we are, stymied again. Didn't know or doesn't remember. That seems to be the way on too many counts.

Frustrated, I pull into the lot and park. Once inside, we settle into Dad's front corner table. Joy rushes over with coffee, which is some comfort. Anne rushes over with the newspaper. Lily rushes over with a menu for me. She already knows that my father wants bacon, eggs, and cinnamon toast, and I just double the order.

With a great rustle, he immerses himself in the paper. Around us, voices are early-morning low. Forks scrape on plates, teacups on saucers. The shop is half-filled, though a pair of young parents with toddlers arrive minutes after we do. Of the patrons already there, several faces are vaguely familiar.

"Dad," I cup my mug and lean close, "do you know any of these people?"

He looks up, then around the shop before meeting my gaze. "Is that a trick question?"

I chuckle. "I'm sorry. No. No, it's not. I just can't remember their names."

Glancing around again, he hitches his chin. "Babcock."

I follow the hitch. "John? History teacher?" He was old when I had him. He looks ancient now.

"Retired."

That's good, at least. He put us to sleep back then. I'm sure the man knows everything there is to know about America's wars, but I doubt he would convey it any more dynamically now, and with America's recent history? Disaster. "Who else?"

He hitches his chin farther left. "Hendersons."

I catch my breath. "That's Mr. Henderson?" I stare at the man. He has to be my father's age, to judge from his hands and face, but his hair is too blonde, his Polo shirt too slim, the woman with him too young. "The Hendersons," I breathe. "He remarried?" I ask, but Dad has returned to his paper, which is fine. The last thing I want is for him to ask about the revulsion that has to be showing on my face. The idea that the cad across the room may be my biological father is horrifying to me. That's the downside. The upside is that he doesn't spare me a look. If I was his daughter, he would. And he would certainly know who I am based on who I'm with.

"Are you good, Mom?" Joy asks as she arrives, following my gaze to the pharmacist. "Yeah, aren't they a pair? They've been married for three years. She's younger than his own kids." The last ends on a rising note that screams *Euwwww!*

"Where do you get your information?" I ask.

"Lily. She knows everyone. Lovvvves gossip." She glances

toward the kitchen. "Ah. Okay. They want me," she says, clearly delighted by this, and heads back.

A bit later, as we munch on the last of our toast, I return to the matter of Mr. Henderson. Do I even know his first name? No. Do I want to? *No.* This is one of the negatives of Tom Aldiss turning out to not be my biological father. Whoever is may be worse.

At least, the dad beside me is a known entity. And sad now, actually. He is withering into himself. If I weren't here, he would be sitting alone. For no other reason than that, I'm glad I've come.

The door opens, and a man enters. About my age, he wears a tired tee shirt, jeans, and work boots. The logo on the back of his shirt is fading, but enough remains to have me jumping up to follow him to the cash register, where he is picking up breakfast to go. Close up, memory stirs.

"Mike?"

He regards me with curiosity, then surprise. "Margo?"

"Mallory."

He grins. Mike Hartley is a handsome guy. Back in high school, he was sweet on Margo, but he wears a wedding band now. "It's been a while. I didn't know you were in town."

"That's a miracle," I quip, but fearing he'll take it as an insult, rush on. I keep my voice low, just between us. "I'm only here for a visit, but Jack said you landscaped his half of the bluff, and I'd like you to do mine. Do you have any time?"

"This week?" He winces and, when Lily appears with a paper bag, wedges a battered wallet out of his back pocket. He darts me a little glance as he pays. When he's done and we're alone again, he says as low as me, "This week is packed, summer people back after the winter and wanting work done. But working weekends and all, I take Mondays off. I could come over tomorrow and take a look."

If I've learned anything working in New York all these

years, it's how to shoot for a mile when you're offered an inch. It's also a version of Margo's *Accept what you can't change by changing what you can't accept.*

I brighten my big smile with hope. "How about coming over tomorrow to *plant*?"

He seems amused. "I haven't seen the space. I don't know what you want."

"The space is exactly like Jack Sabathian's, and I want what he has." The names are with me, each one in my mother's lyrical voice. "Switchgrass. Goldenrod. Beach plum. Bayberry." When he scratches his head, I sweeten the pot. "I'll help plant. So will my daughter. And Jack. And *Anne.*" I whisper the last with a quick shot at the kitchen, and there she is, watching us, but I'm not turning back. Jack has to work, of course, and Joy is counting on going with him, but at some point they might help, even for an hour, and Anne, well, Anne won't be able to fight me here. "I'll pay. I'll give you a check there and then." Summer people don't do that. They take their sweet time paying. I remember hearing grumbles to that effect from our electrician, though, in fairness, he was a surly guy.

Mike Hartley wears a crooked grin. "Well, I don't remember this. *You're* tough."

"Thank you," I say with a perky grin of my own. "What time will I see you?"

We agree on a time that allows him to first load his truck with plants, loam, and fertilizer from the nursery. He has barely headed for the door when Anne is hissing in my ear, "I was supposed to do that, not you."

"I'm helping," I insist, but I'm careful to keep my excitement from sounding like gloating. "It's one less thing for you to have to worry about."

"Yuh," she drawls. "And you'll tell Dad?"

"That's the best part," I gush, unable to hold it in. After too much frustration, here is a bit of light. "He and I were on the beach before we came here, and he was the one who raised it. He *told* me to do something. He actually complained that Mom hasn't." I don't mention the paying part. I will happily pay. No doubt, Anne already does her share.

"He thought Mom was here?" Anne asks with a sorrowful glance at the front corner table. Dad is still hidden behind the paper.

"Just confused," I say and put a confident hand on her arm. "I got this, Annie. You go back to work and cross one thing off your list."

Returning to the table, I'm feeling good. I still have calls to make to Paul, who may be able to shed light on Elizabeth, and to Shelly Markham, who may know whether my mother had an affair. And Jack has his to-do list. But this is my first real sense of accomplishment.

My satisfaction lingers through breakfast as one table clears and another fills. When the screen door opens yet again, though, and I see my sister, my contentment fizzles.

It isn't my younger sister. It's the older one.

Chapter 17

Margo. Too chic in her blouse, stacked sandals, and capris. Too formal with her dark hair in an artful coil at her nape and her makeup just so. Too wide-eyed to uphold the rest of the confident image.

She glances quickly around Anne's shop before zeroing in on me, by which time I'm halfway to the door. I want to be pleased that she's come, but her presence here is as shocking to me as it is to her, if the dazed look on her face is any measure. It was her vow never to return, spoken aloud more times than I can count. Just yesterday, when she realized where I was, she was angry.

My whisper is urgent. "What are you doing here?"

"Rescuing you?" she whispers back. Her glazed eyes have landed on Dad, who is studying his crossword puzzle. "I was on my way to the house when I saw your car. Omigod, does *he* look old."

I understand her shock. Prior to coming here, I'd seen my father every few years, but for her, it's been the full twenty. Memory freezes the past in ways that can be good or bad.

"He's not well," I tell her, "and it isn't just his mind. He gets winded with even the slightest exertion, which he wants to ignore—"

"*Hiiiiiii,*" I hear from behind, and, in a flash, Margo's expression changes. Her eyes light with genuine pleasure, her arms open to hug her look-alike niece. It is a warm moment for me, even a comical one. What we have here is conservative versus funky wearing the same face. It has been this way since Joy began choosing her own clothes. But Margo adores her, for which I will always be grateful.

"You. Are. Gorgeous," my older sister says against my daughter's hair. As quickly, she holds her back and looks her up and down. "How old did you say you are?"

Joy glows. "Thirteen and *loving* the nail polish you sent for my birthday. I *adore* that it's free of the worst baddies, like formaldehyde and camphor. The purple is delish," she runs on, still half in Margo's arms, "but my favorite, *favorite* thing is doing alternate nails purple and green, or two purple for every green? Like Gem and Tabitha—*gorgeous* shades. If I'd known you were coming, I'd have done that so you could see." She slides a hopeful look past Margo toward the parking lot. "Jeff and Teddy?" She adores her cousins.

"No," Margo apologizes. "They're on a guys' trip with their dad. They'll be disappointed when I tell them I saw you."

Accepting that, Joy says, "But I'm so glad *you're* here." She spares me a suspicious glance. "Did you know she was coming?"

"I did not."

"Nor did I," says Anne, joining us as my daughter had seconds before.

My sisters hug in a perfunctory way, and I can live with perfunctory. It could be worse. Anne resented Margo for siding with Mom; Margo resented Anne for siding with Dad. I've been the bridge between them over the years, orchestrating our every reunion. But those were in neutral space. Bay Bluff is ground zero.

Would Jack ever have a field day with *that* image, I think. I have a sudden urge to text him.

But Joy is impossibly touching us all with her arms, turning it into a group hug. "I *love* this," she sighs, "everyone together." Her pleasure makes my heart clench. This is the family she wants.

"I was in New York with friends," Margo explains before Anne can ask. "I called Mal to see if I could stop by her place, and when she said she was here, I figured I'd better come, too."

"*Crazy,*" Joy says, still in delight mode, which is probably good, since we three have no clue what to say.

When Margo slips free and approaches Dad, I gesture the other two off. Either they understand that simple is better for him, or Anne just doesn't want to witness the reunion. Whichever, slinging an arm around Joy, she ushers her toward the kitchen.

Dad doesn't look up until Margo slips into a chair. His eyes are blank at first, then puzzled. "Margo?" he finally asks.

She nods.

Sitting straighter, he breaks into a wide smile. "Margo," he repeats, and I breathe in relief. She hasn't talked with Dad since he and Mom split. He might have been furious. Might have told her to leave or gotten up and left himself. Here is selective memory at its best. As tragic as that is, to my peace-loving mind, it's welcome.

"How are you, Dad?" Margo asks in an atypically wavering voice.

"I'm fine. Fine."

"You look fine." She does not. She looks nervous. After what feels like an eternity of silence, she spots his cast. "What did you do?"

He flicks the wrist. "I tripped. You know, all those rocks on the beach. Where've you been?"

She has no idea where to begin, simply sits there looking bewildered.

"Chicago," I put in, as if it's just a reminder to him. "With her husband and sons. How are they?" I ask Margo, who readily grasps the line I've thrown.

"They're great. They're in France," she tells Dad. "Dan took the boys there to do the whole World War I tour. That's one of the reasons I went with my friends to New York."

Dad is frowning. "When did you get married?"

"Seventeen years ago."

"Do I remember the wedding?"

He hadn't been there, hadn't been invited. Actually, Margo had eloped. She said it was what she and Dan wanted, since he had a difficult family situation as well. After the fact, we had a small celebration in Chicago for which Anne had come, but that was it.

"I don't remember things like I used to," Dad announces, blue eyes spearing Margo in challenge. "I have Alzheimer's disease. My brain is going. Did she tell you?" he asks, cocking his head toward me.

Margo kindly avoids implicating me. "Are you sure that's what it is?" she asks instead.

"Know what happens?" he instructs. "You start forgetting small things. Then you forget big things. Then you forget how to walk. And talk. And eat. And breathe. That's when you die."

"Jesus," Margo murmurs. She and I have run through this progression, but hearing Dad say it unnerves me, too.

He snorts, darkening. "Got nothing to do with him, or he'd change it. It's a bad way to go. Knowing it's coming." His eyes are suddenly distant. Returning to his puzzle, he makes markings with his pen, not whole words, just letters here and there.

Margo's eyes meet mine. She's thinking about the medicine route, which we've also discussed. When I give an infinitesimal headshake, her expression asks, *Why not?* in a way uncannily like Joy's hands-open *duh* look when confronting the obvious.

Because, my adamant eyes answer Margo, I've tried convincing him but he refuses, and anyway, this isn't the time.

Accepting that for now, she sits straighter and looks around. "This place is adorable. So, who do we know?"

Henderson has left without a glance at me, for which I'm very happy. "Uh," I scan faces, "over there, Mr. Babcock."

"My history teacher?" She passes over him before doing a double take, then, gawking, returns to me. *"Ancient,"* she whispers, but her gaze has shifted. It is now riveted on Lily, who is approaching a table with four breakfasts perfectly balanced, two per arm. "Who is *that*?"

I explain the relationship to Elizabeth, as well as how Lily came to be here, and neither of us holds back the eeriness of it. Jolting Dad to talk is the point. But he remains placid, his mind either elsewhere or empty.

Then Anne whips out of the kitchen and makes a beeline for us through the mosaic of tables. She leans close to Margo. "Can we talk? Outside?"

With an almost imperceptible nod, Margo gets up. When Anne gestures me to come, too, I hold back. They haven't seen each other in nearly nine months, and I do know what's coming. It's the same indignant, why-are-you-here discussion Anne had with me. I don't imagine Anne will mention being pregnant, so she doesn't need me to support her in that. I figure I'm better off at this table, holding the fort with Dad.

But she gestures again, insistent now. *I need you with me,* her eyes say. She wants a moderator. After a quick look at Dad, who is blissfully unaware, I follow her out. Truth is, I have my own agenda. If Anne is abrasive, Margo may turn and leave. But now that she's finally here, I don't want that.

As it happens, Margo is quiet. When Anne asks the expected question, she isn't belligerent. She seems torn, eyes avoiding ours and wandering instead to the base of the square. The shops are open now; a sprinkling of tourists walk from one to the next. The clouds I saw near the horizon at dawn are drifting closer.

Margo says, "I should have come a while ago."

"Yuh," Anne scoffs, "like twenty years ago?"

"I couldn't then. But after Mom died . . ." Her voice trails off.

"Like since you lost one, you should go to the other? Like since you had Mom's money, you should go after Dad's, too?"

I put a warning hand on Anne's arm, but her only concession is to lower her voice. The underlying rancor remains. "For what it's worth, he left it in trust for the sake of the house."

Margo is visibly offended. "I'm not here for money. I wouldn't take it from him even if he offered. I have plenty. So, forget money." Her tone moderates with a return of doubt. "Think Mom. There were things she told me . . ."

We wait through beats of stillness. My anxiety rises. "What, Margo?" I coax.

She is silent—and not for effect, though she is perfectly capable of that. Her uncertainty clearly has to do with whatever it was that Mom said.

"You're making me nervous," I advise in a low singsong.

Finally, tentatively, she speaks. "Dan has been after me to talk with you, with you both, because it's been eating at me. She was angry when we first moved to Chicago, and even after her life came together there, she would get heated when she talked about Dad. She did have feelings for him."

"He had feelings for her," Anne corrects, as though the two can't both be true.

"What *is* it, Margo?" I'm convinced by now that it has to do with whoever fathered me, that Margo doesn't want Anne to hear because she will latch onto Mom's infidelity as proof of blame for the divorce.

"Did you know that Mom and Elizabeth went to school together?" Margo asks.

I'm taken aback.

Anne is puzzled, too. "School? Like high school?"

"College. They were friends before Dad met either of them."

That's not what I remember. "I thought they met after the houses were built here."

"Well, that's what we were told. But they both went to U Penn. I checked it out."

"It's a huge school," Anne argues. "Are we supposed to believe that they met there, two individuals out of thousands, and then ended up enemies here?"

"They weren't enemies back then. Mom said she and Elizabeth were together at a party in Philly when they met Dad."

Anne laughs at that. "Party? Dad?"

Ignoring her, Margo says, "He was at the law school there those same years. Mom said he started dating her, then had an affair with Elizabeth behind her back."

"And Mom agreed to live in a house right beside her after that?" Anne asks in disbelief. "What woman would do that? Come on, Margo. You always said Dad played around. What's new here?"

"Mom loved Elizabeth."

The words hang in the air.

"Loved," I echo.

"As in, *loved*?" Anne asks.

"Was attracted to," Margo confirms. Her voice is apologetic, but not in doubt about what Mom said. Rather, she regrets betraying a confidence.

I'm dumbstruck. Nothing in my mother's manner ever led me to think she was drawn to Elizabeth in any way, the very least being physical. "Mom *said* that?"

Margo folds her arms, though whether to brace herself or show strength, I'm not sure. "She did."

"That's *crazy*," Anne decides. "You say in one breath that Elizabeth slept with Dad and in the other that she and Mom were lovers?"

"I didn't say they were lovers," Margo snaps and lowers her voice. "Mom and I used to meet for dinner after work sometimes. That night, we were sitting at the bar waiting for a table. You know Mom and martinis. One's her limit, but she had two. She went on about a co-worker who had just come out after raising four kids in a traditional marriage, and then, out of nowhere, there it was. She smiled when my jaw dropped, but she didn't take back the words. She claimed she and Elizabeth never acted on it. Women didn't back then. But the way she talked about Elizabeth that night, well, I could hear it. She was mesmerized. She loved that Elizabeth was independent and strong. She loved that Elizabeth had ambition."

"Okay," Anne argues, "maybe Elizabeth was bi, but Mom was straight. She was with Dad. And," she looks hard at Margo, "with other men."

"*He* says," Margo counters.

"Elizabeth was with Richard," I point out, trying to defuse the moment. "Being with men is what women did before it was okay to be gay."

Anne turns on me. "You think Mom was?"

"I don't know, Annie."

"And Dad knows?"

"You tell us," Margo suggests. "You're the one who's closest to him." It's a throwaway line. Obviously, if Dad had said something to Anne, she wouldn't be so shocked.

"But she *was* with other men beside Dad," Anne says.

"No proof of that," my older sister warns.

I may be the proof. But Margo doesn't know that, and this isn't the time.

Anne waves an impatient hand. "Okay, so what's the point here, Margo? If it's true, what does it have to do with anything? Is there a scandal about this? Is something about to hit the news? Does Jack know his mother was gay? Did we ever see them together? And what in the hell does this have to do with Dad? Or with Elizabeth's disappearance? Was Mom in touch with her after she vanished?" Anne asks, her dark green eyes more imploring than incensed. "Or did she just run off so she could be free? And if they loved each other, could we really have missed that?" I think of the photos in the attic, which may show something. But Anne isn't done. "Mom and Elizabeth hated each other at the end."

"Hell hath no fury," I say, but Anne is staring at Margo.

"Do I remember wrong about that?"

"No," Margo says. "But that was at the end. Before Mom agreed to marry Dad, she made him swear that he and Elizabeth were done. She believed it, until he got involved in Elizabeth's business."

"Involved how?" I ask, edgy now in a different way. None of the options Jack and I had tossed around included Tom's active involvement.

"When it started to fail, he helped her save it."

"How?" my younger sister challenges in disbelief.

"By cooking the books."

Anne rolls her eyes and, having clearly reached her limit, raises both hands. Her voice is suddenly temperate, as if what we're discussing is no longer real. "Okay, I have my own business to run. I'm going back inside. If you want to stay at the house, Margo, that's fine, but if you want to make Dad out to be a criminal, forget it. He's an old man who is losing his mind. What's the point?" Foregoing an answer, she opens the screen door and leaves.

I watch until her mesh form dissolves into the kitchen, then eye Margo. "Do you really believe he committed fraud?"

"I have an easier time believing that, than believing Mom was gay," she says. Now that it's just me, she seems to have exhaled. "He was capable of it. Lots of his clients cooked the books. He would know how it's done, and if he didn't, someone else in the firm would. I don't know the details, Mal. And maybe I shouldn't have said anything. It's been gnawing at me for the longest time, but maybe Anne's right. What's the point?"

"The point," I say, thinking of Jack, "is learning as much as we can about what happened that night. If Dad is the last living witness and he's losing it fast, this is our last chance."

The frustration of it—the sadness—is suddenly overwhelming to me. As I look around searching for comfort somewhere, my eyes land on the picnic table where Jack sat yesterday. Where is he this Sunday morning? He must have friends. His life can't be just work and books in the house on the bluff. There has to be more.

When Margo goes back inside, I pull out my phone. *Where are you?* I type into a text box, but the words are too demanding. Deleting them, I try again.

You'll never guess what I just learned. Seconds later, I delete these, too. I have no idea what Jack will think of a relationship between his mother and mine. Texting isn't the way to share it.

Guess who showed up this morning, I finally type, and this one I send.

Moving farther from the door, I watch for an ellipsis cloud, but none appears. Finally, desperate, I text Chrissie. Her ear would be nearly as welcome as Jack's. She and I may not go back to childhood together, but we're just as connected.

And doesn't *that* give me pause. If my mother was gay, am I? Is that why I've never found a man I liked enough to commit to?

But no. I've never been sexually attracted to Chrissie. Never been sexually attracted to any woman. To John Sabathian? Yes. But no one else.

Can you talk? I type and send.

Seconds later, my phone rings. "Tell me," she says without preamble.

As I walk around the square dodging Sunday visitors, then pass under the pergola to stand at the top of the beach, I fill her in, one subject to the next. Having always asked about Elizabeth's mental state that night on the boat, Chrissie is intrigued by the business failure part, which feeds into the therapist's concern about suicide. For both of us, though, the issue of my mother's sexual orientation is new.

"Margo said that?"

"She did."

"And you believe her?"

Chrissie does not know Margo. "Why on earth would she make it up?"

"I don't know." I hear bewilderment, then a pause, then recovery. "So, if it's true, how do you feel about it?"

"I have no problem. Clearly my mother did. Forty years ago was one thing, but she was on a date with a guy when she died. That was only ten years ago. She could have come out of the closet at that point, but she didn't."

"She was still of a certain generation," Chrissie says. "And what about you? Are you wondering about yourself?"

Trust Chrissie to cut to the chase. I sputter a laugh. "Don't I wish. I salivate over my old lover every time I see him."

"Jack?" Chrissie whispers eagerly. "Do you?" The therapist is gone. She's all girlfriend now.

"Yeah. Not good. It's doomed."

"But it might be fun."

"Fun with a ton of angst afterward," I say and my phone dings.

I read, *Who showed up?*

Margo! I text back and return to Chrissie. "And then there's the issue of who my father is. Maybe it's Dad, maybe it isn't. I know, I know, a cheek swab. But what excuse do I give for that without upsetting him?"

"Maybe now that Margo's back, now that all three of you are there, he'll open up."

Why? texts Jack.

Because I'm here. Where are you?

In Providence neutering cats.

"What do you *want* the truth to be?" Chrissie asks, and even though I have a gazillion questions for Jack, I steer myself back.

It isn't an easy question. My memories are of this family, these parents, this life. And yes, I'd like to know why Tom Aldiss always treated me like I was one step removed from the rest. Still, the familiar is familiar. If my childhood memories prove wrong, where's my anchor?

Thinking aloud, I say, "Margo and Anne will always be my sisters. I'll always be Mom's daughter—and Dad's daughter, just like an adopted child is. Do I dream that there's more? It's a double-edged sword. I'd love to have a Dad who adores me unconditionally, but if there is one out there, where has he been all my life?"

"What about siblings?" she asks. "Would you want more of those?"

"Only if they're you."

Is neutering cats on Sundays an alternative to going to church? I text.

Did I ever go to church?

No.

Feral cat colony. Trap Neuter Return. Good deed. What did Tom say to Margo?

He knew her. Smiled. I think to tell him her news, then think again. *When'll you be back?*

In Westerly? Tonight. I'm going bowling with the police chief.

Bowling? Seriously?

His favorite sport. I'll let him crush me, then beg him to leave Tom alone. Is Margo staying?

She won't say. She's troubled.

About?

I'll tell you later.

When?

Later.

When?

LATER.

Come on, Mal. Throw me a crumb.

Text me when you're home.

We are on our way back to the house, Margo driving Dad in her rental and me following in my own car, when the skies open. That makes it a perfect afternoon to spend in the attic.

First, though, considering Jack is taking steps with the police, I have my own phone calls to make.

Chapter 18

You've reached the law offices of Aldiss, Schuster, and Finn. Our regular hours are Monday through Friday . . .

I'm not sure who Finn is, likely a big-name lateral who joined from another firm after Dad took the bench. But Paul is my interest here. I follow the prompts until I'm connected. And, finally, there is his voice. It always held kindness, and it warms me now. Naturally, since it's Sunday, he's out of the office, which brings another memory. The office was his second home. I remember Mom saying that with a kind of sadness. She wanted a fuller life for him. Perhaps he has it now?

I consider leaving a message but hold off.

His home number is on the list by the kitchen phone. That list has been there for twenty years—no, *longer,* since it's in Mom's handwriting. Anne has crossed out some numbers and added others, but Paul's is still there near the top. It leads me to voicemail as well, which leaves his cell. Twenty years ago, he wouldn't have had one, and there's no other Paul number on the list. If I ask Dad or Anne, they'll come back with more questions than I want. Even leaving a message is a risk, lest Paul ask Dad or Anne why I've called. But what's my alternative?

"Hi Paul," I say brightly, "it's Mallory Aldiss. I'm in Bay Bluff—yup, back after all this time visiting with Dad and

Anne—and a ton of memories. You were always part of our life here. I'd love to touch base." I give him my cell number, add what I hope is nonchalant encouragement, and disconnect.

Next up is Shelly Markham. She isn't on the list by the phone, so I open the drawer where Mom always kept the town directory. Unfortunately, the one here is for the current year, and there's no Shelly Markham in it . . . because she's in Florida.

I Google her name on my phone, but nothing comes up.

I can ask around for contact information, at the very least the town in Florida where she lives.

But no. I can't. Not without stirring up dust.

I'm trying to come up with a plausible excuse for asking someone in town about her, when my cell rings. Seeing a Rhode Island area code, I answer with care. "Hello?"

"Mallory? It's Paul. What a treat to hear your voice. Visiting in Bay Bluff, are you?"

My caution vanishes. His voice is as warm as my memories of him. "I am. It's overdue, I'm afraid. But I hadn't seen Dad in a while."

"Is he all right? I mean, other than the usual?"

"Yes, he's fine, other than that."

"Are you here with your daughter?"

"You know about her?"

"Of course. I see your father often, and what he doesn't tell me, Anne does. It's Joy."

"Yes, and true to her name. She's been wanting to spend time with Dad. I figured we should do it before he gets much worse." My voice thickens with concern. "Can we talk in person, Paul?"

"Not today. I'm sorry. I'm not in Bay Bluff. I bought a place in Lenox a few years back. The Berkshires are different from the shore, and then there's all the music here."

Another memory returns, making me smile. "You love

music. Longhair Paul. We used to tease you. I'm sorry for that. I love classical music now. So does my daughter."

"Both of you? That's good to hear. And yes, I'd like to talk in person. I'm driving home tonight. Maybe tomorrow?"

We agree to meet Monday for a late lunch in downtown Westerly. By that time, I reason, Mike Hartley will be close to finishing the bluff plantings, Joy will be with Jack or Anne or Margo, and Lina will be with Dad—all of which leaves me free for a clandestine meeting.

When I return to the living room, Margo is on the sofa, exactly where I left her. Her legs are crossed at the knee, her hands folded in her lap, her eyes fixed on Dad as he does his puzzle. He is so intent on it, that I wonder if the focus is a concerted effort to keep his mind sharp. He doesn't look up when Margo leaves the sofa and joins me at the door.

"Not a great conversationalist," she whispers as we move into the hall.

"What else is new?" I hitch my head toward the stairs. "There are boxes of photos in the attic. Look at them with me?"

I'm halfway up when I realize she is lower, slower, studying the family shots on the turret wall. "Funny," she says when I join her, "you take one family picture, and it's a novelty. The next year, you add a second and see how the kids have grown. By the next year, there are three pictures, and it's become a routine. By the time you get four or five, you have a tradition. Family pictures are heirlooms, way more valuable than anything money can buy."

"You have them." I'd seen them myself, there on her living room mantel.

"Mine are candids, even selfies now. I hated these posed ones. Elizabeth took them." She frowns at me. "Why was Elizabeth always the one who suggested it?"

"Was she?"

"Dad couldn't have cared less. Mom liked them. Maybe she did it for Mom?" Margo climbs to another photo. "Annie smiles in every one. Was she that clueless?"

"She was innocent."

"Did she not see that our parents were unhappy together?"

"Eventually. Obviously." I lower my voice—not that there's anyone around—but still. "Margo, did Mom say anything else the night she was drunk?"

"Not drunk," Margo replies, rising another step to study the next picture, "just tipsy. If she'd been full-out drunk, I wouldn't give as much credence to what she said."

"Tipsy then. Was there anything else?"

"Like what?"

"Like . . . well, maybe about *why* she and Dad weren't happy."

"No. She was confessing, not analyzing. That's your friend Chrissie asking."

It isn't. It's me. But the instant passes. Continuing up the stairs, I head for the guest bedroom. I've barely unfolded the attic ladder when the warm air tumbles down.

"Whew," says Margo from close behind. "Stuffy."

"Yeah. But filled with goodies," I sing as a lure and head up. The rain is steady on the roof, relegating the ocean to a distant roll. The smell of it blends well with the faint mustiness here. I don't mind either today. They're comforting in the sense of shelter.

Going straight to the box labeled *Mallory's Photographs,* I open the flaps and lift as many prints as I can safely hold, then settle on the edge of *Anne's School Papers.*

"It's exactly the same," Margo says from the top of the hatch. Having left her stacked sandals at the base of the ladder, she makes little sound as she crosses the space. "Barely dusty."

"Lina must clean here."

"Lina?"

I explain. It would have been a perfect lead-in to asking what Margo remembers about Roberto Aiello, only she is suddenly lost to all that's here. After running a finger across the span of legal diaries, she skims her palm over the shoulders of Dad's suits, then, gasping, weaves toward the "things" corner and rummages through board games.

It looks for all the world as if she's pleased to be here. And there's another question to ask. *Why did you come?* To rescue me? I don't think so. Once, she swore never to return. Maybe, having found that I was here, she came to tell us about Mom. But Mom's been dead for ten years, and we three have been together at least half a dozen times since, and she hasn't said a word. I wonder if there's something else on her mind.

"Is everything okay at home?" I ask.

"Of course." She shoots me a where-did-*that*-come-from look. "Why?"

"No reason." Trying to make a joke, I ask, "Think Mom was hiding anything else?"

"Nah." She tosses it off with such carelessness that I believe her. Then she squeezes in beside me on my makeshift bench to look at the prints in my lap.

The photos on top are nature shots, black-and-whites that I processed myself, and while she admires them, I'm more interested in the people ones beneath. Mainly in color, they're not as artistic as a jellyfish or an arcing wave, but they bring back more memories.

Margo is quickly into these, too. We laugh at one where she is white-nosed under zinc oxide, and one where she and Anne blurred jumping the waves, and one of Anne with her hands raised in despair when her sandcastle is wrecked by a rogue wave.

"Memorial Day?" Margo asks, lifting another.

"Must be. That's the town clambake. There'd have been twice as many people if it'd been Fourth of July or Labor Day."

"I liked Memorial Day," she says as if only now realizing it.

"Me, too. The town was still ours then." Forearms on thighs, I look closely as she holds the print. "There's Jack and his dad. Do you see Elizabeth?"

"Nope." She points. "Mom, Dad, the Mahoneys—remember the Mahoneys from down the street? Total geeks." Her finger moves. "Who am I talking to?" She sucks in a breath. "Omigod. Michael Hartley."

"Yup. You'll see him tomorrow. He's coming to put plants in on the bluff."

"He was hot. If I'd stayed here, I might've been into him."

"Are you sorry you didn't—stay here? I mean, if things had been different?"

"No," she says. "I like my life."

The next few prints are from the same event. I hand her several and study others.

"Are we looking for something special?" she asks.

"Mom and Elizabeth together," I offer, though there's so much else here to potentially see. "Mom and Dad together. Dad and Elizabeth together."

"Here you go," she says into the sound of the rain on the roof. "Mom and Elizabeth talking with Paul Schuster. Paul Schuster," she repeats softly, clearly remembering the man. "*Nice* guy."

I'm about to tell her that I talked with him, when she holds out another photo. "What does this one say?"

We're at the firepit on our own beach. Mom and Elizabeth are scraping sticks down to the green with pocketknives, which I so remember doing myself. But they're on opposite sides, not connected at all. "That they don't like each other?"

"That they're deliberately avoiding each other?"

"That we're making s'mores? I don't know, Margo. Does this get us anywhere else?" I look closer. "So sad. Jack's dad is alone over there by the water."

"Richard."

"Did he and Dad ever talk?" I ask.

"What could they talk about? They had nothing in common. He isn't still around, is he?"

"No. He teaches at Berkeley. He doesn't look happy here." Lonely, is what he looks. Forlorn. Abandoned, like Jack. Had he been a different sort of man, the two of them might have been close to make up for Elizabeth's distance. But Richard just . . . couldn't and, in his super academic eyes, Jack felt stupid. Rather than try to compete, he went the other way. From what I could see, he turned his life around only after his father left. *Sad*.

"Richard never smiled," Margo remarks. "What did he get out of that marriage?"

"Jack," I say pointedly, thinking of all the man squandered.

Margo's eyes touch mine before her finger taps on the tall figure with long hair and a defiant expression. "And how is our boy?"

Our boy. I smile at that. It's a little jab that goes nowhere. Margo knows she and Jack would have bombed. "He's fine," I tell her and, in that instant, wonder if Jack is better off now that his parents are gone. Both of them were emotionally dysfunctional. His childhood rebellion may have saved him from that. He is levelheaded, at least, where animals are concerned. I'm familiar with TNR programs. They rely on the volunteers. Jack Sabathian volunteering? "Interesting, actually," I say. "He's still here, but he's different."

"Aren't we all," Margo murmurs and, that quickly dismissing Jack, reaches into the carton for her own handful of photos.

For the next few minutes, we sort through them in what would have been silence had the rain not pulsed against the roof. It slows, then picks up, gusting and calming in the sky's mimic of the surf. Margo shows me a shot of her working with Mom in the potting shed, then sets it under her thigh in the unobtrusive way that speaks of appropriation. I show her a shot of the three of us, our backs to the camera as we sit shoulder to shoulder at the end of the dock, silhouetted against a mackerel sky.

"Mom took this," Margo muses. "She was artistic back then. It's like there's a part of her that she left behind when she left here."

"Didn't we all?" I say, thinking just then of goodies like sunrise and sunset and rain on the roof.

But Margo is distant as she studies the photo. "I did. No part of my childhood made it to Chicago."

"Have you missed it?"

She doesn't answer at first. Her made-up face is carefully composed, but those green eyes, so like all of ours, are troubled when they rise from the print. "Last week I'd have said no. Hell, twenty-four hours ago, I'd have said no. Then I heard Dad's voice coming through your phone, and a window opened. I tried to close it again, tried all last night, but I couldn't." She is so poised, so in control but for the pain in her eyes and her voice. "Memories are always there. Y'know?"

I do. "They're like freckles under makeup—"

"Hold that thought," she cries and, in a flash, is backing down the attic ladder. Had it not been for the rain, I'd have heard where she is going—her old room? Downstairs? Out to her car?—but her footsteps are lost.

While I wait, I push deeper into the box of photographs. The memories they bring are different from the ones I carried with me to New York. Those were dark. They were of loss and confusion, unanswered questions, distrust. But the ones in my hand are lighter. They conjure fun and closeness and love. Yes, love. Even in candid shots of Dad, who shoots daggers at my camera while actively, proudly posing for me holding a boat line in one shot and extracting a clam from the sand in another, there is feeling. I've always focused on the negative. Nightmares kept me away from this place, and staying away kept me from hurt. But what about comfort and warmth? There was positive here.

Margo returns with her iPad. "My next column," she states, and though she sits beside me again, she is distracted typing notes.

Leaning in, I read, *We can look the other way when a memory intrudes, or deny that it ever existed, but it doesn't go away. Memories shape us as surely—and invisibly—as DNA.*

I reread that sentence. She's hit the nail on the head. But she isn't done.

I'm visiting my childhood home for the first time in years. The trip was a spontaneous thing, or so I tell myself. I wonder now, though, if I've been waiting, just waiting for the right time, maybe waiting until the pain of staying away became worse than the pain of coming home.

Her fingers still, then fall away from the keyboard. Raising resigned eyes to mine, she says, "Memory is life experience. When we deny it, there's a hole where it should be."

I'm still thinking of that hole an hour later. She's given a name to what I sometimes feel. It comes at odd times, down times, times when a dream wakes me or when I hear the sea in the dark and sense a vague emptiness, a distant shadow, the motif of a song that I don't know, but do.

Having taken a raincoat from the mudroom hook, I've come down to the beach. Rain falls on my hood, my shoulders, my bare feet. It falls on the sand, thick drops dappling what was dry before and leaving a new sheen on the rest. Meeting it, the waves rush in with the force of the storm to break like dominoes along the shore, and retreat. The clouds overhead aren't dark, just dense.

Growing up here, I used to find these clouded days soothing. Rather than a complex world of color, there is one, and the simplicity is striking. It also haunts. Standing with my hands deep in the pockets of my wet raincoat, I sense that emptiness off in the distance.

The sound of the sea soothes, I tell myself, then repeat the thought to drum it in. But that distant emptiness haunts, perhaps more vividly now that I'm here. It reminds me of past pain. Maybe, too, it calls me back.

So, was I waiting, like Margo, just waiting for the right time? Did Jack's phone call open a window that I couldn't shut again? And if so, what now? Is it possible to live in the moment of today's Bay Bluff, when the place is overrun by the past?

Chapter 19

The dilemma continues to haunt me as we ready for another dining room dinner, this time plus one. Ignoring the rain, Joy has gone out for fresh flowers to augment yesterday's arrangements. She enjoys working in the garden, enjoys doing what her grandmother did before her. I feel guilty having kept her from this. But I wasn't ready to be here.

I'm not sure I am now. All three of us? With Dad? And more questions than ever? And Anne not her usual sunny self and Margo not her usual confident self? And Billy Houseman? And rain enough to frizz all of our hair?

Oh yeah. The hair. Even if we didn't all have Mom's green eyes and more-or-less heart-shaped faces; even if we weren't all roughly the same size and build, the hair would give us away. Anne may have her burgundy streak, Joy her neon scrunchie, Margo a Swarovski comb at her crown, and me a tortoiseshell clasp on the right. To a one our faces are haloed by frizz.

Anne has brought in Italian from the restaurant of a friend in Westerly. Antipasto, rigatoni bolognese, charred cauliflower, pappardelle, with a separate side of penne and white sauce for Joy—it's a divine spread for a precarious gathering. Although we work together putting the food on platters, there are so many elephants in the kitchen with us that it's an overcrowded place. When we're together in New York, we focus on noncommittal subjects like books, movies, and UGGS. Here, Anne prattles on with local trivia—a film club forming in Bay Bluff, a tapas place opening in Weekapaug, an independent bookstore thriving in Mystic. It would be sweet and upbeat, if there wasn't an undercurrent of desperation to it. There is no mention of accusations against Dad, no mention of Mom's relationship with Elizabeth. Alzheimer's disease is off the table, and, given the risk of it spilling into dinner with Dad, I'm not raising the issue of my own parentage. A baby would have been something to discuss, if neither of the men were there.

There isn't talk of Billy either. Anne dares Margo with a defiant look—just dares her to challenge his presence. But Margo is in the same state of uncertainty as when she first arrived that morning. *Why am I here?* Even after the words she wrote, I hear her thoughts. Hell, they're my own. *Is this supposed to fill the hole in my life? Is this me?*

I try to break the ice. That's my job in this family, though whether tied to DNA or life experience, I do not know—and doesn't that issue give me pause?

Dad is something else. With the table even fuller tonight than last, he sits at its head looking from face to face, unaware that his pleasant expression is both out of character and blank. He's going through motions that, in this particular moment, he doesn't fully understand. When Anne raises her wine glass to toast our reunion, he raises his. "My daughters," he says, echoing her words, but if he feels nostalgia, it doesn't show. When Anne rounds the table, blaming his casted wrist for a missed buttonhole on his shirt, he docilely lets her fix it. Other than using a spoon where a fork is called for, he has little trouble eating. He nods when someone else nods and murmurs a *yes* here or there. But he doesn't take part in the conversation, and his enjoyment seems superficial. As the meal goes on, his salty brows lower, his thin mouth thins more.

I have Alzheimer's disease, he told Margo this morning, and everything about him now suggests he is thinking of that. Deep down, in whatever pockets of clarity he finds, he is not happy.

Nor, despite her chatter, is Anne. She doesn't do more than touch her lips to the wine. When Bill asks her about it, she draws in a breath and rolls her eyes to blame this big family situation for her lack of appetite.

Joy saves the meal. Seeming armed with an endless supply of questions, she asks Bill about prison food, asks Margo whether her cousins are going to summer camp in July and, if not, whether they can come here. Before I can remind her that she won't be here in July, she asks Anne about a funny-looking purple plant in the front shrub bed. She asks Dad whether he likes sushi and, undaunted when he eyes her blankly, tells him of the time we made it. She asks Bill whether he wants another tattoo, then quickly changes the subject before anyone can mention her birthmark.

What I hear is curiosity and nervousness. She doesn't know the things I've discussed with my sisters, but she does know something's up.

Then, innocently enough, Margo sets her fork on her plate and asks Anne about the shop. "You were doing a great business this morning. Is it like that every day?"

Anne lights up. "Summers, yes. I'm closed Mondays and Tuesdays November through April, but the locals all know that, and they're mostly who's around. I feel bad doing it, because they're *so* loyal, but it's nice to be able to sleep in during the off-season."

"So, times like now you're there every day?" Margo asks.

I hear surprise. Anne hears criticism.

She cools. "Who else would be there?"

I'm guessing she'll need to rethink that in seven months, when Margo suggests, "A partner? A manager?"

"There's no partner, just me, and I'm the manager. It isn't a big place, Margo."

"Assistant manager, then, to fill in when you can't be there? How many others?"

"There are four of us full-time—including two in the kitchen—and another two part-time. And a bookkeeper off-site."

"Who does the ordering—food and supplies?"

"Me."

"Marketing? Social media?"

"Me."

"Really," Margo says.

I hear awe. Anne hears doubt.

Wanting to soften the look on her face, I say, "She admires you, Annie. So do I. You're the businesswoman of us three. Who'd have known it when we were kids?"

"You mean, because I wasn't as good a student as either of you?"

"No," I say evenly. "Because you were never the banker when we played Monopoly."

Joy laughs. Fearful Anne will take that the wrong way, too, I eye her sharply, but she is all innocence. "What? That's hysterical. What other hidden talents do each of you have?" She grows a grin as she looks from face to face. "It's Truth or Dare. I mean, that's a perfect question. What's your hidden talent?"

"No dares," Margo says. "I know what those are like." She's thinking of her boys, for whom dares typically involve burps and farts. I suffered through one of those games and agree with her. No dares.

Looking awkward, Bill stands. "Well, folks, it's been nice, but I'm outta here." After holding Anne's eye for a minute, he is gone.

Taking a cue from him, Dad wanders off.

"Okay, no dares," Joy concedes—and still I think to stop her, remind her that this isn't a group bonding event during school vacation at the Y, that we're adults, that we don't need an ice-breaker. Only I want to hear what my sisters say.

"No dares," I remind them, then concede, "Anne's hidden talent is business. Margo, what's yours?"

"Writing obits," Margo says.

Anne looks like she may laugh. *"Obituaries?"*

"Someone has to," I reason to forestall that laugh. "It's providing a service at a time when people need help."

"I'm talking *public* obits," Margo tells Anne, "the kind that run when a national figure dies. We do them ahead of time so that they're ready to run. I'm good at it." Dismissing Anne, she looks at Joy. "What about you?"

Joy jolts back and points at herself. Apparently, she hadn't thought she'd be in the game. "Hidden talent? Uh, uh." She shoots me a defiant look and sits straighter. "Folding socks."

"What kind of talent is that?" Anne teases.

I answer for my daughter. "You'd be amazed the shapes her socks take." I'm being facetious, of course. Her socks come out of the dryer in the shapes they went in, meaning pulled off in a wad inside-out. "Deer, rabbits, *cats*—"

"Your turn, Mom," Joy cuts me off. "Hidden talent?"

I consider. "Making chicken soup."

"But you don't cook," Anne argues.

"From scratch?" Margo asks.

"My daughter insists on organic, so yes, it's from scratch."

Before Anne can say that the meal we've all just eaten is far from organic, Joy raises her hand. "Okay, next question. Dream birthday gift."

"Breakfast in bed," Margo says. "I'm always the one who has to make breakfast."

Anne snickers. "Me, too, but I choose to do it. *My* dream gift is a horse."

"A horse?" I ask. "Where did that come from?"

"I've always wanted a horse. Remember the horses in the Fourth of July parade?"

"Remember the street sweeper that followed them?" Margo asks.

"Remember us sitting on the curb watching?" I add.

"And laughing," Anne says. "Remember the candy the riders threw?"

"To distract us from what was happening at the other end of the horse," Margo says. Standing to gather dishes, she asks Anne, "Is Dad okay?"

Anne reaches for the drinking glasses. "He's good. He'll be reading or puzzling or staring. It's his usual after-dinner thing."

"My dream birthday gift," Joy announces in a loud voice, "is my father's name."

No one speaks.

She looks at Margo, Anne, then me. "What? You know I want that. I've always wanted it."

"I've explained legal contracts," I say and grab the depleted pasta platter.

"That doesn't mean it can't be my dream."

I hand her the platter. "Kitchen," I instruct, and once Anne ushers her there, I collect unused silverware.

"Don't be angry with her," Margo says, holding the dirty dishes while I return the silver to its drawer.

"I'm not. I'm just surprised she said it in front of you all."

"Us all? Anne and me? We're family. You've told us she wants that."

"I know." My anger fades. I close the drawer. "It's a touchy point for me. Evokes guilt." And isn't that hypocritical? Here am I, desperate to learn the identity of my biological father, and I deprive my daughter of it?

"Want to talk about that?" Margo asks.

"Not really." After scooping up dirty linen, I follow her into the kitchen.

"Can we still play?" Joy asks, meaning *Am I forgiven?*

"Absolutely." I dump the linen on a chair and rub my hands on my shorts. "What's next?"

"Forbidden desire."

"Forbidden desire?" Anne echoes, sounding alarmed. I actually think her alarm is real. She's afraid of being laughed at. Or of saying something about being a mother.

Putting a hand on her arm, I look at Joy and clarify, "You mean, like what do we want that we can never, ever have in real life?" When Joy nods, I tell Anne, "We can do this." I broaden my gaze. "I want a PhD in Art History."

"Seriously?" Margo asks.

Anne answers with a sigh. "It's in character. She's the artsy one."

But Joy, my too-insightful daughter, has taken it one step further. She understands that if I weren't a mother, I'd have had other choices, and, stricken, says, "I'm sorry."

"For what?" I ask. To hug her would give credence to what she is thinking, so I simply touch her cheek. "It's forbidden, because I chose to be a photographer long before you were born. I love my work. I would not love being at school again. In another life, though, I'd teach fine art."

"Dad would approve," Anne says. "He always thought photography was a faux art."

"Christ, Anne," Margo scolds.

"What? It's true."

Joy redeems herself by cutting in. "Your turn, Margo. What's yours?"

"Forbidden desire?" She takes her time crossing to the sink, searching for rubber gloves in the under-cabinet, pulling them on. Then she turns and holds up a hot pink finger. "Once, just once, I want to sing with Bradley Cooper."

"Well, *that's* a good one," says Anne. "You can't sing."

"None of us can," I point out and break into *Happy Birthday* to prove it. Joy covers her ears, but I'm smiling at the memory it brings. "If we celebrated a birthday anywhere but home, people around us would laugh. We were awful."

"Still are," Margo says, "but that's the point of this truth. It's something I know I can't have, but that doesn't mean I don't want it. Okay, smarty pants," she goads Anne, "what's yours?"

Smarty pants. If that isn't a flash from the past, I don't know what is. It was Margo's favorite epithet, used as many times on me as on Anne, and with the same goading now as then. But this isn't the time to goad. Anne is too sensitive. I can't believe Margo doesn't see that.

Anne continues to spoon leftovers into plastic containers— to spoon them slowly and with great care. I'm starting to wonder whether she's too threatened to confess her forbidden desire, when she raises her eyes. They land hard on Margo. "I want a week alone with Mom."

I don't know what to say.

Nor does Margo, to judge from her silence. Finally, she says, "You hated Mom."

"I never *knew* Mom. You got her the most. You had her all to yourself for two years. Then you came along, Mal, and yeah, you had to share her with Margo, but two is better than three. I was third. I got the dregs. If Dad hadn't paid attention to me, no one would have."

I can understand her wanting Mom's undivided attention. We all did. But her vehemence? Her resentment? Her loving Dad more because she felt Mom loved her less? I always thought her loyalty to him came from the fact that he coddled her.

Feeling horrible now, I ask, "Did you really think that?"

"Yes."

Margo looks as disturbed as I am. "But everyone babied

you. You got three times the attention either of us got. You had older sisters. I never did. We looked out for you in school. I never had that."

"I wanted Mom," she repeats, glaring now.

"Maybe I'm glad I don't have siblings," Joy states and, when all eyes snap to her, adds a meek, "Moving right along . . . secret *hiding* place?" To reinforce the diversion, she says, "Mine is the leg of the snowsuit I wore when I was a baby."

There is silence. I'm not sure any of us can recalibrate so quickly. Then again, I'm not sure any of us can fully process Anne's declaration, least of all Anne, who is suddenly looking more wounded than angry. There are years of lost love in her expression. How to process that?

We need time. Seeming to realize it too, Margo and Anne take visible breaths.

I focus on Joy and say a quiet, "I know."

Her jaw drops. *"You know?"*

"You've always been so insistent about saving that snowsuit for a child of your own, that when I saw the legs getting fatter, I checked it out."

"You looked?" Guarded now.

"Squeezed. When what I felt was not a rat, I backed off."

She is barely relieved. "But now it's no good as a hiding place."

"I said I didn't look. I won't."

She pouts before turning to Anne and muttering, "Secret hiding place?"

"Daisy's box," Anne states. She's still annoyed. But at least she's playing.

"Daisy," I breathe, letting that particular memory surface into an image of something tiny and gray.

"Our cat?" asks Margo. "Our one and only pet? Who was sick from the get-go?"

"I loved her," Anne declares, daring anyone to refute that.

"What *happened*?" Joy asks Anne, before turning on me. "I never knew you had a cat."

"She didn't live long," I explain.

"Three months," Anne says. "She was born with a neurological thing, and I held her and hand-fed her and kept saying she needed medical treatment, only no one listened to me."

Margo clearly remembers that part, too. "There was nothing we could do," she says.

Anne looks about to argue, then relents. "Maybe not. We had her cremated. The ashes came back to us in a little wood box. It was mine." To Joy, she says, "Every year on the anniversary of the day she died, I used to sprinkle a few of those ashes around outside."

"I didn't know that," I say and glance at Margo, who seems as ignorant as me.

"When there were none left," Anne goes on, "I used the box for whatever I wanted to hide. Since everyone still thought Daisy was inside, they wouldn't touch it."

"Poor cat," Joy whimpers and links an elbow through Anne's in consolation.

Anne looks at me. "What's yours?"

"Secret hiding place? Here?" I smile. "Empty film canisters."

"But they were tiny," Margo argues.

"So were the earrings that I didn't want either of you to borrow. What about you?"

My older sister's eyes dart uneasily at my younger sister. She takes a tentative breath, murmurs, "Speaking of earrings," and clears her throat. "There was a removable wood panel near the electrical outlet in the potting shed. I was watching when the outlet was installed. Remove the panel, and there's a kind of shelf."

We wait.

Finally, I ask, "What does that have to do with earrings?"

Brows lifting in apology, she looks at Anne. "Those pearl earrings of Mom's that you wanted?"

"Mom lost them," Anne says.

"Unless some rodent is wearing pearl earrings, they're still on that shelf."

Anne gasps. "You hid them so she couldn't give them to me?"

"I wanted them myself."

"I thought she didn't want me to have them!" Pulling free of Joy's arm, she backs away from us. "How could you do that, Margo? Didn't you know what those earrings meant to me?"

"No—"

"Did you ever think of those earrings all these years? Did it never occur to you, *especially* after Mom died, that I might want them?"

"No!"

"Well, I would have. Even after all this time, I'd have liked to know she really did want me to have them, but you couldn't be bothered. There you were living your sweet life in Chicago while I was back here taking care of Dad." Her face is tight, her hands balled at her sides. "I've sacrificed, Margo. I've given up a bazillion other lives to take care of him. But you were too absorbed with yourself to chip in, because coming back here might interfere with your fancy-pantsy life. You left me all alone—just dumped everything on my shoulders—because you were too important to do things like dismantle your father's office and pack up his life and take him to the dentist and . . . and buy him *socks*. You're mean, Margo, *mean*." Her voice is jagged. *"Mean,"* she shouts and makes for the door. *"Selfish. Hateful."*

"Where are you going?" Margo cries as Anne flies through the mudroom.

"I want those earrings!"

Margo is out the screen door seconds after her. Exchanging a look of alarm, Joy and I follow. Though I understand what Anne is feeling, I don't know what she might do. Tear the shed apart looking for loose boards? Throw pots? Grab a trowel and hit Margo? When we were kids, she used to pummel Margo with her little fists if Margo made her angry enough. We aren't kids now, but there's something about family being reunited in the family home that unearths long-buried resentments.

And then there's the issue of my guilt. Much of what Anne said to Margo applies to me. I haven't been back to help with Dad. I didn't help with Mom either. So here we are, my sisters and I, still worlds apart.

The rain has slowed to a tepid mist, but with clouds blocking the moon, it's dark. I hold Joy's hand as we run down the stairs, then stop us both. "Maybe you should go back inside with Papa." I want her with me. But that's one more bit of selfishness to add to the rest. My sisters are a worry. It could get ugly.

Joy tugs me into motion. "Are you kidding? I started this. I'm *in*."

Rounding the side of the house, we run over the wet grass. The potting shed is only a dark blob until a light goes on inside. It is dulled by the dirt on the windows, but first Anne's, then Margo's outlines appear. By the time we enter ourselves, Anne is at the far wall, the only one with a double layer, reaching over pots and between tools to pound at planks on either side of the outlet. Squeezing in beside her, Margo flattens a palm on the correct one, angles it in, lifts it out. Her hand is inside before Anne's can make it. This is atonement for her.

Then she screams and jerks her hand back.

Snake, I think in panic.

"Snake?" Joy yelps.

Margo shakes her head as Anne reaches into the cavity. What she pulls out isn't a snake. It is dark and small, but it doesn't wiggle, slither, or coil. That would have been too easy.

Chapter 20

It's a handgun, but it might have been reptilian from the way Anne holds it at arm's length.

"Omigod," Joy breathes.

Margo breathes something less polite.

I am so hit by the implications of a gun existing that I barely breathe at all.

But Anne does—breathes, thinks, acts in ways that suggest she has envisioned this scenario before. Securing her grip on the weapon, she rushes past us out of the shed.

"Stop!" Margo yells.

"Go back to the house, Joy," I order and take off after Anne. The light escaping the grimy windows of the shed is absorbed in an instant by the murk, but I know the way. She has made a beeline for the beach stairs and is racing down. *"No, Anne, wait!"* I shout, because I know what she plans, and she shouldn't, absolutely *should not*.

The rain has picked up again, thickening the pungent smells of vegetation and marine life, but nothing slows her. Racing across the wet sand and down the sodden dock to its end, she hauls back, puts everything she has into a side-arm swing, and hurls the gun far out to sea.

Stumbling to a stop beside her, I watch in horror as it disappears. Given its import, it should make some sort of show before going down. But if even the smallest splash occurs, it is lost in the rain-roiled waves.

"Anne!" I protest, dismayed, *"why?"*

She turns on me, voice rising over sea and rain. "Why *not!* I don't want a gun around. He threatened Jack, he'll threaten other people, he just loses it sometimes without knowing what he's doing, and now you and Margo are here—and *Joy,* do you want a gun around *her?* What kind of mother are you? What kind of *awful* mother wants a gun anywhere *near* her child?"

"You said there was no gun, you swore it," I charge, refusing to look back when footsteps patter from behind. I'm suddenly, powerfully livid at Anne—livid that a gun did exist, livid that it is now gone, livid that she didn't consider anyone's wishes but her own. Mostly, I'm livid that she doubts I'm a responsible mother. She stood up there on the bluff all but crying at the thought of raising a child alone. But everything I've done for Joy all these years, I've done alone. It was me, only me—no Bill, no Dad, no Lina, no cozy little Bay Bluff to help—and I've produced an incredible person, so clearly I've done something right.

Anne may be right. I haven't been here for Dad. But I'm a good mother. She has *no right* to question that. And I'm a good sister, if keeping the three of us in touch is any measure. She didn't help with that, not one bit. It has been me, all me, spending a lifetime trying to keep peace.

Well, fuck that. Birth order only goes so far. Attack me, and finally, belatedly, wholeheartedly, I attack back.

Here on the dock in the dark under a steady rain, I let go in a voice that is fierce after years of restraint. "You call Margo selfish, but you're the selfish one, Anne. You had no right to do what you just did. It was thoughtless and uncaring. What happened that night happened to *all* of us. Just because we weren't here doesn't mean that gun didn't shape our lives. It's haunted us for twenty years—was *the* biggest question—and you just threw away all the answers. What in the hell were you thinking?"

Eyes dark, mouth tight, there is little sugar in her heart-shaped face. "That gun would tell us nothing."

"How do you know? It had a story. If we'd been able to confront him with it, he might have talked. If it had a serial number, it could have been traced."

She doesn't blink. "Why? You want to stir up the whole sordid story again? I mean, God, Mallory, it's not like a medical examiner can match a bullet to a body. There's *no body*."

"That's not the point!" I shout. The ocean air blows through my increasingly wet clothes, but it's not cold that shakes me. It's anger. "The point is, we might have learned something. He denied having a gun that night. If we'd been able to trace this one to a later manufacture date, we'd have known for sure that he was telling the truth. If he didn't buy it, we might have been able to find out who did. Maybe it belonged to Elizabeth. Maybe Dad tried to take it away from her and it accidentally went off. Maybe she deliberately shot herself."

"Maybe Anne bought the gun," Margo says from my side. The poised Chicagoan is gone. Like the rest of us, she is soaked. Joy is beside her, and while I want her back at the house, out of the rain, and away from ugliness, it's too late to shield her. To her credit, she knows to keep her mouth shut.

Not Anne, who cries, "Are you kidding? I would never buy a gun. I don't want to *touch* a gun."

"But you knew he had one," Margo says.

"I did not."

"You knew it was in the shed."

"I did not! What is *wrong* with you?" She points a shaky finger up at the bluff. "Did you not see me back there? I didn't even know there was a loose panel! You did, Margo—and if I hid a gun there, wouldn't I have known about the earrings—

earrings Mom meant for me—earrings that *you stole*?" Perhaps remembering them now and wanting to get them, she tries to dodge past us, but we are three blocking her one, all four of us bedraggled. And I'm not done.

"It was Dad then," I say. "Dad hid the gun there."

"Why does it *matter*? The gun is gone! He can't use it. We're safe. That's one good thing about Margo being a thief—it led us to the gun—and anyway, Mallory, why should I listen to you? Put you to the test, and your true colors show. I always knew you were on her side." Her gaze broadens. "If either of you cared for Dad, you'd know I did the best thing."

"Just because the gun is gone doesn't mean it didn't exist," Margo says.

"It *didn't*," Anne insists. "That gun had *nothing to do* with what happened to Elizabeth."

"Well, wouldn't it have been nice to prove that," I say. I'm growing desperate, like she is an impenetrable wall getting thicker by the minute. "I have tried so hard, Anne—have tried to keep things calm between us—and all you can think about is who's on whose side? What about the common good? What about working as a threesome? What about consulting each other and reaching a consensus? Did it not occur to you that *we* might have thoughts about disposing of the gun? Did you not think to ask?"

"You would have said no."

"Because *no* was the responsible thing to say," I argue. "Listen to yourself. It's great that you're an optimist, but there's a difference between optimism and naiveté. Optimism is the hope that things will work out well. Naiveté is the refusal to be realistic when they don't. Being naïve doesn't work now, and trust me it won't work in seven months—" I trip at the words and quickly add, "or twelve months or twenty months." But the damage is done.

Anne's face changes into something I've never seen.

"You're right about not being my sister," she seethes with a venom that the rain can't dilute. "Whoever your father is, he must be a rat. You're not Dad's. You have *none* of his good in you. You're the bastard daughter, Mallory," she spits, "the *bastard*." When she pushes past me, I'm stunned enough to do nothing.

She doesn't run, simply stalks back down the rain-coated dock to the beach as we watch in shock.

"What was that about?" Margo says into her wake, then to me, "What was *that* about?"

I push wet hair back from my face. "Anger," I reply, but I'm trembling harder than ever. When Joy's cold fingers slip between mine, it's a lifeline. Pulling her close, I tuck her hand against my churning middle. "I'm sorry you had to see that." Suddenly, brutally aware that I'm the mother, she the child, and we're standing in the rain, I wrap an arm around her and start us down the dock. "I didn't think it would get so bad."

"What was she talking about, Mom?"

"What *was* that about?" Margo repeats from my other side. I pick up the pace, but she stays close. "'Whoever your father is'? What in the hell did she mean by that? And seven months? That's a magic number. Is she *pregnant*?"

Joy might have missed that part had Margo not pointed it out, but I'm too devastated to do more than mutter, "She'll have to tell you herself," and hurry across the sand. The night is too dark, too wet, too empty at the edges for me to be here another minute.

"She *is*," Margo declares as we hit the stairs. "Is it Billy's?"

"You'll have to ask her," I say, not trusting myself with another word. Having botched this whole thing, I'm numb. I can't possibly imagine the awful scene to come inside.

Even before we reach the top of the stairs, though, headlights slice through the rain. With the angry crunch of tires on wet gravel, Anne whips the Volvo around. By the time we've fully crested the bluff, red taillights have shrunk and, seconds later, are gone.

"Good," Margo states as we head for the house, but the declaration does nothing to relieve me. Like the gun that is gone but remains larger than ever, so is Anne. Here, though, there isn't a tiny bullet hole but a big gaping wound.

Hurting, I pass through the mudroom and, ignoring the half-cleaned kitchen, release Joy's hand and head for the stairs.

Joy runs to catch up. "Are you okay, Mom?"

"Just need a shower."

We all do. I go first, then Joy, then Margo. None of us linger. Soap and hot water can't wash away the damage. Then we're all three in my room, sitting cross-legged on the plaid quilt wearing dry shorts and shirts and in various stages of towel-drying our hair.

Margo is the first to set her towel aside. "Speak," she orders.

And I do try. But words won't come. This trip has become a nightmare, making clear thought impossible. I don't know what she wants to hear, don't know what *Joy* should hear. I've been the decision-maker all these years, but I can't pick words now. I want to call Anne a liar but can't. I want to tear into myself for giving her secret away but can't. I want to *vomit* or in lieu of that, lie down in this bed, turn off the lights, pull the covers up to my ears, and blot out the world. But I can't do that either, with my sister and daughter waiting.

"Mom?" Joy whispers in concern. She's never seen me like this.

I've never seen me like this, either. Helplessness is a luxury I could never afford. I'm so unpracticed at it that the onrush of emotion is paralyzing.

The best I can do is to wave a hand. *Not ready,* it says, and they accept that.

"Papa," Joy murmurs to Margo, who nods.

Climbing off the bed, she goes downstairs to check. I'm rocking gently, doing everything in my power to put my mind in a different place. Except, the gray fringe of my nightmares is closing in, made sharp by fragments of Anne, Mom and Dad, Margo and Joy. Jack is in the muddle, but he is no fragment. He is my safe place. He always knows what I'm feeling, always understands, always fills the void.

I need to reconnect with that safe place. But I can't leave Joy now. Or Margo. Margo has to be hurting, too.

"Anne will be back," she whispers.

I don't want her back. That's the thing. I'm not up for another confrontation, any more than I can talk about the one we just had. Even after Joy reports that Dad is asleep in his chair, I continue to rock.

Margo slips out only when Joy is beside me again, as if by silent agreement they won't leave me alone. Likewise, they ask nothing. Margo returns with three mugs of hot chocolate topped with globs of whipped cream, and though the gesture is the sweetest, I can't drink. Hot chocolate, here, in this house, is so thick with memory that it would clog my throat.

My phone chimes. Grabbing it from the desk, Joy sets it in front of me on the quilt. It settles into a fold that obscures the screen, and for a minute, I don't right it. If Anne is telling me to go back to New York, I'll have a problem. If she is calling me a bastard in print, I'll have a problem. If she is saying that she won't be back for two weeks, I'll have a problem.

Margo angles the phone, reads the screen, and turns it to me.

Just got home. Will you come?

"Jack?" she asks.

I nod.

"Go."

"I can't. What if Anne comes back?"

"She won't," Margo says softly. "If she's with Billy, he'll calm her, though how anyone covered with tattoos can be calming," she mutters, "is a mystery. Go, Mal. If she comes back tonight, I'm here. I'm in charge. Joy will sleep with me."

Again, I think of all they haven't asked. "But what she said—"

"—can wait," Margo cuts in, both commanding and gentle.

Leaning forward, I hug her, then put a hand to Joy's face. She's always such a talker that her silence unsettles me. When I draw back with the question in my eyes, she simply says, "Go, Mom."

I'm not sure she's okay. But Margo is already reaching for her, and right now, there's no one I'd trust more.

Leaving the bed, I step into flip-flops, pull on my sweat-shirt, and lifting its hood, run down the stairs.

With each step on the bluff stairs, each loping stride across the sand, everything else falls away. All I can think of is running through the rain to get to where I need to be.

He is tall and solid as he holds open the back screen. His hair is a mess, though whether from shower or rain I nei-ther know nor care. The rest of him is gray—gray eyes, gray sweats, gray tank—and the irony of that? Despite those bits of gray in my life that I hate, he is everything I want.

Those gray eyes hunger. He is pleased that I'm here. One look at my face, though, and he sobers. Drawing me inside, he lowers my hood and pushes his fingers into my hair until they cradle my scalp. "What happened." It isn't so much a question as a statement of dread.

Being here with him after an eternity without is such a re-lief that I find strength. I don't speak, simply rise on tiptoe, wrap my arms around his neck, and hold tight. He smells of warmth and soap, distantly of beer, mostly of Jack.

I hear a whimper and feel a wet nose on my thigh. *Guy.*

Ignoring the dog, Jack holds our heads inches apart. "Tell me."

My mind dredges up single words from the debacle on the dock—*ugly, gun, broken, gone*—but only one thought is a phrase. "Make me forget?" I beg. He said sex did that for him, and I want it now.

Guy whines.

Ignoring him, Jack lowers his head to mine. I feel his face in my hair, his breath against it. "Talk first," he insists.

But I can't. The restraint I've perfected in years of raising Joy is gone. Angling back, I frame his face and stare into those eyes. "Make. Me. Forget." Pulling his head down, I kiss him the way he kissed me yesterday in nearly this very same place.

Reality is slow to return. I fight it for everything I'm worth, wanting to stay forever first on the kitchen counter, then against the stairwell wall, then in Jack's boyhood bed which, true to his word, is just as it was when we were last here. What we do now, though, is very different from then. Back then, Jack was in charge. More sexually adept than me, he taught me what to do. And it's not that I've become the expert since I left, just that my need for him is an adult need and greater than ever before.

I demand, initiate, *take*.

That is the first time, the one in the kitchen, all the fiercer after the seconds it takes for Jack to race up, shut Guy in the master bedroom, and race down. The time on the stairs is Jack's answer to me, typically precarious with his feet, an elbow, and my bottom all on different treads. And the third? In his bed? Slow and sleepy and sexy. It is what we have never, ever done.

The hair on his chest is damp under my cheek, his heartbeat still a rapid *ka-thump ka-thump* when he turns us so that we're face-to-face. I can see him in the dim light of the bedside lamp—his mussed hair, flushed cheeks, the way he sucks in a breath when I spread my fingers over his belly. He wants me again, quite clearly. But there's something else in him now, another change with age. We used to communicate about everything except sex. We were too young for that. Sex was sex and, frenzied as it was, untouchable with words. No more.

"Where did you learn all that?" he asks in a thick voice.

"You."

"You never—"

I stop the thought with my fingertips. "Just you."

He lets that stand for a minute, our heads sharing the pillow, his eyes holding mine. Then he circles my back to cinch me in. His voice vibrating against my cheek. "Tell me what happened tonight."

"No."

"What do you mean, no?"

"Not now. Don't ruin now."

I feel a ripple of frustration in him, but he accepts. Because he understands, as I knew he would. So, I hold reality off a little while longer. But reality is like the gun thrown into the ocean. Just because it disappears from sight doesn't mean it's gone. It is there, under however many fathoms, like the princess and the pea, which I used to read to Joy just as my mother read it to me.

"Three hours," I murmur as sleep hovers. "Set your phone."

He snorts. "I'm not setting any phone."

"I'm serious, Jack. I can't sleep here the whole night."

"Why not?" In the next breath, he answers. "Huh. Joy. But Margo is with her."

"I can't, not the whole night." I could talk of the responsibility Anne claims I lack, but I don't want to go there. I could say that I have never spent a night away from Joy since she was born, but I don't want to think of why I am now and where it goes from here.

I don't look up. My decision is final.

"Five hours," he bargains.

"Three."

"Four."

"Three point five."

"Done," he says and, wrenching away, is thundering down the stairs and back up with his phone, dropping it on the nightstand, turning off the light, and sliding his long, naked body against mine.

I fall asleep breathing him in. And for those few minutes— few hours—I feel whole.

After releasing Guy from the master bedroom, Jack walks me home. Hauling me up against him on the back steps, he gives me a last thorough kiss. It's his mark, bestowed with what used to be smugness but is only worry now. I've told him about the gun, the argument, our mothers, but I didn't allow for discussion. So, his worry could be from one of those things. Or from us. But I refuse to let him ask how I can really return to New York after what we just did. When he starts, I cover his mouth with my hand and shake my head in warning. Now, he simply, devastatingly, places a sweet kiss on my forehead and lets me go.

There is no sound when I creep in through the beach door. I already know that Anne's car hasn't returned, but the fact that night lights are the only ones lit says that Margo has been down to check.

Anne is with Bill. She has to be. The hope that the Billy Houseman we knew as kids should turn out to be our savior is bizarre. But it's the best we have.

Chapter 21

Joy is sitting on the bed when I wake up, and the fight with Anne, the gun, my time with Jack all return. Needing a bridge into mother mode, I focus on the ocean sounds through a show of sleepiness, peering at her first through one eye, then both, before stretching.

"Are you okay?" she asks softly.

I nod.

"Jack helped?"

"Good to talk with," I say.

She grunts. "Mom." She knows exactly how I spent the night.

"Good to talk with," I repeat, because I'm not getting into that. What Jack and I did was pure escapism—friends with benefits—the ultimate for-old-times'-sake. I don't want to explain that to Joy any more than I want to dwell on it myself.

But my worry is needless. She is more concerned about her aunt.

"Anne never came back. Margo says she spent the night at Bill's, but do we know for sure? What if she had a car crash, like the one that killed Gram or the one we saw driving here Friday?" she asks with a frightened grimace. "But she has to be at the shop by now. Wouldn't she be there?

I mean the baker gets there at four in the morning to make muffins, but Anne *is* the shop? She opens at six thirty. She *has* to be there."

"She will be."

"And what about us, Mom?" Her eyes are clear green and worried. "What do we do now? I was the one who wanted to come here way more than you, and now it's a big fat mess. All because I wanted to play Truth or Dare? Like, I keep going back to that. If I hadn't—"

I squeeze her hand. "No, babe. It would have happened anyway. It needed to happen. And it was good to find the gun."

"Good? There's nothing good about a gun. And now it's gone, but Anne hates us."

I jiggle her hand. "She doesn't hate us."

"The things she said—"

"She was angry."

"Bastard daughter?"

Lifting my head, I squint toward my cell. "What time is it?" The sun is well up. I hear gulls.

"Seven."

"I can't do this at seven," I breathe, sinking back as the details of last night's fight pinch at my mind.

"But what do we do now?" Joy repeats with even greater urgency. "Do we stay or leave? Do we take Papa down to the shop? I don't know if I want to be with Anne if she's going to be that ugly. How can sisters treat sisters like that?"

"Sisters are people first," I say. No, not the discussion I want to get into now, but I am my daughter's mother, and the buck stops here. More to the point, knowing her as I do, this daughter won't let it go. "Sisters are related, not identical. They have different personalities and different life experiences."

"But you grew up together. You lived in this house together as many years as you lived away. You ate the same food and celebrated the same holidays. You rode in the backseat of

Papa's old wooden Jeep, and you ganged up on him. Doesn't that count for anything?"

It did. Absolutely. But shit happens. It's part of life. How to prepare her for that? How to explain family angst in a way that doesn't put her off family altogether? My greatest dread in conceiving Joy as I did and raising her alone isn't in not having back-up when we both have the flu. It's in passing on the belief that living alone is best.

"Family can be a challenge," I say, "but the alternative is worse. That's why we're here, Joy. My sisters and I experienced life together but differently, and we've been apart for twenty years. What you're seeing now is a . . . rapprochement."

She knows the word. She singled it out of a book not a month ago. We discussed its meaning, as well as the beauty of the sound. Ra-proche-ment. Soft *proche,* French *ment.*

I had hoped the memory would lift her spirits, but she pouts. "A rapprochement is happy. This isn't."

"It will be. 'The best way out is always through,' Robert Frost says."

"I know, Mom. You've told me a gazillion times, but you didn't say *through* meant war."

"It isn't war. It's negotiation."

"Like give and take? Like bargaining? I didn't hear that last night, and anyway, where does that leave us now?" Her voice quivers. "Anne let me work at the shop, but I don't know if she will anymore. If Anne doesn't want me around and Jack doesn't want me around—"

Sitting up fast, I take her shoulders. "Anne wants you. She loves having you here. Anyone watching can see how proud she is to have you at the shop. You're her family."

"Jack isn't, but I thought he liked me. He promised I could be his intern, and now it's Monday, and I'm still here."

I smile, grateful to have definitive word on this, at least. "He's coming for you at eight."

Joy's pretty heart-shaped face, framed with wispy curls, lights up with elation at this news, but only for an instant. In the next, the worry is back. "Then what about Anne? What if she's expecting me to go down to the square when I wake up?"

"I'll text her."

"But what about *Papa*?"

Papa is in his own world. I had begun to think of morning as his good time, but not this day. He doesn't look up when Joy and I enter, doesn't respond when she says a bright, "Hi, Papa." Still in his pajamas, which is itself unheard of, he sits at the kitchen table with his hair uncombed and his salty brows knit. He looks to be brooding. Actually, he looks defeated, to judge from the way his arms hang at his sides.

The smell of fresh coffee is strong. Margo has likely been the one to put it in front of him, but he seems oblivious to her as she leans against the counter holding a mug of her own. There is warning in her arched brow when our eyes meet. Last night is on hold. Tom Aldiss is front and center.

"Good morning, Dad," I say. He glances only halfway up. "Joy wants breakfast before she leaves," I add, careful not to identify who she'll be leaving with, since Lord knows how he'd react to that. "I'm making her eggs. Do you want some?"

"I'll make them," Joy offers in a magnanimous tone. The pleading look she shoots me says she doesn't know how to deal with Dad and wants an out. "Fried?" she offers him. "Scrambled?"

His mouth tightens. "I have no toothpaste."

"Sure, you do, Dad," Margo says and goes in search. She's heading for his room, apparently braver than me when it comes to entering. Either that, or, like Joy, she's just wanting something else to do.

"Scrambled," I tell Joy, and am about to point to where

the skillet is when she finds it on her own. "Make a bunch. We'll all have some."

She takes what she needs from the fridge and heats the pan.

"She's a good cook," I tell my father. "Well, for eggs. She takes after me when it comes to the rest, which is *meh*." I wait for him to scold me for that. He believes women should cook. Actually, scolding would be better than no reaction at all, but no reaction at all is what I get. He is . . . I have no clue where.

Margo returns. "The toothpaste was on your dresser, Dad," she says off-handedly, as if someone else had put it there, which we know isn't the case. "I put it back in the bathroom." Retrieving her coffee, she takes a seat.

Nope, not another word from his mouth, I tell her with a disheartened look.

"At least the rain stopped," she tells Dad, then me, "it's gorgeous out, a good day for planting. What time is Mike coming?"

"Nine," I say.

No reaction from Dad, though it's certainly another opportunity for him to scold. If he has forgotten giving me permission and only remembers not wanting to pay someone else to do what he thinks my mother should, that would be something. But he remains unconnected. Maybe he's picturing Sunny Side Up and expecting us to take him to the square? I remember Anne telling me of the time he went down in his pajamas. I hope he doesn't plan on doing that now. Then I wonder if he plans things at all, or if they just happen with the random shift of thought.

"Wait'll you taste my eggs, Papa," Joy calls from the stove. "They're delish."

And they are. She has added spinach, cheese, and the last of the grain salad from Saturday night. It's our favorite way of disposing of leftovers, our composting cuisine, and while an occasional creation doesn't work, today's does.

Between bites, Joy describes our most notable egg failures with grand distaste, but her eye is on the clock. At five before eight, she goes to the window in the dining room to check the front drive. Margo starts to ask. I gesture her silent, but that game is done when Joy shouts, "He's here! I'm going."

I rush to the front door, only to be hit by ocean air and screen when she is halfway down the walk.

Margo is beside me. "Who is *that*?"

The car is black. Thanks to the rain, its newness shines.

"Jack."

Having pulled up at the end of our walk, he leans across to open the passenger door.

"Driving a Tahoe? Not his usual clunker?"

"Twenty years, Margo," I remind her, then explain, "He needs the space in the car for cages and supplies. And for his dog," I tack on, feeling a wave of guilt at having shut the dog off by himself last night. "Jack is a vet," I add, watching to see if he looks our way. I see the chestnut of his hair and glimpse purple scrubs but no face.

"But why's she going with him?"

"She talked herself into an internship. This was before she started working at Anne's." With the briefest glance our way, he waves and leaves. I want more, but don't know what, especially with my sister right here. So, taking a cue from my daughter, I ask as the truck disappears, "What do we do about Anne?"

Margo says nothing. Arms folded, she is watching me from the door frame. With her wavy hair loose, her face clean, and her eyes probing, she looks so much like the Margo she used to be that it's scary. Or flattering. She's aged well.

I wait, but she remains silent. "What?" I finally ask.

"Do you love Jack?"

"I always loved Jack."

"Still? Now?"

"I don't know. Maybe. Like an old friend."

"Is that what last night was about?" she asks innocently enough.

What does she want to hear? That all we did was talk? Or that Jack started bad-mouthing Dad, so I left? Or that he called Margo insane regarding our mothers? None of this is true, but I'd be willing to say any of these things if that will end it. Saying what people want to hear is my forte.

So here I am again, caught between pleasing others and asserting myself. And suddenly, what Margo wants me to say doesn't matter. I can't please others all the time. Last night proved that. There is a me inside that appears to have grown bigger than the me I was back then. If I am who I am now—if I am who I want to be—I have to act it.

"Last night," I tell her, "was about my needing comfort and his being the one who could give it."

She is quiet for several beats. Then, "I'm sorry."

"For what?" I snap, still in assertive mode. "There's nothing wrong with my needing Jack. He may be irreverent, but he is honest and smart. He understands what I'm about, and he cares. If you're going to talk about how awful he was twenty years ago—"

"I'm not," she interrupts. "What I meant was that I'm sorry *I* couldn't be there for you."

Having been ready to argue, I'm suspended while the apology registers. Then I laugh in relief. "You covered for me with Joy. That was the best."

"So," she gives me a reprieve from Jack, "is Anne pregnant, and why did she call you the bastard daughter?"

"I can't find my comb," Dad says as he comes from the kitchen. Breathing heavily, he collapses to sit on the stairs. "Someone took my comb."

"Who would take your comb?" Margo asks gently enough, but he is visibly struggling.

"I don't know, but it isn't there. I can't find it." Eyes clearing, he looks from Margo to me. This isn't paranoia, I realize. It's stark honesty. The words come out in a rush, as if he knows how brief his window of lucidity may be. "I can never find things. I don't know where I am. I don't know where I'm supposed to be. I can't work. I can't drive. I can't finish my crossword puzzle." Planting his feet apart on the lower tread for balance, he puts straight arms on his pajama knees, his cast barely breaking the cuff. "Listen to me," he orders, the Tom Aldiss of old. "It's clear. Right now. She says every old person is like this, but they're not."

"She?" Margo asks.

His brow tics as he searches. "Anne," he finally says, and his blue eyes drill us again. "You're both here now, so I'm telling you. I don't want this. I want to end it. I tried to get pills, but my connections are gone. I'd drive over the bluff, but she hides the keys. So, I have a gun."

We both gasp. I'm telling myself that suicides don't announce their intentions as clearly as this, and that when they do it's only a cry for help which we're here to answer, when Margo says, "Well, you did have one, only we were worried about it being in the potting shed where anyone could get it, so we disposed of it."

I prepare for an outburst. I'm thinking that he looks frail, that surely Margo and I can subdue him until help arrives. But his thoughts have snagged on something she said.

Incredibly, he smiles. "The potting shed," he breathes. "*That's* where I put it. I forgot." The smile fades. "See? I don't remember things. It's been a long time since I put it there."

"Did you have it on the boat with you?" Margo asks. "That night?"

I'm thinking of ways to prevent suicide, who to call, how to talk down a man like Tom Aldiss. But Margo is right raising this. It's an opportunity we can't ignore.

"What night?" he asks.

"On the boat."

He gives a quick headshake. "No gun on the boat." He frowns. "Didn't I say that?"

"How did you get a gun?" I try, to which he snorts.

"Any fool can get a gun."

"When did you buy it?"

"Oh. I don't know. Maybe last year?" His gaze moves to the dining room window, eyes distant again. "It's self-protection."

"Against what?" Margo cries. This is the first hint that she is as disturbed by the discussion as I am. "There are no intruders here."

"The future," he says. "When my mind goes, but my body stays. I don't want to live that way."

Crossing to him, I sit on the stairs. "That's not the answer."

"What else . . ." He shrugs, but it's the look on his face that moves me. It is gentle in ways I've never known, gentle and apologetic and sad. Here is a humble Tom Aldiss wanting to end his life.

I grip his arm. "Don't, Dad. Please. You have lots of good times. Can't you still enjoy them?"

"Enjoy what?" he asks and proceeds, with tragic insight and total lucidity, to add to the list. "I can't write an opinion. I don't understand the ones I read. I can't figure out how to use the phone. And who would I call? People call me to see how I am. I've known them my whole life. They have to tell me that. It's embarrassing. Same with going into town undressed."

"You were wearing pajamas," I correct, only then realizing my mistake.

"She told you. Embarrassing," he says, seeming oblivious to the fact that he's also wearing pajamas now. "And Lina. Babysitter. I'll need more than that soon."

"Not soon," I argue because I hate this. For all the times he was difficult, this is the worst. He is begging us to understand why he hates his life in ways that would have had me on my knees if I hadn't been perched on the stairs.

He rumbles on. "I don't know what I like for breakfast. Don't know the beach. Don't know shells. I can't find clams. I can't take the boat out."

"I'll take you," Margo offers, on the stairs with us now.

But he's focused on me, just as I always wanted him to be, though not in this situation. "That little girl plays the piano—"

"Joy."

"—and I don't know the names of the songs."

"Can't you just enjoy the sound?"

"But I don't know the names."

"But we're all here, Dad," Margo reasons, "all three of us, plus Joy. Don't you want to be with us?"

He looks up, seeming surprised to see her. "Where's your mother? She should be home by now."

His blue eyes fade as they slip from Margo to me. "Ach," he says, "the potting shed. Potting." Pushing himself up from the stairs, he wavers. Margo catches one arm, me the other, and we boost him to his feet. "I'll talk with her."

He opens the front door, looks out, then closes it and returns to the kitchen. On his heels, we follow him through the mudroom, but when he lets himself out and, leaning crookedly on the railing, starts down the steps, Margo catches my arm to hold me back.

"Give him time," she whispers.

"How much?" I ask as he plods unsteadily over the grass.

"I don't know. But he's talking with her. It's all she ever wanted."

We watch him open the door of the potting shed as he has apparently done many times these last twenty years. We can't see him once he's inside.

"What if he tries something?" I whisper, afraid to say it louder.

"Like what?" she whispers back. "We found the gun. It's gone."

The words are barely out of her mouth when we hear a sound that can't be anything but.

Chapter 22

I tear free of Margo's hold. Yes, we took the gun, but that sharp crack suggests there's another. What had he said—that any fool can get a gun?

My father is no fool. I race across the grass thinking that if he bought a new one each time he forgot where the old one was, he might own three or four or five. And how many more hidden panels are there?

Always that little bit faster, Margo reaches the door first and screams. Tom is on the floor in a crumple of pajamaed arms and legs, skin white, eyes open and unseeing. Falling to her knees, she shakes his shoulder gently at first, then less so. "Dad? *Dad?*"

He doesn't blink or twitch. There is an utter stillness to him. The only sounds in the shed are frightened ones coming from Margo and me.

Having raised a child on my own, I know the drill, but reality is something else. What to do first? I manage to cry, *"911."* Then, *"CPR!"*

Dead weight is all I can think as we roll him to his back. While Margo starts chest compressions, I race back to the house for a phone. After calling 911 from the kitchen, I tear upstairs for my cell, run back to the shed, and crouch on

Dad's opposite side. Margo's body jolts with each push of her arms, and my own heart is pounding, but he doesn't move.

"Anything?" I ask.

She shakes her head *no* without breaking the rhythm of her palms on his chest.

Anne. I call her, but she doesn't pick up. I try a second and third time in quick succession, prepared to keep at it—when she clicks in with an annoyed, "I'm working."

"Dad shot himself," I shout before she can hang up. "He's on the floor of the potting shed, and he isn't breathing. You have to come home."

"Oh please, Mallory," she mocks, "I'm not an idiot. He can't shoot himself. I got rid of the gun."

"He must have had another—Annie, you need to come!"

She falters then. "Is this a joke?"

"No joke," I wail, staring at Dad's lifeless body. "He shot himself!"

Then I realize that he hasn't. If he'd shot himself, there would be blood. But his head is intact, and there is blood neither on his pajamas nor pooling out from under his body. I don't smell it either, just a wisp of something match-like fading into the ubiquitous smell of the sea. Bewildered, I look around and, yes, a handgun lies on the cement floor by a stack of clay pots, though whether he fired it himself or it went off when it dropped, I can't tell. All I know is, gunshot is not the problem.

"Heart," I say with dawning horror, recalling the shortness of breath I had seen several times and ignored. "It must be his heart."

Anne must be remembering the same thing, because she says a frightened, "Okay," and ends the call.

"He gets breathless," I tell Margo in a rush. "Remember how he sat down hard on the stairs just now after walking two steps from the kitchen? He was worse walking up the hill from the square and even going down the beach stairs yesterday morning. I knew there was a problem, but he kept saying there wasn't."

"He knew," Margo says with one downward push, then with another, "Didn't want. Intervention. But he came. For the gun. He wanted to die."

"He can't die *now*," I argue in a high-pitched voice, "not when we've all just come, not when he's still thinking straight, not when there are still so many questions."

"He. Wanted to die," she repeats through gritted teeth.

She is angry. But so am I. "He is *not* allowed to tell his heart to stop."

"Tom Aldiss. Makes his own rules."

"Do you feel anything?"

"No!" Her bark shakes me. Margo is the oldest, the strongest, the smartest. One word is all it takes.

"Is there anything else we can try?"

"No!"

"Can I take over for you?"

"I'm good," she says, which is a crazy remark but one I understand. She needs to do this herself. Through the rhythmic up and down of her body, she says, "Meet the EMTs. Bring them here."

I don't want to leave her alone, but she needs this, too. Tom Aldiss is her father, no questions asked. Whether justified or not, she will be feeling guilt for not being part of his life all these years. This effort to save him is redemptive for her.

My car is still alone in the driveway. Phone in hand, I call Jack, fully expecting voicemail, relieved when he picks up.

"She's fine," he says with a smile, but his voice is low, like he's with a client, which would give me pause any other time, just not now.

"Something happened to Tom!" I blurt. "I think he had a heart attack. I think he's *dead*."

Jack sobers. "Where is he?"

"The potting shed. Margo's doing CPR. I've called 911, but, God, how long do they *take*?"

"Not long. Do you want me to bring Joy home?"

"No, uh, not yet." Squeezing my eyes shut, I finger my forehead and try to decide. "Uh, maybe. No. I don't know." Yes, I want Joy with me, but no, I do not. She was barely three when my mother passed and has no memory of death. Schoolmates have lost grandparents, one an estranged dad, but Joy's emotional involvement with those was nil. This is immediate and personal, the darkest moment of life. I want to shield her but am not sure that's right.

"How much of this should she see?" I ask Jack, and there is nothing rhetorical about the question. I need his opinion.

He is silent for a beat before offering a soothing, "Nothing yet. The uncertainty will be hard, and she's happy enough here. Call me when you know more."

With the crackle of tires on gravel, the Volvo appears.

Ending the call, I meet Anne, who races past me toward the potting shed. I'm picturing the scene inside, with Margo pumping on Dad's chest, when a heavier crunch of gravel marks the climb of the ambulance up the bluff.

They do everything they can. When he doesn't respond to CPR, they try defibrillation, and when that doesn't revive him, they try an IV, even intubation.

Nothing.

We are a frightened trio, crowding at the door of the shed since there is no room for us inside, what with three large paramedics and their equipment. We don't know any of the men; Margo and I have been gone too long, and if Anne knows names, she's too upset to say. She knows the police, who were alerted by the 911 call, and start arriving, one squad car after the next, but she pays them little heed. Her focus is Dad. Repeatedly, she begs them to get him to the hospital, until Margo says a soft, "They're doing it right."

"But it's not working!"

"They'd have to stop CPR to put him into the ambulance," she explains in a tempering voice. "They don't want to do that. Better to work on him here."

"She's right," one of the cops says from behind us, to which Margo adds, "It's protocol."

But Anne is indignant. "How do *you* know?"

"Dan's mother had a heart attack. This is what they did."

"Like you were right there? You *hate* his mother."

Margo's voice remains low. "After his dad died, we were all she had. We were the first ones she called when she felt chest pains. It was the middle of the night. We arrived at the same time as the ambulance, so we saw what they did."

I'm not sure whether Anne accepts Margo's authority, or whether she is simply worn down by fear, but she grows silent. And so, we huddle there at the door, craning around for whatever glimpses we can get of Dad when the men switch places. They are in constant touch with the hospital, low voices alternating with a radioed one. None are hopeful.

Ten minutes pass, then twenty. After forty minutes with no response, they sit back on their heels, arms limp, radio silent. The eyes that meet ours hold regret.

"There has to be something else," Anne protests, "maybe this is just a blip, maybe he's just zoning out because he isn't always completely clear with his thoughts, but he is totally *healthy* . . ." She is still talking when, apparently notified by the cops, Bill appears at the door and draws her out.

Margo and I squeeze farther inside. "Is there any chance?" I don't hold Anne's false hope, but I have to ask.

The paramedic who was in touch with the hospital says a quiet, "He was gone when we got here. This long without a heartbeat . . ." He doesn't have to finish. Six minutes is the limit I've read, and Dad has gone nearly sixty.

There is a moment of silence then—and another, and another. Even the surf seems to have stilled, though whether in helplessness, disbelief, or tribute to Tom Aldiss I don't know.

But reality won't allow for more. Reality demands . . . something.

"What now?" I ask, bewildered. No one has moved.

"Autopsy?" Margo leans close to whisper to me. "Do we want to know conclusively whether he did or did not have Alzheimer's?"

"No," says Anne from behind us. Calmed by Bill, she sounds rational. "He didn't want to know."

"Organ donor?" I ask.

"No clue." This, too, from Anne. Pushing between us, she drops to the floor, uncaring that she's in the way of the men who will be gathering their equipment but determined to see through her role as Dad's caretaker.

Relieved that she's there, I leave the shed and call Jack, who picks up after a single ring. "He's gone," I say.

"Oh, sweetheart. I'm sorry."

I haven't cried up to this point, but his voice brings tears to my eyes. I'm thinking of loss, so much loss, and disappointment, so much disappointment—and of want and need and desire, so much of those, too.

"I'll bring Joy," he says.

"Please."

"What should I tell her?"

I hesitate. It's my job to tell her that her grandfather has died. But Jack has to give a reason for rushing her home, and either he lies about that or . . . what? What would be best for my daughter?

"Tell her he collapsed," I suggest, but even in such a short time, seeming by instinct, he gets Joy all too well.

"She'll ask more."

"Tell her the paramedics are here."

"What do I say if she asks if he's dead? Kids jump ahead. I would."

"What would you tell her?"

He considers it for only a beat. "I'd tell her the truth. But I'm not you, Mal. You're her mother."

"Okay. Tell her if she asks." Joy may not be a full adult, but she's halfway there. A straight question warrants a straight answer. And while I have no reason to trust Jack to give it with the sensitivity I would, I trust him completely.

It makes no sense—not my trusting Jack, not the anticlimax in the potting shed as the paramedics load up, not Tom Aldiss leaving the house on the bluff for the very last time.

It makes no sense that Bill Houseman should be Anne's strength, or that I'm the one to snatch up a missed scrap of gauze from the potting shed floor, or that the ambulance is barely gone when several townsfolk drive by to lay flowers on our front steps in honor of a man whose honor they had once seriously doubted.

It makes no sense that while Margo insists that her husband and sons not cut short their trip, I am eternally grateful when, after delivering Joy into my arms, Jack stays—and that Anne says nothing.

It makes no sense that when Mike Hartley arrives with a truckload of switchgrass, beach plum, bayberry, and goldenrod, we insist he plant them, at least, Margo and I do. Living and green is what we need. Anne only comes around after Bill points out that Tom wanted it.

Taking Joy with him, Jack goes to the bluff to direct Mike and save us those questions, at least. There are so many others we can't answer—like where and when to bury Dad and dressed in what—like whether the funeral should be at the funeral home, the church, or the graveside and who should eulogize him—like whether he even wants a wake—and even before all that, there's the urgent issue of organ donation. Death isn't a topic we ever discussed with Dad, and if Anne doesn't know, who will?

One name comes to mind and, suddenly, having him here is a must. Paul Schuster is a grown-up. Technically, we are, too, though right now it doesn't feel that way. It occurs to me, as I key in the call, that when it comes to the death of a parent, a child is a child regardless of age.

When Paul answers, I blurt out the basics, after which I break down. I didn't cry when Joy arrived, simply held her while she did, and I do come close to crying each time I look at Jack, who is in our house only because Dad is not. But while my eyes tear up seeing the empty chair in the living room as I make this call, it isn't until I hear the voice of Paul, who was such a stable part of my childhood, that my control dissolves.

He murmurs disjointed words of comfort, seeming as upset by my tears as he is by my news. Like Jack, though, he is able to think. "Tom and I did talk about this. No to organ donation, despite my efforts to change his mind. As for the rest, it's all on paper. I'll bring that." And fifteen minutes later, he arrives.

Paul Schuster's is a welcome face, framed as it is by kind memories. Though never as tall and thin as my dad, he moves with a fitness that belies his age. His face is lightly lined, his brown hair faded. He wears slacks and an opennecked shirt, carries a worn leather briefcase, and has hazel eyes, which I only notice now because of their compassion, to which I cling. He is there for us. It's a steadying thought.

I'm not the only one who finds strength in Paul. My sisters do as well, to judge from our collective composure as we sit at the kitchen table listening to Dad's letter—which is so *him* that, in other circumstances, we would have laughed. He spells out in detail what he wants in these first days, naming the director of his funeral home of choice, his preferred style of casket and desire for peonies on top, and the location of his plot in the town cemetery. A draft of his obituary is attached, as if he knew of Margo's hidden talent and was leaving the finished version to her. He wants to be buried in his judicial robe, and he wants people to be able to pay their respects for one full day and one full day only. He is specific about that. Tom Aldiss is controlling from the grave.

But we don't mind. We now have direction, little jobs to do at a time when we're still in shock.

This is what funerals are for. They keep the family busy to distract them from the actual loss.

Physical activity works best. For us, that means cleaning the house. If the flowers that have shown up on the front steps are a sign, people will be following. The town grapevine is in full swing, reports Lina, who is otherwise silent and always efficient. Though we'll have to be the ones to direct her on what to toss and what to keep, she immediately sets to neatening and polishing. She also digs out the large coffee urn that hasn't been used in years.

I have two other priorities. First comes the planting on the bluff. Since I arranged to have it done, I'm the one who stays behind to supervise while Margo and Anne go to the funeral home. And they're the right ones to work with the director there. Anne lived with Dad all these years, while Margo, his firstborn, thinks as he does. And me, who may or may not be his biological daughter? Better at home.

Not that I don't feel guilty staying. Theirs is the heavier task. But their doing it together is a good thing. Margo insists on driving, and Anne, clutching a wad of tissues, doesn't argue, so they're meshing on this at least. I want to think it's a harbinger—because it occurs to me, as I watch Margo's rental disappear over the crest, that with Dad gone, we're alone. Whether we keep in touch is up to us. Whether we find common ground on which to move forward is up to us. Whether we have any relationship *at all* is up to us.

And then there's Paul. While my sisters welcomed his presence in the kitchen, I'm not sure they feel any further connection. I do. With Dad gone, Paul's here, and he has answers that I want.

Once Margo and Anne have left, I walk out to the bluff. Though Jack and Joy are up to their knees in plantings, they are quickly with me, Joy full of frightened questions. Where have her aunts gone? Where is Papa right now? Even, albeit in an awkward whisper, what will she wear to a funeral, since she didn't bring anything black?

They both also ask how I am. Joy's concern I expect. Jack's is a gift. When, at my urging, Joy returns to the planting, he lingers, holding my hand for a few last moments.

"If you have to go back to work . . ." I say, offering him an out.

"No. My partner is there. She'll cover."

I know little about his work. I never asked, and the timing is crazy now. But isn't this a distraction, too? "Who is she?"

"Sara Donovan, married, three kids. A couple years back, we merged our practices. I cover for her when her kids are sick. She'll cover for me now." He wraps a hand around my neck, support of the first order.

"Thank you," I say, clinging to the warmth of suede-soft gray eyes before he turns back to the bluff.

Returning to the house, I join Paul on the front steps, where I offer him the same out I offered Jack. "If you have to go back to work . . ."

He smiles sadly. "I'd rather be here. Tom is—was—a close friend."

Was. The correction startles me, which is ridiculous, since that's why Paul is here, since that's why these flowers are here and why my sisters are not. How to process my father's death? I feel so many conflicting emotions that I jump right up again, put a hand on the top of my head, and say to Paul,

"Uh, uh, would you give me a minute? I mean, please don't leave, but just, uh, just stay right here?"

"Of course."

And I'm off, running inside and up the stairs. I need my camera, my security blanket, which waits, patient and steadfast, in the bedroom. Gripping it, I feel calmer. This is who I am when the rest of the world is in flux.

Outside again, I jog to the bluff to document the planting. Joy continues to add fertilizer and water to the hole in which the bayberry bush beside it will soon sit. She knows exactly why I'm doing this at this particular time. We've talked about my need for the Nikon. She has accused me of hiding behind it when I don't want to mix with parents at school concerts. Bless her, though, she says nothing now. And Jack? After staring at me in mute sadness, he, too, goes back to work.

When I return to Paul, I'm more composed. Setting the camera down with its nose aimlessly aimed at a vivid blue hydrangea, I put my palms together and, feeling decidedly sheepish, press them between my thighs. "Sorry about that."

Paul is easy. "I understand. You didn't expect this when you left New York."

I chuckle. "Nope."

"For what it's worth," he says on a wry note, "I didn't expect it either when we agreed to meet for lunch." He grows serious. "I saw Tom every week. I probably should have come more often, but, well, there just wasn't much to say. I'd tell him about a new case or about some gossip in the firm, but I don't know if he wanted to hear it. He always knew who I was. But there were times, especially lately, when he barely acknowledged me. It was anger. He didn't like the man he'd become, and I exemplified the one he used to be. Lately, if I lasted here ten minutes, I was lucky." He pauses, then says, "So, was I coming to visit for him or for me?"

Though his confession suggests the latter, the little I remember of Paul argues for the former. He always struck me as selfless, in stark contrast to Tom. Tom craved attention. He was the center of his world. Would he have appreciated the effort people made cutting flowers from their own gardens and driving them here? I'm not sure.

"He was a complicated man," I say, looking out at the sea. It is still there, the sea is, always there and comforting in its constancy.

I feel Paul's eyes on me before they shift away. "He had a good heart."

I don't know about that, either. But this is a time to remember the positive, or, at least, to try, and I do have the best of intentions. But Tom is gone, and here is Paul, who knew him well and may be our only source for answers. "He left questions."

Paul looks at me again. When I meet his gaze, he sighs. "You mean about Elizabeth?"

"Yes. And his relationship with my mother."

He considers that. "He loved your mother."

Well, there is the matter of her adored peonies, which he wants on his casket. And he has certainly referred to her enough in recent days. But is that because I'm here, or because he feels guilty for not being a better husband, or, simply, because he only remembers things from the past, like the early days of their marriage?

"Did he?" I ask Paul, wanting his opinion. I do want it to be love. Totally aside from the anguish that finally led to divorce, I want some of what we grew up with to be real.

"In his way."

I'm not sure what way that is. "They were divorced, so something clearly went wrong. What did he feel for her?"

Paul lifts a single brow. "Love, loyalty, fondness. Hate, distrust, obligation. Definitely complicated."

Like my relationship with Jack, I think. But the thought is soon overrun by other questions. "Where did Elizabeth come

in? Did you know that she and my mother were friends before either of them met Tom?" Yes, he knew that, to judge
from the pinch of his mouth. "And then, twenty years ago?
What happened that night? *That. Night. So* many questions
there. What was Elizabeth's frame of mind when they went
out on that boat? Her business was tanking, wasn't it?" As
her lawyer, Paul would know, *does* know from the distress
on his face. But he may not feel free to tell me, and I don't
want him to leave, so I rush on. "Margo remembered hearing a gunshot that night. Dad swore he didn't have a gun. We
now know that he did. But did he have it back then? And if
so, did he use it? Did she?"

We weren't on the boat. We can't know for sure. After
hearing everyone else's opinions all these years, though, I
want to hear his.

But not yet, I realize with a jolt. Not. Yet. Right now, right
here, I have a window. Margo and Anne are in town, Jack
and Joy are on the bluff, and we're alone, Paul and I. Here's
my chance.

"There's something personal," I begin, "and it's probably
insane, but if anyone would know, you would, and I may not
have time again to ask."

His expression softens with the kindness I recall. "You'll
have time, Mallory. I'm not going anywhere."

"But this is really personal, not for anyone else's ears."
Anne knows my suspicions and no doubt Margo will soon,
but they don't have to know I've asked Paul. "There are
times—*were* times when I wondered if Dad loved me."

"Of course, he loved you."

"As *his* daughter?"

Several beats pass. "Am I hearing something else?"

What the hell. He's right. Beating around the bush is stupid. "Was he my father? Biologically? Was my mother the
unfaithful one of the pair?"

Paul knew both of my parents. He talked law with Dad

and most everything else with Mom. By rights, he could be on his feet in protest, scolding me for even thinking such a thing, telling me I'm wrong. But he is calm. The only sign of surprise is a straightening of his spine and maybe, just maybe a tic in the crease at the corner of his eye.

"Did he ever give you cause for doubt?" he asks.

"Not in words. But I annoyed him."

"Annoyed, how?"

"He frowned when I entered the conversation. Like my existence grated on him."

"Did he ever—"

"No," I cut in, sensing where he's headed. "He never hit me. It was all disapproval. I wasn't smart enough—photography was a bogus art form—I didn't have the right friends—Jack Sabathian was trouble. He was an exacting father, but at least the others understood why. I never did. He just . . . treated me differently from them." I barely breathe. "You were his closest friend, Paul. Did he ever say anything to you?"

Paul frowns in contemplation. "Tom was a prideful man." He doesn't dismiss my charge, though. "Did your mother ever say anything?"

"No, but I never asked. I felt like my place in the family was conditional on my not making trouble. Asking my mother—putting her on the spot—might have done that. I kept hoping she would say something herself. Then she died." Feeling the tragedy of that, I put my elbows on my knees, chin on my hands, eyes on the horizon.

Beside me, Paul is silent. But, of course, he knew the circumstances of Mom's death. He had sent me a condolence note so thoughtfully written, so kind, so true to my mother that I cried over it. I still have it back in New York in the hand-painted box Mom gave me when Joy was born. She had meant it for things I wanted to keep for Joy, like the tiny band that circled her ankle in the hospital nursery, photos from those early years, and baby teeth retrieved by the tooth fairy. Now it also holds mementos of Mom herself, like the hoop earrings she wore the last time I saw her—and the very beautiful note from Paul. She didn't envision my using the box for these, didn't plan on dying so soon.

"I'm sorry," he finally says. "She should not have died that way."

"Not when she'd finally become someone she liked."

His kind eyes are pensive. "I always sensed a restlessness in her"—he smiles fondly—"the proverbial bird in a cage. Was she finally fulfilled?"

"Very. More confident than I'd ever seen her. That's one of the reasons I agonize. I could have asked her. She was in a good place. I kick myself for not doing it."

"What about her will?" Paul asks. "Was there anything in it to give you a hint?"

I consider how much to say, but wills are in the public domain, are they not? "She left me more money than the others. The lawyer said she did it because I was a single mother, and my sisters were okay with that. So maybe that's the only reason?" I ask, studying his face for a clue.

"Maybe," is all he says, seeming mystified, too.

"Part of me wonders whether she did it because she figured Dad—Tom—wouldn't leave me a cent—and if that's the case, it's fine," I insist, lest Paul think me a gold-digger. "I have plenty of money. I don't need his."

Paul sighs. "I can't tell you about that. I didn't do his estate plan. Nate Yeager did. He's in the firm. He'll be in touch."

In the ensuing silence, I hear Jack call out something about beach plum, then Mike shout something to Joy, but their words are swallowed by the surf. I'm thinking of taking up my camera again, when Paul says a quiet, "You look like your mother, you know."

It is at the same time a most flattering and frustrating statement. "Yeah, well, that's one of the problems. If I looked like Tom, we'd know."

"None of you look like Tom. Your daughter is beautiful, by the way."

"She is," I say with a helpless little smile that is erased in the next instant by a sharp, loud noise inside the house. For a breath, I remember the gun in the shed that did not kill my dad. But no. This is the clatter of a dish or a pot, and I feel a twinge at not helping Lina. What I'm doing out here on the steps is selfish. But I'm not ready for it to end.

Neither, apparently, is Paul. "If not Tom, who?" he asks.

"Beats me," I say in an attempt to lighten the charge. "Jack says there were rumors."

"About your mom?"

I nod. "Kind of horrifying, I know. But Jack heard them. You never heard any?"

He looks frustrated, my mother's champion even now. "I'm on the far side of Westerly. I don't hear much of what's said on this side. Who are the possibilities?"

"Pharmacist," I say. "Roofer. *Gardener*."

He winces. "Roberto Aiello?"

"You know the name?"

"Definitely. Tom was so jealous of the man that he made Ellie let him go midway through the summer season. Aiello was known for liking women, so your dad had cause. But he shared his suspicion with the wrong person, and it got back to Aiello, who threatened to sue for libel. Your mother asked me whether he had a case. That's how I know the name."

"Did Mom say whether she was ever involved with him?"

"She was not," he says with certainty.

I'm about to ask how he can be so sure about this after being circumspect about the rest—whether he asked Mom outright about Aiello—when his eyes shoot to the road. A car has appeared on the cusp of the hill and pulls onto the berm at the very start of the large open circle, as far from Mike Hartley's truck as possible. The couple who climb out are casually dressed and carry foil-covered plates. I draw a blank on their names.

"Chief Justice Walker and his wife," Paul reminds me and, standing, extends a hand for mine.

I hesitate, feeling instant panic, thinking that greeting mourners will make this real, that I'm not ready and don't know what to say and would rather be anywhere else. I'm that child again, a child of the late Tom Aldiss.

But Paul's warm hand firmly draws me up. Close to my ear, he says, "When a sick person dies, we see them at their worst. Then friends come to share good memories, and it helps. Let's remember Tom at his best."

Chapter 23

Sad news travels fast. We've decided to wake Dad here at the house, since it's the place that he most loved, and though we designated tomorrow for formal visiting, that doesn't stop others from coming today. After the judge and his wife leave, two of Dad's former law clerks drop by, as do several of his law partners and, as the afternoon progresses, a steady trickle of locals.

I tell myself that this keeps us from dwelling on the mechanics of death. Paul is certainly right about people wanting to share good memories. Does it help? At a time when you need to smile but can't? Margo can do it. She is the ultimate grown-up. Anne is the ultimate child and, as such, is allowed to break down and be coddled by these people she has known forever. And me?

Ideally, I'd be on the beach with the waves. Was it just yesterday morning that I'd been there with Dad, when he was short of breath, and I did nothing? Would it have mattered if I'd dragged him to the local ER? Would he have allowed it?

This last question is a crock, of course. It puts the blame elsewhere to ease my guilt.

But I'll always wonder, which is why I need time alone to process what was and will be. If I talk, I want it to be with Margo and Anne about our issues—or with Joy about death and her grandfather—or with Jack about truths that Tom Aldiss now takes to his grave. I want to talk about the future.

But death defines its own moments, and mourning with friends is where we have to be now.

It isn't until eight in the evening that we're alone, by which point we're too tired to talk about ourselves or anything else. It's just the four of us nibbling bits of a chicken-ziti casserole from a neighbor, and the farro-and-vegetable dish that Anne's assistant manager brought with Joy in mind. Not that Joy eats much more than we do. Hunger isn't a priority, any more than working through our differences is. We're respectful in a hands-off kind of way. We give each other space.

Margo goes upstairs as soon as the kitchen is clean. Anne takes off for Bill's. That leaves me alone in the living room listening to Joy, who is in the sunroom picking out pieces on the piano. They're slow, sad ones, a few strains of "Someone Like You," then strains of "Fix You." After a silence comes the opening of Bach's Brandenburg Concerto No. 4, which I never thought of as sad but which grows more so as allegro slows to adagio. Then nothing.

I wait for her to join me. When she doesn't, I cross to the sunroom door. Elbows on the keys, face in her hands, and shoulders hunched, my Joy is joyless.

"Oh, baby," I breathe, rushing to the bench. As soon as my arms are around her, she begins to sob. Swaying, as we did when she was a baby, I rub her back until the tears slow. She wipes them with the heels of both hands. After a ragged exhalation, she regards me with tragic resignation.

"I almost had a grandfather."

My heart breaks. She so, so wanted this. I could kill Tom Aldiss for stealing it from her—which is a ridiculous thought, but I'm that upset for her. Death is a life lesson none of us escape. I know that. I just wish it had come later.

Then I remember Margo's words. *Accept what you can't change by changing what you can't accept.* My father may have died nearly in front of my daughter's nose, but I won't have her thinking the timing was all bad. I can change the narrative. Can't I?

Touching her cheek, I say with vehemence, "You did have a grandfather, Joy. You *do*. You'll always have memories of this time with him. You made his last days happier."

Her nose and cheeks are red from planting that morning on the bluff in the sun, and her eyes are swollen and damp, but they hold hope. "Did I?"

"Absolutely. You played the piano for him. He loved that. He loved that you served him breakfast at the shop and made him breakfast at home. He loved that you look like an Aldiss woman. He even loved thinking you were Margo."

"Until Margo showed up."

"But you brought her to him first. He was so happy seeing you, Joy. I will never, ever forget the look on his face when he saw you at the clinic last Friday, and when he reached for your hand and then didn't take his eyes off you the whole way home. You'll always have that memory. Papa wasn't naturally a happy person, not in the sense of being cheery or jovial and lighthearted. But when you played this piano for him, when he was sitting here beside you, he was peaceful. You gave him that."

"Really?"

"Yes," I say with the confidence of a new memory now inked in. And if that memory is an exaggeration of the truth? It doesn't matter. Joy isn't the only one who needs it. The idea that my daughter helped my father in his last days comforts me as well.

Unfortunately, my thirteen-year-old needs more. "But why did he die so soon after I came? And why like that? He was supposed to die of Alzheimer's."

Well, I've thought about that, too. "There's an upside to

it," I reason. "He didn't want to live to be a vegetable. This was cleaner."

"Did he know it was happening?"

"He knew his heart was weak."

"But when it happened, did he know?"

"That he was having a heart attack? I don't know."

"Was he in pain?"

"He was unconscious when we reached the shed, so I'm guessing no."

"But we were *here*," she argues, sounding hurt. "Didn't he want to spend time with us? I thought he liked being with me."

"He did. Oh, baby. He didn't choose to have a heart attack. It just happened."

"Does that mean it could happen to you?"

A heart attack can happen to anyone. But that isn't what she means. She means, if my father had a heart attack, might I one day, too? Genetically speaking, yes, if I am Tom's biological daughter. But am I? For a split second, I think of the scrap of gauze that I've squirreled away. It has bits of blood on it, and while I didn't think corpses could bleed, ongoing CPR must have caused leakage when they inserted an IV line.

Will I use it? I can't go there yet. As for what Joy heard, we haven't discussed Anne's accusations, and now isn't the time.

Framing her face with both hands, I look her in the eye. "Anything can happen to anyone, but if I have trouble breathing, I'll see a doctor. I am not going anywhere, Joy. Got that?" When she nods, I thumb the last tears from her cheeks and smile. "Want to read?"

The switch takes her off-guard, but the new light in her eyes says I've hit the jackpot. She wags a finger between us. "Together? Tonight?"

"Papa would want that," I say, and the thought is a good

one, if, again, more wishful than true. My father never read to me. He never read to *any* of us. Despot that he was, he thought we should read to ourselves. But I do like to think he approved of my reading to Joy. It plants another memory for my daughter that may not be based on fact, but that will benefit her in life. "Yes. Papa would want it."

So we read. Though we haven't finished *The Art of Racing in the Rain,* Joy picks *Number the Stars* from the bookshelf in my room. She isn't as familiar with Lois Lowry as I was at her age, and there is an argument to be made that reading about the Holocaust is no more appropriate than the other after the day this has been. But the book, which made such a deep impression on me that I remember it to this day, is about bravery, heroism, and ultimate triumph. So we climb into bed and start.

It's a distraction for Joy. Likewise for me, but only at first. As her head grows heavy on my shoulder, I feel the weight of our future and, with it, the same confusion I felt earlier. We're not facing a World War, certainly not one in which Joy can be snatched from me. Still, I feel fear. I want to see the future but can't—not about my daughter, not about my sisters, not about an ongoing role of Bay Bluff in my life.

Midway through chapter three, she falls asleep. Closing the book, I treasure the weight of her head on my shoulder for a while. Then she turns away onto her side, breaking the contact, and my tether is gone. The night is dark, the sea sounds powerful through the open window. I am insignificant against it. I feel lost.

Slipping deeper into the sheets, I listen for movement in the rest of the house, but the utter stillness only reminds me that Tom Aldiss is dead. How to process that, when my feelings for the man are so mixed? I try to distract myself thinking of the people who came by today, but their faces blur. Jack, my parentage, new info on Elizabeth, Anne pregnant—these issues have been put on hold by death. I don't even feel better when I think of New York. Job, condo, friends—all seem like another world, distant and distinct.

The ocean floods the darkened room with the rumble of the tide. I might as well be out there, floundering in the night waves, because I can't see a freaking thing. Always before in my life, I've had direction. I've known where I wanted to go. Hell, five days ago I did. But something has upset the balance. Dad's death? Being in this place again with Margo and Anne? Seeing faces from the past? Being with Jack?

Being. With. Jack.

I'm trying not to think about him, but it isn't working. I can push thoughts of him to the back of my mind, but they slip forward again. That's what this place does to me. He's always in my head, hovering like a gnat.

After swatting him away yet again, I cave. I'm tired of fighting. With all else that's going on, I want to be weak.

Slipping from bed, I pull on my sweatshirt and run quietly down the stairs. Minutes later, I'm on the beach, that much closer to both the ocean and his house. The latter is dark, save the kitchen light. I could cross the sand, climb the steps, and open the door.

But my feet don't budge. They're asking me why I would go there. And they're right. I have to get through this myself. It's what I've done all these years. It's what I'll do again when I leave this place.

Resolved, I settle into the lounge chair. I've no sooner tucked my feet under my bottom, though, when he comes out of the shadows. I'm not sure where he was hidden, but here he is, sliding a hand from my head down my neck to gesture me forward. *Resist,* a tiny voice cries. But that quickly I'm lost. Once I'm forward, he swings a leg over the lounge behind me, lowers himself, and draws me back between his raised knees. My head fits into the crook of his neck, but, having surrendered, that isn't enough for me. I know what's coming tomorrow and need an infusion of strength.

Jack has always offered that. Turning sideways, I wrap my arms around his middle and press my face to the spot under his jaw where stubble ends. The scent of his skin is as familiar to me as my own, memory and reality for once just the same.

I'm right to dread Tuesday. It is as grueling as I imagined. I've always thought myself to be socially adept, certainly when it comes to making small talk. Isn't that what a peacemaker does? Or a mom sitting with other moms at the Spring Sing at school? Or a photographer whose client trails her from room to room to room?

But endless hours of small talk with a steady stream of people coming to pay respects to my father? Exhausting. Years later, thinking back on this day, I will remember the most glowing of the comments—the people Tom helped, the friendships he held, the justice he served. Paul was right about that. They did capture Tom at his best.

Today, though, it all blurs. As crystal clear as memory and reality were on the lounge chair with Jack last night, not so in the house on Tuesday. Whether I'm in the living room with the pastor, in the kitchen with a high school friend—of whom there were a bunch—or on the front porch with the woman who served as U.S. Attorney for the State of Rhode Island while Dad was on the bench, the moments run together like streaks of sand swamped under an incoming wave. I remember Joy being by my side much of the time. And Paul maintaining a low profile while serving as the impromptu facilitator of the event. And Jack, whose presence may be controversial for Anne but acceptable for the rest of the town.

By evening, when the last of the visitors have left, we are too exhausted to think about burying Dad the next day. That's the point, I guess. The kitchen is packed with food that Lina has efficiently stored, but she, too, has left. And Anne, who needs to reclaim a semblance of control, decides to grill chicken. No matter that there is more chicken than anything else in the fridge, she can't fathom eating any of *that,* she declares in distaste, and sets to work.

I'm not about to argue. The truce between us is fragile. Far be it from me to risk breaking it.

We let her direct us—*salad bowl there,* she orders Joy with the hitch of her chin, and *thin-slice that zucchini,* she instructs me with a nod at the cutting block. She sends Margo to the market for fingerling potatoes, sends Bill to the package store for beer. Then she spots tall, tousle-haired, stubble-jawed Jack planted against the dining room jamb, and when he asks what he can do, she stares.

Leave, she's about to say when I step in front of her. Truce or not, I can't be silent. Jack is here for me, maybe even for Joy. "Please?" I whisper.

Her eyes snap to mine, and I brace myself. But her tone is surprisingly mild. "Dad would not want him here."

"Dad won't know," I offer in apology. "*Please? Let him help."

I'm not sure whether she feels he'll be a buffer between us, whether she concedes for the sake of Bill, who does like him, or whether she's just too tired to fight. But after a minute, she says, "Fine," and looks at Jack. "You, set the table."

Joy laughs.

Anne shoots her a dark look before grabbing the grill brush and heading out back.

My daughter rounds innocent eyes on me. "What? He can scrape the grill. He can vacuum the living room or . . . or fix the doorbell, which, FYI, does not work. What does he know about setting a table?"

"Oh ye of little faith," Jack murmurs with a smirk and, straightening from the jamb, pivots into the dining room.

After slicing the zucchini, I join him. He has managed to find the basics and is circling the table with napkins and plates. Leaning against the peach-painted wall with my arms folded, I consider the absurdity of what he is doing—and where—until he's done, at which point he puts a shoulder to the wall close beside me. This is the first time all day that we've been alone.

His voice is low. "Doing okay?"

I lean just that little bit sideways so that we touch, my form of self-medication. His warmth always loosens me up, and I need that after the day that was. "Weird," I say. "So many people. To hear them talk, he was beloved. Is that seriously what they remember?"

The corner of his mouth twitches in a smirk, just barely contained. "It's selective memory. They wanted to help you. Did they?"

"Some. I had no idea he went to bat to help the Eigers' son get into Harvard. Why didn't he tell us that?"

"Maybe because he didn't go to bat to help you get in there. Maybe because he was too busy making your life miserable."

I want to scold him for speaking ill of the dead, but if his bitterness is loyalty to me, how can I fight that? "Maybe he did talk about it," I whisper. "Maybe I just don't remember."

But Jack's eyes have drifted off. I follow them through the front hall to the living room, where they focus on Dad's chair. It still bears the imprint of his body. None of us fluffed its cushions, not even Lina. Incredibly, as though there was a sign with Dad's name, it stayed empty all day.

"Hard to believe he won't sit there again," I say, to which Jack threads a piece of hair behind my ear, then snakes an arm around my shoulder and tugs me close. It isn't until he speaks again that I realize I'm comforting him, as much as the other way around.

His voice is reverent. "For me, it was the dressing table where my mother did her hair. I used to hate it, because when she sat there, she was getting ready to leave." I look up at him, but the memory has him in full grip. "The chair was a stool with a low back. It fit all the way underneath. When I was six, or eight or nine, I don't know, I used to pull it out, like she had just left it and would be back. Dad pushed it in. I pulled it out again." Taking a deep breath, he returns to me, looking down with eyes that are sad and resigned. "Yeah, it's hard to believe. All of it."

I brush my cheek against his shirt collar, then draw back and touch it in awe. He had worked early that morning, but had showered and changed before coming here. A pressed shirt and slacks? So not like the Jack I remember, but apparently like the Jack he is now, because there are no price tags in sight.

He cocks his head at the empty chair. "Tell me what you feel."

"You, first. About him." If this is a moment of truth, I want it all. There was no love lost between my father and Jack. Jack has a right to blame Tom Aldiss for that empty dressing table. I'm okay with his being happy Dad is dead. Isn't that poetic justice?

But "happy" isn't the word he uses when his eyes fall to mine. "Relieved."

"Really." Milder than I thought. "That he's dead?"

"That there's one less wall between you and me."

Not knowing how to answer that, I ask, "What else?"

"Do I feel? Scared."

I don't need any elaboration here, either. With my father gone and Anne hostile and Margo soon returning to Chicago and me to New York, what becomes of us as a couple is a huge question.

"Bad timing, huh?" he asks with an unapologetic look. "Selfish of me?"

"Confrontational," I reply, then plead, "I can't go there, Jack. Right now, I'm only thinking of now. Dad is gone. He can't answer our questions."

"Yeah, and that's another thing," he says. "I'm fucking pissed at him for leaving us up in the air."

I almost laugh. This is more my Jack. "Maybe he told us everything he knows."

"Everything? Like what happened in the days leading up to that night on the boat? Like what he knew about my mother's family estate? Like whether he was your biological father?"

Turning to fully face him, I jiggle his arm. "Don't be angry. Not today."

He raises his brows and looks to the ceiling. I'm not sure what he sees there, but when he returns to me, he is calmer. Something new, this self-control? Maturity? Compassion? Sheer force of will?

Whatever, it is welcome. "Besides," I say, "Paul will help."

"Has he said anything?"

"Not today. It was enough that he made introductions when I didn't remember people. I mean," I wince, "old high school friends? I'd already seen Deanna Smith and Joe Di-Minico, but . . . Alex LaRouche? Angie Ballantine? Mark Miller? And there was Paul, whispering names in my ear. He's definitely on our side."

I do believe that. Paul will help us get to the truth. First, though, we have the funeral to survive.

Funerals have a way of stretching on when the deceased leaves a long list of hymns, readings, and eulogies, with the names of people to deliver them. The hymns and readings are a mystery to us, since Dad wasn't a regular worshipper. The eulogies are more predictable. One is given by a fellow judge, one by the lieutenant governor of the state, one by Paul. Tom didn't name any of us to speak. We can only guess that when he wrote his letter, he didn't know whether Margo and I would even come. And Anne, well, Anne is not the kind of speaker he wants to paint a lasting picture of him. For one thing, she is a woman and Dad was a man's man all the way. For another, he would have known she would be too weepy to say much.

What do I remember of this day?

I remember Margo's husband and sons appearing in time for breakfast after flying in from Paris. She had told them not to come, and given that none of the three really knew Dad, the fact that they cut short their trip to be with Margo is special. I'm envious of that. More, I'm relieved that Joy has her cousins with her.

I remember wearing the little black dress that Margo ordered online yesterday for early-morning delivery today. The eminent personal shopper, she chose different ones for each of us. I may have a full wardrobe of black in New York, but I'm not in New York, and neither Joy nor Anne has anything remotely appropriate to wear to a funeral. *Jeans and Joe* does have a sundress rack, but the offerings are beachy and short.

I remember the church choir singing "Be Thou My Vision," which took me right back to childhood Sundays with Mom, and "Eternal Father, Strong to Save," since Dad was a JAG in the Navy, and "Amazing Grace." I remember the arched windows running the length of the nave, clear-glassed and multipaned, and the pastor's voice, another throwback to my childhood.

I remember wanting to sit beside Jack—who wore a tie and jacket and looked so respectable that I hated it—but ending up between Anne and Joy. I held Joy's hand, or she mine, while, sitting in the row behind, the so-respectable man in the tie and jacket put a hand on my shoulder at discreet moments. I remember the godawful ride behind the hearse to the grave by the sea.

Dad does have a beautiful spot. It is deep into the cemetery, in one of the older sections within sight and sound of the surf. Gathering here, we are fewer in number, mostly those who were closest to him. I stand with Jack and Joy—because Anne is with Bill, and Margo with Dan, Teddy, and Jeff, and, really, is there anyone to question it? Jack and I were best friends back then. It stands to reason he would support me now.

I remember a string of graveside prayers, the lowering of the casket, and Joy clinging to me when the first clod of dirt hit mahogany. I remember needing to touch each of my sisters as we turn to leave. And then there are others to thank before they walk back across the grass to their cars. Seeing blonde hair in retreat, I realize it is Lily and wonder, briefly, if she is here to make sure my father is well and truly gone.

Then I stop short, and not out of guilt at this uncharitable thought. A woman stands alone, facing us from the very rear of the gathering. Dressed all in black—black blazer, slacks, and glasses—she looks vaguely exotic or would, if not for her hair. Though exotically dark, it is pulled into a messy bun that has nothing to do with style. Her beach waves simply won't otherwise behave. I know. We've discussed it dozens of times.

"Look, Mom!" Joy cries on a note of delight, but I'm already running forward.

"Chrissie," I say and hold her tightly for a long, long minute. "You did not have to come."

"Where else would I be? You're my best friend."

"Thank you," I say. Drawing back, I take what feels like my first deep breath in hours. Chrissie represents such a sane part of my world that the sight of her brings instant relief. "Did you just drive up? I didn't see you in the church. You should have sat *with* us."

"Oh, no," says my friend. "I didn't make it to the church. Bad traffic out of the city, and Kian had a nightmare accident in his Captain America undies that I couldn't leave for the nanny, so I was late. And anyway, I'm here under the

radar, just for you. And Joy," she adds with a brighter smile
and open arms for my daughter. "Joyzie. I'm *so* sorry about
your grandfather." The hug barely ends when the direction
of those dark glasses shifts to the man who has come up by
my shoulder. "This is Jack." Suddenly shy, even nervous,
she holds out her hand.

"The notorious Chrissie," Jack remarks. I've named her
as one of the reasons I love my life in New York, but whether
he respects that or resents it is up in the air. I can't see his
eyes. Like Chrissie's, they're behind sunglasses. "You look
familiar," he says.

"Because she looks like me," I explain. Chrissie and I have
always joked about this.

"I do," she says with a tentative smile—which dies altogether when her focus moves past us.

Turning my head to follow, I see Lina approaching. She
wears a dowdy navy dress and clutches a small purse, neither of which is out of character for a woman who works
in the shadows. But the look on her face? It is light years
removed from the who-*are*-you stare she gave me in the
kitchen Saturday morning. The one she is giving Chrissie
is . . . what? Hurt? Shocked? *Angry?*

Chrissie's eyes remain hidden, but I sense a silent panic.
She seems frozen, barely breathing, like she has no idea what
to do. I slip an arm through hers to let Lina know that she's
mine, but it helps neither of them. Chrissie opens her mouth
to speak, closes it, and swallows.

There are several beats of ominous silence before Chrissie capitulates. Seeming to realize she has no other option,
she takes a shaky breath and says, "Hi, Mom."

Chapter 24

Mom? What the . . .

I look from Chrissie to Lina for explanation, but neither seems to know what to say to the other, much less to me, and the silence doesn't bode well. Chrissie *always* knows what to say. She is the ultimate diplomat, the ultimate mediator, the ultimate friend. She has never once in our seven-year friendship told me anything that wasn't the truth.

But . . . *Mom?* A tiny window of betrayal cracks open, just enough for appalling thoughts to snake under and in.

My Chrissie's full name is Christina, which can also be shortened to Tina, which is the nickname by which Lina's daughter was known.

My Chrissie's last name is Perez. I don't know her maiden name, because it never mattered. We relate to each other in the present, and in the present, I know that my Chrissie's father is dead and that she is estranged from her mother, who refuses to accept her biracial husband.

My Chrissie is three years younger than me, as was the little sister of my friend Danny Aiello. My Chrissie has a brother Dan. Margo would point to her husband and remind me that Daniel is a common name. But that common?

"Why are you here?" Lina scolds with the hushed intimacy

only a mother and daughter would share, which rattles me even more.

I catch Jack's eye, looking for something he knows that I don't. He may remember Tina Aiello better than I do. He may have seen Tina in recent years and see no resemblance at all between that woman and this. But he is no help to me here. His twitch of a headshake says he's as confused as I am.

Chrissie isn't confused. This is the kicker. I can't see her eyes. They are hidden behind her sunglasses—*hidden*—like mine were when I climbed from the car at the square last Friday afternoon and wanted to stay anonymous. Chrissie wanted that, too, but she has been found out. To judge from the sudden flush on her cheeks, she is mortified.

Turning her back on Lina, she clutches my arms and says in a desperate whisper, "I'm sorry, Mal. I never dreamed she'd be here. If I'd known, I wouldn't have come. I wanted to be at the funeral for you, but the last thing I wanted was to make things worse. You don't need this right now. I'm going to leave, just drive back—"

"You are not," I cut in. Staring into her barely-outlined eyes, I see my own reflection. The blend of the two is as freaky as anything else. "The damage is done. What's going *on?*"

"Not now," she begs softly. "Not here." In the next instant, though, her attention shifts. Focusing past me, she gives the tiniest shiver before breaking into an uneasy smile.

"Hey," Margo says, coming up by my side. She isn't suspicious, just curious.

"Margo, this is my friend Chrissie, from New York," I say as casually as possible, but here is another thought. These two never met in the city, and through no fault of mine. When my sisters were coming to town, I repeatedly invited Chrissie to join us. I even appealed to her therapist-other by saying that if she met Margo and Anne, she could understand me better. But either she had to work or Kian was sick or Dante wanted to spend the weekend at the Jersey shore.

Now I see why she was evasive. She feared Margo would recognize her, which lends credence to the fact that she's known for a while that she was hiding a very, very important fact from me. I want to know why, and I want to know now.

To Margo, I say, "Can Joy ride back to the house with you, so Chrissie and I can talk?"

"But I want to stay," Joy argues. She senses something is up. Of course, she does.

Margo puts a possessive arm around her shoulders, gutting the protest, and gives Chrissie a warm smile. "Mal has mentioned you so often I feel like I know you. Thank you for coming."

I feel like I know you. How ironic is that, and Margo not even connecting Chrissie to Tina? Not that the lack of recognition is surprising. Margo is two years older than me, meaning five years older than Chrissie, which is a huge span in school, and Chrissie has changed a lot—at least, I think she has.

My memories of Tina Aiello are vague. I recall a girl who was dark-haired and pudgy, who was smart but shy and wore tee shirts and jeans to fit into the crowd. My Chrissie struggles with body image issues. We've discussed it many times. She still carries extra weight on her hips, but you'd never know it from her chic way with tunics and long blazers. As for being shy, the woman who struck up a conversation with me seven years ago on an adjacent stair climber at the gym wasn't shy. She was confident—and friendly and interesting and fun, all of which raises the horrendous thought that it was all a carefully-conceived plot—that she'd known exactly who I was—that she had deliberately chosen that particular stair climber—that she had been *stalking* me.

No. Not stalking. Or maybe, in a watered-down sense of

the word. But a pathological stalker? No. If Chrissie Perez was that, I'd have seen other elements of psychosis in her, and I've never seen a one. We're that close. Still, if this brilliant woman, this sensitive woman, this *loving* woman hid such a crucial fact from me all this time, what does that say about our friendship?

I need answers, but not with Joy listening. This is between Chrissie and me. And while Margo can't possibly know what's going on here, she has taken my daughter in hand. Again. And I'm grateful. Again.

So I remind Joy, "Your cousins are here, babe. They want *you*."

Joy wants them, too, which is why her leaving doesn't take any more convincing than that. But she doesn't go before asking Chrissie, "Will I see you at the house?"

And how to answer that? Worst case scenario, Joy and Chrissie may *never* see each other again. I'm agonizing about that, when Chrissie tugs on the side braid that falls thick and vibrant over my daughter's collarbone. "I may have to head right back, Joy. But somewhere or other I'll catch you. Go, be with your cousins."

When Joy gives her a parting hug, I realize something else. Chrissie is good at equivocating. She knows how to be vague in a way that sounds definitive but that doesn't say a hell of a lot. A therapist does this. A friend should not. Chrissie could have told Joy she would see her tomorrow morning, or next week in New York, or next month at the Jersey shore, because Dante's place is large. But any of those promises would lessen her options.

The evidence mounts. Right now it's circumstantial, but I sense that's about to change.

After Joy leaves with Margo, Anne and Bill linger at Dad's grave watching workers fill in the rest of the dirt. Jack stands with Paul a short distance from us, and with the rest of the mourners heading for their cars, it's Lina, Chrissie, and me.

"Why are you here, Mom?" Chrissie asks Lina, but she sounds confused, not accusatory.

"She's Dad's housekeeper," I explain.

"Why are *you* here?" Lina hisses at Chrissie again.

I answer this as well, perhaps more sharply than I might have, but I'm in a rush to move past the preliminaries. "We're friends in New York," I tell Lina, though all the while I'm staring at Chrissie. I want her to know that I'm waiting. "She's here to support me." A beat passes. "Aren't you?" I ask, hating the bitterness in my voice.

"That was the idea," Chrissie says with a snort. "Clearly it backfired."

She looks hurriedly around. Then, telling Lina that we need a few minutes alone, she grabs my arm and leads me down a paved path, past headstones and under trees whose leaves whisper in the ocean breeze, toward a stone bench facing the sea. As we walk, I smell age and foliage and ocean, even a trace of honeysuckle wafting from nearby bushes. I also smell Chanel's Gabrielle, which I gave to Chrissie last Christmas.

Her voice is breathless as we walk. "I know you have to be back at the house. This might have waited if my mother hadn't seen me."

"Waited how long?" I ask as we leave the grass and reach the bench. Her hand has left my arm, removing this last bit of connectedness.

I don't sit. I can't. I can barely even hear the sea, so if Chrissie thought that would calm me, this plan backfires as well. And here is another memory, poking at me like a bratty child. How many times have I told Chrissie about my love of the sea? How many times have I described growing up beside it, seeking solace in the fact that it is always, always there?

These were doors that I naïvely opened, that she knowingly ignored.

"Tell me, Chrissie. Now." The warning in my voice is for real. Our friendship depends on what she says. As it stands, I'm feeling lied to and betrayed. The one relationship that I have relied on most these past few years is in serious jeopardy. If there isn't truth, there isn't trust, and if there isn't trust, what is there?

She puts the back of her hand to her nose. It is a gesture I know, one that means she is trying to decide what to do. Only this time, she isn't grappling with her three-year-old's all-out, on-the-floor temper tantrum.

Finally, her fingers go to her sunglasses, which she removes. Her eyes are frightened, which is good. I'm glad it's not just me.

"When I walked into the gym that first day," she begins, leaning against the stone bench, then straightening again, seeming unsure which to do, "I had no idea who you were. I swear it, Mal. It was pure coincidence that we ended up next to each other. Then we started talking and just kept at it." She is begging now. "I'd never clicked with anyone like that before. And the conversation had nothing to do with hometowns or parents. It was about the gym and kids and baby fat, and when we went for coffee afterward, we talked about work. Do you remember?"

I nod but am only marginally relieved. "That was the first of, what, a thousand conversations, during any one of which you might have told me who you were? When did you make the connection?"

Her eyes widen, like she fears what she is about to say. After a last pause, she blurts out, "When we exchanged names and phone numbers."

"That first day?" I ask in horror. Fine. She hadn't planned it in advance. Still. "You knew *all* this time? You knew and didn't tell me?"

"I wanted to," she cries. "I really did."

"Why *didn't* you?" I shout with a ferocity that sounds harsh even to me. But hell, I'm not the peacemaker with Chrissie. That's one of the things I love—loved—about our friendship. I don't need to be in control.

Her eyes grow teary. "I don't know," she whispers. "We were at Starbucks, sitting between a geek on a computer and a couple who could have been our parents, listening to every word we said. You gave me your information, and I typed it in my phone, and seeing it there in print, I realized I knew it. But it seemed too bizarre to be true. And if it was true, I wasn't sure how I felt."

I drew back. "What does *that* mean?" If she was embarrassed to claim me as a friend because of the Aldiss-MacKay affair, I would scream.

But no. Chrissie wasn't that petty, which is small solace in this shitty situation. In place of it, she is off on a different tack.

"I had issues with Bay Bluff. My growing up years weren't the best. My mother and I were always at odds, my dad was a serial cheater, their marriage fell apart. Suddenly there you were at the gym, my best friend in waiting, and we hit it off so well that I knew I'd met someone special. But I didn't want you to be from Bay Bluff. I didn't want *any* connection to Bay Bluff. Just to be sure, I asked where you were from. Do you remember?"

No. I do not.

Actually, I do. After I told her I was from Westerly, she said she was from New Haven, and I assumed that was where she'd grown up. I continued to assume it even after she explained that she and her husband had lived there before moving into Manhattan. Technically, she hadn't lied.

Still, I'm devastated. "How could you not have said something, Chrissie? You learned we were from the same itty-bitty little village—I mean, what were the odds? Okay, so you didn't want any connection to Bay Bluff, but we were miles from there, miles from the people we'd been. Weren't you even a little *excited* about that?" A normal person would be jumping up and down. To immediately click with someone and then discover a kind of karma connection?

"I *was*," Chrissie insists, sheltering herself with an arm over her head. "You have no idea. But I didn't say anything that day—I don't *know* why—and time went on, and I loved that you were my New York friend, and we grew closer, and you held my hand through my struggle to conceive and then my nightmare pregnancy, and Kian was born, and I fell in love with Joy, and the time was never right, because saying something after years of silence was *impossible*."

I could almost understand that. Marginally calmer, I ask, "But why now? Why risk coming back here and being recognized?"

"Your Dad died."

"And that made it worth the risk?" I ask, skeptical. She and I are on the same wavelength so often it's scary, but I'm not there with her now.

"Yes."

"*Why?*"

"Your dad died," she repeats, suddenly disciplined, suddenly the woman who coaches lost souls, the woman who understands love and grief and regret. "Whether or not he's your biological, he was your dad. I knew you'd be feeling lost, and conflicted, maybe even guilty that you haven't seen him more. I knew this whole—" she gestures widely back at the cemetery, "*business* was going to be difficult for you, and I knew your sisters would be here. I wanted to be here for you, too."

It's the proper response, but I know Chrissie too well. There's more. Her look right now is . . . frightened, pleading, *pregnant*.

Facing the sea, for all the good it's doing, I brace my hands on the top of the bench. Its roughness gives me traction as I consider how to proceed. But bluntness is the only way. Diplomacy is beyond me. "What aren't you saying?"

She doesn't answer.

My eyes fly to hers then, because suddenly, I *see*. She's from Bay Bluff. She's Roberto Aiello's daughter. She's heard the rumors. "You think we're sisters!"

She hesitates for several seconds more. Maybe she's waiting for me to elaborate. Maybe she's hoping I'll deny it and offer evidence to the contrary. Maybe she's praying I'll confirm it, saying I suspected it all along. But how could I have ever suspected it, when she's kept me in the dark all this time?

She must have realized that, because her words burst out, like horses breaking from the Derby gate. "It makes sense, Mal—us looking alike and thinking alike. I don't believe in chance, and I don't believe in cosmic voodoo, but what are the odds that we'd end up beside each other in the gym? So maybe it was meant to be, and maybe I was afraid to let you know who I was, because I suffered through talking about Bay Bluff with my own therapist, and it was too painful to repeat. Maybe I wanted it so badly that I was afraid to give you a chance to say it was not." She takes a breath, as reality slows her down. "Then your dad got sick. I couldn't say anything, because it was inappropriate. And once you were back here, you were with him and Anne, and then Margo came, and there was everything you were learning about your mom. When was I supposed to tell you, Mal?" she pleads. "Would it have helped in the middle of all that if I'd told you we were sisters?"

"You're not," Paul says in a voice that is kind but firm.

I don't know when he and Jack approached, but here they are. I've been so lost in Chrissie that after years without Jack, I'm actually startled to see him again. In that surprise, he is a momentary distraction. He has taken off his blazer and tie, rolled the sleeves of his shirt to the elbow and pushed a hand through his hair—stunning in all regards.

He has been a rock these last two days.

My rock.

But so has Paul. And since he's the one who has just spoken, my attention slides there. "You sound sure."

"I am, Mallory. I told you that Monday." He eyes Chrissie. I'm not sure if she knows who he is, but between his dark suit, the lines on his face, and his manner, he exudes quiet authority. "The rumors were unfounded. Eleanor Aldiss was never with your father that way."

Chrissie frowns at Lina, who has come to us right along with the men. "He told me he was," the older woman says in self-defense. That explains the scrutiny she gave me Saturday morning. She was looking for Roberto in me.

Paul's voice is gentle, but all the more weighty for its reluctance. "If he said that, then he lied. I know," he returns to me, just me now, "because your mother denied it. I believe her, because she never lied to me." Quietly, he adds, "And because I know who is."

I press a fist to the center of my chest. "Who is?"

Chapter 25

The world recedes. Oh, I'm sure that the ocean continues to roll and its breeze stirs the trees. Birds still call, squirrels still rustle, insects still buzz as they did during the pastor's words. All I hear now, though, is the pulse of my own blood.

Paul is silent as well. Not so his hazel eyes. *This isn't the time,* they say. *We're burying your father today. If it's waited this long, will just a little longer hurt?*

The words are familiar. Haven't I just heard them from Chrissie? She has fallen into the periphery, but I answer Paul with the same insistence I did her.

Yes, my eyes shout back. *Now.*

Releasing a breath, he looks skyward in apology, then at the waves in frustration. But the expression that finally meets mine holds wry amusement. My insistence has surprised him—and not in a bad way, says the small twitch at the corner of his mouth.

Appreciation is not what I need right now.

Sensing that, he sobers and tics his head toward the paved path that skirts the ocean. A low sea wall rises at its edge, two feet of artfully-placed stone packed with mortar to block sea surge. Its flat-brim mosaic of slate and rust is wide enough for mourners to sit. But Paul doesn't have sitting in mind, not before an audience.

"Walk with me?" he asks, though it isn't really a question. He is already moving past the bench toward the path.

Suddenly, I do feel a second's qualm. *Do* I really want to know? Do I really want to know *now*? He's right. This isn't the best time. But I've waited so long, wondered so long—not to mention the tiny part of me that wants it to be now in sheer defiance of Tom Aldiss, who also kept me in the dark.

I am turning to follow him when Jack touches my arm. His eyes are the gray of soft flannel and worry. He wants to know if I'm okay, or want him to come along. The sun glances off his chestnut hair, the tip of his straight nose, his light beard. Knowing he's here is all I need.

Managing a small smile, I shake my head and set off. I'm safe with Paul. Years of childhood memories tell me that. I catch up with him in an instant, and we walk silently along the path for a bit. Funny, but I feel no rush now. Paul was always measured. He'll take his time, but I can trust what he says. *If there isn't trust, what is there?* And he is, truly, all I have left of my parents' generation.

We follow the path as it curves along the shoreline. Finally, he stops in the shade of a weeping willow. His hands are in his pockets, drawing back his suit jacket in what should be a relaxed pose. But he is tense. I see it in his face, his ramrod-straight back, even the set of his loafered feet.

He is about to speak. I can still stop him.

No. I cannot.

As he looks toward the waves, the past arrives. "I've known Tom for forty years. We met at a law conference in Boston and his mind was the best legal one there. People were always drawn to him for that. I was no exception. I want to say he was drawn to mine the same way," he slips me a self-deprecating smile, "but he was more interested in the fact that I lived in Westerly. He vacationed here as a child, and it was where he wanted to settle. Our forming a law firm was a natural offshoot of that. We rented space and hired associates and were just getting off the ground when he signed papers to build the house."

He darts me another glance to check that I'm still with him, willing to let him set the pace. And honestly, I thought he would blurt out a name as soon as we were far enough from the others. Yes, I'm impatient. But I understand his wanting to start the story at the beginning on this day of remembrance. Besides, there is something about his voice—a personal, heart-felt shade—that, while not quite hypnotic, slows me down.

"He was dating your mother then," he continues. "The house was not yet finished when they got married, so the wedding was in Newport." He smiles at that. "It was an extravaganza. Tom had lots of friends and even more acquaintances, and he wanted them all there. Ellie didn't know them. But she did know me. I was her fallback. She kept coming to talk with me when the rush of faces got too much."

"Was the marriage doomed from way back then?" I ask.

"Oh, no." His eyes are sincere. "She was good with company after she got to know people. Once the house was done, they entertained often. Bless her, she always included me."

"You were her rock," I say, understanding it even more these last two days.

"Your Dad was too, in his way," Paul insists. "He was solid. Predictable. She knew what she had to do to please him."

"And when he started having affairs?" I ask. I understand Paul wanting to lead me gently toward my mother's infidelity. But I also want to think she was provoked.

He raises one foot to the stone wall, leans an elbow on his knee, and circles one set of fingers with the other as he slides me a look of regret. "Not good. She was hurt. Angry."

"Was he—" *shagging* is the word I almost say before filtering the thought, "having an affair with Elizabeth then?"

"No, I know there was some history, but Eleanor was okay

with Elizabeth. The two of them had an understanding. I'm not entirely sure what it was, but they were comfortable with each other. Living so close may have helped. Each could see what the other was doing, and Elizabeth had her own marriage to protect. Besides, your mother knew that Elizabeth didn't suffer fools lightly and would have no qualms telling Tom, even during a family event, when he was being a prick." His eyes widen. "Sorry."

His gallantry is sweet in an old-school way. "Don't apologize. He was one sometimes." Thinking of that, I wonder how far his prick-ness went. "Was he ever physically abusive to Mom?"

"Not to my knowledge. But he was demanding."

This I knew. I had seen it for myself—demanding husband, demanding father—which brought me back to why we are talking now, Paul and me, about who was unfaithful and with whom.

I refocus. "So my father had affairs."

"Yes."

"Mom knew."

"Yes."

"Did she have more than one herself?"

Removing his foot from the wall, Paul straightens. "No. There was only ever one. It was meaningful."

Something about his quiet intensity, the way his eyes hold mine, starts my heart thumping—and not because I'm about to learn what I've been waiting for ages to hear. I have a sudden horrendous thought that the answer won't be at all what I thought.

"How do you know?" I whisper, afraid to breathe.

Willows are notoriously messy. This one has dropped silver-backed leaves along the sea wall. Paul picks one up and rubs its slender length with thumb and forefinger.

"Paul?"

His eyes return to mine. His mouth—that kind mouth—

tips into a self-conscious smile. Despite the waves, the cry of a gull, even the distant drone of an airplane at this very minute, the silence is deafening.

I take a step back. But where to go that the truth won't follow?

"You?" I whisper.

He huffs a laugh, both awkward and apologetic. "Not what you expected?"

"You were my father's best friend. You were part of the family. It can't be you."

His smile is rueful. "Those things made me the perfect candidate. Your mother and I grew closer. And no one suspected."

"But . . . behind his back?"

"We didn't plan it, Mallory. It just happened. Things like that do."

"It meant nothing?"

In a flash, he is earnest. "It meant everything. I had loved your mother for a very long time."

"Did she love you?"

He considers his answer, picking his words with obvious care. "She did, though I think in a different way from me. I was a friend, not necessarily the love of her life."

But she was the love of his life. The implication is there, which raises a raft of questions relating to her life after the divorce.

I can't go there yet. I'm stuck on the basics, trying to imagine the idea of Paul Schuster and my mother together. On one hand, it's a no-brainer. Paul was often at our house. He liked being in the kitchen with Mom, while Dad wouldn't be caught dead there. Paul chipped in with domestic things that Dad considered beneath him. My mother and Paul were easier with each other than either of them was with Tom.

On the other hand, seeing my mother and Paul working

together in the kitchen is very different from picturing them in bed. Naked? Limbs linked? Passionate enough to produce . . . *me*?

I cover my face with a hand. There are too many emotions to sort through. For the sake of survival, I distance myself, as if their affair was between people I didn't know.

My hand slips away. "Was it one night only?"

He seems vulnerable, upset by my reaction. But what had he expected? Unbridled excitement? *Oh, biological dad, I love you so much?*

As he lowers himself to the sea wall, his eyes are older, begging me to understand. "I loved your mother. That started early on. But she loved your father. I had no idea why, but she did. Then he had one affair too many."

"So it was revenge?" I don't want to think this is how I was conceived. Actually, I'm wondering whether Paul is right at all. Oh, I'm sure he and Mom had an affair. He couldn't imagine that. But the idea that he was around our family all those years harboring this huge, intimate, marriage-blowing secret—*me*—is beyond the pale. Besides which, he loved my mother. He's said that twice now. If she didn't love him the same way, there might well have been other men Paul refuses to acknowledge.

"Not revenge," he says. "It was more a cry for help. She felt rejected by Tom, and came to me. She knew how I felt and, at that point in her life, she needed to know she was loved."

It sounds innocent enough. Still, Paul helping Eleanor meant cheating on his best friend, not to mention that he hasn't answered my question. I repeat it. "Was it just one time?"

He runs a hand down the back of his head and gazes at a far-off barge. "It went on for a bit."

"What's a bit?" my out-of-body person asks.

His eyes find mine. "A few months."

"And before and after? How do you know she didn't have others?"

"I told you that earlier. She said it, and I believed her."

"Why did it stop?"

"With us? Guilt."

Guilt? About cheating on Tom Aldiss? But what about me? If I am Paul's biological daughter, what about *me*? It'd be one thing if my biological father was the gardener or the electrician or the goddamned roofer. I'd expect any one of those to cut and run. But Paul? Mr. Kindness? Mr. Caring? Mr. Responsibility? I would have expected more of him. *And our talk on the front steps on Monday?* I specifically asked him about all this!

In a heartbeat, I'm furious about silence and evasion and secrets, about all that went on that I knew nothing of, all that might have helped me growing up under Tom Aldiss's critical eye. Angrily, I say, "You watched me all those years, thinking I was your daughter? Did you not know how miserable I was—how I felt there was something wrong with me that my father treated me the way he did?"

"I knew," he admits in defeat and, sensing my upset, pushes up from the wall. I'm not sure if he wants to protect me, belatedly, with his height—or use it to protect himself.

"And you did nothing?" I ask.

"What would you have had me do?"

"*Tell* me," I say, like it's the most obvious thing in the world.

Paul is suddenly as intense as I am. "And put a wedge between you and your sisters? And risk you resenting your mother—or blurting the truth to Tom at some point, which might have caused him to treat you worse or even disown you?"

"Or break up the law firm?" I add, because I'm not ready

to see him as an icon of altruism. There were selfish reasons for what he—what *they* did. "Didn't you feel like a fraud?"

"Every blessed day," he says with vehemence. "But what would you have *had me do,* Mallory? *What?*"

I don't know. Still, my anger remains. I am angry at the situation, at all those lost years, maybe even at the awkwardness I feel now, which I never before felt with Paul. I can't process the fact that he is my biological father—am so not in control of my feelings that I resent him for that, too.

"What if you aren't?" I ask. I know I sound spiteful, even infantile, but that's what anger does. When he looks confused, I say, "What if you aren't my father after all? What if Tom was the only one with my mother during the time she conceived?"

"They were going through a rough patch for months before and after. They didn't have sex."

"She said."

"I'll happily take a DNA test."

I think of that scrap of gauze. It would tell me if Tom and I match but, if not, it wouldn't tell me who does. "What if she *was* with someone other than you?"

"DNA test," he repeats.

"Why did she never tell me?" I ask. "She divorced Dad. She could have told me then. Did you ask her not to?"

"Absolutely not. I wanted her to tell you. I begged her—" He stops short.

"Then why *didn't* she?" I cry with a resurgence of the emotions I had felt so often since my mother's death. She didn't know she would die so young. But I was a grown-up. I had a baby of my own. I deserved to know the truth. "Didn't she trust me?"

"It was Tom she didn't trust," Paul says. "She didn't know what he would do if word got back to him." He pauses, pained. "How can I say things like this today?"

"How can you not?" I fire back. "He's gone. *She's* gone. We are not."

He considers that. "True. And you're right to be upset with Eleanor, but you have to understand. She worried he would destroy me, or destroy you. Tom could be vindictive. There was this lawyer—"

"Newcombe," I say, remembering the name well. I remember my father's vitriolic comments at dinner, when he got so caught up in ranting to Mom that he forgot we girls were there. "He accused Tom of accepting a bribe in exchange for giving a defendant a light sentence."

"Tom got him disbarred."

"Rightly so?" I ask. I can't say that I always wondered. My father's venom was so lethal that I had to believe his version.

Paul releases a small breath. "I can't say."

"Won't say."

He fixes me with a look of gentle chiding. "It's not my place, Mallory. Tom isn't here to defend himself. I just ask that you understand why your mother did what she did."

Or didn't do what she didn't do, I think and suddenly picture Chrissie's guilty face. These were all sins of omission. And Paul? I'm not yet ready to rationalize his fault.

"How do I know you don't just want this to be true? You never had kids of your own, so maybe you want to think I'm it?" Before he can say *DNA test* again, I rush on. I'm being irrational. But the whole *situation* feels irrational. "How do I know you aren't just the last man standing?"

His words are low but firm. "Because I know things another person wouldn't know. I saw things another person wouldn't see."

"Like?"

"A birthmark."

My heart stops. My mother's birthmark—*Joy's* birthmark—both hidden where only someone with intimate knowledge of a person's body would ever see. I stare at him, but he doesn't blink. Either he is an expert liar who is repeating something my father told him—though why the impersonal Tom Aldiss would tell anyone something as personal as that is beyond me—or he has seen that birthmark himself. Since I have never before had cause to think Paul Schuster a liar, and since there is no other way he would have seen it, I have to accept that he and my mother had an affair. And if I accept that, I realize with a start, I have no reason to doubt the outcome.

Overwhelmed, I back away.

"Mallory."

I hold up a hand, warding off any paternal words as I struggle to accept. There's still the matter of where he's been all my life, why he didn't come forward either after I moved to New York or after Mom died. There's still the matter of where he was when my daughter—*his* granddaughter—was born. Tom wasn't around. Paul might have been.

I feel bitter about it all, confused by a world that apparently considers the whole truth and nothing but to be optional. Mostly, I feel swamped. Too much is shifting underfoot—my relationship with my sisters, my faith in my best friend, my father's death. And yes, I'll always think of Tom Aldiss as my father. But the rest? I've lost control of things I thought I knew.

Paul says my name again. Ignoring it, I turn and run. I have no destination. All I know is that I'm grateful Joy isn't here, grateful that the heels Margo bought me are low, grateful that the sea wall path takes me away from where I've just been.

After following it along a wide arc, I see the parking lot ahead. The hearse is gone, for which I'm grateful as well. I see Chrissie's CR-V, Lina's Civic, and Paul's Lexus. I see the Volvo that says Anne is still here, and a dirty truck with the cemetery logo on the side and a wheelbarrow in the back.

I also see Jack's Tahoe. Fortunately, it is unlocked, and while it's hot inside, I don't care. Pulling out my phone, I text him.

I'm in your truck. Can we go?

Chapter 26

Jack trots up to the truck minutes later. His face is damp with sweat, and his frown lines are pronounced. Eyeing me with worry, he tosses his blazer in back, starts the engine, and turns on the AC full force. Then he reaches an arm sideways and cups my head in his palm. There is a calm in the gesture that belies whatever turmoil those frown lines betray.

He does not ask who my biological father is. Does not ask about Tom or Elizabeth. Does not ask if I want to let Chrissie know I'm leaving or if I need to call Joy. All he asks is, "Where to?"

"I don't know," I whisper, feeling lost, but I've grabbed his hand and am holding on for dear life. Jack is a rock in my world of shifting sands. "Just drive."

He heads out of the lot. "Home or away?"

"Away."

He turns left. We pass the florist with purple petunias cascading from hooks on the porch, pass the pharmacy, pass a dozen homes with wood siding painted each its own shade of gray. I see the strip mall in the distance, the one with the Urgent Care where I had first seen Dad last Friday, but before that particular memory can sink in, I spot something else.

The Hideaway, once known as Tuck'er Inn, nearly hidden under its prim canopy of ancient maples and oaks.

"Here," I say, and a swarm of forbidden thoughts take root.

Jack eyes me in alarm when I wave him urgently toward the small parking lot. No doubt thinking I'm about to be sick, he swerves into the space nearest the road. But I wave again, this time toward the office.

Shooting me concerned looks every few seconds, he backs up and drives closer. By the time he has parked, his alarm has lowered to wariness.

I hold his gaze. "Take a room."

"A room," he repeats with a speculative emphasis on the *m,* because something in my eyes has tipped him off.

"A cottage." My phone dings; I ignore it. "The sign says there are vacancies."

"I see that," he says, "but we just buried your father—"

"—who lied to me all these years," I say, and the dam bursts, "who was married to my mother, who lied to me all these years, who was best friends with a man who lied to me all these years—and speaking of best friends, I have one of those, who, thank you very much, has *also* been living a lie. Call *me* a liar for sneaking around with you when we were kids, but not a single person was hurt by what we did. Same with the way I conceived Joy, not a single one of them was hurt, and I actually did consider that. I nearly didn't do it because I was worried one of my parents would be hurt, and when I decided to go ahead, I told them exactly what I was doing and why. Did they return the favor? No. Did they tell me what they had done and why? *No.*" I'm breathing hard. "So yes, I want a room—and don't tell me it's inappropriate right after a funeral. I want to do what *I* want to do for one solid hour, because all these years, no one has thought of *me,* and it's about *time* I'm a priority. I don't want to think of another person." I stop short. "Well. Except you. Unless you can't." We both know I'm not talking about his getting back to work.

I don't tack on the last as a deliberate distraction, but it does the job. He snickers and says in a voice deep enough to have come from the part of his body that we'll need, "Are you kidding? With you?" My phone dings again. "Want to check that?"

"No." I switch it to mute. "Please? A room?"

He doesn't need to be asked again. In a heartbeat, he is out of the Tahoe, striding toward the inn's office and disappearing inside. I don't agonize while he is gone, don't have a second thought. Nor do I look at my phone. Joy is with Margo and is fine. Chrissie is with Lina and is not fine, but deservedly so. Same with Paul, who is likely alone. Neither of them was concerned about me all those years; I don't need to be concerned about them now.

Call me disrespectful or perverse. Call me *selfish*. But I've earned this.

Jack reappears with a wooden key fob in hand. Seconds later, he is backing out of the space and jouncing us along a dirt path behind the office. The cottages there are named after birds, as in The Piper, The Robin, and The Wren. Ours is The Swan, which I will later think of as metaphorical but now simply take in.

Leaving the truck from either side, we meet halfway to the door. He unlocks it, sticks in his head and sniffs, then moves aside to let me enter first. He's right; it smells clean enough. The light is dim, but dim works. I'm vaguely aware of blue and white, of a double bed, a nightstand, an armchair and a dresser, not to mention air that hasn't moved in days, but my urgency outstrips it all.

When I reach for the zipper at the back of my dress, Jack's arms circle me, hands displacing mine at the tab. Before he pulls, though, he pauses.

"Are you sure?" he asks, and for a split second, the rest of the world is there.

But I don't want the rest of the world right now. I don't want any *part* of the rest of the world right now. For the first time in thirteen years, I don't even want to think of my daughter, though I can't quite say that aloud.

Rather than speak, I rub the creases between his eyes with the pad of my thumb, run that thumb down his blade of a nose, then press my face to the spot on his neck just under the scruff of his beard. His skin is musky and damp. Two seconds, and I'm lost in it, but only until my zipper rasps and I feel a freedom on my back where there wasn't seconds before. Drawing away, I reach for his belt. My fingers have barely begun to fiddle with its buckle, when he pushes them aside.

Practiced in unbuckling, he doesn't have to look. His eyes hold mine, and I swear they've gone molten. Molten should be dangerous where footing is concerned, but Jack is my safe place. The danger for me is back at the cemetery, back at the house, back at wherever Paul Schuster has lived all these years during which he didn't bother to identify himself as my father. Jack Sabathian may have changed in the twenty years I've been away, but the heart of him has not. Lifting a hand, I touch his mouth, then the bristle of mustache above it.

"Do you need help?" he whispers and shoots a heated glance at my dress.

With deliberate motions, I kick my shoes aside and shrug the dress off. Bending at the waist, I free my hair, which Margo had neatly knotted that morning, but with which the humidity at the cemetery has wreaked havoc anyway. I remove pins and an elastic, then, straightening, toss my hair back. I'm reaching for the clasp of my bra when I realize that, although Jack's belt hangs undone, his hands are still.

"Do you have a problem?" I ask. I've never used this particular tone with him during this particular activity, but I'm still in the grip of defiance. And this is Jack, who knows defiance like a second skin.

Smirking, he says in a husky voice, "Yeah, I do," and drops his hands to his sides. "You are too fucking beautiful. Take off the rest."

Words and voice—both are a turn-on. Simmering inside, I remove the bra and step out of the panties, dropping both on the chair with my dress. When I turn back to him, his eyes are on my naked body. For a minute, I don't move—and not out of shyness. Shyness was when we first made love, when I was grateful for the night, which hid the fact that my right breast was fractionally smaller than my left and that I had nicked the notch at the top of my thighs in an attempt to remove the hair there. Shyness was when I was grateful for a moonless night that hid the details of *his* body, which I desperately wanted to see but didn't dare, and, besides, we were rushing to do "it" before we were caught.

Last Sunday night, I had wanted to lose myself in his body and forget the rest of the world, but my need here is different. This need is for certainty, and Jack offers that. This need is for defiance, and what we're doing in this cottage offers that. This need is to feel my own power as an antidote to being powerless in so much else.

Standing before him, I watch his gray eyes smolder and his arousal thicken behind the placket of his fly. He wants to touch me but is controlling himself, and something about that control snaps mine. Closing the little distance between us, I go at his clothes, tangling with his hands when they go at my breasts.

"Jack," I breathe roughly, "help me."

"You're doing a fine job all by yourself," he rasps but takes pity on me with the last of his clothes. The instant his pants are off, he takes my thighs from behind, lifts me so that I straddle his hips, and, telling me to hold on, tosses the duvet away with a single hand and takes me down to the sheets.

In the next breath, he is inside me and then, with only the slightest shift of his hips, deeper still.

We both cry out at the sense of completion before we've even begun to move. And then we do. I may be the defiant one, but Jack is incapable of passivity. He is over me, under me, behind me, driving me higher, as I do him. I'm not sure when I lose control of the situation—whether it is with the first orgasm or the second. But, somewhere along the way, my defiance burns up, leaving only desperate desire in its place. And then, after a final, screaming climax, it, too, is spent.

Panting, we collapse on the sheets and lie side by side on our backs with our fingers laced between us. As reality returns, I grow aware of the warmth of the room, the scent of sweat and sex, the richness of the afternoon light that slips through a gap in the drapes.

"This was for all the times we didn't dare come here when we were kids," I say but in a whisper that is more nostalgic than rebellious.

"This wasn't about that, and you know it."

Yes. I do know it. It was about defying my present-day life by focusing in on the one thing that has always rung true. Rolling onto him, I settle my legs between his. He is flaccid at last, and though I know that his ability to rebound is epic, I can't resist this last press, body to body. I chafe his scruffy jaw with my knuckles. "Thank you."

"My pleasure," he says with a smug look on his handsome, flushed face.

"Do you feel used?" I ask.

"I feel loved."

"But I used you."

His eyes sharpen, and smugness is gone. "We use the people we love, like when we're hurting and angry and there's no one else we can sound off to. And if we're too young to realize why we're doing what we are and too dumb to understand the consequences and too stubborn to apologize, we end up not talking for twenty years, and during that time, that whole time, we're alone."

I swallow. He's right about this, too. But the direction in which the conversation is headed isn't one I'm able to face in the midst of the rest. So, I close his lips with my hand and whisper, "Not yet, Jack." The red readout of the nightstand digital says it is two. "My hour is up."

"Take another."

"I can't. There's too much . . . too much . . ." My voice wobbles. I take a deep breath to steady it, but the breath wobbles, too. There's too much with Paul, with Chrissie, with my father and my sisters, and, yes, with Jack. That quickly it all rushes back, like an eavesdropper tumbling through a door that has unexpectedly opened.

Jack's face blurs, and, to my horror, I roll away to cry.

Immediately, he sits and scoops me close. My tears come even faster then, because he *is* my safety net, and I've fallen a huge distance. How calm and organized my life was six days ago, how in control. And now?

Safety nets don't ask questions or murmur empty platitudes. Safety nets don't say anything at all. They're simply there, holding you until you exhaust yourself. Then, maybe they wipe at your tears with their fingers—or Jack, with the heel of his hands. And still they say nothing until you, and only you, speak first.

A safety net doesn't need apologies, still I feel the need to say, "I'm sorry. That was a poor show of defiance."

"Are you kidding?" this safety net asks and turns back into smart-mouthed Jack. "Look where we are. Look what we're doing. Look what we're wearing."

"Or not," I say in a meek quip. "But crying?"

"Anne sobbed through the funeral. You did not. This is your time."

I give him a *yeah, right* look, which may or may not have

registered, since my eyes are still wet, so I say, "Crying for Tom? I'd like to take credit for that, but it's so much more." Hearing the words, I stop, look at Jack, see his curiosity. I owe him.

"It's Paul," I say very quietly.

He frowns. "Paul."

"My father."

"Paul?" His brows rise. *"Paul?"* He makes a face of utter disbelief. *"That* Paul?"

I feel an unexpected spark of protectiveness. "What's wrong with it being him?"

"Uh, nothing—nothing," Jack stammers, looking as muddled as I must have back at the cemetery with Paul. "It's just—*how?*"

I tell the story quickly, sharing as much as I'm able, because, while Paul's revelation isn't as strange the second time around, it remains upending. I barely make it through the basics before the bottom line returns. Paul is only the final straw in a muddled haystack. "I come back for a week, and my life is turned upside down!"

"Or right side up," Jack says.

While on mute, my phone has been busy. There are texts from Joy, from Chrissie, from Margo. There are three VMs from New York, one each from my Sotheby's broker, my stylist for Saturday's shoot, and the hair salon reminding me that I have an appointment for a cut next Tuesday.

I read Joy's texts before I'm even dressed. She says she's on the beach with her cousins and when will I be there? *On my way,* I text back, and quickly add *Twenty minutes,* to which she immediately replies, *Bring Jack. He'll die at who I'm with,* to which I reply, *Who are you with?* to which she simply sends an angel emoji.

I read the texts from Chrissie while I'm in the bathroom, knowing I'll feel like a fool if I start crying again. I don't.

But I ache. *I'm sorry sorry sorry,* she writes, *you are the one person I never ever wanted to hurt.* In a follow-up sent seconds after the first, she writes *I can't bear to lose both a sister and a friend. If we can't be sisters, can we be friends?* And a third text nearly on top of the second, *I love you, Mal.*

Not knowing what to say, I say nothing.

We're back in the Tahoe when I open Margo's texts. The first reads, *You OK? I'm worried.* The second reads, *Anne told Bill. He wants wedding, she says no.* And the third, *Dan wants to stay to Sunday. Should we call Watch Hill or is crowded OK?*

Jack squeezes my thigh, which his hand has not left since we both buckled in. "Anything good?"

I sigh. What the hell. My sister hates me anyway. And Jack doesn't gossip. "Anne is pregnant. Only you don't know that. She just told Bill, who wants to get married, and she's resisting."

"Why?" he asks halfway between curiosity and disbelief.

"Maybe," I reply with no small amount of guilt, "because we thought Bill was a loser—well, until we got to know him. Face it. His past isn't stellar."

"Nor is mine."

"You were never in prison. And okay, he got cleaned up and is on the other side of the bars, but there are those tattoos—and okay, I'm fine with them, too, but maybe Anne isn't. Maybe she worries about the people he's with all day long. Maybe she thinks Mom would be turning over in her grave." With a jarring realization, I add a bleak, "Or Dad."

Jack squeezes my hand to grant the sympathy of that. Despite what he knows now of Paul, he thinks the way I do. Tom Aldiss raised me. He is Dad.

But the subject is Anne. "Maybe she's afraid of marriage," he offers.

I'm startled. "Why?"

"Same reason as you."

Afraid of marriage? Me? Who has managed a good job, a great condo, and single motherhood without a husband, thank you? I remember the discussion we had, Jack and me, about power and control. I don't want to think Jack is right.

"I'm not afraid. Uh-uh. Oh, no. Don't turn this around on me, Jack. I told you why I haven't married, and it has everything to do with not finding the right guy. That's not scared; it's smart. As for Anne, Bill is the right guy. He loves her."

"I love you," Jack says mildly, just part of the argument.

"And I love you, but that is for another discussion." Determined, I change the subject. "The immediate issue is Margo's family. They're staying through the week. She's looking for vacancies in Watch Hill. Any suggestions?" He wouldn't know about vacancies, but he would know about the best places to stay. Margo wouldn't step foot inside a place like The Swan. The thought makes me smile.

"What's wrong with the house?" he asks.

"Nothing, but you saw the size of the boys. Both of them are approaching six feet, and the guest room bed is a very old double. All those legs?" I give a doubting sputter.

"That's a nice problem to have," Jack says with something akin to envy. He might have liked a brother, might have liked a big family having to crowd into a house. "A first-world problem. Can't they squeeze in for a few nights?"

"Not Margo's boys."

"So use my house."

"For Margo's boys?" I ask in surprise. Jack doesn't know them, barely knows Margo after all this time. He doesn't owe her any favors.

But, of course, he would be doing the favor for me. What he says next, though, turns that around.

"For you and Joy," he says, like it's a no-brainer, like I should have been thinking this myself. "You and Joy stay with me. Then Margo and her family can be with Anne." When I stare at him in alarm, he shrugs. "I have room."

"You have dreams."

"Those, too, but think about it, Mal. Joy would love it. She kept Guy with her the whole time she was at the clinic. He's dying to sleep with her."

"He told you that?"

"Very clearly."

"*I'm* not sleeping with Guy."

The look he gives me now says that I'm daft. "Why would you? Guy sleeps with Joy, you sleep with me."

"Uh-huh. With Joy in the next room?"

"Down the hall."

"Like we were quiet just now?"

"That's just it," he says with a crooked grin and a whisper of conspiratorial excitement. "Think of the fun we'd have trying not to scream. Is that a turn-on, or what?" He is incorrigible.

I clear my throat. "I'm not ready for her to see that."

"See what?" he asks, all innocence as he turns at the tri-road onto the one for Bay Bluff. "She doesn't have to *watch* us."

"You know what I mean, Jack. She's only thirteen."

"Which is old enough to know what happens between a man and a woman."

"It's a different thing when the woman is your mother and she is in bed with a man in the next room."

"Down the hall."

"Seriously, Jack."

"Seriously, Mal."

There's so much more to this, but I'm distracted by his mockery. When it is lighthearted, as his is now, it is fun. We know each other so well that it works.

"Will you consider it at least?" he asks.

"When?" I ask in frustration, because there *is* so much more to it that I need to think. Our staying with Jack goes beyond who sleeps in what room. It makes a statement not only to Joy, but to Margo and Anne. I have to weigh the pros and cons. "Margo needs an answer."

"No sweat," says Jack. "You have three minutes."

We arrive back at the house looking unsuspiciously messed thanks to the breeze that sweeps us up the minute we leave the Tahoe. Given that there are no strange cars in the drive, meaning mourners who might be inside, my first thought is to change out of this godawful funeral dress and into beach clothes. Actually, that's my second thought. My first is seeing what Joy is up to. On the beach? With her cousins and . . . someone else?

Crossing to the edge of the drive, I take off my shoes at the spot where grass begins, continue barefoot to the top of the beach stairs, and start down. Joy and her cousins are on towels closer to Jack's house than ours. I'm puzzled by that until I see who she's with.

"Fuck," I hear as Jack sees the same thing. Passing me on the stairs, he trots the rest of the way down and takes the sand in long strides.

Joy and the boys, all wearing sunglasses, are sprawled on beach towels in states of careless relaxation. When my daughter spots us, she scrambles to her feet. To her credit, a coil of leash is thick around her wrist, and her hand is on Guy's sandy head, letting him know he is safe.

Now she wants Jack to know. Smiling proudly, she holds up her wrist.

He slows, which actually makes me more nervous. The fact that he doesn't want his pit bull alarmed by even *him* speaks to the danger of the beast. Not that wilted-ear, wrinkle-skinned, woe-eyed Guy looks terribly dangerous. He actually looks comfortable with Joy and content in the afternoon sun.

"How did he get here?" Jack asks. His anger is muted, but it is anger.

Joy loses the smile. "I brought him. He was whining. He had to pee."

"He's trained to hold it in."

"But he's been stuck inside since, what, nine o'clock this morning?"

"So you let him out? *Joy.*"

"Well, the back door was unlocked," she argues and holds up her free hand in a what-do-you-expect gesture. "I thought for sure it'd be locked and figured you'd have a key hidden somewhere, only I couldn't find it. Guy knew I was there and started to bark, so I tried the door just in case, and, just like that, it opened."

"Just like that," Jack repeats.

I say nothing. He is trying to figure how to handle her. I want to see how it plays out.

"Should I not have?" Joy asks. Her eyes are hidden by the sunglasses, but her voice is innocence personified. "Should I have left him alone and uncomfortable?"

"He didn't have to pee."

"He peed the instant I let him out. Has he never had an accident while you've been away? Never? *Ever?*"

Jack scowls.

"So why should he suffer?" Joy goes on. "He knows me. He knows I won't hurt him. He wanted to be down here with me, and with Teddy and Jeff, and I know how to introduce him to new people."

"She was careful," Jeff says. At sixteen, he has the voice and body of a man.

"We took it slow," says his fourteen-year-old brother, not quite as mannish but almost.

Joy preens under their praise. But she quickly turns back to Jack. "Don't be angry," she pleads. "I understand that you don't want him to attack a stranger, though I honestly don't think Teddy and Jeff would sue you, since we're all friends. But, like, I wouldn't have let Guy attack them. I put the leash on him before I let him out, and it hasn't come off once, and anyway, I didn't need to worry at all, because you have done *the* best job training him. If my cousins *ever* had a doubt about owning a pit bull, they don't anymore." Her head tips toward Jeff. "Am I right?"

"Totally," says Jeff.

"Teddy?"

"Mom might not agree, but I do."

Grinning, she faces Jack again.

I'm thinking that my daughter has manipulated him into a corner, when he turns to me in frustration. "Don't you have anything to say?"

"No," I reply with a smile. I'm about to say something like, *You handled that well,* which wouldn't have been the smartest thing for me to do, when, in a perfectly-timed distraction, my phone rings.

Paul Schuster, says the screen, and something tightens in the pit of my stomach. Where unfinished business is concerned, Paul is right up there. I need to tell my sisters about him. I need to tell Joy.

But not now. Until I come to terms myself with who he is—with who *I* am—Paul is off-limits to the others.

I hold up a palm to my daughter, warning her to respect Jack. Then I point to the phone and head away from the group on the sand.

Chapter 27

Slowed by indecision, I stare at the screen as I walk through the sand toward the stairs. I'm certainly calmer than I was at the cemetery, but Paul's confession remains hard to grasp. Having made tough decisions about my own child, I understand that he did what he thought was right. And then there's the matter of a co-parent. I had the advantage of making decisions myself; Paul did not. My mother had a say. I could be angry at her, but she is dead. And Dad is dead. And here we are, just Paul and me.

I don't know what my relationship with him is supposed to be. Don't know where it is headed. Don't even know what *name* to use when I think of him.

After a last few seconds of hesitancy, I click in with a simple, "Hey."

Silence greets me, and for a split second, I wonder if I'm too late. But no, he hasn't hung up. I can sense him on the line.

Finally, tentatively, he says, "Are you all right?"

Am I all right? Of *course,* I'm not alright. I have a slew of challenges lying in wait.

But that's the big picture. The small one—the one involving just Paul and me—has changed in this very instant. It feels more defined now that we're on the phone, as if the hardest thing was reconnecting after I walked away. The fact that he has called me, rather than the other way around, feels like caring. It feels like a cushion that will make things a little more comfortable as we work out what's to come.

"I'm fine," I say with a sigh. Having reached the beach stairs, I lean against the wood rail. Paul is, after all, the answer to a question that has haunted me for so long. Not the answer I expected. Still, an answer. "I just needed a little time." I gulp in a breath. "About the things I said—"

"I understand your shock," he interrupts. "I understand your disappointment, even your anger." His voice gentles. "But I don't want to lose you, Mallory. I've waited a long time to tell you all this."

I swallow and say, "Yes." I don't say, *You might have told me sooner,* because that is water over the dam. A peacemaker doesn't rehash the past but tries to move on.

It strikes me that if all of what Paul has said is true with regard to his relationship with both my mother and my father, he may be a peacemaker as well. That doesn't forgive him the deception, simply softens it.

"You'll have questions about your mother and me."

I do. But face-to-face seems better than the phone. "Where are you?"

"Look up."

There he is, standing on the bluff a short distance from the stairs. His suit jacket is gone, sleeves rolled in a way that suggests he is ready to work on what exists between us. And with that thought, I'm intimidated all over again. Yes, intimidated. I may not have identified it as such at the cemetery, but this man played a major role in creating me, which is an intimidating idea in and of itself. Add the fact that I can't seem to break the lock of our eyes, and I definitely feel . . . lesser.

I need moral support. And why not Jack? He has questions for this man, too. If Paul is willing to answer them, if he trusts me enough to trust Jack and give us answers we both need, he will have passed a test of sorts.

"Be right up," I say, but the instant I break the phone connection with him, I head back across the sand, open Margo's text, and reply, *You all take the house. Joy and I will stay at Jack's.*

The man himself is still talking with the three on the sand, but he is on his haunches now, scrubbing his dog's chest. When he glances my way, I wave him over. He says something to Joy before leaving, and since Guy is still wrapped around her wrist, I assume he has okayed it. By way of confirmation, she sends me a thumbs-up.

Jack reaches me with his head vaguely cocked. I can't see his eyes through his sunglasses, but the crease between them is shallow. He is curious is all.

"Paul's up there on the bluff," I say with the tiniest hitch of my head behind and up. "Let's ask him about Elizabeth."

He glances at Paul, then returns to me with a disbelieving snicker. "Now? Don't you want to talk about the other?"

"I need time to take it in. This will buy me a little. Please, Jack? He owes me this." My phone dings. It's Margo.

That's a statement, she texts. *Where are you?*

Right outside, I type back. *Talking with Paul. But don't book rooms.*

As soon as I send off the text, I show the screen to Jack. He has to lift his glasses to read it, and his eyes quickly brighten. "Yes?"

Nodding, I pocket the phone, slip my fingers through his, and draw him along with me. Paul meets us at the top of the stairs. He studies first Jack, then me.

"I told him," I say quietly. There's no need to elaborate. The only subject between us, really, is the fact of who Paul is. "Jack is the only one who knew my doubts all these years."

"You're that close?" Paul asks, his gaze drifting between us again.

I can't read his expression—don't know if he approves or disapproves and why either should matter. Feeling a thread of my earlier pique, I raise my chin in defiance, but the effect is diluted when the sea breeze whips my hair across my mouth. Gathering it in my free hand, I hold it to my neck.

Before I can speak, Jack says in a typically male, typically Jack declaration, "We're that close. We share everything." In a gesture of directness, he shifts his sunglasses to the top of his head.

"Including things about Elizabeth," I add, lest Paul think I'm just along for the ride. Everything about that night concerns me, too. If Jack's focus is his mother, mine is Tom. With him gone, it's now about memory. I want to correct whatever parts of that may be wrong. "There's too much we don't know. You handled her business affairs. You have answers we need."

Paul looks like he's about to object. I'm sure he'd rather be talking with me alone, perhaps explaining himself more or sharing what he wants our future to be. Hell, he may be feeling like my asking him about Elizabeth at this particular time is emotional extortion. But he does owe me.

Jack gets it going. "We know my mother's business was on the verge of collapse. We know she had a falling out with her brother. Tom rambled about a man named Doe, likely Ronald Doe, the lawyer in Albany who handled her family trust. Doe is dead, or I'd be asking him these questions. My mother was the executor of the estate. I've searched her files for information connecting these things, but there's nothing."

"Tom talked about robbing Peter to pay Paul," I say. "You're the Paul. The Peter is Elizabeth's brother, but he won't talk with Jack. Nor will anyone else in the family."

"Except his granddaughter," Jack puts in. "She's here in town for the summer. You've probably seen her? Looks like my mother?"

Paul is bemused. "The blonde at the funeral today? I assumed it was coincidence."

"No. She's working at Anne's for the summer," Jack says and drops the heavy part. "Her college major was investigative journalism."

His brows knit. "Doing research? For a book, an article, an *indictment*?"

"We don't know. But she can't have gotten far if she hasn't talked with you. You're the one with the answers."

Paul turns to me. "Is this why you called Sunday?"

I feel a moment's guilt for having an ulterior motive, but the bigger picture has taken over. This isn't about my parenthood. It's about a broader set of events that affect us all.

"When we realized you were the Paul in 'robbing Peter to pay Paul,' yes, I called." But I soften as I remember that call. "Hearing your voice brought back other things. Good things. You were always a comfortable part of our family. And you were always nice to my mom."

A corner of his mouth quirks at the compliment.

Pressing the advantage, I say, "Elizabeth's business meant everything to her. If she knew it was failing, what did she do?"

I'm not sure if there is an expiration date for attorney-client privilege. But Paul has to be realizing that with Dad now dead, Mom and Elizabeth both gone, and Jack and I being next of kin, secrecy is overkill.

Glancing around, he spots the long bench at the spot where the Sabathian drive forks from the circle. It is half-hidden by rangy junipers whose blue-green hue camouflages the weathered wood. A gnarled oak rises behind, offering shade.

Heading there, he waves us along, but when we reach it, he doesn't sit. Nor does Jack. I do. Crossing my legs, I tuck my still-blowing hair under the shoulder of my black dress. Then I sit back in silent expectation.

After a minute, Paul cedes. "There was money taken—borrowed," he adds with air quotes and eyes Jack, "from her family estate."

"Did you advise that?" he asks.

"No. It was done before I learned of it. Your mother wasn't proud of the company's decline. She was hoping money from the estate would shore it up and that she could repay it with no one the wiser." He stops short.

Jack finishes. "Only it didn't pick up."

"No." Paul's voice gentles. This is Jack's mother he's talking about, and Paul Schuster is nothing if not kind. "She truly did think of what she borrowed as a loan, but when the business continued to tank, she was in trouble."

"And you suggested . . . what?" Jack asks in annoyance.

It is less that I feel a sudden loyalty to Paul, than that using him as a scapegoat just isn't fair. Reaching out, I grab Jack's fingers again, hoping to calm him.

Paul says, "She was in the process of considering various options, when the lawyer for the estate did an accounting."

"Ronald Doe," Jack says.

"Yes. He noticed the missing money and asked your mother about it. As executor of the estate, she could explain it away, but the money was still gone. She was terrified that if Doe looked too deeply, she would be charged with embezzlement, in which case she might lose everything. She and I talked about downsizing the company, selling it, even declaring bankruptcy." He sighs. "Well, I talked about it. She listened, but she kept insisting that if she hung in a little longer, things would improve." He slips me a look of regret. "When things kept sliding, there was only one person she trusted enough to go to."

"Tom," I say. The conversation with my sisters is fresh in my mind. We were speculating, but, setting my own resentment aside, I don't want our guesses to be true.

Paul says a quiet, "Yes."

"What did he do?"

Glancing back, he looks at our house. He is thinking that we just buried Tom and that he doesn't want to be saying this. I'm thinking, for the second time in as many hours, that he can't stop now.

When he turns back to me, he is resigned. "He taught her how she could cover up what she'd done."

"How *she* could," Jack says.

"Yes, *she,*" Paul insists. "Tom wouldn't do it himself."

"Because he didn't want to screw up his chance of a judgeship?"

"Because he had principles. Say what you want about his autocratic approach to life or his temper, but he didn't break the law."

"But he knew how to do it."

The two are glaring at each other, Jack fighting for Team Elizabeth, Paul for Team Tom. Jack is the taller, more brooding and imposing of the two. But Paul has age and experience, which give him a certain gravity.

"Actually, he didn't know himself, not this specific situation. But another of our partners did."

That was one of the possibilities my sisters and I raised. Easier to swallow, perhaps.

"Oh, Tom was crafty." Paul snorts, half in admiration, half disdain. "He asked so many detailed questions—all in the hypothetical, mind you—that the other fellow thought he was researching a novel, like the next John Grisham. The partner asked me about it, which is how I found out. Tom never discussed it with me himself."

"Which makes it hearsay," Jack argues and, pulling his hand from mine, cocks both of his on his hips.

"True," Paul says.

"Did you ever ask him about it?"

"No. I didn't want to know. Tom and your mother had a strange relationship. There was a tie between them that

I never understood." He eyes me. "I asked Eleanor about it once, but she dismissed it so quickly I never asked again."

I could guess at her reasons and was just as glad. Infidelity, romantic competition, bisexuality—any one of these might muddy the waters of her relationship with Paul. As the product of that relationship, I wanted to keep it simple.

"I do know," Paul went on, "that when the company continued to flounder, she went back to the trust. Since she now knew how to fudge the numbers, and since she hoped that a larger infusion would do the trick, she took more—basically drained the estate's reserve."

"And you know this how?" Jack asks, still in attack mode.

Paul answers him, glare for glare. "Tom told me in the months after the accident."

"Accident," Jack mocks.

"Accident," Paul states and shifts back to me. "He agonized, Mallory. He truly didn't know what happened that night. She was there one minute and gone the next. He did not hit her, and he sure as hell didn't shoot her. Whether she jumped or fell, he just didn't know."

"But why were they out there that night at all?" I ask, reliving the frustration we all felt at the time. "The ocean was churned up—"

"Not when they left. Tom was firm about that, and the forensic report supports it. It was foggy, but nothing that his chart-plotter couldn't beat. The squalls were a ways off." He broadens his gaze to include Jack. "She begged him to take her out. She needed his ear, needed his sympathy, his advice."

"Did he give it?" I ask.

"He told her he didn't know what to say."

Jack's voice rises. "Did he advise her to kill herself?"

"Pu-leeze."

"Or disappear?"

A chuffing sound is Paul's response.

"How do you know?" Jack demands. His eyes are granite

hard. This is the man I fled from twenty years ago. I hadn't known how to handle him.

Paul seems to. In the face of anger, his composure grows. "Because I know Tom," he says levelly. "I also know how difficult the last few years were for him. His mind wandered. I'd be sitting with him, and without warning he'd be back in time. Often it was to that night, and he was asking me what she'd been thinking. He kept saying there had to be another way, that nothing could be so bad to make her disappear like that. I'm not sure he knew what he was saying or remembered saying it after he had—but beneath it all, there was a method to his madness. I don't think his illness allowed him to lie."

Jack rolls his eyes. "Dementia guarantees the whole truth and nothing but the truth?"

"Even before dementia. He was law-abiding."

"So the cops got the whole truth? Did he tell them any of what led up to that night?"

Losing a tad of his composure, Paul lashes out, "Would you have wanted him to tell the police that she stole from her family's estate and then covered it up? Or that she planned her disappearance so the problem would go away? Because he did think that. For years, he held onto that hope. But the fact is, Jack, he didn't know. He didn't know the whole truth."

Jack wraps a hand around the back of his neck and says nothing. Wanting to bring him back, I grab onto the edge of his pants pocket and give a little tug, but he seems unaware.

"Look at it this way," Paul argues. "Everything I've told you makes sense. When it came to money, the company was a sieve. There's no hearsay about that. I saw the figures first-hand. Then your uncle suffered a personal crisis, and the estate was unable to help. Elizabeth told me this. She was horrified. She couldn't sell the company. There were no buyers. So she had to watch her brother lose his business, his home, his wife and kids. He became a broken man, and she blamed herself."

"And therefore committed suicide?" Jack asks. He and I have discussed this. We all did, back when it happened, albeit bewildered, since we lacked this background information. I tug at his pocket to remind him of earlier conversations we've had on this vein, but he is lost in the thick of it.

"I don't know," Paul says. "Tom didn't know."

Jack snorts. "Tom knew."

But Paul is sharp. "It's haunted him these last twenty years. He blamed himself for taking her out on the boat that night."

"He should," Jack declares. "If you know a person is suicidal, or just suspect or even just fear it, you do *not* give them opportunity. If you care about a person the way he supposedly cared about my mother, you do *not* take them out on a foggy night with warnings of micro-bursts on the marine channel, and if you find yourself in the middle of one, you put on a fucking life jacket." Tossing both hands in the air, he stalks off down the drive toward his house.

"Jack," I call, twisting to watch.

His head is downcast, eyes refusing to see more. In the sole indication that he has heard my voice, he raises a palm halfway, *let me be, you have nothing to say that I want to hear, you're on the wrong side.* And there we are, twenty years back.

Only we aren't. We're twenty years older, twenty years wiser, and, regardless of where our relationship is headed, I'm not letting words come between us. I may be an inveterate peacemaker. But making peace won't work just now.

Bolting after him across the gravel, I shout, *"Wait."* But his long stride doesn't falter. Finally catching up, I grab his arm. "Walking away accomplishes nothing."

He turns on me. The glasses on his head do little to tame

his chestnut hair, which is nearly as wild as his eyes. "It makes me feel better." His voice is dark. "He was your father. She was my mother. Nothing has changed."

"It has so." Ignoring everything else in the air around us, I hold his gaze. "We're all brilliant in hindsight. Of *course,* he shouldn't have taken her out if he thought she was suicidal, but did he think that?"

"You're defending him."

"Shouldn't I?"

"He never defended you."

"Right, and we now know why. So that was a flaw of his, but the issue here isn't me. It's your mother. I don't believe there was anything malicious in what he did with her that night."

"She *died.*"

"And we don't know how it *happened,* but do you seriously think he wanted her dead?"

He opens his mouth to argue but stops.

"Right," I repeat, relieved that he is listening. "Think of his behavior when he returned to shore that night. Think of what Paul said about his recent visits. We know he was tormented—because, I'm sorry, Jack, even apart from the principles, Tom wasn't much of an actor. If he had been, he might have treated me better all those years, which is neither here nor there right now. We do know that your mother's death tormented him. We even know it tore his own marriage apart." I lift a quick hand. "And yes, there was reason for that totally apart from her, but what happened that night and the scandal in the days after clinched it. I'm not taking sides. I'm just trying to make sense of this."

His voice lowers in defeat. "How can I do that? I'll never know what happened. Any answers there might have been are buried with Tom."

"I'm saying," I beg, with a hand on his chest, "that maybe he didn't have the answers, and that maybe we *don't* get them in life. And that maybe we can talk things through this time instead of walking away."

With the ocean flowing and ebbing somewhere below the bluff, Jack studies me. He knows I'm right. I can see the sadness in his eyes. But his jaw remains taut. Good intentions aside, a habit of twenty years is hard to break.

Blowing out a long breath, he looks over his shoulder at his own house, as if debating whether to head there or back with me. Suddenly, a visible tension pulls at his shoulders and spine. At the top of his front steps, hidden in a far right corner on the porch, is the image of his mother.

It's Lily, of course. But given our discussion, if the sight of her jolts me, I can only imagine what it does to Jack.

With a guttural WTF, he takes a step toward her before spinning back. His finger gestures me to Paul, then straightens in promise. *We aren't done.*

Understanding that he needs to talk with Lily alone, I do everything I can not to look back as I return to the bench. Paul is sitting now, bent forward with his elbows on his knees and hands clasped between. He looks up when I lower myself to the other end.

"That's her?" he asks softly.

I nod. "Weird timing."

"What do you think she wants?"

Beats me, I say in a grimace.

"What do *you* want?" he asks more gently.

"For Jack and Lily?"

"For you and me."

With a mildly hysterical laugh, I lift a bewildered look to the drifting clouds. "Everything, nothing, time, memory, experience, talk—I don't know." Back at his face, I scowl. "How can we not know so much about the most important things in our lives?"

He should be as puzzled as me. The question is a cosmic one, and I've asked it rhetorically. But his eyes warm in the way of one who is older and wiser preparing to lecture. I'm thinking that I'm not ready for a lecture from this particular man, when I see empathy in that warmth.

"Because life isn't static," he says. "It keeps changing. We think we know where we are, then something happens and we're somewhere else, and we have to find our way all over again. Sometimes, like with Jack's mother, there just aren't answers."

Haven't I just said the equivalent to Jack? I'm gratified to hear it from Paul. He is wise in ways I've always appreciated, and what he says makes too much sense to reject the words simply because of who he is. Besides, this doesn't sound like a lecture or even advice. It sounds like a discussion.

"All those memories—" I recall frightening times with Tom, frustrating times with Mom, family times with Paul always on the sidelines, "—should they be ditched for being wrong?"

"Not ditched, just amended. And what about new ones?"

New ones, I think.

"You and I are both alive and well," he says. "It's an opportunity."

Well, it was. But I say nothing. Truth is, Tom's antipathy toward me notwithstanding, I feel traitorous declaring affinity for another father so soon. How can I simply negate a lifetime of memories in favor of new ones, even amended ones?

"This is sudden," Paul acknowledges. "My timing stinks. I'm sorry." He sits back. "Trust me, I didn't plan this. But could I keep quiet after what Tina Aiello said? Of all the times I anticipated my confession," he adds in self-derision, "the day of Tom's funeral wasn't one."

"Would you have told me—ever—while he lived?"

He studies a distant point. "Probably not. Tom was one of my best friends, and still I hid this from him. I didn't see that I had a choice. What good would it have done to tell him?" His eyes find mine again. "For what it's worth, it never occurred to him to ask. He never dreamed it would be me, for which I feel all the more guilty, mind you. I never lied. But I did tell only half-truths. Like Tom with the police. Like so *many* of us. So, are we just taking the easy way out? Or are we choosing the lesser of the evils?"

He's asking me? Like I'd know? I kept secrets from my sisters about having non-Aldiss thoughts, failed to ask personal questions of a woman I called my best friend, stayed away from the man I loved for twenty years—all in the name of keeping peace. Was any of it the lesser of the evils?

"But I repeat," Paul says, "Tom was my friend, and now he's gone. I can argue that he's been gone for months, even years, but death gives 'gone' a new meaning. You know?"

I nod, although I'm nowhere near as philosophical about death as he is.

He lifts an arm toward my shoulder but it falls before making contact. Touching is something he isn't sure he's earned, and he's probably right about that. Like death, perhaps, our connection gives touching a new meaning.

A quiet urgency remains on his face. "I turned seventy last summer. Now a good friend has died, and I think of my own mortality. I think about years I missed and ones I may still have."

I think of those as well. And it isn't that I'm brooding about mortality. I'm too young, too healthy, too optimistic. Call me in denial, but no one my age plans to die, least of all someone with a thirteen-year-old daughter. Margo and I joke about this, joke about her taking Joy, joke about a drama-queen daughter being the antithesis of her sons. The joking has a point, though. If anything happens to me, she will be a wonderful mother to Joy, and that is the sum total of my last will and testament.

No. For me, it isn't about death. It's about things that I've missed and now want.

Paul's urgency settles into a plea. "Like I say, we have an opportunity. Do we use it or just let it go?"

Chapter 28

Just let it go, begs the part of me that clings to resentment. Granted, that part is shrinking fast, but it isn't entirely gone. With its dying breath, it wants to stoke the hurt of being ignored by Paul all those years—to shut him out of my life as he did me and deny him the pleasure he might have had if he'd acknowledged our relationship before this.

But that, I realize, would be shooting myself in the foot. Joy has always craved family. I can see how happy she is in Bay Bluff. Even with Dad's burial so fresh, there she is now, down on the beach holding court with her cousins and Guy. I would never spring Paul's identity on her so soon. We need to mourn Tom first. Then, when the time is right, we'll talk.

She'll like having a still-living biological grandfather on the only side of her lineage that she knows. And she does like Paul. Hell, aside from this one massive sin of omission, what's not to like?

But there's something else. If I'm being honest, Joy isn't the only one missing family. Jack's phone call may have been the catalyst for my return home, but the trip has had its high points. The me who lives in the moment has enjoyed breakfasts at Sunny Side Up, snippets of warm talk with Anne, even Truth or Dare with my sisters and daughter before it went downhill. All I have to do is look at the photographs in the attic to remember what being with family was like. Or look into Jack's eyes to remember what we had. The memories aren't all bad.

I may not be philosophical about death, but I am, suddenly, about this. When we don't have something in our lives, we tell ourselves that we don't need it, that we don't *want* it—because the alternative is aching for it, which breeds a sense of loss. So, we remove it from the picture we make of our lives. What we don't see, we don't miss.

Then, as Paul said, something happens, and the view changes. In the process of refocusing, we see pieces that we do, in fact, miss and want restored.

That's where I am right now. I need to repair things with Anne. And with Chrissie. Jack is a whole other story. I'm not sure where to go with that.

Paul is the easy one. He is patient and sincere, and he isn't going anywhere. I'm not ready to throw myself into his arms. I need time to absorb everything he's said. For now, though, I want him to know there's hope.

Sliding a little closer on the bench, I slip an arm through his and, feeling shy but certain, let it stay.

The rest of the world gradually reappears. The circular drive is rimmed with cars, but they are all ours—two rentals plus Anne's, Bill's, Paul's, and mine—meaning that mourners have taken pity on us and gone home. The sea breeze rustles in the shrubs, the surf gathers and rolls, threads of teenage laughter rise from the beach. Margo emerges from the house and stands for a minute at the edge of the porch to listen for the kids before going back inside. She hasn't seen us. Our funeral garb fades us into the bench.

The crunch of loafers on gravel grows closer, until Jack rounds the bench and drops into the space I've just left. Subtly, I slip my arm from Paul's and, once Jack is settled, ask a quiet, "What did she want?"

He lounges defiantly—legs fully extended, ankles crossed, arms folded—and stares straight ahead. "She offered to leave town."

"Offered?" That's a surprise.

"With Tom dead, she has no one to haunt."

"Did she *say* that?"

"No," he concedes without meeting my eyes.

He saw my arm in Paul's, I realize, and, sensing a meeting of minds of some sort, doesn't know where he stands in the mix. Does he think it's two against one now? Like it's a competition?

"She didn't say she was haunting him," he grudgingly admits. "But she did say she'd been hoping for answers. I told her I wanted them, too, but that it doesn't look like we'll get them."

"What about the book or whatever she was hoping to write?" Paul asks.

"She claims she isn't. Claims there isn't enough to say, so there's no point. Claims she's lousy at investigative journalism anyway, since she doesn't have the guts to prod."

"And you believe her," Paul says mildly enough, not even a question, still Jack turns to glare.

"Yeah, I do. She didn't call you, did she? She didn't call the cops. She knows everyone in town from working at Anne's, but she hasn't called anyone."

"How do you know?" Paul asks, still mildly but asking for trouble. I want to tell him to just *shut up*. But the damage is done.

"Because," Jack barks, "I'm not a rookie. I've been asking people questions for twenty years, so I know how to ask them about her without tipping my hand. She hasn't approached them. And she hasn't approached you. She knew you were Mom's lawyer but couldn't get herself to call."

"Did you tell her what Paul just told us?" I ask.

"Hell, no," he replies, only marginally softer. "It's not her business. The money's gone, my mother's dead, we'll never know for sure what happened on that boat. End of story. So why not let her stay in town? She needs the money. And she likes it here."

"She said that?" I ask.

"Yeah, and I believe that one, too. I've seen her on the beach. And working at Anne's. She's having fun. She isn't a bad kid."

"What about the PI?"

"They broke up."

"That didn't last long."

"No, but I don't know if that's good or bad. I feel sorry for her. She seems lost. She could be a server anywhere, but she has a connection to this place. And then there's Anne, who doesn't need the complication of finding a replacement. So, anyway, I told her not to leave. I said it'd be a helluva lot easier keeping tabs on her if she's here in town."

"You didn't say that," I chide.

"Sure did," he says with a snide grin. "Naturally, she took it totally the wrong way, like I'm a relative looking out for her welfare. But I'm just being realistic. She can go back to Boise and do research if she wants. She can do research from wherever. If she's here, she's visible."

"I buy her interpretation," I say. "You're a softie."

"It was a decent thing to do," Paul adds.

Jack straightens. Unfolding his arms, he extends one behind me so that the side of his hand hits my shoulder. He doesn't hold me exactly. But it's a statement. "Some of us do know what decency is."

"Jack," I warn, knowing where he's heading.

But Paul is up for the challenge. "Okay. Spit it out."

"She grew up being hurt." No doubt who the *she* is. "With Tom dead, that's over. I don't want it starting up again from you."

"And how might I do that?" Paul asks.

"Paul," I caution, knowing how tenacious Jack can be.

"No, no," he reassures me, "this is good. Let's air it." He sits forward just enough to squarely face Jack. "How might I hurt her?"

"By disappearing again."

"I never disappeared. I was always here."

"Skulking in the shadows."

"I don't skulk, and if I've been in the shadows, it's out of respect for Eleanor and Tom."

"And now?"

"Now, what?"

"Are you promising things you can't deliver?"

"Like what?"

"Affection. Loyalty. Support."

After following the dialogue, back and forth, side to side, I'm on Jack. "Excuse me, but I don't need—"

"And *you've* given her those things all these years?" Paul fires back at him. "From what I understand, you've been AWOL for twenty."

"It's not—" I try but am overridden by Jack.

"We were young and hot-headed."

"You were hot-headed. I can't imagine Mallory ever was."

"Jack and I—" have discussed this, I might have said had I been allowed to finish, but Jack is unstoppable.

"Which shows how little you know her. She's independent. She does not need anything from you."

When Paul mutters into my right ear, "What *is* he to you?" and Jack into my left, "What is *he* to you?" I've had enough. Jumping up from the bench, I raise both hands. My voice is low and fierce. "I don't like fights. I've spent a lifetime avoiding them. If you . . . *boys* . . . need to argue, you can do it without me."

Whipping around, I head for the house, then whip back.

"But I will fight. I have a life and a daughter, and I won't have either of you interfering with that. Got it?" Before they can speak, I leave.

I'm still simmering as I enter the house and spot Margo. Legs crossed, she sits on the living room sofa beside Dan, but there is nothing relaxed about her. Deeper in the room, Anne is stern in the wingback chair by the sunroom door, with Bill at a nearby window, looking out. Before I've taken two steps, all faces turn to me.

I glance from person to person. The silence here is nearly as forbidding as the first clod of dirt hitting mahogany this morning. Feeling a thread of hysteria, I ask in a high voice, "Have I missed something good?"

For a minute, there's nothing. Then comes a rush of replies.

"Just sitting."

"Exhausted."

"Finally alone."

I'm not sure who said what, but the occasional crushed cocktail napkin, partially eaten pastry, and used tumbler speak of guests who returned to the house from the cemetery. *From the cemetery.* Hard to believe the funeral was just today, so much has happened since.

And there is Dad's chair, still with the markings of his body, waiting for him to return.

Something snaps in me. Are hollowed cushions really a tribute to the man? We need to find a way to move on.

Crossing the room, I reach for the loose cushion resting against the large back one—then abruptly pause. I look back at my sisters. "This needs to be fluffed. Can I?"

"No," says Anne.

Margo says nothing, clearly wary of ruffling Anne—which makes me the monkey in the middle—which, ironically, I often was when we were kids in the backyard, playing the game. But I'm not about to push the issue. There are other ways to move on.

Unsure what the best one is, I sink into the sofa facing Margo and Dan. All of them do look exhausted, for which I possibly hold a little blame. "I'm sorry for deserting you."

"It's not like you were playing golf," Margo remarks.

Anne is quiet. With the funeral over and the antipathy of Sunday night hovering again in the air, I expect belligerence from her, certainly distance. Looking at her, though, I have no clue what she's thinking.

I wait for Margo to speak again. She's our leader, isn't she?

Or maybe we need silence. Yes, I tell myself. Silence. I sit through a minute or two, trying to think of Dad or Mom, trying to remember. Only the memories aren't coming to me, not with so much to say in the here and now.

Clearing my throat, I glance at the men. "I'd like to talk with my sisters. Would it be—would you mind?"

They're moving before I'm done, dying to get out. And why not? The air in here is grim.

Once we're alone, I approach Anne. Crouching, I grab either side of her chair cushion. "I'm sorry, Annie—sorry for what I said about the gun. We were all upset and said things that were angry and unfair."

She stares at me. Her hair is loose now, its waves tipped with the frizz we all know, but the burgundy streak that I've come to like seems more truculent than fun. I search her face for my little sister, but that little girl is grown.

So I speak to the woman she is now, who may be more sensitive than I give her credit for. "I'm sorry for what I said about you being naïve. Your optimism has always been one of the things I most love about you."

Her eyes fill. "You think I killed him."

I recoil. "Why would I think that?"

"Because I didn't take him to the doctor when I knew how breathless he got. And I did know it. I'm not stupid. I didn't take him to the doctor about the memory thing either, and if I'd done that, the doctor might have discovered the heart problem, and if he had, Dad might still be alive."

Shifting my hands to her knees, I give them a little shake. "Would Dad have been happy with that?"

"No! He didn't want any of it! But that isn't why I didn't take him to the doctor. I did it for me. I didn't want to know he was sick. It was my fault, not his, *mine*."

"No," I insist, but she races on.

"He was my life here. Oh sure, I have the shop and friends, but Dad *is* this place. He built it, and he ruled it. You both have other homes." Her gaze widens to include Margo, who has come close. "Not me. I've lived in this house my entire life, and I've lived with him that whole time."

"Oh, Annie," I breathe, seeing her loss in ways I don't see my own. She's the one whose daily life will be different. Of course, she would feel Tom's death more intensely than either of us. "I'm sorry."

"But I'm *not* sorry it's been that way, don't you see? We've been good here together, Dad and me. I understood him. I worked around his moods, and he loved me for that. The house has been filled with people, and now it's empty. Everything has changed."

"Not everything," I say, thinking of all of us here now.

Margo adds, "Not Sunny Side Up. Not Bill—"

"—who wants to *marry* me," Anne wails.

She sounds panicked, which I don't understand. "But that's *great,* Annie. You were afraid he wouldn't."

"Wouldn't want to be tied down to a baby, but then when he said the word *marriage,* I freaked out. Like, marriage is forever—I mean, it wasn't for Mom and Dad, but you should be thinking forever when you go into it, shouldn't you? I have no idea what kind of husband he'd be. I have no idea what kind of *father* he'd be. I mean, he works in a prison."

"So did Dad—well, almost," Margo says, stretching it even with the qualification, though I'm not sure the remark registers with Anne, who remains centered on Bill.

"He has a criminal record, meaning he spent time on the *inside*. And his tattoos, all those tattoos?"

"I thought you liked them," I say, startled again.

"I *do,* but tell me the truth, I mean, seriously, is he the kind of man Dad would want me to marry?" When neither of us is quick enough to speak, she says, "See? You agree. Okay, sure, Dad got used to seeing him around, but that's a whole different thing from my being married to the guy. And having his baby? Dad would *die*."

Squeezing her knees, I whisper, "Dad is not here."

"Besides," Margo adds in a very Margo, very Tom, very firm tone, "even if he was, it's not Dad's decision to make. It's yours."

From the look of the tears that have begun to trickle down her pale cheeks, this doesn't comfort Anne. "That's fine for you to say—for both of you. You've been making decisions for yourself all these years, but I haven't."

"You absolutely have," I inject. "Look at the shop—"

"Dad's been part of my life. And I wanted it that way. I liked knowing he was here. I liked knowing he depended on me to keep the house running, and when he got forgetful, I liked being able to help. I didn't rush him to the doctor, because I wanted things to stay the way they were. I'm an enabler—that's what I am, an *enabler*—and now he's dead."

"Annie." I grasp her arms to be closer to her heart. "There is no correlation between what you did or didn't do and his death. *He* told me that he didn't want doctors or medication. But you, you made his last years happy. You didn't cause his memory problems *or* his heart problems. You made his life better in spite of them. Think of him having breakfast at your shop. Going down there gave him purpose. He loved it."

She seems hesitant, but the ghost of hope in her eyes says she wants to believe.

Margo joins in. "You blame yourself, but what about us? We weren't here. You did it all. But what's the point of our agonizing over it," she pleads. "It's done."

"You mean, he's dead," Anne says.

"Which," I argue gently, "is what he wanted. It is, Anne. Don't you think so?"

She doesn't answer.

Softly, Margo says, "He would have shot himself if his heart hadn't given out first."

Anne considers that as she looks between us. "You don't blame me then?"

"Blame you?" I echo. "You were his savior. We are infinitely grateful for that."

"Infinitely," Margo stresses.

"And now?" Anne asks.

I'm not sure what she's getting at. "Now?"

"What happens?" She makes a triangular gesture.

She's right in bringing us back to this. It is what we need to discuss.

"We're sisters," I say, then, looking awkwardly between them, add, "uh, half-sisters. I do have a different father."

I'm wondering if the time is right for this, when Anne bursts out, "I shouldn't have said what I did, Mal. I'm sorry. You're right; we were upset. It doesn't matter who your father is. We're all Mom's, and we were raised together. I know you felt Dad treated you differently, but he thought of you as his, I'm sure he did."

Margo is watching me closely. "Do you know for sure?"

"Shy of a DNA test? Pretty much." Mom's birthmark notwithstanding, I want to know beyond a doubt. Paul offered.

I'll accept. It may be the only thing I'll ask of him, other than not to hurt Joy.

"Who?" Margo asks.

But I draw the line there. "It doesn't relate to who we are."

She would have prodded—I know Margo, she would have—if my younger sister hadn't been elsewhere. "Dad left me the house," Anne blurts out, looking frightened, afraid we'll be upset.

Letting the other go, Margo says, "As he should."

"Agreed," I second.

"But I don't want to be alone."

"You won't be," Margo assures her. "We'll be back."

"You will?"

"Annie," I smile in disbelief, "of course, we will."

"Even without Dad here?"

Margo snorts. "Especially without him here."

I'm more nuanced. "If you're asking whether you're enough to bring us back, the answer is yes. Of course, you are, Annie."

But she is eyeing Margo. "You'd come, too? Even with this place being more Dad than Mom? It always will be," she warns and tears up again. "I used to think of the potting shed as being her. I'd go in there a lot. I'm not sure I ever will again."

Anne kept the door oiled, then. Not Tom. It's a nice turn.

But she isn't done with Margo. "So you won't have the potting shed either. Mom isn't here anymore. What's to bring you back?"

"You," Margo says.

"How? *Why?* After all these years?" Anne asks skeptically. "The only times you've seen me have been on neutral ground and, then, only because the family diplomat," she flicks her chin at me, "arranged it. You didn't go on those trips for me, and if I'm all there is for you in Bay Bluff, you won't come here either."

Margo is suddenly pissed. "Where have you *been,* Anne? Have you never read *any* of my blogs? Half of them are about you!"

She draws back. "Me?"

"Yes, you. I write about siblings. How we're permanently connected. What being sisters means. When it works and when it doesn't. Why being sisters is more than being friends and how we suffer when a sister is lost. Loads of women I know are estranged from a sibling, but I write those blogs because of us. I don't mention your name—trust me, I wouldn't do that—but you're right there."

She has no reply. Nor do I, actually. But one of us has to speak, so I say, "I didn't realize."

"That I was talking about us?" Margo asks in surprise. "Then either I went overboard being obtuse—or you didn't want to see it. I wrote those blogs to say how much I missed my sister." She looks at Anne. "You."

Anne is teary again. "Seriously?"

Margo rolls her eyes. "Must I grovel?" She catches up Anne's hand. "We will be here. Unless you don't want us."

"I do," Anne cries, looking like she might burst into full-on sobbing. I'm thinking I might, too, my own throat is that tight. But she is suddenly scowling. "As long as you know, I'm not marrying Bill. He can be involved with the baby, he can even live here with us at the house, I have no problem with that, but I am not rushing to lock myself to him just because of a baby. If you did it without a man, Mal, so can I."

"But Bill loves you," I remind her.

"Then maybe in time, but not right now."

She looks at me, then at Margo. There is a sense of expectancy in her that has nothing to do with Bill or the baby. We're back at the *what-happens-now* question.

But I do have the answer. I won't tell them that the words come from Paul, because he doesn't—shouldn't—have a place in this circle of three. Nor will I force it on either of them. For one thing, with Tom barely in the ground, this is a time to remember him. For another, forcing isn't my way. But the idea offers definite direction.

"What if we were to start making new memories?"

Chapter 29

I needn't have worried about infringing on Tom's memory. His absence, even beyond those hallowed, hollowed cushions of his chair, is a stark presence in the house. If it isn't his pen on the floor by the chair, it's his glasses in the key bowl in the hall or his boat shoes parked side by side at the back door.

That said, even if these things hadn't kept us subdued, caution would have. The truce between us is fragile. No one wants it broken.

That goes for Jack as well. I'm not sure how he ended it with Paul outside, but he is suddenly, solicitously, with us in the house. He runs to the market for cookout makings, then keeps the kids busy readying the firepit while my sisters and I prepare salads, chips and salsa, and trays of garlic bread, condiments, and s'mores makings.

Another time, Margo or I might have noted the stereotype of women in the kitchen, but given Anne's career, we don't dare. Besides, there is something soothing in filling a traditional role here together. There's a sense of the torch being passed now that the last of a generation is gone.

More than once, I think of Paul, who was with us over the years for so many family gatherings. He is grieving for his friend. That should be reason enough to invite him to join us. But I'm not ready to reveal the other, and whether I can have him here without giving it away with a careless word or look is up for grabs. The last thing I want is to muddy the waters of this intra-family truce.

That said, I am sorry he's alone. Finding a free minute, I slip off to a private part of the porch to phone him, then change my mind and text. It's the coward's way, I know. But I'm giving myself permission to be that for once.

Was he very difficult? I type. After sending it off, I return the phone to my pocket and am heading inside, when he texts back.

He says he loves you. Mutual?

As I study the words, I think about the irony of sudden honesty. But how to answer?

It is a minute before I reply. *I always did.*

Past tense?

Maybe present too. We're different now. Figuring out what to do with these new renditions of us, homes and careers and all, isn't easy.

Don't overthink it, Mallory.

Fine for him to say. But how can I not? What happens between Jack and me impacts my daughter's life.

Or maybe Paul is right.

Can we talk tomorrow? I ask.

Of course. I'm around.

I'm about to return the phone to my pocket when I think of Chrissie. I could text her, too. Or call. But I'm not ready for either. As hopeful as I'm feeling about other players in this drama, I'm still in the dark about her. Though family ties may fray, they never completely break, but friendship is different. We pick our friends. We can unpick them. Her lack of forthrightness gnaws at me. Granted, I'm super sensitive right now. It's possible she's a scapegoat for my upset.

But overthinking won't help that, either. I need time.

* * *

If the goal is creating new memories, a cookout on the beach works. Everyone chips in carrying things down from the house, cooking at the firepit, spreading blankets, and passing food around, but the real fun begins when the burgers and dogs are gone, the live dog is banished to Jack's, and Margo's boys take up with a soccer ball. Joy, who is no athlete, insists on joining in, and, taking pity on her, I do as well. Before long, we're all playing. We tell ourselves that it's a tribute to Dad, but it's a way of letting off steam for sure.

Naturally, we end up in the water. It was often that way, this progression from sand and sweat to relief. Also, as it often was, by the time we're toweled off back on the beach, the sun is nearly gone. The sky is orange-pink on the bluff behind and purplish on the horizon ahead, with finger-clouds of every shade in between. We sit comfortably around the fire, which has died to embers that are perfect for toasting marshmallows. When we were kids, this was one of our favorite things to do.

It's different with Tom no longer the director. The fact of his fresh burial is just beneath the surface of our smiles, but the kids are faster to rebound. Given the eagerness with which Joy makes s'mores for every adult who wants one, I know she won't forget this night.

Nor will I. It's a moment out of time, one for updating the past in favor of the future. It'll stand us in good stead once we've gone our separate ways again.

Once we've gone our separate ways again. Funny, how the subconscious can repress a single thought and then, when it pops up for half a second, not be able to push it back down. I have to be on the road back to New York by Friday evening if I hope to work on Saturday morning. That leaves only two more days here.

"Can't we stay longer?" Joy asks that night. She has taken over Jack's guestroom, which would have looked as sterile as so much of the rest of the house, if, within minutes of her retreat there, she hadn't scattered her belongings around. It's deliberate. She's already told me that she hates Jack's ex-wife's taste.

"I have to work," I say, clearing the bed enough so that I can pull back the duvet. "This job has been on the books since before we left."

"But I like it here, and Teddy and Jeff aren't leaving 'til Sunday. Can't you put the job off until Monday?"

"Nope." Propping up the pillows, I wave her in. "The client runs a business out of her townhouse, so a weekday won't work." I rummage around for the Lois Lowry.

"Then leave me here for the weekend and come back Monday." When I dart her a doubtful look, she says, "Or Margo can drive me back?" As I snag the book from the easy chair, she suggests other options. "Or she can put me on the train in Providence and you can meet me at Penn Station, or I can take—"

"You are not taking an Uber or anything else." Sidestepping Guy, who looks to be asleep on the bath towel Joy dropped on the hardwood floor, I climb onto the bed.

"Well, then," she tries sweetly, green eyes wide with possibility, "I can stay here until you *do* come back. Wouldn't that work? I mean, we discussed the possibility when we first decided to come—"

"You discussed it," I remind her, but gently. Despite the dread I felt before we came and the angst we've experienced here, a tiny part of me doesn't want to leave. Sensing that a stiff upper lip is needed for both of our sakes, I say, "I gave you the week, which was more than I wanted." Had we left last Sunday as I initially planned, I wouldn't have had a chance to reconnect with Jack. Life would have been simpler then.

Joy sits cross-legged with her hair in a mess around her face and, taking my hands, positively beams. "But aren't you glad you stayed? Think about it, Mom. If we'd left last Sunday, we'd only have had to come back for the funeral, and then you'd have missed those last days with Papa." Her smile fades. "And with everyone else." She grows worried. "What happened with Chrissie?"

"We, uh, had a misunderstanding. We'll work it out."

"It has to do with Paul, doesn't it." She isn't asking, isn't even letting her voice rise at the end.

"Indirectly," I say but leave it at that.

When my silence drags on, her expression darkens. "Are you ever going to tell me?"

Suddenly, it seems silly not to. She isn't a baby. She heard what Anne said Sunday night on the dock. The fact that she's waited this long to ask speaks of a respect for my needs that is actually quite mature. How can I make her wait longer?

Without elaborating on what was wrong with my parents' marriage, I give her a short, cleaned up version of the story of my conception and Chrissie's *mis*conception of it. Joy is far less interested in the Chrissie part than the other.

"Paul?" she asks with a curious smile. "That's so nice."

Her calmness startles me. I might question her loyalty to the man she so recently called Papa. But I know my daughter. Her way of dealing with loss is to fill the hole. Besides, parentage has always been a vague concept to her, given that she knows nothing of her own biological dad.

But I don't have time to dwell on that, with her bolting onward. "And there's *another* reason for my staying here. If he is my grandfather, shouldn't I spend time with him?"

"Joy—"

"*He* can drive me home." She pauses, eyes suddenly keen. "Or Jack, what about Jack?"

"What about him?" I ask, though my heart knocks. I know where she's headed with this one.

"I mean, here we are in his house, and in an hour, there

you'll be in his room. Are you seriously going to pack up and leave in two days?"

"Are you seriously going to pack up and leave in two days?" Jack asks so identically that I wonder if he and Joy discussed it earlier.

Granted, several hours have passed since such a discussion would have taken place, and last I checked, she is asleep down the hall. Prior to that, though, we lie in her bed and talk. There's no reading here. I'm not sure if she fears Jack will think she needs a goodnight story. But how can I argue with talking? Guy seems to agree, since soon after we settle into it, he rouses enough to jump up onto the foot of the bed, stretch out on Joy's lime tank top, and go back to sleep.

The thought that he might wake in the night and lunge at her throat has crossed my mind. But Jack is right. The vicious pit bull is a stereotype that does not seem to apply to this dog.

And the stereotype of a headstrong Jack? Headstrong can be good or bad.

I do have to give him credit. He doesn't mention my New York plans when, after I leave Joy to her book, we settle on the back porch with glasses of wine. Out there, we talk about everyone else or nothing at all. The silence of the latter, accompanied by the night sea, is pleasantly arousing. It isn't until we are upstairs in a state of post-coital half-sleep that he pops the immediate question.

Drowsy and warm, I press my fingers to his mouth and whisper, "Don't ask that." The moment is too sweet for reality to intrude.

Headstrong Jack whispers back, "Fine. No asking. *Begging.* Stay."

We are lying face-to-face in a mess of white sheets. His

long legs tangle with mine, an arm at my waist holds me close. I want to think he's too tired to be fully aware of what he is saying, but no. Not Jack. His eyes are wide open, reflecting the night.

I slide my fingers along his stubbly jaw, pleading for time with a look.

And he sees it, oh, he does, but he isn't dropping the bone. "I can't let you go."

"I have another life."

"Another man?"

"No, but a home, a job, commitments."

"Change them. Move here."

I exhale into a dismayed laugh. "How noble."

"I'm serious."

"So am I. You want me to drop everything I've spent twenty years building? To trust that what happened between us then won't happen again?" I keep my voice to a whisper, but my vehemence is clear. "It isn't just me. Joy has a life, too."

"She hates her school."

"Did she say that?"

"Yeah, she did. She says people here are more friendly."

"She hasn't met any kids here yet, and if she were to, it could happen here, too. She goes against the grain. She says what she thinks. Kids her age don't necessarily like that."

He arches a brow. Oh, he knows. He lived this himself.

"Jack," I complain softly, but his large hand climbs higher on my bare back, not letting go at all.

"If she's unhappy there, can't she be unhappy here?"

"Jack."

"Seriously."

"And what about me? My work?"

"Okay. What if you kept your place there and went back and forth?"

"With Joy where." It isn't a question. It's a problem.

Jack is unfazed. "Here. Anne wants her here. I want her here. *Paul* wants her here."

Dropping my forehead to his chin, I close my eyes. "You're not making this easy."

"I won't let you walk away from me again."

"Who walked away from who?"

"Whom. But I'm not letting either happen again."

I open my eyes. I want to make him happy, really I do. He has been a godsend to me since I've been back, and I do love him. But I loved him before, and it wasn't enough. "Your way or the highway?"

"Not this time. If you can't live here, I'll move to New York."

For a minute, I don't know what to say. Then, just shy of stammering, I protest, "You can't do that. You have a business."

"It's called a practice," he says with a trace of humor, "and don't tell me New Yorkers don't have pets."

Of course, they do, and of course, he could find work there. But I can't even *begin* to imagine what a Jack-in-the-city life would be like. Maybe he was right when he said my life in New York was about control. The unknown terrifies me.

"Jack," I sigh.

"Mal," he sighs back.

Don't overthink it, Paul advised, *ten* times easier said than done with so much at stake.

"Slow," I suggest.

His frown lines deepen. "What does that mean?"

"It means this is happening too fast. I've been here five days. That's not enough." Five days is too short a time to make a major life decision.

"I agree," says Jack, but he takes my words differently. "Five days isn't enough. I want years. You've been missing from my life, Mallory."

Sliding my hand down his throat to his chest, which is

warm with texture and broad under my palm, I beg, "Slow? Please?"

He tries. Really, he does. Jack's version of slow is simply not talking about it. But he's there even when he isn't, hovering in the back of my mind. When Margo and I muster the courage to enter Dad's room, spot Mom's dressing table, and remember the way she let us play there, I share Jack's memories of Elizabeth and feel all the worse for his loss. Just at the moment when Joy and her cousins are trying to decide how to spend the afternoon, Jack comes from work like a knight in shining armor, collects the three, and drives them back to the clinic to help socialize a litter of King Charles Spaniel pups. Dan and Margo insist on discussing Jack's obvious devotion, and when I call Paul for advice on what to do with Dad's books, he asks if Jack is behaving.

On the plus side, the truce with my sisters holds. Anne is better being at work than not, although she is subdued, clearly grieving. She also looks exhausted, which may have to do with the baby, or with Bill, or simply with having us all here.

Naturally, Jack is with us for dinner. We've decided to purge the fridge by eating whatever friends brought that is still fresh, and the extra mouth helps. Naturally, he hangs around afterward. Naturally, he walks Joy and me back to his house when the others begin to yawn. Naturally, we feel like a family of three.

It would be cruel, if it weren't so nice. Same with our lovemaking that night. Though I sense a desperation in his stamina, he doesn't ask if I'll stay.

Joy does. By Friday morning, she is mentioning it more and more. We're having a late breakfast at Sunny Side Up— Margo, the boys, and me. Joy is serving, but each time she stops at our table, she ups the ante. If she isn't sneaking extra donut holes to her cousins, she's telling them how *awesome* the town beach is or how *cool* it would be if *all* of them had red BAY BLUFF hoodies—and, *Mom, would that be the craziest photo ev-ver?* Finally, I wander into the kitchen to see how Anne is doing and casually raise the issue. When she lights up at the prospect of having Joy stay on, I'm sunk.

I can't stay, myself. Aside from the fact that two people have cleared their Saturdays to assist me, I owe it to this particular broker.

She's my top referral source, I explain when Jack oh-so-tactfully asks if I've made a decision. *I don't want to lose her.*

Say it's a family emergency.

She's a businesswoman. She wouldn't understand.

Try her.

I don't reply other than to say, *Taking the kids into Westerly. Anything special we should see?*

Wilcox Park. And bookstore.

Though the bookstore is new since I left, I remember the park. It proves to be an amazing photo trove for both statues and kids, and the bookstore—well, Joy and I are likely in higher heaven than Margo's crew, but we know how to wreak the most damage in the shortest time. We are at the checkout counter with our arms full, when Jack texts.

Will Joy stay with me?

Margo wants her with her.

Until when?

Next week.

You'll come back for her?

Yes.

And stay a while?

Depends on work.

Stay a while.

I need time.

I've given you time.

Time is not a day or two or three.

Neither is love. It's forever.

I let this text go, too. For one thing, when it arrives, my sisters and I are in the office of Dad's lawyer. The will is a formality, but we figure we ought to hear it while the three of us are here.

For another, I don't know what to say. He's right. And yes, I love him. But the logistics of making it work are daunting.

He's with us again at dinner. Anne is more civil toward him now, though I don't know whether she's getting used to him or simply knows that once I leave he won't be around. I've already transferred Joy's things back to our house and put my own in the car, all but my camera. It's still in action, capturing the kids watering the new plants on the bluff, Margo modeling her own red Bay Bluff hoodie, and Anne baking humongous peanut butter cookies.

We're having Thai tonight. Bill and Dan pick it up, leaving Jack with us at the house, for which I'm grateful. I'm acutely aware that the clock is ticking, that even aside from leaving Jack, I'm leaving Joy overnight for the first time in her life. I'm also aware that by the time I return, Margo and her family will be gone, to which end she keeps shooting me soulful looks.

Totally unfazed, Joy is with Jeff, doing a jigsaw puzzle in the sunroom. She feels no qualms about my leaving, is actually excited.

Then there's Jack. He doesn't make a show of checking his watch, but the few times he does, his eyes turn a vulnerable gray. In them, I read fear of abandonment, and I'm hopelessly torn. It takes a concerted effort to think of my life in New York.

I'm doing that a short time later with something akin to desperation. Leaving Joy is easy; we'll be in touch the whole time, and she does need this separation. What is it they say, *a mother raises her children to let them go?* Besides, she's with family.

Jack is alone.

My eyes are glued to the rearview as I drive forward, etching an image on my brain that is as indelible as one my camera might make. He stands apart from the others, as if my departure breaks his link with my family. Tall, singular, and apart, he is helplessness personified. I feel the same watching him. How easy it would be to step on the brake and put the car in reverse? Hell, I wouldn't even have to back up. If I stopped, he would run forward, I know he would.

But my life waits, my life waits, my life waits. So, I tip down over the crest of the road, erase that heart-rending sight, and drive on.

Tourism is winding down at the square. Beyond it, I pass the stretch of beach with its salty houses, lush hydrangeas, and Mahoneys, Santangelos, and Wrights. I pass the banks of mailboxes at dirt driveways that burrow off into the trees. Once I'm through the three-way intersection, I see Gendy's, then fiddle with the tripometer to avoid seeing Jack's clinic. When it, too, falls behind, I tell myself it's for the best. Only, the best feels like shit and, coming up on the left, The Hideaway is as emotionally potent as the other. Pushing on past Urgent Care, I turn onto Route 1 heading south and I tell myself that I'm safer, even more so after I've driven around downtown Westerly, through Pawcatuck, and onto Pequot Trail.

When I finally hit the highway, I give myself a mental high five. I-95 is neutral ground. Exits stream past my window—90, then 89 and 88. There are no choices here. It's straight highway driving, only modestly busy at this hour. Cueing Pandora to a soothing Mozart, I take a few long, slow, deep breaths. At the Exit 87 mark, twenty-eight minutes have passed since I left the bluff, but the hollow in the pit of my stomach remains.

Ignoring it, I drive on. By the time I pass Exit 86, I'm thirty-two minutes away from Jack and still hurting. Desperate for a distraction, I call Chrissie.

Chapter 30

The speakerphone comes to life after a single ring. "Mallory," she says with a loud sigh, sounding infinitely relieved, like she's had the phone in her hand all this time, waiting for my call, and is only now allowing herself to breathe.

Not sure what I feel myself, I stick with a simple, "Hey."

Several awkward beats pass. Signs for Exit 84 are headlight-lit in the encroaching dusk. Groton is behind and New London ahead, while Bay Bluff is farther away with each turn of the wheels.

Cautiously, Chrissie asks, "Where are you?"

"Driving back to New York. You?"

"Here already. Hey, Joy," she calls out, assuming my daughter is in the passenger's seat.

"She's back in Bay Bluff," I say, but I don't want to think about Joy either. "When did you leave?"

"Wednesday night." Her voice wavers. "There was no point staying."

My first thought is that she's talking about our tattered friendship. Then I recall the other piece, which I've been too mired in self-pity to see. Of *course*, it would be absurd to think she's been in Bay Bluff with her mother all this time. "Lina?"

"Lina."

I remember the woman's hard stare last Saturday, when she was looking for her husband in my face. That was bad enough. Recalling the scene at the cemetery, I can't begin to imagine what Chrissie must have felt when Lina hissed at her—her own daughter, whom she hadn't seen in years. "She's tough."

"You have no idea," Chrissie drawls. Neither of us laughs, but the mood softens a bit.

Taking warmth from that, I watch Exit 84 come and go. *I'm sorry,* my dovish self wants to say, *sorry that you had to confront her because of me.* Only, I wasn't the one who caused their rift. It happened before Chrissie and I ever met. She didn't talk about her mother often, I realize, but thinking back on the times she did, I recall little things she told me the woman had said. They weren't pretty.

"How can a mother be like that?" I ask. "It's not like she has four other daughters."

"If she did," says Chrissie, "I'd be off the hook. Since I'm the only one, she expects me to be her clone. My daring to deviate is a cardinal offense. She wrote me out of her life."

She had said this of her mother before, but having now seen the woman in the flesh, not to mention in my family's employ, I am particularly aggrieved. "Because your husband is *Hispanic*?"

"Because he isn't Italian or Catholic or from Rhode Island. Because I choose to live in New York. Because she assumes I'm crazy rich and not insisting she live with me, which is ridiculous given her distaste for my husband, my child, and New York, but that's how looney she is."

If anyone can deal with looneys, it's Chrissie. "You couldn't talk her down on Wednesday?"

"Hell, no. She's as bullheaded as ever. She says—get this—that I publicly humiliated her. Like anyone recognized me before she approached?"

"I'm sorry, Chrissie. Is she any better to Danny?" He left home, too, which is an interesting fact in this new light.

"Danny is male. The rules are different. Whatever he decides to do is considered upward mobility. I'm the one who's supposed to preserve the heritage. I'm the one who's supposed to take care of my mother the way she took care of hers. She considers me a traitor for not doing it."

Not even Jack being put on his mother's back burner seems as bad as Chrissie being shoved into the fire. I'm thinking about the miracle of her having such a happy marriage and raising such a normal child in spite of all that, when a car veers in front of me from the left lane and takes the Exit 83 off-ramp.

I'm in New London now, thirty-seven minutes gone from Bay Bluff.

"Do you?" Chrissie asks. "Think me a traitor?"

Her meekness returns me to the discussion—and yes, I did think her a traitor at first. Now that things have calmed down and I've put Lina's face to Chrissie's heartache, I see her side of the Bay Bluff issue. She regrets not being forthright seven years ago. I know that. She certainly regrets the way things played out this week. Can I seriously hold a grudge? We're all flawed, aren't we—all brilliant in hindsight.

We love the things we love for what they are, Robert Frost wrote, and I do love Chrissie Perez. Hell, at some subconscious level I must be accepting her for what she is, if here I am, rushing to call her when I need a friend.

She adds a mournful, "I really wanted us to be sisters."

I have to smile at that. Everything she said about clicking with me is mutual. Maybe there's a Bay Bluff gene swimming in our blood? "It would have been nice."

The line is silent for a spell, but it's a comfortable break.

Then comes a quiet, "Do you know for sure we're not?" It's her last ditch effort to make it so.

I'm forty minutes from Bay Bluff, approaching Exit 82 and

Waterford, and, just like that, I'm close enough to Chrissie again to say, "I do. It's Paul."

She gasps—and, just like that, is as indignant as my BFF Chrissie could be when she feels I'd been wronged. "Where's he *been*?"

I make a sympathetic sound, half laugh, half grunt. "Same place you were, believing silence was the best way to go."

"Ouch," she whispers.

"Sorry, I didn't mean—"

"You did, and you're right. But out of the goodness of our hearts. By the way, I don't remember him from Bay Bluff."

"He'll visit in New York. You'll meet him." Forgiveness is easy once it's done. Of all the sins of omission I've learned of this week, Chrissie's is the simplest and most innocent. It feels *so good* to connect with her again. Besides, I want to know what she thinks of Paul.

"And Jack?" she asks. "Who adores you, by the way."

Jack. Who wanted me to stay. Who begged me to stay but whom I just left. Whose face I see reflected in each exit sign I pass. Whose name alone twists at my heart.

Trying to make light of it, I tease, "And you saw this in, what, ten seconds?"

"Ten minutes, and he was looking at you like you hung the moon."

"That's being dramatic. But I left him. Again. He may be hurt enough to get over me."

"Is that what you want?"

A car speeds by at what has to be eighty-five, its driver desperate to get somewhere or other. So am I, but I follow the rules of the road. I'm desperate to restore order to the life I've made for Joy and me in the city. After a week at the shore, though, that city life looks different, feels different, may never be the same.

Exit 81 flies by. I'm another few minutes closer to Manhattan, another few minutes farther from home.

Home. Such an interesting word. Is it where you park your body? Your family? Your *heart*?

"Mal?"

"It's a tricky situation."

"Does it have to be?" she asks, so much like Paul's *Don't overthink it* that I do wonder if I'm the problem here. But she persists. "It was a difficult week for you, but weren't there good parts?"

Jack, I think. Anne and Margo, I think. Jack, I think. I think Joy on our beach, moments of lucidity with Dad. Again, I think Jack.

Chrissie thinks bigger. "Broad view."

Zooming out, I consider. "Reconciling past and present. Figuring out who I am."

"Did you?"

I'm about to say yes. But the word won't come. Instead, I blinker left to pass a Camry going under the speed limit, then blinker back into the middle lane. Having passed Waterford, I'm nearly in East Lyme.

"There's still Jack," I admit and glance at the clock. Forty-five minutes have passed since I left. I wonder what he's doing.

I'm picturing him wandering the beach with Guy. Or reading in that godawful sterile living room. Or . . . or staring at the unmade bed in his room and thinking of me?

As therapists do, Chrissie has let these minutes pass in silence. Finally, gently, she says, "What about him?"

"It's hard to describe."

"Try."

"He was so a part of my life once upon a time. Then not." Just thinking about it, I feel a spreading hole. "Then again this week. It's like we picked up where we left off before . . ." She knows enough of my history to finish the sentence. "I mean, it was different. We're different now. Maybe more realistic. Definitely more mature."

She waits. Then, "And?"

"And nothing. In some ways, it's better than ever with him and, in others, ten times more complicated."

"Since when have you been afraid of complicated?"

"Since Jack," I say with a derisive laugh.

"Because you love him?"

"Yes, but isn't it possible to love someone and not be able to make the logistics work?"

"Love isn't about logistics."

"It can be," I argue, but my best friend sees it differently.

"What if he is who you are?"

"Excuse me?" I ask, not because I haven't heard, but because the question is huge.

"You went down there looking for answers. What if he's one?"

"Oh, Chrissie, I don't know," I say, shaking my head in a way of slow doubt. I'm not sure whether I don't believe it, or whether I simply don't want to.

Suddenly, though, the doubt lifts like fog at the shore, because it makes sense. I do believe it. I want to. I don't want Jack and me to be done. He is so far and above any other man I've ever met, and no, I don't need a man. But here I am, looking at the clock every two minutes, feelings more lonely with each exit I pass.

Jack Sabathian *is* part of who I am.

The certainty of it sinks in as I drive south on a darkening highway, back toward a life that I've successfully shaped and fully control, but that still won't be whole. And suddenly, half-whole isn't enough.

"Uh, Chrissie," I say with abrupt urgency, "I think I need to go back, have to turn around at the next exit—where the hell *is* the next exit?" I've barely said it when it appears. Blinkering right, I take the off-ramp, drive under the highway to the opposite on-ramp, and head back to Bay Bluff.

* * *

What took me fifty minutes southbound seems to be taking forever on the round trip. The northbound exits are more spread out, I swear they are. I don't listen to music or take deep breaths, because trying to relax is futile. Same with going the speed limit, though I do stay within ten over.

I'm gripping the wheel as hard as I can in an effort to keep my mind off what I'm doing. Futile effort there, too. Because it's crazy. *I'm* crazy, heading in the wrong direction when I have to work tomorrow morning. But little images keep slipping through my mind—dream thoughts, like our driving back to New York together, his watching me at work, our walking around the city, eating at places where I've always wanted to eat, sleeping in my bed, waking up together. I have no idea where Joy is through all this or, for that matter, Guy. Still, the dream wisps come.

I could just call him as I drive. Why don't I call? I didn't have to turn around to do that. I can even pull over at the next rest stop and do it.

But no. We have to be face-to-face. He has to know that I'm not running away this time—has to know that I will not abandon him, even if it means driving back to New York tomorrow at dawn. He needs to know that he is part of my life, that he will *always* be part of my life.

Realizing this myself, I feel a burning need—and not between my legs. It's in my chest. The heart sitting there now is too big for just Joy and me. It needs Jack in it, too.

The miles creep, one after another after another. Finally reaching Exit 91, I take the ramp at warp speed, or my modest equivalent thereof, and head for Westerly. It's nine-thirty, meaning dark enough to steal through yellow lights and roll past stop signs with minimal fear of detection by the town's finest. Breezing by Pawcatuck, under the railroad bridge, and into downtown Westerly is smooth enough, and the emotional landmarks that come after? Since my heart is already fully involved, they've lost their particular punch.

The square is deserted. Accelerating past, I angle up the bluff road. Of the two houses that loom at its crest, only the Aldiss one is lit.

Jack's is dark and its driveway empty, but that's the one I turn down. Refusing to be discouraged, I park and, hurrying to the front door, ring the bell. When he doesn't answer, I ring it again and put my ear to the wood. No footsteps. No whine of a dog. Running around to the back, I rap on the wood, then bang. When neither raises an alarm inside, I try the knob, but the door is locked tight. Gone? Refusing to believe it, I turn to scan the beach, but the only movement there is the shimmer of a light surf, pearlized by the same moon that shows no man and his dog planted in the sand, looking broodingly at the sea.

There are perfectly good explanations, I tell myself. He may be dealing with an emergency at the clinic, or running with Guy on the long beach near the square—or, since I didn't see his truck when I passed there, at another beach entirely. Maybe he's at the bowling alley with the police chief again, drowning his disappointment in beer. He'll be back, I tell myself and, returning to the front of the house, take up position on the steps to wait. Two minutes into that, I try his phone. It goes straight to voicemail.

Naturally, my eye is drawn to the Aldiss lights. When a figure moves past the living room window and stops, I hold my breath. I don't want Joy running out. Call me a coward. Call me *irresponsible*. But what I'm doing here isn't about motherhood. It isn't about correcting a memory, though so many were proved false this week. Nor do I need the Nikon to save this moment. I'm living it in real time, alone, waiting for a man who has a life of his own and may or may not have been serious about changing it.

Cell in hand, I allow another thirty seconds for imagining the questionable places he may be, the women he may be with, and the reasons I was an idiot to turn around on the highway and race back. Then I try his phone again. Nada.

Where are you? I text and wait. And wait. And *wait,* with no ellipses on his end.

After what feels like forever, I pocket the phone and, devastated, hug my knees. I tell myself that he's a grown man with his own life, that his silence doesn't mean anything bad. But how can it not, with his supposedly loving me enough to want to spend the rest of his life with me, with my having rejected him again, this time after he begged—*begged*—me to stay?

My eye keeps drifting back to the house with the lights, the one in which my family is living, breathing, waiting. Sitting here alone, I wonder if that's where I belong, if the past will always be a barrier between us, if I'll always be too much of an Aldiss for Jack.

Anne appears at the front door. Even in silhouette, she is defined by the same careless topknot of hair that had set her apart from Margo and Joy earlier this evening. Slipping out onto the porch, she closes the door carefully behind, though the effort at stealth is wasted. Or maybe it's just that Margo is as attuned to her now as they both are to me. Before I can move, they're side by side at the edge of the porch, staring at Jack's house.

I'm up in a flash. Maybe I'm wrong, maybe Jack is somewhere completely innocent, somewhere without phone reception. Maybe he's so heartsick that he turned the damned thing off. But I don't know, just don't know, and the thought of a life without him is bleak.

The dim light that escapes from the house is soft, but it must have captured my chill, because Margo takes those last few steps with open arms. Not to be out done, Anne joins the hug, and there's nothing weak about her arms. Warm as Margo's, they support me well.

Finally, Margo draws back. "What happened?"

"I blew it," I say, not quite crying but close. "I left, and now he's gone. He won't forgive me this time."

"Are you kidding?" Anne asks in disbelief.

Margo shares her doubt. "Did he say that?"

"No. But I can't reach him. Doesn't that say something?"

"You've been trying him all this time?" Anne asks, curious now.

We're standing so close that our voices are low. Still, with a quick look behind, Margo guides us farther from the house and into the shadows. As always, she's right. I'm not sure what the others are doing and don't want Joy out here yet. For now, my sisters are enough.

I don't mention talking with Chrissie, just tell of my time on the highway, passing exit after exit, feeling worse and worse. "It wasn't until East Lyme that I realized I was being stupid. I should have called him then, but I honestly pictured him right here waiting for me. I mean, after everything he said, you'd think it, wouldn't you?"

"Not with Jack Sabathian—" Anne says. She catches herself, but only after sarcasm has leaked out, history rearing its ugly head.

A week ago, I might have agreed with her or, at least, let it go. But my loyalties have shifted.

Actually, not. I'm still loyal to my sisters. My loyalties have simply broadened to include not only Jack, but a more cogent reality than one I've embraced in the past.

"Do you honestly think that, Annie?" I ask softly. "After everything he's done this week? He's been supportive and thoughtful. He's been respectful of Dad—not a single snide comment—and he might have gloated. Another man would have. Another man might have said Dad got what he deserved and justice was finally served. But Jack didn't. He's been with us through this whole thing, despite all the answers about his mother that he'll now never get. He's been good with Joy—*great* with Joy."

"And with you?" Margo asks.

Glancing at her, I shrug. "The best."

"Then you were right to come back."

"But you have to work tomorrow," Anne protests, playing the devil's advocate as Tom's longtime caretaker would inevitably do.

"If I'm on the road by four, I can make it."

"Without any sleep?" she asks, but the answer is on my face. I could talk with Jack long enough to miss sleep entirely, and it would be worth it. "Would you marry him?" Clearly, marriage is on her mind.

"If he asks."

"Elizabeth's son?"

"Elizabeth's son."

"After everything she did to our family?" Anne asks but more feebly, like she's running out of options.

I might remind her that whatever had happened, we'd done to ourselves. But it is done. *Done.*

So, simply, I say, "Yes."

"What about Joy?"

"Joy can handle him."

"But . . . but your career, her school, the condo?"

"I don't *know,* Annie. I don't know how *any* of it will work out. All I know right now is that I want to be with him. I love him. I always have."

Margo gives me a crooked smile of concession. "He was always yours."

Anne says nothing. But really, what more is there to say? A complicated situation is as simple as that.

So we stand in the shadows of the house, all three of similar height, hair, face shape, and eyes, a hand or arm touching in the comfortable way of shared blood, and we'll always have that, my sisters and I, even if not with the purity we were taught. Our silence is broken by a voice from the house, though I can't tell whose. I hear the ocean and want to hear it more, want to hear it forever.

Then I hear something else. So do my sisters. Our eyes turn to the road, where the crunch of gravel and growl of an engine grow louder, nearer. I barely breathe as the lip of the road comes into gauzy focus with its tiny rocks, bits of stray grass, and wrinkles of blown sand. Seconds later, twin orbs rise as the Tahoe crests the bluff and turns onto the Sabathian drive.

When its headlights hit my car, its taillights abruptly blare red. Leaving the truck running, Jack is out and sprinting forward. He tugs open my door, looks inside, slams it shut again, and makes for the house. Scanning the front porch in passing, he lopes on to the back. For several aching moments, I lose him.

Then he reappears in the truck's headlights. Putting a hand on the top of his head, he looks around. He seems confused, bewildered, *desperate*. His eyes land on our house and hold, before somehow, impossibly, finding us in the dark. After staring for a minute, he starts forward, then stops. I left him. He isn't sure why I'm back, isn't even sure I *am* back. I'm with my sisters. For all he knows, I've cast my lot with them. For all he knows, I'm only back for Joy.

Giving me a not-so-gentle nudge, Margo says in an exasperated whisper, "What're you *waiting* for?"

I barely hear. In this watershed moment, words are as faint as the moon. Same with the ocean, the salt air, and the shadows that surround us, because Jack Sabathian has my full attention. My sisters will always be my past and present. He is my future.

What am I waiting for? Nothing. Nothing at all. In the next breath, I'm off.